OUT OF THE
DARKNESS

Robin Magaddino

WWW.PPP-PUBLISHING.COM

HICKORY, NORTH CAROLINA

Powerful, Potential & Purpose Publishing
Hickory, North Carolina
Gloria Coppola | gloria@gloriacoppola.com
www.ppp-publishing.com

Publisher's Note: This is a work of fiction and all the characters are figments of the author's imagination. Any resemblance to real people, living or dead, is unintentional.

Book Layout and Cover Design
Carol Anne Hartman | cahartman.com

ISBN 978-1-7376603-5-4

Printed in the United States of America. First edition printing 2022.

This book is dedicated to my husband, Joe and daughter, Martina, who gracefully put up with reading all the innumerable versions of this story and never asking if I was finished.

My niece Nicole for her unflagging support.

And to my mother, Martha Owen, 1917-2006, who encouraged me in all my adventures.

CONTENTS

"Never doubt that a small group of thoughtful committed people could change the world. Indeed, it is the only thing that ever has"

—Margaret Mead

CHAPTER ONE

L ike death, I wait for no man. At least that's my plan.

I trudge back to the pond from the point of the hill, where I was able to scope the valley. I let my binoculars drop to my chest, the strap cutting into my neck.

I'll add the trumpeter swan and six duck species I spied on the river to the list I started almost an hour ago. I'd left the field notebook on one of the hefty light bollards around the pond when I began walking around to warm up.

My fancy cowgirl boots, the ones I've saved for a special occasion, are not made for hiking over sharp landscape stones. The colorful flowers stitched across the toes and up the sides of the black boots, that go so well with my black leather pants, are getting nicked on this unexpected stroll. I lift my bottom onto the oversized landscape light with a little hop and, crossing my legs for warmth, lay the binoculars aside and grab my notebook.

He's late. I'm waiting. My old patterns are coming back to haunt me after I thought I was over them. The last time I tangled with a man, I swore that I would never wait again. Never be manipulated in this way.

So what if I'm jilted by a boyfriend at this age. I didn't even want one, but internet dating moves fast and so did JB.

I'll give him three more minutes. I check my phone for missed messages and to start the count down.

It's freezing now that the sun dipped behind the Salish mountains. If we'd agreed to meet at a nice restaurant, at least I'd have a glass of Chardonnay in my hand.

Thinking of wine, which I used to drink by the bottle, reminds me of my life's career. I hug my middle and lean forward into the triggered stress pain. Breathe, breathe, inhale, exhale.

Working in the good-old-boy world of corporate multinational mining was brutal. Only pride made me last so long. I was not only the token woman, but the token environmental specialist, writing impact statements, meeting and negotiating with locals. I'd been propositioned and threatened so many times that I quickly learned to keep it professional, be better at my job than anyone else and put up with words like hard-assed bitch to my face.

My life was worse when I spoke at conferences of my peers. Corporate biologists are considered pariahs by their own kind. Sell-outs to big business against the environment. To make changes, I told them we needed to engage with the enemy.

I spent many nights drinking alone and crying in my hotel room while the other biologists flocked together in the bar.

Well, I showed them all. The settlement for whistleblowing gave me a tidy retirement at age forty. Now at fifty, I am somehow being played for a fool again. I need to figure out how. I keep wondering if the corporation sent JB as an annoying payback.

I circle my arms overhead and inhale deeply, then exhale and lower my hands to cover my heart. I'm grateful that it's in the past.

I zip my leather bomber up to the top, snap the corduroy collar around my neck and fish the leather gloves out of my pocket to slip on.

Finally! Here he comes, drifting around the curvy road and gently coasting to a stop in the parking place at the bottom of the path. I lift my hand to wave and, hating myself for it, to forgive.

His engine unexpectedly thunders to life, thrusting the car up the manicured lawn towards me. I freeze in the headlights then lean out to jump. Too late. Tumbling through the air, I see the stars, then the lake. Then nothing.

"Row-set-ah." A familiar voice says my name one syllable at a time, a mantra-like Row-set-ah. My eyes flutter uncontrollably, can't focus on the face. Instead, the threads of the Emergency Medical Technician patch are clear before my eyes. Every stitch on the circle seems inches wide. The woman leans closer to move aside the damp hair sticking to my face. "Rosetta, can you hear me?

Eve Birdwoman's eyes are wide, her forehead wrinkled and lips stretched tight. Seeing my best friend's face like this is a shock. Her usual dead-pan expression is gone. The patch on her khaki-colored fishing vest turned ambulance-jockeys catchall moves away as she lifts her blue gloved hand with blood smeared fingertips.

She looks down when I yelp. Eve's round, Blackfeet Indian face instantly rearranges itself with a calm, mothering smile, like a blanket unruffled. Her face would be calm if a volcano erupted overhead. *Strong in the Face of Danger* says a sign over the inside of her front door. "Breathe and center your thoughts, like in yoga class, Rosetta," Eve prompts. My teeth clench against the fear and pain and no breath comes. No one is going to call me needy.

"You're okay, Rosetta. Everything's okay," she repeats. "I can't give you pain meds for a little while. Can you stand the pain?"

I blink and she mistakes it for a yes. Not going to whine. "Don't move," she adds unnecessarily. That's funny, I think. I have no strength do anything anyway. Her dark eyes show no emotion when she drapes my forehead with a large gauze pad resembling a Depend adult diaper.

"Damn, Eve, am I going to die here?" If energy was visible, I'd be glowing like a red-hot engine. If only I could move. I desperately want to stand up and run. I wonder if I'm dying.

The inside of an atom couldn't look busier. Everyone is in motion, calling first from here, from over there, back here again. Slamming car doors join the cacophony of voices. Orders direct the tow truck to back up towards the pond.

I cringe from the loud clanking of chains pulled across the metal truck bed. The winch motor squeals as men pull out the steel cable.

Choking diesel fumes drift across the lake to my face, join the aroma mix of latex gloves and leather boot polish. Eve leans down to adjust my hair. "The car's about twenty feet down caught on the ledge." She looks up at a splash. "Someone's swimming down to hook the tow line to the axle."

"Where's JB? The bastard tried to run me down."

"Don't waste any time thinking about him," Eve says, holding my hand. "It's ok."

My eyes begin to fill and I squeeze my eyes shut to hold in the flood. Something is not ok. Excruciating pain in my left hipbone feels like I'm in a steel bear trap. The cold and helplessness remind me of when the stack of hay bales tumbled over on top of me a few winters back.

Wait. Since it was alfalfa bales in the barn for the pregnant sheep, it might have been six years ago. Wait. Is it good to know that I'm confused? It was the spring the mountain lion ate two lambs, which was the same year my two beehives swarmed and fled the farm. To top it off, I went to Belize for a month of work and my house sitter found the heads of my three, half-grown geese on the lawn where great horned owls picked them all off in one evening. So, it was five years ago.

I feel so disoriented. You're alive, Rosetta, focus.

A few ewes squeezed through the door to lay down next to me, chewing their cud and keeping me warm with their breath and long fleeces. It took two long hours to free myself and crawl on hands and knees back to the house through the frosty evening.

"Rosetta, Rosetta, where did you go?" Eve is holding my face, slapping my cheeks. "You're shivering."

If only my foot can go over there, maybe I'll scoot there and crawl away from this trap. My breath catches and tears spurt out. Damn! Sharp rocks hold me fast to the earth. The world is tipping. Damn, damn, damn. "Eve, remember our pact about being helpless—If I end up paralyzed or brain-damaged, without a doubt, snuff me out."

Eve huffed. "You'll be ok if you remain still. You're wedged between these butt ugly steel light bollards."

"Why couldn't they install small, normal landscape lights? Someone is on the way to remove one. You'll be free in a moment. It's fine." She always talks so matter-of-fact that I do feel fine.

We could be talking about rubbing a scuff mark out of my favorite riding boots. Eve's comforting voice can persuade everyone into compliance, no matter if it's at the community planning meeting or a high school football game. No one can escape Eve's charisma.

The oversized yard lights have their purpose. The five pairs of pillars stand around the spring-fed lake and, from a distance, look like gnome couples contemplating the quiet water. Each bollard is four feet high, two feet square, and stands about eight inches from its neighbor. Downward aiming louvers direct the soft light toward the ground. They make a great perch for bird watchers like me. What birds show up. Anything special? Oh, yes, a pair of wood ducks. What's that big white bird flying in?

"Rosetta, wake up." Eve shakes me, flicking my ear with her fingernail.

"I like the lights, Eve," I wheeze.

"I know you do," Eve whispers back to me, her face close enough to feel her breath and smell the wood smoke scent of her skin. "Are you ready to get a move on?"

One of the blessings, or mortifications, of small-town living, is that you personally know the ambulance jockeys who come to your rescue.

"Hey, hey Roe. What did you get into now?" Pryor Miller, the builder of luxury homes by day and finish carpenter at my Stone Mountain Art Gallery and Coffee Bar by night, hovers above my face. "You couldn't make it to the party for the new ambulance, so we brought the party to you."

At the first vibration of his pager, Pryor and other EMTs leap and speed, hazard lights flashing to the firehouse or directly to the accident. They've always seemed overzealous until today. Pryor's young face contorts in shock at my bloody and bruised appearance. His dark curls fall over his face when he jerks back.

This afternoon's fund-raising barbecue at the firehouse to show off the shiny new ambulance happened without me. I delivered my pasta salad for fifty people to the volunteer fire department around four o'clock. It seems like a lifetime ago.

Red and white checkered plastic tablecloths fluttered on the long tables lining the fire station lawn.

The Tamarack Falls Fire Department Auxiliary worked alongside the firefighters to host fundraisers. It was hard for me to hand off my director duties to someone else, but I had other plans. The poor Auxiliary will clean up the party all by themselves tonight because everyone else came to my rescue. I get to see the new ambulance after all. Ooh, my chest.

It hurts. Remembering the food along with the coppery reek of blood makes me feel like retching. Other smells fill me; dirt, diesel fumes, sweat, pine oil disinfectant from Eve's jeans, crushed grass. The camping trip when we were sixteen. Eve crushed the long green grass beneath our camp kitchen. Fumes from my auntie's old primus stove filled the air when we failed to get it started. The next time we flicked the lighter, a loud whoosh burst out with a flaming white fireball. We fell back in tandem, scrambling across the campground. Eve grabbed pine oil from a jar in her pack to dab on our faces and fingers. Is that white fireball still growing? Wait, is it an angel?

"Are we losing her? Try this."

"Ouch. Stop it." The sharp thumping on my forehead ceased. Kelly and Eve bend close. "Stop hurting me, damn it!"

I think I'm feeling stronger. Maybe I can get out on my own.

"Thank God you're in Eve's yoga class Rosetta," Kelly says, bringing her smiling face close to mine, "or you wouldn't be able to twist like a pretzel and not break something. It looks like the bollards broke your fall and saved you from sliding over more of these sharp stones." Kelly reaches forward to jab at the metal box. "The damn louvers are holding you down."

Kelly taught a self-defense-for-women class I sponsored. Her tall muscular body brought contrast to the willowy look most women strive for. She was a New York firefighter until after 9/11. To regenerate her health, she moved her kids and husband here to open the Firehouse Kitchen Restaurant, creating a famous dinner destination in our little village. "Hey, hot leather pants, woman. So tight. They'll be toast after the emergency room. We'll get your jacket and boots off now."

These poor leather pants and jacket have been locked in the dark for twenty years. They attracted me from the back of my storage closet, begging to hug my body today. The few times I wore them I felt like a superhero. After all, I did fly today.

Eve held my head immobile while Kelly pulled something warm and wet from beneath my shoulders, replacing it with a thick layer of towels. The blood odor goes away with the fuzz.

Pointed chunks of granite made my head wound bleed a lot. Whatever had been my pillow must be soaked. I think of a tennis racquet contacting my forehead in high school, the river of blood running down my bare face, and the hysterics of my doubles partner.

"Hey, you in there?"

Our paramedic, blue-eyed 'Ooh-la-la' Brent, eye candy of the ambulance service, begins to gently squeeze every inch of my body. His large, strong hands glide over my face, down my shoulders, back, wherever he can reach—one arm, chest, belly button, around one hip, legs, ankles, feet—asking over and over again, "Can you feel this?" My body tingles beneath his palms. Is his hand between my thighs? My eyes find Eve's, we manage a tiny smile. Ahh, I can only imagine. A ten-star rating for Brent.

Since I pass the feel test, he says, "We're wedging a board beneath your back to support your weight. If these lights weren't so close together, we could slide you out."

Fingers walk around my body, lifting me more onto my side. Pryor maneuvers a board down to my hips, lifting me off of the pillar. Now, the sharp louvers of the opposite bollard cut into my stomach.

Kelly and Brent hold me firmly in place while Pryor gets to work removing the bollard. He ties his hair into a short ponytail and flips his ball cap on backward.

Pryor aims his tools to unscrew the bolts fastening the corners of the bollard to its cement pad. His ratcheting power-wrench whines out of control. Pryor curses as the first bolt sheers off. After the slow removal of the other three bolts and some hammering, Eve counts "One, two, three" and the bollard slides away.

A swift sleight of hand follows. Three sets of hands gliding the backboard onto the ground and sliding me up until my whole 5'8" body was on the board. Eve's hands never leave my head to keep my neck from bending.

"What do you feel now?" Brent's talking to me. His hands caressing over my legs and arms again.

"Better," I croak.

"I can walk." I try to roll onto my side, intending to push myself up. "You go, girl," laughs Kelly, as she gently strong-arms me flat onto my back again.

Eve cradles my head on her entwined fingers to help Kelly slip on my stabilizing cervical collar. They add one rolled towel next to each ear, then pass webbed straps through slots in the back-board edges over my head. As I reach up to reduce the constriction, Brent gently pushes my hand down to my side and asks for the spider straps. He and Kelly deftly tighten the web around me.

"Her teeth are chattering," Kelly points out.

"Adrenaline wearing off." Eve places a hand gently over my heart. Then she places a mask over my nose and mouth and straps it to the neck brace. "A little oxygen will make you feel better."

Brent maneuvers my boots off, one at a time, and commands me to push my feet into his hands. The added gentle massage is heavenly. When I open my eyes, a circle of faces blocks the view. Some I know by name, most are strangers—Marry Kat, a short woman with long, rainbow-colored hair is a reporter, I don't know the cowboy chewing a matchstick, a big man with concern in his eyes, the sheriff? Why are so many people moving into our small village?

I focus on the face of my auto mechanic, Jackson Jones, also one of my closest friends. We have a constant, cut throat rivalry for bird sightings. We haunt bird feeders or marshes to get the earliest bird of the season and be the first one to post our sighting on the Birding Hotline.

I'd let my birding lapse as JB became a distraction. Jackson is one up on me with the black-legged kittiwakes migrating through our valley in February. Looking for a feathered rarity, I glance at the sky to see if the right bird will immediately fly across my limited field of view. Out the corner of my eye, I see Jackson's head tip back to follow my upward gaze.

Tears flow down Jackson's face. He is a big, sensitive guy who can't stand blood. I'm sure he heard this emergency call on his kitchen table police-scanner and came running because he knew they were talking about me. Jackson is one of only two people who knew I'd be at Larsen Lake this evening. Pryor picks up my original head pillow and throw the blood-soaked Carhartt jacket over to Jackson. I vow to buy him a new one before next winter.

"What's happening?" I shout. My eyes cross as I accelerate towards the sky. The four medics, each gripping a corner of the board, circle the end of the pond to carry me straight down the steep hill toward the open ambulance doors. Tall Pryor and Brent carry the front, followed by the shorter Kelly and Eve. This is a rehearsal for my final parade, four pallbearers hurrying my coffin towards the grave. Eve and Kelly quickly strap me onto the waiting gurney.

Pryor leans over before they lift me inside. "Hey, hey, enjoy the ride." A quick smile crinkles his eyes and off he goes.

CHAPTER TWO

The clanging sound of the metal doors slam, startling me.

"Hey, hey, tell me when you're set," Pryor announces cheerfully from the driver's seat.

Eve and Brent crowd close and inch themselves sideways next to my head. The white glare is blinding. Every inch of wall holds Plexiglas fronted cabinets to organize splints for broken bones and bandages for every wound. I cough at the smell of rubbing alcohol and new vinyl. A computer monitor and oxygen nozzle gleam brightly. No dings or scratches mar the toxic disposal canister or fire extinguisher. The old ambulance felt like a converted camper in comparison. I'm the first customer of this expensive new purchase. I feel special.

"We need to get our girl to the hospital ASAP!" If I am the first victim, then Pryor is the first driver of the first rescue with the new ambulance. He's giddy. Our girl? As if. Who last called me that? My giggle turns into a grimace at the sharp pain in my ribs. Is giggling a side product of suffering?

"What's that noise? Are you choking Rosetta?" Eve squeezes my arm.

"I think she was laughing," says Brent, frowning down at me.

"Let's do it." Eve gives the orders today.

The engine purrs to life. Pryor eases the ambulance slowly around the parking lot potholes and sways onto the county road. It's very disconcerting to lie face up, head forward, speeding towards a place you can't see. This is pure torture for a confirmed back-seat driver like myself. The ambulance's strobe lights wink off the forest and reflect through the back door windows. Pryor flips on the siren when he turns onto the highway. Traffic parts before us like Moses crossing the Red Sea as we accelerate toward the hospital thirty minutes away. Crazy how we measure distance in minutes instead of miles in Montana. JB thought it was the funniest thing. When people ask me where I live, I always describe it as eight minutes away from the village. It's eight miles and it could take longer if I get behind a motor home, stop for deer to pass or if the road is icy. So many *ifs*.

The Crossroads Café is only a few minutes from home by car. If I ride my bike, it's fifteen minutes in May, or nine minutes in July when I'm in better shape. I wonder if JB can ride a bike or a horse? If I ride my bike into town, I can use the shower at my new art gallery. If it gets finished. Am I always so detailed oriented?

Last summer I rode my horse to the café instead of my bike and it took half an hour to get there when the mare stopped to take a good look at every horse, cow, elk, deer and dog along the way. The canter home lasted less than ten minutes. "Huh, huh, huh," I giggle and all I hear is a long moan.

The blood pressure cuff pinches. "Hey, open your eyes." I'm shocked back into reality. Brent shoves my shoulder and asks a checklist of questions about my pain and feelings. Eve bends close to tell me she's going to administer fluids on the way to the hospital. I hope for a bottle of water, instead, I get a needle in my arm.

The morning I picked JB up from the airport, I almost turned back at this intersection. That will teach me to trust my intuition.

How could I be meeting an online date, a stranger, at the airport, when I planned to only meet for coffee?

How'd he talk me into it?

"Rosetta, open those eyes for me." Replacing the blood-soaked gauze from under my head with a dry one, he reports that my scalp has almost stopped bleeding. He rests a warm, comforting hand on my forehead. Did this man know Reiki energy healing, too? Without warning, his thumb presses down on my eyelids, rudely pulling each one up in turn. Pointing a small penlight quickly into my eyes, he nods his satisfaction. "Pearls," I think he says into the air. I don't care what kind of compliment he gives me; Brent's score comes down from ten stars to nine.

"Almost finished," Eve says, pressing the last piece of tape across the needle and plugging in the tube from the hanging bag of saline solution. They continue to talk, but it's as though someone turned down the volume. Did Eve bring on the pain meds?

Almost finished with his job, JB told me. Plan to retire soon, he announces. It had the insincere feel of someone lying to themselves. Was that his first lie to me? Now, I remember, I never told anyone.

Far away, I hear Brent telling someone this is Tamarack Falls Ambulance. "We have a fifty-year-old female with a head wound, rock gouges between nape and crown, forehead hairline sliced by metal outdoor lights, and possibly internal bleeding. Thrown about twenty feet by a vehicle hitting a landscape light she sat on. No, it didn't strike her. GCS down from 15 to 13." There is a short pause. "Eyes closed until asked to open them. Yes, confused, short attention span. Perspiration beads across the patient's forehead, she says, are a hot flash. Loosening clothing and applying cold compresses to wrists and forehead." He says our estimated time of arrival is twenty minutes. Eve applies the cool compresses and leans in close to my face.

"Talk to me," Eve says, shaking my shoulder and leaning over to shine a penlight into my eyes again. "What day is this? Who's the vice-president? I politely respond, "Can that Italian man get me a cappuccino?"

"Dream on," Eve answers.

Brent is still talking. I block him out. "Cervical collar"… blah, blah, blah… "Oxygen"…la, la… "no cerebral"…bee-bop… "IV." I snort.

"Christmas day," I quip. Eve gives me her 'not funny' look.

"Kidding," I try to smile. My face feels tight, and I move my mouth and jaw side to side. It reminds me of the clay facial I had for my birthday last winter. After so many years without a date, my girlfriends pooled their pennies and treated me to a complete surface enhancement from head to foot. The green facial clay left pink circles of bare skin around my lips and eyes. My photo of the day looks like an Andy Warhol pop art painting. It dried to pottery harness when the technician joked with my friends and forgot me.

Eve reads my mind; she has a way of doing that. She rips open a package of moist gauze and removes the air mask to pat at my nose, chin and lips. "Breathe with me and relax." She works her way up my face, applying more moist pads to clean off the blood. "Slow your breathing. Count." She loosens the straps over my torso. "Unclench your hands. Relax your belly. Inhale 2, 3, 4. Exhale 2, 3, 4." She tears open an antiseptic wipe to dab at the scratches and scrapes. Will the waste of foil packets never end?

I gulp in a breath and blow it out into the mask, searching for relaxation. "Hey, who the heck is the vice-president?"

Eve continues to hum and clean my face. Brent drones on in the background.

"Doesn't anyone appreciate my sense of humor?"

The siren of a second ambulance speeds past us back towards our beginning point, the forty-foot deep, spring-fed pond perched on a hill above the Larsen Lake Golf Course. Old Man Larsen fenced the pond from animals and shooed away ducks to keep the water free from contamination. "There are special critters living down there in the dark that lived here before Indians came over from Asia," Old Man Larsen told me and countless others. He pronounced it "doun dair in da dark" with his cute, singsong Norwegian accent.

Mr. Larsen attached the Larsen Lake Protection Clause to his deed, sold the three hundred acres to developers, and skipped snow country for Costa Rica. The golfing community gave it a wide berth, making a natural area for two hundred feet around the pond, from the steep grassy hillsides up to the shoreline and the forested hill behind it. The only intrusion was a gravel path, a few benches, plus the tall, attractive bollards lighting the way and providing me an elevated perch while I waited for my special date, JB.

It was warm for early April and the evening sun already headed towards the horizon. New birds showed up every day. Varied thrush trilled from treetops, Canada geese and whistling swan honked and hooted from the river and slate-sided juncos skipped through the short grass, their clipped chirp like a spark of electricity. Two months ago, a resident pair of bald eagles clasped talons together over the village in the spiraling descent of their courtship flight and already incubated their eggs. No one reported the beautiful black and white osprey, but it was early and Canada geese still occupied most of the old osprey nests atop telephone poles.

A green line of the exposed forest followed the stark white of the melting snow up the mountainsides in the warm weeks of spring. The pink tinge of alpenglow brightened up the mountain peaks as the sun dipped behind the smooth forested ridgelines on the west side of the valley.

A small, spiral notebook sat in my lap, a short bird list growing on the page as I tried to distract myself. I expected JB earlier. He was the second person who knew where I would be this evening. I wore a baggy leather bomber jacket over a blue silk blouse and slim-cut, twenty-year-old leather pants I somehow still fit into, tucked into my boots. Every few seconds I told myself to leave before it got colder. Or darker.

It was dusk. He was late. He was always late come to think of it. How annoying. My cell phone was quiet. I checked the screen for the tenth time in two minutes to see if a text message mysteriously appeared. Great horned owls hooted from their nest site on the forested hill.

A shooting star! A lucky sign!

I drew a birthday cake in my notebook with 50 scrawled on top like candles and, underneath, a package with the letters JB jotted around it like a ribbon. I sketched out a mind-map starting with the day that brought me here. My name is in the middle circle. Branches go out to the clay facial and painful Russian body scrub, mani/pedis, my tipsy birthday celebration, girlfriends posting me on a dating site. All this girlie stuff made me uncomfortable. I wasn't used to pampering myself.

Hello beautiful appeared as the only answer just after midnight.

JB called, came and conquered the town. That was early February. Now is early April. I'm not waiting much longer. What do I know about him? Big fat nothing. I had the impression we would move our relationship forward tonight. What will it feel like to dip into my hot tub together?

Headlights came creeping around the curves of the quiet road. Excuses for his lateness flooded my mind. I've managed my anger so far. Maybe he stopped for gas. Maybe he picked up a take-out picnic dinner. His Mustang slowed to enter the parking, gliding into the slot closest to the path. I lifted my hand to wave, giving a futile cheer. Everything is so jumbled in my mind.

My mouth gaped open when the sound of the screaming engine broke the evening quiet. In seconds, the glancing blow on my perch launched me skyward. As I flew through the air, the car soared off the steep mound, engine still revving, angling up and away from me. I was high in the sky. Scary high. The car ascended, reached the peak of its arc, did a belly flop, immediately tipping nose down. I floated up and up, weightless, in slow motion, like an out-of-body experience. Suddenly things sped up. The water was beneath me, and then not, as I smashed to the gravel on the far shore.

The spring water will be a little less pure now. The last thing I saw before hitting the ground was a splash and the taillights of JB's brand new Mustang disappearing into Larsen Lake.

CHAPTER THREE

Under his breath, he whispers, "You're a code red, babe." Blood rushes to my head when Pryor abruptly breaks the ambulance to circle the old Kalispell County Courthouse. Brent radio's the hospital that the priority-one patient will be there in eight minutes. He and Eve exchange fretful glances. She's been holding my hand the whole ride. One thing I know for sure, code red is not a good sign when talking about anything, from a forest fire to terrorist attacks.

Eve never leaves my side when the emergency room doctors and nurses transfer me from the ambulance to the hospital gurney. She rattles off what happened to me. Someone asks her for my insurance information and insultingly wants to know if I'm on Medicare.

Brent reports on my physical conditions and symptoms. I watch him lean flirtatiously into one of the emergency room nurses, whispering a bit too loud, "She's out of it." Two more stars struck from Brent's rating. With a chuckle, he adds, "Thick skull." Brent's rating plummets from seven stars down to one, and that's only for his good looks.

Eve looks pained as I grip her hand in what might be my last death hold. Both our knuckles are white, and her fingers have a definite purple tinge. "Eve, remember you are the executor of my will. Please keep Meg but find a good home for my horse."

Pryor folds his tall frame over me, squeezes my hand, says the work will continue unabated at the art gallery. "I'll keep you updated and send pictures." He leans closer, "Don't go talking about your last will and testament. You're a survivor." He signals Eve, and she brings her face close to mine. "Don't leave me," I whine. She needs to ride back in the ambulance to pick up her car and call someone to look in on my horse and dog. "I'll be back in a jiffy."

"Don't go," but in a blink she disappears.

People are talking over each other, shouting instructions and words I can't understand. More white lights in the eyes. My jaw goes slack, and drool makes a path down my cheek. Two people examine my neck, reporting there are no external wounds. A needle glides into my arm and blood fills vial after vial. Scissors snip. I feel my leather pant legs loosen and my shirt and bra whip off like a vaudeville act. My pants and panties are gone, and I feel a finger briefly inserted into my anus. "Sphincter good, no blood," someone reports. I struggle against the finger assault. "STOP!" booms through the room. The same voice, oddly calm now says "We're going to take care of you, ma'am. Can you tell us where it hurts?"

This doctor must be a comedian. Where doesn't it hurt? My eyes scrunch shut. My hands involuntarily fly in to cover my Brazilian waxed womanhood, mentally adding it to my bodily aches and pains. Can't he see the pain is everywhere, inside and out? With a face that must look like a Mayan mosaic mask of pale skin and purple bruises, my eyes flutter open. I lick my lips to deliver my smart-ass retort. Whoa, now. Who's this? The doctor is a twin to television's Dr. Kildare of my childhood. He's super tall. He's hot. I want to get into his… "Take a cleansing breath," Eve's spirit whispers in my ear. He's young enough to be my… something. "Another cleansing breath," the whisper insists. I might be old, but I'm not dead. Damn, a searing hot flash comes on. Salty droplets pour into my eyes.

A shuddering "Aahhh," escapes my lips, not as smart-assed as I'd hoped.

"Right. Get her ready for CT scan and X-rays."

Doctor Kildare's tall clone has longish, sandy hair falling across his hazel eyes. The five o'clock shadow outlines his chiseled cheeks and angular jaws. He whips back his hair like a model as he looms over me, leaning closer, making an appraising inspection. I try to suck my body wrinkles smooth. He lifts my arms one at a time to check for fractures. When my hands fall to my sides, I see his eyebrows lift. Is he blushing? Enjoy buddy, is all I can think. His huge hands glide over my skin, squeezing, pushing, prodding, lifting, running a few fingers down my back from my neck to my tailbone. A shiver runs through my body. Someone pulls a warm sheet over me.

"No CT scan," I croak. "Radiation."

"We need a picture of your head and CT is better for trauma." He announces that I might have cracked ribs, a fractured pelvis or spine, ruptured spleen, and probably a concussion. I should cooperate and be as still as possible. Before I can refuse, the nurses close in on the bed. He nods, satisfied we're all following his orders, and leaves the room.

I hope to God he hadn't seen the sexy underwear I chose today. Hopefully, they made it into the trash. Silly, since he saw everything the underwear tried to embellish.

A few minutes later, two nurses push me on a long, zigzag trip down the hallway for the CT scan. This hospital seems to be in a perpetual state of remodeling and construction. We pass through a temporary open ward of empty emergency beds all in a row looking like a scene in *The English Patient*. "Watch out," they ignore my mewing. Every jostle is agony. The rush of passing doors makes me nauseous.

"One, two, three," they count, lifting me onto the scanner bed. The air is cool and smells sterile. My knees rest on a pillow. This is the first time someone asked if I was comfortable. Finally!

The nice technician slides a soft paddle next to each ear, nodding for the nurse to remove the neck brace. A clean, lightweight sheet covers me from neck to toes.

"Please promise that you will not move or turn your head. Lay still and relax," the technician instructs. "We're only scanning your skull and neck this time. Ten minutes tops."

No one gives orders here. Everyone knows his or her job. A tiny screen above my eyes shows the nurses and technician in the next room. One smiles into the camera and gives me a thumbs-up. My bed makes a leisurely trip into the open barrel-shaped scanner.

The peaceful, rhythmic thrum of the air conditioner and squeak of the machine is relaxing. JB is standing next to me.

I want to know where he's been? My eyes are covered by a filmy haze, so I can't see his expression. We argue about inconsiderate people and the invention of cell phones. I startle awake to "one, two, three" and the trio hammocking me back onto the traveling gurney. My neck brace is already in place. I notice that I'm dressed in one of those hopeless hospital gowns—little more than a sackcloth with strings tied in the back. We quickly weave our way back to the emergency room. The place is noisy, full of coughing people and a few wailing children. They can damn well wait. I was here first.

Most of the emergency room repartee is a blur. An X-ray machine wheeled in and out. They fall as quiet as nuns when another doctor comes in, asking questions with a voice that sounds like a slow, old tractor coughing to life. They take turns filling him in, adding, "Yes Doctor John, no Doctor John," in answer to his questions. One nurse offers, "She hasn't opened her eyes for the past 10 minutes." The sheet flips down, bringing a cool draft from my shoulders to my belly button.

"Hmmm," he growls. I feel a cold, rough hand on my breast and a sudden, firm twist of my nipple. My entire body jerks in protest and my eyes squeeze tighter. I clench my teeth. The nurses gasp and one tells Dr. John to please not do that.

"Well," he grunts. "At least we know she's not paralyzed." A nurse replaces the sheet, pulling it up to my chin, and tucks in a warm, light blanket for added protection. She leans close to my ear, "Sorry about that."

The women damn old Dr. John for a few seconds and switch to talk about the new Indian restaurant, Calcutta, their dining choice last night. One doesn't like green cardamom pods or cilantro; the other thinks coconut milk is too fattening. Eating and cooking ethnic food is one of my favorite pastimes, so I put in my two cents. "What's the point of eating Indian without coconut milk and cardamom?" Did I say it out loud? "Cilantro, you either love it or hate it." No one argues. My eyes are still closed. They must think I'm unconscious, even after the alarming nipple pinch. I can't make my eyes open. A few times in my life, I've felt I wanted to wake up, but my eyes stayed shut as if I were in a morphine stupor. A startling "muh" escapes my lips, and the talk turns back to me, particularly to my haircut, which they destroy with their snipping scissors.

One nurse gently cradles my head in her hands, and the other sits on a stool, reaching underneath to slash off the hair as close as possible. She uses an occasional spray of warm liquid to wash away the gravel and blood into a shallow pan and loosen up more matted hair. The snipping is driving me crazy. It seems to go on forever. This afternoon, I paid ninety-five dollars for this elegantly simple 'do' of rich auburn hair color, with creamy highlights. The hairdresser admitted it was a vast improvement over the dull, wicked-witch-of-the-west gray genetics handed me. Soon I hear the buzz of electric clippers.

The last nurse in the room speaks quietly to me in her gentle voice. "Now honey, don't you worry about anything. I know shock brings on a coma-like shutdown of the senses, but you can likely hear me. Set your mind at rest that you will be ok but might have a long rehab in your future. My name is Angel and I'll be one for you tonight."

Plastic crinkles as Angel cleans up the room. "Land sakes." Then, "Victoria's Secret. Hmmm." There is a long pause, followed by more rustling. She must be shaking out my clothes and putting them in the garbage bag. Angel chuckles. "Well, you're a braver woman than I am. A little red demi, push-up piece of lace for a bra and string panties with a bit of flutter along the hips."

She has a pleasant laugh, but I can't even smile. "I have got to take lingerie buying lessons from you, honey. I think you can salvage this little bitty panty." She sums it up with a chuckle followed by another "land sakes." I don't tell her this underwear set is a six-year-old, never-worn gift from an aunt pulled from the bottom of a dresser drawer. "I'll send this home with your friend Eve, along with your pocket contents."

"You must have had a hot date tonight. I'll bet he'll be in here as soon as he hears about your accident. I heard something about a car driving into a lake. Not having your seatbelt on saved you this time, but you keep it buckled from now on," she admonished, giving my shoulder a gentle pat.

"You'll be off to the ICU as soon as they get a space ready for you. You beat the evening rush at this ER, so for now, I'll look after you."

Angel uncovers one arm and begins washing me with a warm

cloth, humming a hymn I remember from my teens when I sang in church and school choirs.

The song has a comforting melody. Can I call this tune a Negro spiritual anymore? Is it an African-American spiritual, or have we demoted it to a mere hymn? I remember some words.

My home is over Jordan. Deep river. I want to cross over. So high, how could I be so high over this pond? What's that roaring? A motor? The pond surface reflects the setting sun. Green leaves are way up there near the violet sky. Can I touch them?

When I wake again, Angel is singing another tune while she washes my feet. When she reaches the part about *a band of angels coming after me*, the evening comes into focus. It's quiet now. All distractions are gone. The shock of the night creeps in, tightening around my throat and chest like steel bands. My hot date will not be rushing in to comfort me. That band of angels did not show up to carry me home. Did angels or demons carry JB home?

A trickle of tears runs out the corners of my eyes, down my temples. My angel notices and presses a warm, soft cloth across my eyes to soak up the steady flow. In the background, I hear loud buzzing, beeping, and shouting and have the sense of going over a waterfall.

CHAPTER FOUR

It could have been worse. My all-leather armor of pants, bulky bomber jacket and cowgirl boots shielded me from more cuts and bruises. If only I'd worn a helmet for this big date. Ten days in the hospital had been hell. The rehabilitation ward applied a whirlwind of treatments, sipping liquid food, more X-rays than I've had in my entire life, humiliating sponge baths and bedpans.

With the first whisper of spinal cord injury and cervical fracture, I reminded Eve to pull the plug if I could never walk again. My body tingled and burned, like when my foot's gone to sleep, and blood begins to circulate again. Was my whole body asleep?

Luckily, I could swallow, but couldn't hold the glass of water. Plus, the bump on the head gave me temporary blackouts on activities like finding my mouth with the spoon, buttoning a shirt and filing my nails. My friends found it hilarious, I found it confusing.

This body tingling was not a paralyzing broken spine but peripheral neuropathy. Although I hadn't seen his face, I recognized Dr. John's voice immediately. He was the resident expert on my problem. He covered my skin with electrodes to administer low levels of electric shock. Although Dr. John never outright apologized, he also treated me with gentle massages, guided meditation, omega-3 oils, a kiss on the forehead, and physiotherapy, as I'd requested, instead of drugs.

Amnesia came and went. I couldn't remember the names of the other art gallery partners. I surprisingly remembered the name of a young girl when her mother told me she was missing. Who is she?

Eve introduced me to Colette, the pottery-making queen, who brought me fresh vegetable juice and protein smoothies daily. Then Jade, who appeared with her drums to sing me healing songs. Eve came with her shamanic crystals and Ayurvedic herbs. Jackson supplied pizza for himself and Angel.

A blur of half-recognized village residents, neighbors, plus my fellow yogis and Tai Chi classmates, made brief appearances. It was like making new friends.

Flowers filled the room. Some included condolences for JB's death. No tears came. I sent them all down the hall to other patients. Eve hired two high school girls to care for my yard and boarded out the horse and dog to a nearby equestrian center. A continual buzz of activity surrounded me in my hospital room. The rehab center was a tomb by comparison.

Misty images of JB darted through my mind like a specter. I couldn't stop ruminating on what JB did to me and what he did to himself. I tried to distract myself by watching continual television, catching up on soap operas I hadn't seen in thirty years, and it was as though I hadn't missed a show. She was still cheating on him and he still wouldn't divorce his wealthy, evil wife. What had the writers been doing all these years? The evil wife had one after another of sleazy affairs, with men who were a generation or two younger, and was now plotting the death of the husband's mistress instead of her husband. What's with that?

When screams filled my night, Angel showed up to soothe me. JB, The Jackass Bastard she christened him, would never hurt me now. It wasn't true. Dreams of headlights, white and blinding, coming closer. Was he screaming profanity, telling me to say my prayers when the car ripped up the hill? The kind, funny JB, was he the myth or the truth?

I'd started dosing with self-administered painkiller, slurring like a sad drunk each time Sheriff Trammel hulked his ex-footballer frame into my room. He seemed like a tough dude in high school, but Trammel finally admitted the tears were getting under his skin, ruining his ego. He sent a young female sheriff deputy to take my statement and give me the low-down on what happened at the accident scene. The car didn't seem to have a mechanical malfunction. JB hadn't had a stroke or heart attack that might excuse him from transforming into a kamikaze driver. His behavior was a mystery.

The doctor and physical therapist let me go a couple of days early and we were mutually glad to be rid of each other. No broken bones, spleen or serious tissue damage plagues me, other than a throbbing morning pain in my hips and lower back.

Being in my own home was a dream come true. Daily yoga and pranayama connected my bruised body and my brain back together. My garden was overgrown with vegetables to juice to rid me of my sugar addiction from hospital food. I hiked and jogged up mountain trails and swam in the cold river most days. My head wounds closed up, leaving stitch marks and angry red zig-zags. My new hairstyle is the shredded look. It suits the way I feel, ugly, dirty, tarnished. The trauma specialist told me to write down my feelings, forgive myself first and forge forward. It's the whole stupid idea she tells me over and over, "Focus on the things you can change and not on things you can't." Idiotic.

Furious or festering were my go to thoughts about JB. Replaying the incident made me want to curl up in the corner, numb, terrified, and despondent, like a yo-yo swinging the entire length of my emotional string. How long does it take to stop crying? It had nothing to do with JB. The tears of fear come when I imagined the approaching headlights, my body flung up and over the pond, my breath knocked out when I slammed onto the rocks, wondering what happened.

CHAPTER FIVE

Today's the day. I love snuggling my Border collie, Meg, under the cozy down comforter, but time's up. The early afternoon nap revived me a little. "Come on, girl. Let's take a short walk before I need to leave." She never leaves my side during the slow walk around my rancho *piqueño*. Today, my friends are waiting. My public appearance was requested.

The Cinco de Mayo celebration takes over the sunny main street in Tamarack Falls, bringing out vendors and artists, musicians, and dancers. *Hola, bueno, sí, donde está el baño.* All my Spanish language lessons, plus the sense of celebrating, escape me.

May is one of our wet months, but rain and sleet have held off and we're experiencing a warm, dry day. Fortunately, I won't have to struggle with an umbrella. Unfortunately, I will see almost everyone in town, endure the inquiries and chatter about the incident. I'll get all the questions over in one afternoon.

Friends will come looking for me if I don't take the first step. My phone chirps with harp music, displaying a picture of Michelangelo's angels from the Sistine Chapel. My nurse, Angel, warned she would text to make sure I got out the door.

I had a lot of downtime at the hospital and Angel proved to be tech-savvy. For entertainment, she taught me how to make my smartphone a lot smarter.

Angel explained how she traded in her engineering calipers for a nurse's stethoscope when she'd grown disgusted by the good-old-boy attitude of her employers. She had nothing good to say about mining, whether it was oil, coal, or minerals. She thought she could make it more environmentally friendly. It didn't work out.

Her daddy, disappointed that he no longer had an engineer in the family, told her to do whatever made her happy, but, please never, ever fall for an auto mechanic like himself. One afternoon, she laughed when she disclosed she was disappointing her daddy once again by falling for my mechanic friend, Jackson.

I was doubly shocked because I never knew Jackson to go on a date. He was my androgynous friend—my fun and comfortable comrade. We were pals.

I startle as the phone vibrated again and proclaims "Hey, hey, hey, hey, hey." I realize I've zoned out into la-la land.

"Hey, Pryor. I've just parked at the corner. Be there when I get there." He'd kept me updated on work at my gallery and now he requires my human presence to make the last few decisions.

I look over the filled street. Tourists flock here and artists flourish. Colette, Jade and Eve are all professional artists, which means their work is creating art to earn their living. I'm more of a gentlewoman artist, painting when I feel the muse and selling when I take time to frame the pieces. I don't know why they agreed to be gallery co-owners with an artistic slacker like me. I felt both elated and guilty when they took the time to visit my little hospital room.

Teddy Bear's picnic sings out of my phone, bringing me to attention. "Hi, Jackson, I'm on my way." I listen to him and finally interrupt. "No, I am not daydreaming again. Really. No. Thank you. I can walk on my own today."

I have on natural linen slacks, wrinkled from sitting in the car, a white cotton blouse and a bulky poncho of orange, green, and white I'd picked up in Mexico long ago. I've healed my body, so my heavy wooden cane is more for psychological than physical support. A temporary handicap tag allows me to park next to the barricaded end of the street.

The village hugs itself around a small bay where the Swan River meets Flathead Lake. The town father carefully platted house lots and a block of commercial lots on the main street but never considered village people might want public access to the bay. A few buildings in town have a narrow view past the two-story condos marching along most of the shoreline. It's the hazard of having no development plan, a common Montana affliction because they regarded land use planning to be akin to communism.

"Rosetta." I hear an echoed whisper of my name down the street.

"Look, it's Rosetta."

"Wow, she looks pretty good, considering."

"Ugh, her hair. She must be one of those town characters we keep hearing about." I turn to see three well-dressed women in high heels, strangers. I let it go, it's the truth.

Stay in the middle of the street, stay in the middle, the middle road is safe, I repeat in my mind. Hobbling past a marquee filled with tables and chairs and a children's dance troupe, a row of artists' easels stood in front of me, displaying menus from every restaurant. Each chef in the village chose cuisine from different districts in Mexico. Our tickets allow us to sample every meal.

A few old friends stop to hug my fragile frame, wishing me a speedy recovery. I know they're talking about the cane. The limp is unnecessary, but it feels safe to appear pitiful. If people focus on my outside injuries, they'll ignore my crippling emotional crisis. I feel like I'm barely balanced on the head of a pin, waiting to tip and shatter.

Accusatory glares rain towards me, as though the accident was my fault. I hold my cane out in front of me like a kung fu staff, ready to flick it upward to ward off oncoming Mustangs or any human who comes toward me too fast. The doctor calls it post-traumatic stress disorder and assures me that time and therapy will make it disappear.

I have an appointment at the art gallery to go over paint and floor samples. First, I'll run this gauntlet alone. I see the street anew, as if for the first time. Quaint and cozy pops into mind, a place I'd visit during a road trip. The main street of town hosts cute gift shops, galleries, real estate offices, bars and restaurants. Condos for offices and vacation rentals crown most buildings and surround the little village.

Every few steps, someone stops me. Short answers are best. "Tell me, how are you?" Fine. "What can I do to help?" I'm all good. "Sorry for your loss." Thanks. "I liked the guy. Are you sure he tried to run you over?" Yes.

A group of high-school girls rush in, causing me to blink and stumble. They re-balance me and say how they missed me at the last few birding walks down the nature trail, how I missed the arrival of the osprey in the nest by the river, the crazy news about Kendra's taking off for parts unknown. I love how genuine they are, being themselves around me, like friends.

I read the summer theater billboards for *Fiddler on the Roof* and *Dancing in the Rain* to escape the questions and comments that keep coming. "What were you thinking, bringing a stranger to the village?" I looked down at the scrunched-up face of the oldest town resident whose chin comes up to my chest. Instead of screaming about the mistakes in her long life, I ask about the library fundraiser she organized. She smiles and tells me all about it.

Sweat pours down my face from my restraint, as well as the walking. Trudging past the kitchen shop, the county library branch and the community art center takes forever. People who want to talk follow along with me.

I nod to another art gallery owner. He's standing next to the fashion designer whose studio is across the street from my gallery. A new microbrewery is under construction at the corner. Local reporter, Marry Kat, is interviewing the event's organizers on a small stage in front of a tv camera, her long, color-streaked hair drawing all the attention. The fly fishing shop is busy. As I approach my destination, the followers drift away.

Pryor and Jackson stand side-by-side at the door watching my progress. Pryor curls forward, defensive, crossed arms shielding his chest, while Jackson, hands on his hips, spreads his feet in a power pose. They have already fallen victim to my tantrums about not wanting help and are expecting another blow-up now.

As I come closer, Pryor hustles me through the entry to escape the street. He knows I despise crowds. I collapse onto the stool they have waiting inside the door. Jackson grabs my arm. I feel light-headed and wobbly.

"Thanks," I say when he steadies my stumble.

"No sweat. Do you need a drink?" Jackson asks gruffly. He loves having someone to take care of. It's so annoying when it's me. Although I grouse at him, I suspect an occasional helping hand might be a good thing. My gut tells me there's something out there I need protection from. My neck is stiff from continually looking over my shoulder. He hovers over me, pushing a glass of iced tea into my hand. "You look like hell," he offers.

"What do you think?" asks Pryor, roughly shoving Jackson away and sweeping his arm around the room. "I have paint chips for you to look at. Here are the floor samples I picked up this afternoon. As soon as you decide the colors, we'll get 'er finished."

"It's great," I utter, unenthusiastically, observing Pryor's face fall. "I mean it. I'm exhausted from the walk." Sweat droplets run down my face. He offers me a handkerchief from his back pocket. I wipe my face without looking and sawdust grit sticks to the moisture on my brow.

I "ooh" and "ah," to make it up to him. We look at the color chips for a while. An art gallery needs muted values, neutral colors that go with everything and don't add any distraction to the artwork. I'm amazed at how many lights hang from the ceiling. We hired a consultant who specializes in art galleries to design and install the system. It's all controlled by one panel behind the sales counter.

"Let's get you upstairs to see the apartment," says Pryor, hoisting me off the stool.

"Stop slouching," interjects Jackson. "You're too young to lose inches."

Pryor glares over at him and keeps a firm grip on my arm as we go up the ten stairs, turn on a landing, and climb up nine more steps. Jackson follows with a hand on my butt in case I fall back. At the top landing, he reaches past me to push open the arched door. A blinding flood of light streams out.

We head over to the windows. "We have a view." I clap and do a little dance in place, and the boys put out their arms to catch me. The view of the bay looks out perfectly between the two nearest condominiums. I can see the public dock, the bridge over the highway, the impending sunset and paddle boarders in the bay. Privacy walls cover the ends of a narrow deck outside the glass door. It's everything I dreamed of.

Turning our backs on the bay, we stroll towards the street side, with Pryor giving a running commentary of the open efficiency kitchen, a walk-in closet, the laundry/bathroom combo, and into another large room. With no walls dividing the large open spaces, the bed could be anywhere, and the sitting room could be everywhere. The ceiling is slightly vaulted, and a sunlight tube comes down over the kitchen, lending a delicate airiness to the space.

"Leave it like this," I told Pryor. "No interior walls. We can host gallery functions here and even rent it out for private parties. Paint this wall behind the kitchen sink a bright tomato red, outline the red paint with orange molding, and trim this kitchen window with metallic gold and cobalt blue."

"Are you sure?" Jackson hands me the rest of the tea, his face creased with concern.

"Yes. Make the cabinets the same cobalt blue and the counter-top a purple marble with gold flecks." I'm thinking about tiny gold stars on the cabinets, but I can add those later. "The rest of the walls can be Navajo white. Install the gas fireplace over by the bay view windows and I'll buy a Murphy bed so we can fold it up during receptions." I feel powerful, choosing strong colors to chase away my blues, but also wrung out. "If we're going to eat, we'd better get to it." As Pryor locks the door, my reflection in the gallery window stares angrily back at me. I do look like hell.

So many things happened the weeks I was hospitalized and incapacitated. My own injuries are now ancient history.

The talk around the tables that evening was about the disappearance of Maddy McGregor's eighteen-year-old daughter Kendra. I hadn't known it happened the same day I went into the hospital. Kendra attended all the bird walks I led for the school district. She was attentive and loved learning about Native American culture and sign language from an old-timer I included on our strolls down the nature trail. She would have graduated this June, but quit school in March, passed the test for a GED certificate and told everyone she looked forward to getting away from home and landing a full-time job. Lots of kids want to spread their wings and fly from the nest, but Kendra had good reasons to move on.

CHAPTER SIX

"What should I do, Eve?"

"You ask me every day like a broken record, Rosetta."

"Tell me. I can't think straight. I'll write it out when I can place one thought in front of the other."

"Rosetta, we can use my notebook to begin. You dictate I'll record."

We brought a picnic dinner to the craggy outcropping above the lake. The sun offset the cool temperature, and we were alone. We spent the past hour sitting in the gallery, planning how to display art and what to serve at our opening reception.

"Eve, I don't know what to say. It's like the paint pallet of my brain was left out in the rain and all the colors have turned muddy."

The reality of my life was upside down. A nearby stable owner still had my horse, and she seemed happy without me. Eve assigned a second pair of high school girls to take care of my garden and lawn. Friends brought me food and cleaned my house. It was as if I died and wound up in a purgatory of my shortcomings and feebleness.

"Rosetta, say one word so we can start the story."

"Things don't add up, no matter where I start or what direction I take. What was JB trying to accomplish? Was it a prank gone wrong?

Some sort of bet with his friends? If it was something treacherous, he surely hid his dark side from everyone."

"Did you love him, Rosetta?"

"Did I love him? Did he love me? How long does it take for love to bloom with a complete stranger, with whom you seem to have nothing in common?" His final deed tangles around my brain and heart like a piece of barbed wire balled into a knot, taking random turns, locking in at indecipherable curves. "Was it a misunderstanding? Did I give off the wrong vibes? Or was he a freaking fool?"

Judges and juries popped up everywhere to share their verdicts. People are rude.

"It's someone you met online, for crying out loud!" the village busybody hissed into my ear at the grocery store. "What were you thinking?"

As we tapped away at our EFT points, my psychotherapist said, "What if he was a serial killer or an Unabomber wannabe?" That was so 1995 I had protested. " You know all radicals end up in Montana." She clearly had her own issues. "Oh yeah," she continued tapping. "And by the way, I love and accept myself," we repeated while tapping the top of our heads. Eve caught my attention with a bowl of warm rhubarb and strawberry pie from our hamper. "Ok, Rosetta, we should start at the beginning and say how he got here. What do you remember about his background? Ask around to find out what he told other people. Reveal everything you talked about and did together."

"It was sort of your fault he came here."

"I know, and I already apologized." Eve looked out at the calm lake. "I should have protested harder. Put a stop to the online date prank."

"Never mind, it was the wine. Sugardaddymates.com. How is that even a real thing?" I was still mad, but now we were looking for solutions. "What was I supposed to do with those buttons? Wink? Flirt?" We both laugh. They posted my profile before midnight and checked an hour later. There were a dozen winks from the same man. After checking out his photo, I winked back. A few minutes later, he'd sent a flood of flirts. The girls cheered, and after another glass of wine, I sent one flirt back. We exchanged two emails the following morning and somehow, he wheedled my location out of me. The next email had his flight details.

"I don't even know his birthday. Who doesn't share their birth date, family, friends and hometown with a new girlfriend? His profile had no information, either. It was damn creepy. Why did I let that slide?"

"Out of practice," Eve said, straight-faced.

"Why didn't I leave him at the airport? I only wanted to meet for coffee somewhere, not have him invade my car and community." I thought about the burning question everyone had. "Where did he get all that cash? I mean, it shocked the Ford dealership when he said cash and pulled out a roll of actual bills. And the Title company had to jump through some hoops to let him buy that house with paper money. I think they verified it wasn't counterfeit."

"Can we condense that to paid cash for car and house?" asked Eve.

I forgot she was writing it down. "He could charm anyone and always had a compliment waiting. He attracted an audience. As you said, he was a talker and everyone loved his beautiful southern accent, even me. I believe that's why we never ate alone at the cafe, always joining a table or people pulled up chairs to ours. Everyone liked him right away. He was funny, kind, treated the whole place to coffee and tipped like a king." I sighed. "You know he never ate in my kitchen and never invited me to his."

"Hmmm. Did you tell me he went to fundraisers with you? And parties at private homes? Maybe they know something about him."

"I asked all those people. Nada." I will not cry. "He paid way more than anything was worth at every auction and gave the items away immediately. It thrilled the middle school history trip group when his donation covered the cost for the entire class. Oh, and they made the nature trail improvements from his money alone."

"What's wrong with this picture?" wondered Eve. "What are we missing?"

"Well, we don't know what he did to earn that money. Where did he travel every week? If it was a regular job, he could have transacted it all online or from Zoom video chats. Do you think he was laundering the money?"

"I hate to ask, but did you ever have sex or make out?" Eve never blushed, even now.

I color from chest to hairline. "Well, I hate to answer," I shot back. "No, to both. Wait, he gave me one passionate kiss when I grilled him about his work. I think he did it to shut me up. I'm ashamed to say I was so shocked that I forgot all about the question."

"I don't even think I liked the man. He overwhelmed me, entrapped me into being his sidekick. I gave him an excuse to be here." Finally, I tell my truth. "I think I was his first step to changing something in his life. Like the girlfriend before the forever girlfriend. He said he was going to retire soon, but it sounded halfhearted, as though he were lying to himself."

"Well, he's gone now, so whatever it was is over." Eve sighed and closed her notebook.

"I'm not so sure, Eve. It was too creepy. I think whatever we missed will show up on my doorstep."

I type up our notes, including a few things that Eve considered pertinent to give to the Sheriff's Deputy.

What I know about JB Southerton

One: I met him through a website called Sugardaddymates. com. My girlfriends posted my profile on the site during the wine-filled birthday party. The profile said: Not as old as dirt, but better looking; Nosy and in charge, but not a gossip; Lots of friends, so not lonely; Probably still sexy, but no guarantees. He responded right after midnight.

After a few e-mails, JB flew in to meet me. The next day he paid in paper money, not a check, for the new Mustang, then the house.

Two: He was very gregarious. JB attracted people and always had a compliment ready.

Three: He traveled for work. He was away part of every week. One time he said he found things for large companies, a sort of facilitator. He said it was a small niche market. Nothing earthshaking. It may have had something to do with oil drilling because there is a collection of large oil companies less than six hundred miles away.

I quizzed him for days, rattling off a list of jobs as if we were playing twenty questions. When I asked if he supplied wine, women and song, he kissed me hard and told me no more questions. I stopped asking. It had been a long time since a man kissed me on the lips and my brain shorted out. His mystery job didn't seem important anymore.

Four: He was generous with money. He always pulled a gift from his pocket for me. He overbid auction items at fund-raisers and promptly gave away whatever he won. My top-of-the-line espresso maker for my new art gallery was a gift from him.

Five: He never mentioned a family, friend, hobby or home town or any other place he lived or worked, but he had a gentrified Southern accent.

Six: He was always tan. He came here in February already tan. This irritates Montanans to no end because we lose our tans by October.

The End.

CHAPTER SEVEN

I can't stand being home. The cynics are dubious about my explanations. Every time I shop for groceries, I'm bombarded with imagined accident scene reconstructions and hindsight advice. Gossip used to be confined to the beauty shop. We've become a village of clairvoyants and fortune-tellers.

Self-loathing and a guilty conscience loom over me. Somewhere in the recesses of my mind, I know what to do about depression—get outside.

When I tell Eve I'm going camping, the Indian telegraph comes alive. The phone can't stop ringing with protests. I'm still considered the walking wounded. What if I get hurt, ill, have a relapse, a flat tire, a car breakdown, get snake-bit, or encounter a flash flood—all the "what-ifs?" I have to get away and think. I need to find some relief from constant tension, release from the cycle of fear and doubt.

"Listen to me, Rosetta," said Eve, while she gently stretched my neck during Savasana pose in this morning's yoga class. "We need to chat about your camping trip."

Once my mind is made up, all dissenters may as well concede. My friends met me at The Crossroads, for a sendoff breakfast. A few of my book club members show up and shower me with self-help books and CDs for my trip. Several offered to turn my camping trip into a girls' weekend.

This morning's breakfast came with a side order of bad news. A police sting operation nabbed a prostitution ring in the state capital. "The young girls were charged with soliciting, even though they were the victims of traffickers," one shares. "Apparently, there isn't a system to hold or help these girls in any way."

"So many young women are snatched from our next-door Indian Reservations," says Eve, recounting the disappearance of another Blackfeet teen last week. She told me our X-Files heroine, Gillian, made a new movie about trafficking.

"Maddy thinks her daughter, Kendra, was plucked off the street by these girl-nappers. She put posters all over the valley and sent them to every law enforcement office in Montana, North Dakota, and other neighboring states." I pull one out of my bag. I tell the breakfast group the story about their dysfunctional family life, her dad in prison, how he had Kendra dance naked for him and his friends when she was 3 years and older after Maddy went back to work. I'm sure there was more but Kendra didn't tell me or couldn't remember. Maddy always feels so ineffectual and unworthy. At least she put a stop to that. Everyone nods knowingly. It's a small town, after all.

I pack my hay hauler pickup truck and leave before lunch to drive over the mountains and check into a cheap motel at Fort Benton. On the lobby bulletin board is a poster showing a scantily dressed young woman cowering in a dark corner of a dirty cell-like room, plus a list of phone numbers and signs of slavery I should memorize. Covering the rest of the board were announcements for the upcoming rodeo, the local 4-H livestock group schedule, bulls and tractor sales and the university extension service farm and crop tour. The normal parts of country life that feel so foreign today.

More depressed than usual about the screwed-up world and my screwed-up life, I drink too many glasses of white wine in my room and, in the place between pissed and petrified, whimper myself to sleep.

My proposed tent site is a place Lewis and Clark camped with their troop of explorers on the trip toward the Pacific Ocean in 1804. It spreads out over a cottonwood bottomland in the Missouri River Breaks and is little used by campers and boaters. The tiny fishing access is labeled 'No Camping' on the map because it's located on a finger of private farmland jabbing through the government-owned prairie. There are no toilets, drinking water or picnic tables.

The Breaks are aptly named. These steep, eroded, snaking canyons spread out like the crazy branches of a tree. The deeper, wider canyons begin at the river, then dividing repeatedly into smaller and shallower cuts in the landscape, farther away in the prairie.

Most people float the great Missouri River in kayaks, canoes and even jet boats. Sometimes the wide, slow-moving river seems like a traffic-jammed freeway, with one group piling up on the group ahead. When I need a relaxing distraction, driving out to the river to swim, hike, fish and camp alone this is my first choice. If not for rattlesnakes, I'd have brought Meg.

I'd only slept for a few hours and it's not until after lunch when my road veers east, into the glorious unobstructed prairie. White, lacy swirls of virga surround me; sheets of falling rain swooping back up toward the clouds instead of touching the earth. Distant, tall cumulus thunderheads release dark slanted pillars of rain, reaching the earth, draining the cloud until it breaks up. Smaller clouds form, each pouring out a thin stream of rain, as if from a pitcher, and then disappear.

The highway turnoff is a county road winding through farmland toward the Missouri River fishing access. In my mental haze, I don't think about what happens to the brown dusty roads of the Missouri Breaks when it rains. Everyone knows. It's common knowledge. But I'm not thinking. The rain is far away. Maybe this was one of those essential memories the concussion drove out of my brain.

Abundant water graces the prairie all around me. Flowers cover the ground like a patchwork quilt of purple vetch, small white, pink and red flowers, lupine and tiny yellow clover. A good sign. But I'm sort of down on good signs, since the shooting star that horrible night had turned out to be more of an evil omen.

My thoughts loop around the same terrifying memories again and I drive along in default mode. A swirl of fine dust billows behind my tires no matter how slow I zigzag between hay pastures and strips of wheat fields along wash-boarded gravel roads. Once I entered federal land, the track is smoother, and I speed up. I fly over the series of little rises and dips in the road. Driving so fast I can feel the weightless moment in my stomach as I start down each little hill.

These wildlands are home to hundreds of bird species, pronghorn, deer, elk, bighorn sheep and coyote. Even an occasional grizzly joins the black bear, bobcat and mountain lion to hunt in this almost inaccessible country. The road should eventually snake through a steep canyon and down onto the river bottomland, where I would, right now, be setting up my tent, catching and cooking my fish dinner and reading a book next to a campfire.

Instead, I am stuck in the middle of nowhere, with nothing to do, and mired down in the doldrums of my thoughts again. I pound my palms on the steering wheel, swearing out my frustration, finally resting my forehead on my arms to breathe. My wheels are spinning in more ways than one. Why did I putter around so long before I left town? Why did I drive down this dirt road? Why didn't I think about the rain? Why didn't I think? Why? Why?

The cloud probably dropped its liquid early this morning, and by the time my truck entered the wet patch of road, the dust had swelled into what we call gumbo, sucky as quicksand and slick as egg whites. Speeding through the first patch of wet, I start up the rise before noticing my tires spinning and I'm sliding backward. Four-wheel-drive engages at my finger's touch but it's too late.

The road looked so smooth and dusty at the beginning and other adventures had taken me down similar roads. Now I'm mired in the muck. The sign at the turn-off said Missouri Breaks Fishing Access, twenty-seven miles and it's another four miles according to my odometer.

I stand off to the side of the road, my truck and sandals caked in heavy yellow gumbo. My naughty, shadowy ghosts bring on an all-out pity party, my fists still tingle from pounding the steering wheel. Tears start their roll toward the earth, first one at a time, then holding hands in a stream. I kick the front tire, fall to my knees and scream "Why me?" Eve told me not to bottle it up inside. "Let it out," she'd said. "Empty your heart to the universe and it will answer."

It doesn't make me feel any better to think something is hearing me now, even if it is the impersonal universe and jackrabbits. I slap my truck, leaving yellow muddy prints on the blue hood like hand-prints on an Indian pony, and yell unhampered in the privacy of the prairie. Heaven forbid should anyone think me weak or upset or out of control. Crying aloud is pleasant and I really get into it, trying out elaborate yodeling cries, screams, hoots and shouts, adding side dishes of jumps and stomps. In a few minutes, like a cloudburst, it's over. I stand taller, wipe a shirttail across my face and start thinking. I laugh when coyotes yowl a reply.

Should I walk up the road to see if the Missouri River is in sight? Other than sagebrush, rabbitbrush, cactus and bunch grasses, there's very little growing near the road. I can see distant juniper and a few cottonwood trees in a nearby shallow break. The taller conifer and cottonwood treetops showing out of the deep canyon near the river. Maybe I'll find a patch of cell phone coverage along the way. Maybe I can drag some pine boughs back here and try to back out of the mud by sticking them under my tires. Or should I walk back toward the highway and hope for a farmer and tractor to come by?

I grab my water bottle, phone and protein bar and start hiking toward the river. I look back at my truck blocking the road at the bottom of the short rise. Rainwater still trickles down the hill to accumulate around my tires. About twenty feet farther along the flat top of the hill, the road is firmer and rocky. My front bumper almost touches the ground, and all four tires have a thick coating of tan slime, so I know I can't drive forward. It wouldn't do any good. I would be sitting on this little island of dryness because I imagine the other side of the hump is wet as well.

I walk along the level top for less than half a minute and look down the other side. It's not only wet but there is an old, brown jeep stuck almost up to its axles facing toward me. When I stop moving, a swarm of black flies descends upon my face and into my gaping mouth. Through the coughing fit, I untie my cowgirl silk scarf and rewrap it around my face to protect the back of my neck and ears from these biting fiends. At that point, a cloud splits open and a fire-hose of water hits me right on the head.

I slog back to the truck, sandals sinking deeper under this new rain shower and picking up more mud with each step. First, one sandal, then the other, sucks so deep into the muck they stick in place when I lift my foot. I leave them behind, looking like a miniature Stonehenge poking up out of the mud. Gumbo squishes up between my toes. I open the passenger side door and grab my beach towel from the dashboard. I strip off the wet shorts, shirt and underwear, laying them over the back of the seat. The warm towel feels good wrapped around my wet, shivering body. My teeth start chattering now, maybe from the cold rain, maybe from anger, maybe from thoughts of JB. I cover my head, cry a bit and escape into sleep.

Sun beating in through the closed windows brings me gasping back to life. I fling open the door, grab my damp clothes and step outside. The road is still gumbo, my truck is still stuck, but somehow, I feel better. Wide-open spaces can do that for a person. Prying my shoes out of the muck, I carry everything up to the top of the rise so I can scrape off some of the gumbo before getting dressed. I feel a few sprinkles and notice I'm on the edge of a new cloudburst.

The sun is in the western sky and at the right angle to light up a double rainbow in the falling rain to the east. I use my finger to follow the arch from one end to the other, searching the ends for a pot of gold. Under the middle of the rainbow, something moves. It's close, maybe a quarter-mile away. It seems to be tall, dark and bushy. Could it be a bison or a big bull elk? I stand still, so as not to frighten it. After a few minutes, I hear singing. A man's voice singing. I duck down, sitting my bare bum on a short prairie cactus. I scream and leap up. The bushy beast stops moving. I quickly throw on my shirt, as the beast moves closer. I barely finish zipping up my shorts and slip into my sandals, when a mound of pine boughs stops next to the stuck jeep. I stuff my underwear into the back pocket of my shorts.

It's then I notice the branches laid down like a wooden poll bridge from the rocky rise next to the roadbed across the slop, stopping five feet short of the jeep. Dirt spattered limbs are stuck around all four tires: a failed attempt to back out of the gumbo. The man looks at me in surprise.

"*Hola*," he says. "Hi," I answer.

"What's up?" he asks.

"My truck is stuck down in the next dip," I answer, pointing with my thumb back toward the direction I had come from.

"Ah," he says, nodding.

CHAPTER EIGHT

The man of few words drops his improvised travois of two long cottonwood limbs running parallel behind him, spaced apart about as wide as his body. Thin branches are lashed perpendicular across the gap, creating a platform. One end of the travois straddles his narrow hips and is carried in his hands. Rope loops tied to each handle are slung crisscross over his naked shoulders and chest like a pair of bandoliers. The other ends of the limbs are lashed together and dragging behind like a wheeless wheelbarrow. He shrugs off the ropes and a rolled-up shirt protecting his shoulders.

Sweat streams down every exposed surface of his suntanned, athletic body. The travois is piled high with green pine boughs, as well as shorter, groove-covered limbs looking like well-chewed corncobs. Beaver snacks. He must have walked miles to the main river. A rolled-up tarp, fishing pole, hatchet, sleeping bag and jacket stick out from between the branches. The man methodically places the pine boughs parallel with the others, finishing the bridge across the mud to reach the jeep door. He opens it, removes a large bottle of water, chugging it in one, long swig.

A broad-brimmed cloth hat flops down around his brown neck, also covering his forehead and eyes. Flaming black-fly welts stand out along his beltline and neck. Tattoos of dragonflies and birds fly across his bare, glistening shoulder blades. When he tosses the hat onto his front seat, long, dark snakes of hair tumble out as if escaping a cage. Two black, bushy caterpillars crawl across his forehead in place of eyebrows. Nut-brown skin accentuates his blue eyes as he looks at me again. His gaze sweeps down and up my body. Is he sizing up my slim frame next to his buff build?

"So, what brings you way out here?" he asks.

"Birding," I answer back, not wanting to give any more information than necessary.

Pack behavior and the power of suggestion hides in the back of one's brain, waiting to pounce. I keep thinking I'm emotionally fit, that I can breathe, maybe even cope with stress and surprise. Since the incident at Larsen Lake, all free will has left me. I pretend to feel normal, but then I hyperventilate, cry or flinch, involuntarily throwing up my hands in front of my face for no reason.

The extensive discussion of sexual assault on older women at breakfast yesterday comes back to me. Over one hundred thousand women and children are trafficked in the United States each year. How many of them are my age? My friend's service club brought speakers to the valley last year, informing us, in detail, about abduction and human trafficking. They told us to be hyper-vigilant. Who can do that for very long?

My friend drove every one of us to despair with her tales of the ugly tragedy and I told her it doesn't happen in our valley. What was happening here, now? I come out for a quiet camping trip and find myself confronted with a dreadlocked, bushy-browed, brown man in the middle of nowhere. Was his question a trick? What did he want? He's a little taller than my five foot eight. I wonder if anyone will come along to save me and nix the idea immediately.

"Cool. You all alone?" he asks, pulling the hat back on top of his head.

The hair on my body is standing up. I can feel my legs tingling where the hair would have stood up if I hadn't had it cruelly waxed off a few days ago. The casual question could be another trick. I want to run, but I'm glued to the gumbo. My breath is coming in short gasps.

"Hey, are you having a heart attack or something? I know CPR, but we're a long way from help." He says this with concern in his voice.

All I focus on is the simple question *'you all alone,'* and *'we're a long way from help.'* Oh. My. God. Can this be happening? Snap out of it. My alarm goes off, my stomach clenches and my fight or flight response kicks in. I should try flight first. I give myself a shake as he starts towards me. The slippery mud slows him down. I back away and turn to run. I didn't get a chance to fasten my sandals and the Velcro hooks on the straps snag onto the loops on the opposite shoe.

My face plant is slow and graceful. I roll as I go down, so only one side of my face smacks into the sticky gumbo. I end up on my back, winded. The man appears over me, reaching down, his black eyebrows knitting together into a unibrow. An old, childhood horror movie taught me that one eyebrow meant sinister tendencies, vampire, or something bad. Energy rushes through me and I get a fleeting thought of one of my college roommates who had one long eyebrow. I couldn't shake the unreasonable fear. The poor girl had to pluck out the center hairs and keep it clean for the four months we lived together.

My fingernails fly toward his hands and arms, connecting with the smooth skin above his wrists. He's caught off guard and my right knee swings up, striking him on the side of his knee. He yowls, stumbling sideways and off-balance. I jab my foot into his hip, sending him tumbling to his side. Adrenaline brings me quickly to my feet and I take on a fighting stance and begin my attack. I hear and ignore the first rule of self defense: run.

"Stop!" he yells. He is also laughing and rolled into the fetal position, covering his head. "I'm sorry, I'm sorry for whatever I did. I'm sorry." I kick his back and head, my bare, slime-covered feet sliding more than landing.

I must be weak, because between the "ouch, ouch" and "sorry, sorry, sorry," he is still laughing. He's obviously not sorry enough.

What is he, a sadist? "Get off on that beating, buddy? There's more to come." His hand shoots out and grabs my ankle as my heel lands on his ribs. One jerk and I'm off balance and onto my butt. He shoots up and runs a few yards before turning around. I'm up as fast. He lunges forward and grabs my wrist, but I spin out of his grasp, while simultaneously twisting his arm behind him and pushing him away. He raises one of his hands next to his head like waving a white flag; the other hand is holding his ribs where my last kick left a muddy imprint. He shouts "I give up. I'm sorry. Tell me what I did so I can apologize again. Do I even know you?"

Stupid questions deserve more beating. I should run, but I growl and lunge after him. Many years have elapsed between my study of Tai Chi Quan and Karate. I stopped taking classes after college but kept up some of my routine exercises and gentle Tai Chi. My proficiency is not black or brown belt material, but I can sure scare the crap out of anyone who messes with me. I have a collection of jabbing and kicking that is plain mean. Plus, my recent introduction to Krav Maga in self-defense for women workshops is coming in handy.

Here in round two, Dreadlocks rushes me again and slaps away my jabs. He blocks the well-aimed crotch kick with a down-sweep of his hand and blocks my roundhouse punch to his head with his other forearm. He is good, but no match for my jabbing punches connecting with his now unprotected ribcage.

As he curls slightly forward and grabs my shoulders, I slip one hand behind his head and push two fingers of the other hand into his throat above his collarbone, stabbing hard while pulling his head toward the ground. He drops to a crouch, choking, and pivots away. I follow with a foot shove to his butt propelling him, spread-eagle, into the mud and cactus again. I fall on top of him screaming, beating his shoulders, slapping his head. He spins like a trout onto his back, catches my wrists and pulls me close, pinning my arms between using a bear hug and wrapping his legs around mine in a scissor squeeze.

"Calm down, calm down," he first shouts and then says more quietly, "Shhhhh."

I scream, curse and try to give him a head butt. He rolls us over so he's on top, pinning my head with his. I try to bite his ear, but he grips my ear in his teeth first and pushes my cheek down into the mud. I do not beg for mercy. If he is going to rape and murder me I will go down fighting. I begin to gasp for air. The pressure of his weight on my belly prevents me from inhaling. I feel faint and sluggish as my body begins to fade. I relax and he lets go of my ear.

The sudden picture of zebra plays across the movie in my mind. Like an old-fashioned black and white film, it flickers and crackles, starting with shots of the zebra herd running flat out, legs stretched long, moving fast. Then an individual finds himself away from the herd and falters, the lions immediately surrounding him. He kicks, stomps and bites violently, holding the lion pack at bay until one lioness jumps on his back, throwing him to the ground. After a few kicks, the zebra goes into a still, coma-like state to not feel the pain of being eaten alive. I swear to myself I won't die. I try a feeble head butt again when he released my ear. I growl and twist my body, which makes Dreadlocks tighten his grip.

"¡Basta! Please, calm down," he orders. "Don't make me hurt you, please. I don't like to hurt people, but I will defend myself."

He sees me gasping and rolls us onto our sides but keeps a snug hug around me. His sweat smells sweet, mine reeks of fear.

"I'm pretty sure I'd remember someone like you." He gives me a closer inspection. "What's going on? Are you loco? Are you going to stop hitting me if I let you go?"

I nod. The brown man releases my legs and, keeping a grip on my arms, helps me sit up on my knees. I look up into his face. His dreadlocks, eyebrows and face are caked with gumbo. His eyes show only concern. My disobedient chin begins to quaver and tears well into my eyes. He pulls me onto his lap, hugging my muddy body next to his. With one hand still gripping my wrists behind me, his other hand rubs my back, as I lean in and I cry out all my anger, fear and grief onto the chest of this stranger.

I hadn't cried in pain like this when the car hit me. I hadn't cried tears of grief when I identified JB in the morgue. I hadn't cried for loss after we had JB cremated and spread his ashes in Flathead Lake. I had only wept tears of self-pity. Now, I feel relief and release from my horror of the last few months. I cry for JB's sad death, as if he were a lost childhood sweetheart.

CHAPTER NINE

I'm in a vacuum; no gravity, no sound, no movement, no anxiety. The dreadlocked man tells me what to do and, zombie-like, I do it. "Grab your empty water bottles, water treatment bladder, snacks, hat, clean clothes, and a rope." My feet drag, kicking up a stream of dust behind us. I'm numb since we completed our *mano-a-mano* combat.

Devouring half a dozen power bars to fill the void builds my strength and gravity connects my body to the earth once again. My foot catches on a sagebrush and I stumble to my knees, leaving another gouge on my battered body. We walk over the sagebrush steppe. Nothing stirs. The place looks like a smooth blanket of olive green from down here, but from the air it's a maze of jigsaw pieces.

He points to trees growing in the second canyon over, maybe a mile away, which indicates a water source. The manmade trail circles sharply to the north, away from our destination to bypass most of the many gullies. We travel the short distance from here to there by taking the scenic route. After a forty-minute walk through the shrub land we finally stumble down the steep-sided canyon. He'd discovered the developed spring during his earlier wood gathering foray.

I notice the metal pipe sticking horizontally out of a pocket in the steep hillside, directing a delightful flow of water into a long, skinny concrete watering trough that biologists installed for wildlife. The water flows into the trough and out through an overflow pipe on the other end. He instructs me to strip off my clothes and points to the trough.

It's barely broader than my hips and about eighteen inches deep. Lowering myself into the cool water feels heavenly. I lay back and inhale aromas of mud and the musky smell of deer who have rubbed off their shedding coats along the rough concrete. I wash my hair and body as best I can without soap. My clean t-shirt serves as a towel and then goes onto my body to keep me cool. I step into my underwear and nylon hiking pants as he returns holding a pile of wet clothes in front of his hips. He sends me down to wash my own clothes and submerges his skinny behind into the trough.

Can a fight be cathartic? I'm exhausted, but also clearheaded for the first time since the incident. Aristotle suggested we could cleanse a human of excess emotions, like self-pity, anger, or fear, by playing out an experience with the suggestion of intense fear. During our brief fight, the terror was unquestionable. The shift to survival mode broke through my obsession, my continual distress over dating JB. It broke down the wall I built around my mind, my heart. Something dreadful had taken place at Larsen Lake. Now, it's as though someone has slapped me awake. I feel light. Free. Like I've had a colon cleanse.

When JB told me he was traveling in to visit, tension wracked my whole body. The odd twist and turns in our dating, constant second-guessing and dithering never blossomed into a romance. In a flash, my friends come to mind and what they had been saying all along. They continually asked me what I knew about him, what he was like, if he was a wonderful kisser. I blew them off with a laugh, while my subconscious wondered the same things.

I am energized after the cold dip. We proceed toward our cars with Dreadlocks pulling the travois loaded with two full five-gallon water jugs, six small water bottles, more firewood, and our rinsed out muddy clothing. The rain clouds evaporate, leaving behind a hot and muggy evening. The black flies follow us like personal dark clouds. My hips throb from all that kicking. Scrapes and punctures dot my body. His body, also scratched and bruised, emulates a tribal warrior proudly returning from a bison hunt.

"Wait, Mr. Dreadlocks, I have to tell you something."

"Let's keep walking while you talk," Mr. Dreadlocks responds.

"I'm sorry," I shout back. He glances back at me.

"Okay. Bueno." With no reluctance, he walks doggedly towards our goal. That travois must be tough to pull, so I trot up beside him and offer to help. He hands me a loop of the rope that's tied off to one branch of the travois and I slip it over my head and shoulder.

"Yikes." The rope digs into my shoulder. Mr. Dreadlocks reaches back and grabs my almost dry shorts, folds and stuffs them under the rope as padding.

"I love this place," I tell him, trying to strike up a conversation that doesn't involve me apologizing and feeling guilty as hell. "How did you discover it? Few people come out here. My name is Rosetta Stone, but people call me Roe. What can I call you?"

"You mean roe, like fish eggs? You have imaginative friends and parents," he adds, gazing at me with a teasing smile in his eyes. His sensual wide mouth curves up slightly at the corners. I don't know if he'll even tell me his name. Why get further involved with a wacko than you have to. "My name is Enrique. Most people call me Dr. Enrique."

"In-ree-kay, in-ree-kay." I struggle to roll the "r" like he does.

Once he starts, it's tough to get a word in edge wise. He informs me he's writing a book about the ecosystem that Lewis and Clark found here two hundred years ago on their trip through the

Montana Territory. It has been in the research stage for the past four years because he took off two years to serve a prison sentence for stabbing a man. We're tied together and I can only move away about a foot. He reassures me it was in self-defense. I inform him about the collection of historical nature books out there. Yes, he knew other books had been published about this same topic, but he enjoyed doing the research and his writing would be very different.

Enrique had managed a small, private bird preserve along the Yellowstone River. He was the resident botanist and birding expert, meeting up with university professors and students touring the preserve. A disagreement over business practices and money led to the boss getting the drop on him, and Enrique stabbing him. It put him out of the land management business for the near future. He needed to find other means to support him while he finished his book.

"I've only been out of prison for ten days and have accomplished nothing but drive, drink and walk since my release," he admits. "I drove into the mud yesterday morning. You're the first real person I've talked with." He suddenly stops pulling, which jerks me to a halt. I can see why dogs and horses pulled travois. It takes coordination and muscle strength to pull something without wheels. "So, what's with the beating you gave me? Do I look that scary? Is it the dreads?" He gives his freshly washed glistening snakes a shake. "I had to fit into the prison crowd." He searches my face for a moment, then asks, "What are you really doing out here?"

I shrug and stare at my feet.

Enrique sends me to find kindling, fire-starting material of a finer and more flammable nature, to start the cottonwood branches burning. Every plant is alive or damp, so he tells me to look for paper in his Jeep we can use. I totter over the log bridge to pull open the door. My God, it's so neat. My Chevy looks like a pigsty after one day of travel.

A cloth Nature Conservancy bag on his front seat contains several books that grace my library: *The Sibley Guide to Birds; Birds in Place* by Rad Icenoggle; and P.D. Skaar's *Montana Bird Distribution*; plus, *Edible Plants of the North West*. I pull up a couple of shorter books and find *The Journals of Lewis and Clark* and *Undaunted Courage* by Stephen E. Ambrose. Each book has dozens of sticky notes peeking out from the top.

The outside compartment of the bag holds a flattened paper coffee cup full of punch cards from dozens of different latte stands. A lidded metal travel cup, the price sticker still glued to the surface, rests on the dashboard cup holder. I finally understand his drink of choice over the past ten days.

I lean into the jeep to look around. The floor is as clean as a whistle, even under the seats, so I open the console. I have to press on it to get the latch to release. As I back off, the lid springs up like a jack-in-the-box and paper shards pop out, flowing down onto the seat and floor like a tumbling deck of cards. I pick up a couple. They're cup jackets, insulating cardboard tubes that slide over the hot paper cup when you get a latte to go. One's from Banff Bistro in Canada, Caffè Artigiamo in Vancouver, B.C., another half-dozen from Starbucks and Seattle's Best with Seattle addresses. Others came from places near and far in Montana, like Cowgirl Cappuccino, Montana Coffee Traders, True Espressions, Latte Laughs, Latitude 49. Popping the latch on the glove box releases another free fall of cardboard jackets.

"Find anything?" he calls.

I smile, stuff my pockets with cardboard and force the rest back into the center console.

I trudge over the hillside to grab my rucksack out of my truck. The mud already has a dry, cracked surface. Surely, we can drive out of here by tomorrow if it doesn't rain again.

I pulled the pages from my rucksack and read over what I had written about JB and gave to the sheriff, with a few additions I'd thought of over the past couple of weeks.

Enrique soothes a cardboard sleeve between his rough fingertips. "On the first day out of prison, I took a road trip. I took the bus back to the preserve to pick up my Jeep, withdrew a wad of cash from the bank, and took off. As you can see, I missed my espresso and lattes while in the joint." He piles up some sticks, shoves a few pieces of cardboard strips underneath and starts to light the cardboard with one of his wooden matches.

"Wait," I say. "Read this." I thrust the pages about JB at him. "I'll start the fire."

Fire starting is a sacred act to me, so I couldn't stand to throw away this opportunity. Brushing away his crumpled sticks, I build a three-sided tepee of small twigs around shreds of the cardboard, placing sticks and then the thicker branches of beaver wood nearby. Plucking dry brown grass beneath a bush, I form a little bird nest out of a handful of the grass and cardboard shreds and pour an oil-soaked cotton ball from a film canister into the nest.

I grab a small leather case from my pack and pull it apart into halves. One half reveals a flint magnesium rod and the other holds a short flat piece of steel, called the striker. After two smooth scrapes with the striker along the rod, sparks land neatly on the target and the cotton ball smokes. I quickly push the nest inside the tepee of twigs, careful not to smother it. Blowing it into flames and adding more cardboard, twigs and sticks and then the ends of a few long beaver branches, it only takes a few minutes to have a roaring fire. To me, it's like counting prayer beads with a mantra, a method to focus the mind.

On our trip to the spring and back, he'd pulled a pistol out of his rucksack and shot a rabbit and a grouse. He cleans the carcasses and chops the grouse, vegetables, and herbs. By the time he finishes, the dry branches burn into glowing coals and Enrique erects a small steel tripod over the fire and hooks his flat-topped Dutch oven inside the tripod.

Into the pot goes the grouse, along with a few chopped potatoes, onions, garlic, carrots, parsnips, dried chilies, a handful of purslane and other prairie plants for spice. He holds a cardboard box over the pot and adds a few cups of red wine. After replacing the lid, he uses two sticks like tweezers and picks out the larger pieces of hot coals from the fire to cover the flat lid to cook the pot from top and bottom. He laces the slender rabbit carcass onto a forked steel bar that hooks through the top of the tripod to suspend the rabbit over the fire. Hors d'oeuvres, he says. It seems like a lot of meat, but he craves real food after eating the poor excuse for dinner in prison. The aroma smells heavenly.

CHAPTER TEN

Enrique and I sit next to the campfire on our respective camp chairs, sipping wine from my plexiglass wine goblets, while he reads about JB, and I listen to the fire snap.

"This is what you gave to the police who investigated this convoluted fatal event?" asks Enrique as he hands the pages back to me. "It rambles all over the place."

"Remember, I was in shock." I sit taller and defend myself. Why did I add the dating debacle? No wonder I'm depressed. I'm always on the defense now and it is hard work. I want a knight to ride in and slay my dragons, or at least stand next to me and hold my hand. "I'm so tired of thinking about it," I add, slumping forward.

"They probably had a good laugh over the parts about the tan. Not to mention the Sugar-daddy-dates posting and the kiss. Why did you even tell them that? But these other things—throwing cash around, traveling for an undisclosed job, secretive, no known family, attempted to murder you— now those are interesting."

I'd described the scene at Larsen Lake to Enrique during the last half of our walk. Pulling the travois made enough of a distraction so I could talk without thinking too much. It felt good to say it all in one long narrative, and Enrique proved to be a patient listener. I'd pieced together a lot of the story from people who came to my rescue, as well as my firsthand knowledge of the car speeding up the hill toward me. Larsen Lake is about forty feet deep, and someone dove right away to pull him up, but he was already dead. The autopsy indicated he wasn't wearing a seatbelt and had flown over the inflating air bag as the car descended, slamming his head between the steering wheel and windshield, snapping his neck. He didn't have water in his lungs.

"So that's what you think?" I say, looking him over again. "Attempted murder?" Where did this nature nerd, this recently released prison rat, this dread-locked nobody, come up with that idea?

"If so, you're the only one who thinks so."

"Really?"

"Yes, and furthermore, do you have experience in crimes other than stabbing people?"

"Well, I never used it, but I took crime scene and accident investigation courses earlier in my life, and I read a lot of crime novels," he says with a smile.

I laugh. "That's about as qualified as the cops who interviewed me. They all thought it was an accident. The gear shift was in the drive position. They suggested it was some sort of freak car malfunction, you know, like when the Toyota Prius accelerated, and the driver couldn't stop. Or they said JB blacked out for some unknown reason. The car stopped working after being dunked and who knows if JB had medical issues. The medical examiner said it wasn't a stroke or heart attack."

Enrique looks at me, waiting. Waiting for what, I couldn't bring myself to say aloud. The hidden trauma I've been harboring since the incident. Murder? I hadn't asked the sheriff this question. It flitted like hummingbirds through my brain, amorphous and elusive. "Murder?"

"Why did you agree to go to that secluded spot? Why do you think he'd want to meet there?"

"I didn't care why. It would be the first time we were alone, just the two of us, instead of in a restaurant full of people or driving and talking about the scenery." I thought for a minute. "It's really more private than secluded. A risky place for a murder."

"OK, so talk about the location, after the car wreck."

"My old friend, Jackson, was first on the scene. Did I tell you already? I think he heard it on the police scanner on his kitchen table and got there before the ambulance. Maybe someone saw the Mustang shoot up the hill and reported it. I don't think anyone would have checked on my lone car in the lot until the next morning. He probably saved my life." I stumbled over what to say next, but Enrique didn't interrupt. "He placed his coat between my head and the gravel. It was so bloody by the time the EMTs arrived and replaced it. He knew I was meeting JB, hopefully for a more private date." I made air quotations with my fingers around the word date. "On the flip side, maybe he saw the accident. I never asked how he happened to be there first. How could he see me on that hill? It's not really a drive-by kind of place at that time of day, unless you live out that way or are looking for owls."

"Does your intuition tell you why he came there?" asks Enrique.

Without thinking, I blurted it out. "He was looking for me."

"Why?"

"Maybe he was jealous." I took a calming breath. "No. No. Not that. Maybe he was worried about me."

Random thoughts come and go when you think about what happened around an event. It gives new perspectives, other points of view. Other views. Another direction. Looking at it from a different position. Or being another person. What do I see if I am standing in the parking lot? What do I see if I am flying overhead?

"This is what I see happening. I hear the car slow down and pull into the parking lot. I see headlights, but I can still see the car, too, because it isn't really dark yet. It's dusk. There is still a lot of light in the west near the horizon."

I take a slow breath and continue. "The car is idling, slowly rolling into the parking place right at the beginning of the path up to the pond. There's a wide opening there in the low log fence where the pavement is painted with diagonal yellow lines. So, it's not a parking space, but with only my car in the lot, he could have taken any slot."

I squeeze my eyes shut to wring out another memory. "I think he leaned over to unbuckle his seat belt. There is a sudden revving of the engine, the car shoots right through the opening and makes a beeline up the hill toward me."

I stare at the fire, trying to gather my thoughts.

"Wait, I remember the headlights blinded me. They blinked from low to high beams a few times. I thought I froze in my spot, sitting cross-legged on the light pillar, but I didn't. It took time to uncoil my legs. I leaned away to jump, pushing off the pedestal with my hands and feet, almost perpendicular to the trajectory of the car. The car hit a landscape rock and swerved, then hit the bollard as I jumped. That's why I flew across one end of the pond and landed on the shore instead of shooting straight into the water. The revving continued as the car flew through the air."

Enrique knelt by the fire and lifted the lid so he could stab meat and potatoes with his hunting knife. "Almost," he mumbles. "Do you remember what happened then?"

I thought for another moment. "I don't know when the revving really stopped, because I passed out when I hit the ground. I only had a fleeting glance of the car tipping toward the surface and disappearing into the pond."

A moment of realization strikes my heart. "What if JB was knocked unconscious when he hit the light bollard? That's why he couldn't bail out of the car. Next thing I knew, Eve was leaning over me, telling me I was okay." The end of my thought process neared, but I made myself stumble on, over the uneven, rocky part that might be imagination, shock or trauma, or all three.

"Yes, okay, okay. I thought it was attempted murder." I shiver like a ghost has passed through me. "Although the bump on the head didn't kill me, it could have. And if I'd hit the water, unconscious from the blow of the car or a whiplash, I'd be dead. Maybe that's when JB broke his neck." I glance across the fire at Enrique. He's still looking at me. Not with the hard, accusing eyes I thought I saw from people around town, as though they blamed me for the death of JB, the wildly popular newcomer. He doesn't have pity in his gaze, either. Enrique's eyes hold interest, encouragement, support, like he's proud I've remembered something, voiced my innermost thoughts.

"Now that I've said it out loud, I question a couple of other things."

"Like what?" Enrique asks.

"He always wore a seatbelt. The accident report said it wasn't buckled, so maybe I did see him lean over to unbuckle." A couple of breaths later, I continue. "Why did he unbuckle and then speed up?"

"What else?"

"Why the heck didn't he apply the brakes as he hit me? He wouldn't have known I would survive. If he wanted to murder me, I would have been easy to finish off." I ponder a moment. "That's the part that really disturbs me. If he meant to kill me, why kill himself, too? And why the heck did he use the beloved Mustang as a potential murder weapon?"

"What else sticks out?"

I looked from a detective's perspective. "Why kill me? Why not move away? Why not dump me for someone else? No one else has stepped forward to claim him. So, now it makes me think maybe I knew something that I shouldn't. Maybe he'd said an inadvertent word or sign of his secret life and work." I mull that over for a minute. "At the time, I thought it brave and wonderfully free when he purchased the car and the house with no thought of the future. He fully invested himself in the community." What if I was wrong about everything? "Maybe it wasn't his free spirit at all. Maybe he had another reason for wanting to be here in the valley and used me as a convenient excuse."

"Have you examined everything he said to you?" Enrique had me on a roll.

"So many times that my imagination might embellish it. I've even read between the lines. I've examined all my thoughts from our first meeting. I can't find any sign of tension on his part except for that one time, when I pestered him about his work."

"What happened?" Enrique encourages me. "Can you remind me?"

"I even wrote it down in my daily journal because it seemed so funny afterward." I chuckle, remembering. "He kissed me. I haven't had a kiss on the lips for a very long time. He leaned right across the console and pulled my face toward his. I melted on the spot." The feel of his warm lips, the tip of his tongue touching mine, had been so powerful that I can still feel it. The heat rises into my face like a hot flash on a chilly night. I hug my blanket closer around my neck. "I didn't know that it would be the one and only hint at passion."

"Why did he kiss you?"

"It wasn't for romance," I blurt out. My body is burning from embarrassment now and I throw back the blanket. What a fool I'd been. "He wanted to shut me up. He toyed with me, using very elementary psychology to distract me. He was like a magician, a mind reader, or a fake psychic. I guess I was an easy mark." A dark curtain of self-blame begins its descent down, down into my heart.

Dreadlocks bounce as Enrique looks away. "Continue."

"I kept going on and on about his work. He wasn't retired from something that would have ended the whole discussion. He did something he enjoyed. It may have given him some sort of notoriety because I swear, he sat taller, puffed up, when he thought about it. Why didn't he just lie to me?" I consider that for a beat. "I felt like it was something to do with his ego. I felt he was really skilled at it, proud. He called himself a deal maker." I pictured JB telling me this. "What if he wouldn't tell me because it was something illegal. Maybe that's why he shut me down after I suggested he was a distributor of wine, women and song."

"Hmmm."

Enrique is a good listener, but I notice he only speaks when he has something to say. No chitchat.

"So, what about it, Enrique? What do you think so far?" I try to put the ball in his court. My head's tired of thinking about it.

"What if he shut you down because you got close to guessing?" Enrique offers.

"Right." I say, as a sarcastic two syllables. "So, what if he distributes booze or owns a string of cabarets? Nothing so horrible that he can't share it?" My mind starts stepping off the narrow path I'd been walking. I was making fresh turns, moving through the labyrinth, and every labyrinth has its exit. I look at Enrique in wonder. This guy would make a wonderful psychiatrist. "JB didn't warn me that if he told me, he'd have to kill me. Maybe he was illegally importing liquor or was a bootlegger with a string of stills in them thar hills and valleys across the Montana."

Enrique joins in. "Or, speaking of songs, smuggling Mariachi bands across the border."

"Or black market quartets of Italian tenors," I add, singing a poor imitation of Pavarotti out across the prairie. Coyotes answer right away.

We both start laughing and can't stop. Tears stream down our faces. Enrique hugs his sides. I fall to my knees, praying I won't pee my pants. When the laughing runs its course, the companionable

silence, the crackling campfire sparks popping up like mini fire-
works, feel very natural and nurturing. It's great to laugh again, to
really breathe. The accident somehow seems less personal now that
we've laughed about it. My stomach lets out a big growl.

Enrique uses his large hunting knife to separate the legs of the
rabbit from the carcass and hands me one.

"Delicious," I mutter through my full mouth.

"Okay, so what if he was some sort of illegal liquor supplier? Why
come to Montana? We have so many micro beer brewers and whiskey
distillers he could have done it legally. I wonder where his phone calls
came from." I'm surprised by my voice. It sounds like I'm talking
about someone else's life. "Did the police check his phone records?"
Enrique talks while brushing ash off the lid of the Dutch oven.

"I don't know." I have another disturbing thought. "What if it
was something to do with the second part of that question: wom-
en?" I let that hang a moment. "He seemed too friendly, outgoing
and generous to be involved in anything like that. Did I already
mention a girl from Tamarack Falls disappeared the same time as
my injury? Some think she ran away, but her mom thinks she was
kidnapped. What if JB was involved?"

Enrique brings two large plates out of his camp box and dishes
up the stew. We wolf down the meal, declaring it the best either of
us has ever eaten. Night sounds of the prairie serenade us. In the
twilight, we can hear the buzz of two nightjars and watch their
silhouettes zig-zag across the sky on long wings, catching moths. A
few bats swoop through the light of the fire. A large beetle tumbles
out of the firewood and scurries away from the heat. Coyotes yip
and yowl in the distance and great horned owls call to each other in
the forest, where we found our water. The smoke carries that funny
urine scent of burning cottonwood.

"But back to the beginning, if he meant to kill me, why follow
with the suicide? And if he didn't mean to kill me, then why hurt

or scare me and then kill himself? What if he didn't mean to kill himself?" I search the night sky for several minutes, noting a few shooting stars and a couple of satellites moving in a predictable path across the heavens. "I need answers. This has ruined my life."

"Tell me about your life before the incident, before JB," Enrique says.

Raising my face to look at the blackness between the stars, I continue. "There could be a simple, totally unrelated answer to this long list of questions. Some time ago, I was employed by a mega-giant corporation. I was hired as a biologist, writing environmental impacts statements, negotiating with conservation groups around the world. I was hoping to make a difference."

Enrique turned away; his nose pinched as though smelling something nasty.

I hurried on before I chickened out. "Listen, I used to feel the same way about industry biologists. Many of them really are sell-outs. Even I often felt like a traitor, but I really could mitigate the damage done to the earth. Or thought I could."

"I was doing research for another statement when I discovered, by accident, the company had been blatantly dumping its toxic wastes in several countries, violating many international laws. During a global industry meeting, I reported the actions publicly in my speech. Instantly, I became an international environmental heroine and received a whistle blower settlement from a lawsuit. With all the death threats I received, this wasn't a complete surprise. I'm still not sure if it's related."

"You're *that* R. Stone?" Enrique's smile lit up almost as bright as the fire.

CHAPTER ELEVEN

Sometimes, the unexpected can be a happy accident. Like when you're painting a watercolor and color suddenly floods in an undesired direction. You can cry out and madly blot with a paper towel or you can go with the flow. Once in a while, the results transcend the artist's plans. Accepting spontaneity brings in an expression of creativity.

Other times, the unexpected is anything but happy. Like when I was away on the recent camping trip, a tree smashed through the garden fence. Deer promptly jumped the gap to eat up everything that wasn't a weed.

Enrique proved to be my happy accident. He, like myself, is a coffee aficionado, plus he's unemployed and unemployable because of his recent prison release. There isn't anything I don't like about him. He's funny, smart, resilient, cooks, loves the earth and, maybe it's the rebound talking, he's wonderfully attractive.

"Come home with me," I beg. We drove out of the mud the next morning. He camped at the local state park for a week while Pryor finished the gallery's upstairs apartment. I promptly furnished it and moved Enrique in. After a short training at the local coffee roasting mill, he slipped into the position at the gallery like a born barista.

I fired my therapist and Enrique takes over my mental care. My friends fall into his magnetic aura. As a result of my transformation during the camping trip, they hold him in awe. I'm sure they all think I got laid, and who am I to destroy their illusions? Maybe they're all hoping for the same.

Enrique looks good in the tastefully furnished upstairs apartment, decorated with our own artistic pieces. Providing free living space makes up for his paltry wage during this start-up phase of the art gallery. He fit right into our little artists' colony. He can do anything. He said a PhD teaches a person to explore and focus, to think and learn, but no life skills. Those he learned from his family and taught himself.

Enrique invited the four of us partners for a tamale making party to celebrate our new friendships and his new abode. Over the wonderful dinner, he shared the story of how his family migrated between Mexico and California through his childhood and early teens. First working as migrant fruit pickers and then as owners of a grocery and small café. His mama and Abuela taught him everything he learned about cooking their family recipes when he helped in the café kitchen. Once he began high school, they left him to study, play sports and win scholarships. He wasn't the first in his family to get a college education, but he was the first with a doctorate.

Today, I wished for leftovers from that remarkable meal. Exhaustion looms on the horizon for all of us, so I call out for pizza delivery.

"Do you think we can finish tonight?" Jade asks. It's late afternoon before tomorrow's grand opening of the Stone Mountain Gallery and Coffee Bar and we're busy as a beehive. She stands at the back of the room, balancing more of her handmade drums on a cascade of shelves, testing each for tone and clarity one more time.

All four partners help each other arrange art and shelves and coffee paraphernalia. Eve puts the final touches to her jewelry display. Her larger weavings clip onto poles attached to a clever pulley system Enrique devised to raise them toward the ceiling.

"We'll stay all night if we have to," says Colette and sets another Raku pottery bowl on the tables along the edges of the room. Enrique helps hang her hand formed platters and tiles on the walls. My paintings already hang along one wall between the tiles and smaller weavings.

"This is definitely divinely inspired," Eve says. She stands by the door after placing the last bone and turquoise necklace in the window display. We all walk over to stand beside her. Tears sting my eyes. We've created something beautiful together. Our combined individual artworks create a collage of wonder and delight.

"I'm so sorry I have to take off after the opening," Jade says. "All those drum making workshops, Native American powwows, and Rendezvous won't wait. I'll be back in December. I only have five drumming workshops scheduled. Do you mind if I hold the winter solstice Wise Woman Drumming Circle here at the winter solstice?"

"Only if you allow wise men to attend, too," Enrique chimes in.

Jade gives him a lingering hug. She's the youngest one of us. Her tall, lean frame matches Enrique's. As a trained trauma specialist who leads women-only kayak trips in Puget Sound and around Montana, she never had time for anything else.

She detested drum making, a skill she learned from her mother when, starting at age twelve, she had to help stretch stinky wet goat and deer hides over the wooden frames. A few years ago, she forgot what she hated about it and made a drum for her boyfriend. Soon after, she received requests from other friends and then from friends of friends. Now she kayaks for fun and feeds her soul by teaching others to make drums and find the rhythm of joy in their lives.

"Anything for you, dreamboat," she says, laughing and squeezing closer.

"Hey, save some hugs for me. I'm leaving, too." Colette says. "I can't believe summer art and craft shows go 'til September this year. It seems like hardly any break before the Christmas shows begin in October." Colette's slim, short body can easily fit under Enrique's outstretched arm. Her equally short hair has been white since high school, but her complexion is rosy and fresh. She says it's from the clay she uses in her pottery finding its way onto her face.

"That's what you get for being such a great potter," Enrique says, releasing Jade and lifting Colette into a hug and taking a turn in place. "You are unique, like every one of your clay creations."

"I'll be gone all summer and through December selling pottery at craft sales in all corners of the country." She looks like she wants to cry. "This used to be such a joyful time. This year I don't want to go." Instead of returning home to produce more pieces, colleges rent studio space in exchange for her teaching a few classes. Taking only her tools, glazes and mystery powders with her saves lots of time and travel. She promises to send pottery every month.

She and I met a few years ago when I signed up for her tap dance class. Soon after, her foot doctor told her to take time to smell the roses and relax once in a while before she broke down her arches completely. She decided to buy a potter's wheel, so she'd have something to do when she sat down to take a break.

"I'm really going to miss you two," I say, as we all group hug.

This was the first experience at gallery ownership for all of us. I never imagined doing it, but you never know about inspiration and reinvention. I was tired of my life, my same ol' same ol' level-headed flatness. I decided to use some of my settlement funds to color in a dream I had for years.

My job as a corporation's biologist consumed my earlier life. I was on the road and in the air all the time and didn't even dabble in painting until my retirement. It seemed glamorous to many. The money was phenomenal, and I met more famous conservationists than I would have working in a traditional wildlife biologist job. I attended world-wide conferences and spoke at many. The downside was those in the traditional biologist jobs hated me. Looked at me as a puppet of the corporation. A sellout. It hurt.

I never felt disloyal to my calling. That's what it is for those of us who decide to study and protect and promote the natural ecosystems of the earth. A calling. We are pulled to it like a minister or a world traveler or an entrepreneur. Something is born inside you, through you, a compulsion. Resistance is dangerous. It leads to a life of dissatisfaction that I see in those who are stuck in the social system of expectations. My mother and aunt strengthened my wings, lifted me off the nest and let me fly to meet my kismet.

My mom was gone, but my aunt applauded my early retirement. Of course, it wasn't really retirement at age forty-two. However, I ended up with a chunk of change from the whistle blowing lawsuit. My investments would support me for a while until the gallery started paying me back. Plus, I might even sell some paintings.

We are celebrating before our success. Enrique placed his arm around Colette's shoulder. "I'll have the Stone Mountain Gallery website finished this week and will start on your individual site. Maybe people will come here for workshops and art will be sold at such a great volume you won't have to travel so much."

"Where did you say you found this guy?" Jade says. "He's sure no stick in the mud."

We're all laughing and hugging when we turn in unison to see who has opened the door behind us.

Sheriff Trammel fills the frame, blocking the light. His gun, cuffs and radio, hooked to the hip sides of his belt, only widening his substantial girth. His head almost touches the door frame.

"Ladies. Eve," he offers, tipping his head forward a bit, touching the brim of his cowboy hat. His eyes flicker to Enrique, but he doesn't add any greeting. "This looks cozy."

"Sheriff," we all answer in unison. I feel guilty already. What have I inadvertently done now? "What's happened?"

Sheriff Trammel loves to intimidate me and tries to quell the smiling twitch of his lips by running his hand down his full, long, reddish mustache. "The folks at the bakery told me I could find you here, Roe."

Dead silence fills the room. I freeze, barely breathing. Somehow, my name coming from Sheriff Trammel has become a fear trigger. Could it be from all his hospital visits? Making me relive the trauma again and again? Enrique gently touches my back and I inhale instead of turning blue.

"Can we sit down and talk?" Trammel asks. Glancing at the others he adds, "I know there's no use in asking for a private conversation, so anywhere we can all sit will be okay."

Eve reaches around him and twists the dead bolt on the front door, and Enrique leads us all to the center of the room where two gallery sofas sit back-to-back. He and Jade flip one around, so they face each other. I wonder if Trammel's weight can cave in the leather upholstery. As if reading my mind, Eve walks behind the counter and pulls out the sturdy oak chair, "Here, Les. Your chair," she says.

"How are you feeling, Roe?" Trammel asks.

"Great. How about you?" I lie. I freeze when encountering someone who liked JB or hearing something about him. Even after all this time, misguided people still give me the pity stare. Tears surprise me at odd moments.

"Not perfect yet, but making progress," I add, hoping it sounds sincere.

Sheriff Trammel nods. "I understand," he says. "Traumas don't heal up overnight."

Eve breaks the awkward conversation by getting to the point. "What can we do for you, Les?" She's the only person I know who uses Trammel's first name. Les was two years ahead of her in the one-room schoolhouse twenty miles from here. Though younger, Eve tutored Les in math during elementary and middle school. By high school, Les was busy with sports and girls. I was only a grade below Trammel when I moved here my sophomore year, but he was a football star, and I was a science nerd and never the twain did meet. Eve and I, however, were already B.F.Fs.

Eve's hand on mine brings me back to the moment. In answer to Eve's question, Sheriff Trammel reaches into his shirt pocket and pulls out a key with a long plastic tag dangling from a zip tie. Bold, black numbers fill one side of the tag. The flip side displays one word, Southerton. Our small group gives a collective gasp. I hold my breath. The color leaches out of my life again.

"I'm here to give you this." He places the key in my hands. "We've exhausted our next-of-kin search, and the decision was to hand over the house key to you, Roe. The courts will decide how to dispose of his property. I hear the county attorney found the will, but they're waiting for the sheriff's department to release the crime scene. We're not there yet. For now, I was hoping you'd be able to see something we may have missed. You seemed to be the most familiar with him and we all know how you love to solve puzzles."

"I was the most familiar with him," I say, repeating his words. He takes that as an affirmative, but I'm thinking Trammel didn't read the statement I gave to his deputy. Enrique gives a small sputter behind me, coughing a few times to cover an incredulous laugh. Trammel sends a frown in Enrique's direction.

"Sure," I jingle the keys. "I'll see what I can do."

The argument started before the door clicked shut behind Sheriff Trammel. Everyone has an opinion. Everyone voices his or her opinion at the same time.

"You cannot go there alone," Jade declares. "What difference does it make," Colette answers.

"I'm the trauma specialist in the group, and I say no," insists Jade.

"Do you think it's dangerous? I mean, he did try to kill you," says Enrique.

We all look at him.

"Wait. Stop. Quiet!" I shout.

"Listen, we all need to settle down and breathe." Eve lifts her open palms, directing us to inhale and then turns palms down, pushing them toward the floor and repeats, as if directing an orchestra of asthmatics. Heavy breathing replaces shouting.

"Okay, okay. I agree with you," I say. "I won't go there alone. Right now, we need to get ready for our gallery opening tomorrow. JB's house isn't going anywhere."

CHAPTER TWELVE

Fifteen minutes later, we all stand at the front door of JB's house. I turn the key and we flock inside, closing and locking the door behind us.

"Wow," Jade whispers.

We all agree. The house design has a pleasant flow. The wide entry area opens into a vestibule with the garage door and a laundry room on the left, a guest bedroom and bathroom on the right, and then straight into the living room.

Our cluster moves forward together. The next door on the right opens into a small office. The master bedroom door is recessed into a small alcove. The open kitchen stretches out to the left. Fairway Two runs east and west outside the generous windows of the great room. The view is stunning, with the sunset off to the right, the glow on the trees, cliffs, and homes to the left.

I sigh. How happy I would have been to come here and snuggle with JB in the afternoon light. A gas fireplace, framed with gray travertine, fills the wall next to the wide windows overlooking the largest pond and fountains on the golf course. I could have cooked up banquets in the spacious, open kitchen, with gleaming stainless steel appliances and green marble counter tops. I feel myself misting up over my lost possibility. "You know this was a spec house built by the golf course to get the neighborhood started, entirely decorated and furnished by an interior designer," Colette said. "It's been on the market for years, because the economy tanked right after they finished it. It doesn't look like JB changed a thing." Colette attends every Realtor open house for homes over three hundred thousand dollars. Her clients live in such homes, and she claims it gives her a better idea of how to fashion and color her pottery.

"Let's stay together," Eve says. "We don't want to disturb anything before Roe examines it."

"Fat chance we'll find anything," I say. "I can't believe how neat he kept the place."

"Let's start in the bedroom," Enrique suggests.

We all turn to look at him, eyebrows lifting. Colette gives a snorting laugh.

"Men say the cutest things," says Jade, throwing a light punch at Enrique's shoulder.

"Guys take things out of their pockets in their bedrooms at night, or before they do laundry," he mutters. The blush runs from his shirt collar to his hairline. He knits those bushy brows together and pushes us off toward the largest bedroom. A king-sized bed covered with a brown and green comforter and three rows of triple stacked pillows dominates the master bedroom. A cherry wood dresser and mirror take up the wall at the foot of the bed. Two overstuffed chairs and a small table crowd into the space in front of the French door leading to the patio. It reminds me of a Hampton Inn I'd stayed in during my last trip to Seattle.

"All that's missing is the mint on the pillow," Eve says.

She had shared the hotel room with me.

Enrique directs. "Roe, you start in the closet. Go through every pocket, shoe and drawer, and stand on one of these chairs to look at each shelf. Eve and Jade, you check the bed, dismantling it one layer at a time. Check under the pillows. Colette, start in the bathroom. Move nothing, take a photo first. Look and notice if there's anything unusual or out of place."

"And you?" I ask, slightly offended at my orders, which seem like the most boring assignment among the three.

"I'll look in the dresser and under and behind furniture for hidden documents." He handed each one of us a small notebook he'd grabbed from a box behind the counter at the gallery. The simple spiral pads, with the logo and name of the gallery across the front and a short, gold pen affixed on the back, will be given away to our first thousand customers. I suspect we'll have them for years. "Take notes or sketches of anything you want to remember. Use your phone to take pictures of each place you search before you mess it up." Enrique points to his watch. "Let's spend twenty minutes on this first search."

Enrique lifts a chair to examine the underside and then carries it over to the massive closet for me to stand on. Only twenty minutes. Now the closet looks like too much of a challenge. I begin by taking the photos, as Enrique suggested. I guess someone had to be in charge or we would never really search. I would have looked around and called it quits if Enrique hadn't been herding us like a border collie driving sheep to the shed.

I call out, "You all know I've never been inside this place, right?" "Right," they all answer in unison. My complaints during the two months of dating JB hadn't fallen on deaf ears, but the ears had hardened, hearing the same sad song repeatedly. Starting on the left rack, I reach into every pocket in pants, jackets, and shirts. The total number of hanging clothes I write in my little book equals fifteen. Many of the clothes still have the tags. A few pieces came from T. J. Maxx. I always thought his clothes came from Nordstrom's, or at least Macy's. I note this down. *Oh. My. How. Boring.* I write on the next four pages, one word on each page. "Whoa, now," Eve says.

I turn in time to see her jump back from the bed. We all rush over to look at what she'd found, and it changed the entire focus of our search. I had hoped to find some trace of a family or, at least, an inkling of his mystery job. I figured there would be a small album of grandkid photos, college memorabilia, or maybe postcards of recent vacations.

"Don't touch it," Enrique shouts. "I have a roll of plastic bags for evidence." He shoulders past our tight line and pulls off one bag, sticking his hand all the way inside, to the bottom edge.

"Wait," Colette says, as she whips out her phone and clicks a picture. "Pretty clever to duct tape it between the pillows. Most people keep it on the sheet beneath the pillows." When we all stare at her, she adds, "I mean from what they say on those TV detective shows."

Enrique leans over for a closer look, confirming the on-position of the safety latch and picks up the gun with his bag-covered hand, deftly turning the bag inside out to encase the gun. Neat trick. I've seen people do the same when picking up doggie poop with plastic bags along our nature trail.

"Glock." Enrique says, examining the pistol. "A newer version I can't put a name to. It's a little more firepower than most people have under their pillows."

In what seems like one motion, he pops out the ammunition clip inside the bag and pulls back the slide to release the bullet in the chamber. I feel my knees go weak.

"Good find," Enrique says, positively beaming. "Let's get back to work, only fourteen minutes left."

That brought me back to the present. "Give me one of those bags. I might find something, too," I say, trying not to sound defensive. Eve's find confirms my search of the closet is a lame assignment.

I go back to the two coats, one winter coat and a trench coat. Both look expensive. The dressier one is a finely tailored camel hair coat. It's not as long as a polo style, which comes to mid-shin, but shorter, maybe mid-thigh or at the knee. I'm shocked for a moment. Have I already forgotten JB's height? I put my nose to the collar of the coat. It has a hint of his aftershave and something else, maybe a spice or bath powder? Was it new and never worn? Although these can be found on ebay for less than fifty dollars, this one has a stiffer new feel of thick virgin camel wool. The label along the side seam is from Neiman Marcus. The price was probably over eight hundred dollars. I fondle the lapel, wondering if it can be tailored down to my size.

The knee-length trench coat made of firm, brushed cotton, dark and rich in appearance, has oil worked into the fabric. The tag says waterproof. It's fairly new. This could definitely be tailored to fit me. My rain slicker is somewhere in the Missouri breaks, where I left it during the unexpected camping trip with Enrique. I sniff at the lapel of this coat. It has the same spicy aroma. A touch of citrus? It's even stronger on the cuffs. I resist the urge to hug it. I slip my hand into the soft liner of the breast pocket and feel something brush my fingertips.

The thin piece of paper turns out to be a gas receipt. I don't recognize the town's name. Point B, Montana. Is this a clue? Where is point A? Is it the starting point or the end?

"Does anyone know where Point B, Montana, is?" I call out from deep in the closet. I hear a snort from Colette, who's still searching the bathroom.

"Why?" Eve asks. Eve and Jade laugh. "Looking for point A?" More snickering all around.

"Yes, I know it," says Enrique, walking over to the closet door. "It's one of those little towns named after a cattle brand, like Two Dot and Teedee, Montana. The name comes from the brands used by the first and usually the largest ranch in the area. It's way the hell out there in the middle of nowhere, almost on the North Dakota border. I drove there to study migrating birds and ended up getting blown off the road." He was standing at the door now, looking at the slip of paper between my thumb and first finger.

"What's that?" He asks.

"A gas receipt." I hold it up for him to see.

In response, Enrique whips out a zip lock sandwich bag, indicating I should drop it in. "Let's finish up and meet in the kitchen." Enrique orders.

I quickly pull out drawer after empty drawer. The last one has boxer shorts and socks, all in packets of three and all still with their price tags. On the bottom shelf are three brand new pairs of slip-on loafers, the kind he always wore, one pair of black sneakers, and one pair of dark, military looking, high-topped work boots. The boots look brand new, but have a smear of dry, yellow mud in the deep tread of the sole. I stand on the chair. All the upper shelves prove free of clutter and dust.

I join the others in the kitchen, where Enrique lined up plastic bags on the counter top.

There's the pistol, of course, and the gas slip. A dark tortoise shell hairbrush, a toothbrush and toothpaste in another bag. The next holds a few pieces of paper Enrique found in the office. The last bag contains a pair of slippers from under the bedside table.

"Pretty slim pickins, even for a guy who lived alone," Sage says, pointing out the obvious. "What about the kitchen and garage?"

Enrique walks around the corner to open the garage door. The rest of us open cupboards, pulling out drawers, searching in refrigerator and pantry, even the oven and dishwasher. Eve and I circle the great room, feeling beneath sofa and chair cushions, opening cabinets and looking up the fireplace chimney.

"Nothing," Enrique says. "Only a slight trail through the dust from the car tires rolling in and another trail where he walked from the car door to the house door. Nothing on shelves or in storage cabinets. How about the kitchen?'

"Same in here," I answer. "Nothing normal. No food, no dirty dishes, no soaps or cleaning products, nothing in the fridge or dishwasher."

"The guy sure cleaned up after himself," Eve says. "It's as though he was ready to move out at a moment's notice."

"What else is missing?" Enrique asks.

"Dirty laundry, clean laundry, food and garbage," points out Colette. "It's as though he never even lived here. This was a model home four years ago and everything is exactly the same as when it was newly on the market. The dishes, pans, silverware, pictures on the walls, everything is still in the same place it was during the open houses."

I look in the cabinet under the sink. "Only paper towels and new looking dish rack," I say. "Maybe he used a cleaning service."

"I don't think so," Eve says. "The guy was either a nut case or someone who couldn't abide dirt. Maybe germ-a-phobic?"

"Or maybe he was in witness protection," I say, feeling like I should defend the man.

"Or he was hiding out," Enrique says slowly, adding, "hiding from business partners, from clients, or from the law."

"I vote for a nutcase." Sage raises her hand, getting a smile out of Colette and Eve.

"What now? Should we go to the police?" I knew the answer but abnegated the decision to the others. "We don't even know if they've investigated or searched his car. And Trammel did say they searched here first. Did they find anything?"

"We should call him first thing in the morning." Eve says, herding us all toward the door. "We need to finish the gallery for the grand opening."

We all jump and turn toward Colette when she lets out a shriek. "This is so weird." She's holding up the bag with the gas receipt. "He bought gas at one o'clock in the morning at a place six hundred miles from here on the day he died."

CHAPTER THIRTEEN

Preparations for the grand opening of the Stone Mountain Gallery and Coffee Bar drive all thoughts of the gun and the sheriff out of our heads. Colette and Jade finish packing for their respective trips, Enrique manages the caterers and iced coffee paraphernalia, while Jackson directs Eve and I to rearrange artwork yet again. Jackson helps us clean up the last bits of sawdust and fingerprints and makes a few adjustments to the art arrangement. He has another life, so takes off to return to his auto mechanic garage.

We plan a mid-afternoon break to rest before our event and call Sheriff Trammel to make an appointment for tomorrow. Instead, the break happens late, and we barely have time to grab a shower, change, and get back to the gallery in time to unlock the door. I don't know why these things take longer than imagined. Even with all the pre-planning, the caterer brings in the last of the food, after the first guests arrive.

Our friends and supporters pack the place right away. The "wows" make it all worthwhile. Red dots go up on paintings, wall hangings and pottery as they sell. Drums disappear from shelves during the early evening. Later, jewelry flies from the cases and the cash register and card scanner run at full tilt. The box of spiral notebooks grows lighter. My face muscles cramp from smiling so much, but I can't stop. We've pulled it off. A home run the first day and whatever happens after this is heaven.

Marry Kat brought a cameraman so she could write and interview us, plus get some great shots for our newspaper coverage. She was the only reporter who dealt out kindness with the questions about my run in with the date from hell. Her long, rainbow hair is pulled back with a silver and turquoise hair clip she bought from Eve earlier. We hug, and she grabs a few joyful comments from our clients on her way to the food table.

Jackson took time from helping at the espresso bar to stroll arm-in-arm with Angel on a tour of all the artworks. He holds a silver and turquoise necklace against her throat and then takes it to the cash register, along with a wad of oil smudged bills from one of his clients. I see Enrique sweep the bills into one of our eco-friendly bags and hide it beneath the counter, grumbling to Jackson he'd get his change later.

Sheriff Trammel strides through the door, blocking the evening light and shaking hands with guests, as he works his way toward Eve. He needs to know about yesterday's search. As I start towards him, his phone buzzes. He takes it out of his pocket, looks distraught by the text message, and waves me off.

"Later," he shouts back as he rushes out the door. Seconds later, everyone in the volunteer fire and ambulance response unit looks at their phones or pagers. They flow out the door like a school of fish. Eve throws off her shawl and grabs her purse.

"Wait, Eve. Will you be back?" I shout. "Is it something close by?"

"Don't know, but I have to go." She's out the door with the others.

I'm standing with Enrique and Jade. I find Colette's eyes across the gallery. She shrugs. The party pauses for a moment, adjusting to the loss of more than a dozen souls. Everyone looks out the window, wondering.

In the next breath, fresh faces push in through the door and the energy picks back up. The streets fill with folks on their way to dinner or the summer musical theater and many of them will end up in here. Spring rolls and asparagus spears disappear. Desserts and chocolates get devoured along with iced coffee. We showcase what we are about. Art and coffee are us.

Eve didn't make it back to the opening. Colette and Jade helped with a bit of cleaning and then rushed home to finish packing for their trips tomorrow. Enrique and I box up whatever the catering staff left behind for Jade to drop off to the food bank refrigerator. I vacuum, scrub the tile floor at the door and wipe down the doors, while he washes the espresso machine, checks the inventory for tomorrow and washes all the display cases free of coffee cup rings and fingerprints. High heel divots dot the throw rug in the center of the room and there's a foot-long groove on the wood floor where the caterer pulled in a wonky-wheeled cart. We can see the antique streetlamps glowing outside and hear the clock tower quietly strike ten. A short time later, the summer theater finishes, and people mosey along the street enjoying the evening, eating ice cream or sipping hot cocoa. A few knock on the windows and gives us a thumbs-up.

Around eleven, we glanced one more time at the front door for Eve, and a car with no headlights slowly cruises by the gallery. Enrique rushes to switch off the lights and drags me into deep darkness behind the counter. He's still as a statue, like a deer hearing a twig snap.

His muscles quiver through his shirt beneath my hands as I slowly run them up to his shoulders, aware of a ripple of tension. I push against his back as I lift onto my toes to peek over his shoulder, rubbing the length of my body up his. The fire starter sparks. A ragged inhale rocks me, bringing in his scent of cinnamon, coffee and maleness. My nipples yearn for contact with him. The dark, the excitement and a sudden need course through my head, heart and loins in waves. I feel out of control. I exhale into his neck.

He looks over his shoulder at me. "What?" He whispers. "You ok?"

My breath catches in my throat as my eyes squeeze tight. My chin lifts toward his, my lips part in expectation. I feel him slowly twisting to get a better look, as though he's approaching a scared animal. "Don't have a panic attack now, chica. You're safe."

"You're sure?" I ask, trying, but not succeeding, for the breathiness of seduction. To him, it sounds like the breathlessness of hyperventilation. I unglue my body from his back, where my inappropriately timed hot flash has stuck us together. I look toward the door. "What's going on?"

"That car," he hisses, now holding me loosely, but securely, in his arms. I grip the front of his shirt, pulling him closer. "I could swear they looked at this place. The taillights flashed for a second when the car was right in front. Maybe checking to see if someone was still here."

"You know, they had to see the lights go out and the two of us standing here. It was kids, sneaking away to a party, or sneaking home." I don't think we're in any danger, but I dwell on what those kids might have been sneaking out to do. Not able to help myself, I push even closer towards him, warm flutters spreading out from my belly. I imagine he's forming his body to accept me, pushing his leg between mine. I start to wrap one leg around his.

THUNK! Something hits the window. In slow motion, a smear starts near the farthest edge and runs toward the bottom. Whatever hit the glass didn't come through. At least it wasn't a gunshot.

Enrique propels me back and down behind the counter onto piles of boxes and bags. Our bodies twine together. We peek through the small space between the counter and the wall in time to see a hooded figure approach the door and pull it quietly open. We forgot to lock it.

I don't want to wait until the place is trashed, so I reach up and flip on the lights.

"The police are on the way!" I bark out. "Get out!" Thieves are usually so tense they follow simple orders.

"Get out now, before you get hurt." I hear Enrique yell above me.

"Hey, what's with you two?"

"Eve?" I shout, pushing myself up from the floor.

"Were you expecting someone else? And what are you two doing here in the dark at this time of night? And on the floor?" She watches me stand up, disheveled, breathless, and flushed.

My dress hiked up to my hips. Her eyebrows rise and disappear behind her hood.

"He shoved me down when something hit the window. We thought you were a thief," I say.

"Uh, huh." Eve's mouth rolls into a distinct smirk.

"Really," Enrique says. "Something struck the window and right before that someone cruised by in a dark sedan casing the joint."

Eve flips back the hood of her orange, fireproof jacket. I guess the orange was a dead giveaway she wasn't a thief. She stares at us with wide-eyed disbelief.

"Wonder what hit the glass?" I sidestep around Enrique, smoothing down my dress, as I hurry to the front door and out onto the street.

Eve follows. The night begins to chill. The warmth radiating from the sidewalk, and our stone storefront makes it bearable. On the far side of the picture window lay something tucked into the deep shadow at the corner of the building. It looks like a bag or a bundle of cloth. I hug my arms around my body. In the past, I would have taken this sort of thing in stride, not messing with feelings of fear and trepidation. I'd get out and investigate and clean up the mess. The hot flash left my clothes damp and I shiver.

"God, I have to get over this," I mumble. "At least there isn't any glass on the sidewalk."

Eve weaves her arm through mine. "Don't be a wuss. Let's go together to see what it is."

The way she said it made me pull back. Could it be a rag-wrapped brick with a message, or an unexploded Molotov cocktail? Maybe it's the severed head of my horse? Eve sighs, as if reading my mind, and moves us together toward the object, one step at a time.

"It's only a bird." Her voice has an edge of excitement. "Wow, you're right."

"What kind is it?"

"I don't know yet. It's dark out here."

"Is it dead?"

"I'd say so by the way it's still laying here." I find birds around my house that hit the window in the evening, still sitting there stunned in the early morning if the cat hasn't caught them. In the past, a constant stream of injured birds found by friends, strangers, and my dog came through a rehabilitation room in my barn.

"It could still be alive," I admit.

We walk closer until we stand over it. I touch it with my toe and watch the bird's head loll to the other side. That still doesn't mean it's dead. It might be stunned or unconscious. I reach down and slide one hand under its body, supporting the head on my wrist. I lift it up for Eve to examine.

"Is it a dove?" she asks, and then, doing what everyone does, she strokes it with a finger. "It's so soft."

Humans are suckers for something soft, like feathers, fur, or silk. It made me realize how hunting came into existence. Of course, in killing the animal, people possess the part they like so much, the soft outer coating. The meat's a plus, too. I give the breast of the bird a little squeeze to size it up for the pot. It's then I feel the rapid heartbeat.

"It's alive," I say. "Let's find a box."

We hurry back inside, past Enrique. He gives me a puzzled look and then notices I'm carrying something.

"A bird hit the window?" He bends to look closer.

"Yes, and it's still alive," Eve announces, anticipation in her voice.

Even though she's exhausted, Eve is into saving creatures and dying houseplants, as well as people. She expertly assembles a slightly crumpled packing box from beneath the counter. Taking a wad of tissue paper, she creates a ring in the box and covers it with a softer paper towel. I place the bird in the resulting nest and breathe a sigh of relief. Enrique throws me a bar towel and tells me to wash my hands.

We watch the bird for a while. Its feathers appear fluffier, but its head still lolls to the side. Enrique gently moves it to a more natural position, with its beak over the back and tucked under wing feathers.

"It's a domestic pigeon." Enrique notes. "Wonder what in the world it was doing flying around in the dark. These are roosting birds. They gather inside a coop or barn at night."

"Do you think an owl could have gotten in after them?" Eve asks. "Chased it out of its roost and then hit it on the back?" I lean over to blow on it, my breath lifting the feathers, searching for a wound or blood.

"That hardly seems possible," I say, as Enrique bends over to examine the bird, bringing his face dangerously close to mine.

"Anything is possible," he says when our eyes lock together.

I shoulder him aside when I straighten up, turning away to hide my burning face. I don't feel the magical surge of excitement from earlier as he pressed me behind him, protecting me from unknown danger.

We stare at the inert bird body until boredom sets in. "Oh." Eve says, "I didn't have time to tell you about our call tonight."

Eve sits down on one of the love seats and I sit at the other end, gently placing the box between us. Enrique takes a seat on the other short sofa. They still face each other from Sheriff Trammel's visit yesterday.

Eve's text signal goes off again, and she stands up, reading the message. "Sit tight a minute," she says, as she hurries outside, already pressing a thumb against her phone screen.

"If it dies, you want to share it for supper tomorrow?" I smile at Enrique, indicating the bird with my head.

"I have to say, it's pretty cold, talking about the bird in front of it this way."

"Well, I don't think it's a good idea to go shooting pigeons around town but may as well take advantage when one drops into our laps." I laugh, but he doesn't look amused.

Enrique leans forward, resting his elbows on his knees. "I think the older ones are tough, but I'm sure they're still delicious. They must be cooked well done."

"Now you're trying to ruin it for me." I sit back and cross my arms and legs.

I begin nervously swinging my crossed leg. "Look, we can stew it on the stove for a while or pop it right into the preheated oven. We can also poke in some carrots, parsnips or maybe one of those long, firm Japanese eggplants to keep it moist. It will be delightful."

I feel dazed, like I've entered an alternate universe. I'm missing something of significance about the bird. The clock in the back of the store chimes at midnight. I'm sitting in my new gallery and discussing squab dinners, and for some reason, think I might be naked. I'm a nine o'clock bedtime girl and this has to be a lucid dream.

Eve paces back and forth in front of the gallery, gesticulating while she talks on the phone. A couple of cars pass, and she waves. "Must be more quick responders heading home after cleaning up. Whatever it was sure took a long time to finish. Do you think Eve and the crew had a house fire this evening?" I chatter on. "Or maybe it was a serious car accident." Whatever I felt earlier was over now. Maybe the hormone rush came with the fear, the vision of a breaking window. The warrior bravery I felt when the unidentified Eve entered the shop overrode the amorous, vulnerable feeling I experienced with Enrique in the dark. The needy feeling. My adrenaline dwindles and I could fall asleep right here, right now. I close my eyes for a moment to rest and his phrase comes back to me. *Anything is possible.* My eyes fly open.

"Hey, wait a minute," I say. "Do you think I'm some sort of cougar?" My laugh sounds forced and embarrassed. "I'm the farthest thing from it."

Enrique looks at me, obviously unimpressed. He focuses over my left shoulder; the way a cat does after you've given it a dressing down for licking the butter.

"Look, I'm sorry about what happened a while ago. It was the stress of the opening gala. The fear from the crash on the window. A combination of panic attack and hormones. It won't happen again. Stupid excuse, I know." I vomit more words over him. "I'm so sorry. Sorry."

My voice trails off when I see his look of disbelief. Or disappointment?

"I heard that from you on the prairie. You apologize too much." He leans back on the sofa. "You're not a good liar, you know. I hope you don't gamble too much, because you have no poker face. Have people told you that before?" Enrique crosses his arms and legs, his chin tucks like he's holding back what he really wants to say. "And our age difference is so minuscule, you could never be a cougar."

He was six years younger than me according to my extensive google search. "It was a mistake. I really am sorry. Next time we have an art opening and vandalism all in one evening, I'll slather myself with lavender oil as a sedative." I talk myself into a corner, uncertain of how to get out. I thought about JB and how I never felt aroused around him. I never felt safe enough. Never had the opportunity. "I don't think I have anything more to say about the subject."

Don't be ridiculous. I'm embarrassed and I hope he'll drop it. I catch a glimpse of my wilting face in one of the display cases. Dark circles and suitcase size bags melt into the spaces below my eyes.

Enrique shakes his head, chuckling, "We'll see."

CHAPTER FOURTEEN

Eve rushes in, locking the door behind her. "Sorry about that," she says, "The fire chief and I needed to talk about scheduling crews to scrutinize the site tomorrow and what must be done in the next few days."

She looks bone weary and plops down next to the bird again. The bounce of the sofa jiggles the box, and the bird suddenly jerks up its head. It shakes itself, fluffing its body and fluttering its wings, sending loose feathers floating up around the makeshift nest. It's happening so fast none of us can react. The little guy stands, coos, steps around in a circle and leaps into the air. Enrique's hands close gently around the bird when it's about three feet out of the box.

"Wow," says Eve and I together.

"Good hand-eye coordination," I add.

Enrique has this endearing way of breaking into a slight Mexican accent when he talks to animals. He treats my dog with such loving care, as if she is an intelligent being, which, of course, she is.

"Where are you going, my feathered friend?" Enrique kindly asks the bird, as he deftly repositions it in his hands, smoothing down the feathers, placing the neck between his first two fingers and laying the bird gently on its back upon his palm. Making a cage of his thumb and other fingers, he gently blows on the bird's belly. "Let's take a look at you, little *belleza*."

I've banded hundreds of birds in my past life and I'm sure he has banded many more. This is the classic way to hold a bird after taking it from a net. The belly-up position not only calms the bird but also leaves the legs pointing up. In this position, you can grasp one leg between your thumb and finger, holding it steady to receive the open ring of the band.

"Hey, what's this?" Enrique inclines his head toward the bird and then we see it, too. He's holding up the legs, and each one has a ring attached. One is a standard domestic bird I.D. ring, the other one is thicker.

"I don't recognize that. What is it?"

Enrique gives the odd ring a little twist to get a better look. Hidden in the feathers on the other side is a tiny tube about the size of a large vitamin capsule.

"Is that a message pod?" I ask. "I've never seen one before, but what else can it be?"

"Yes, that's exactly what it is. We had a couple of homing pigeons when I was a kid." Enrique says. "My dad would bring them to the farm in Mexico with us, from the house in America. We released them with a message to Mama and Abuela when we started home."

"So, is it carrying anything?" asks Eve.

Enrique pinches the ring, and with his other hand, tries to work the capsule loose. "I can't get it to budge."

He holds it out to me, and I slip on my glasses. It has to come out of the ring to get it open. "We need tweezers. I have some in my purse."

I bring them back in a moment. These aren't your average, eyebrow-plucking tweezers other women carry. Enrique gives a laugh. He knows them right away. The 6-inch-long stainless steel handles with one inch of serrated teeth on both the pinchers identified them as dissecting tweezers biology majors all acquire in college and then collect ever after. They can hold anything, no matter how slimy and gooey. Plus, there never was a better eyebrow plucker.

I reach in and unlatch the tiny metal strip over an eyehook, and the capsule falls onto the bird's belly. Enrique fishes it out of the feathers and places the bird back into its box, stacking my purse on the lid to keep the pigeon from pushing its way out.

"Now, let's see what we have." Enrique goes behind the counter, presses a button on the electronic control panel and the bright overhead lights illuminate the capsule. He picks it up, spinning the ends in opposite directions. It unscrews in less than one turn. I pull his hand close to examine the microscopic threads which held it together. Enrique holds up the other half and Eve pulls out a tiny scroll.

Not too many years ago, a man in England found a pigeon skeleton in a chimney he was renovating. On its bony leg was a red tube containing a secret message sent by the Allies during World War II. The paper was very readable and showed blocks of letters that turned out to be acronyms for recommended strategic offensive measures. The soldiers must have figured it out on their own, since the pigeon obviously didn't make it.

"Is that paper?" Eve asks. It was a rolled tube approximately three quarters of an inch long. "Is it vellum?"

Enrique takes it, rolling the tube between his fingers and thumb. "It's fag paper, you know, for hand-rolling cigarettes or joints." Enrique blushes for reminding us of his prison vocabulary.

"I wonder how we're going to unroll such a tiny, fragile spool." Eve takes it back and holds it up to the light.

"What about this?" I pluck a paperclip from a glass cup by the cash register and unbend one end. "See if this will fit into the middle of the spool like a spindle and then maybe you can unroll it."

Enrique takes it back and fits the paperclip wire into the hole. "Well, aren't we a little MacGyver tonight," he says, smiling. "Here, you can have the honors."

I take it from him and lay it on the counter top. Pushing gently with one fingernail, I roll it sideways. It rolls completely over a few times, so I try the other direction. Right away, my fingernail catches the edge of the paper, and it starts to unroll. I hold it up to the light. It's folded twice toward the center. I use the paperclip, gently lifting one corner and slide my fingernail into the opening, unfolding one flap. It's easy to tease up the other side and carefully smooth it open.

As I hold it up to the light to read the tiny, hand printed script, I think about the pigeon in England and its cryptic message. I'm not sure if this is supposed to be cryptic or not, but it seems clear enough to me. I hand it to Eve, and she holds it close so she and Enrique can read it.

The paper is addressed to me. Is it a caution or a threat? No consequence is mentioned. Is it too late to take back what we've already done?

"Well damn," Eve says. She reads it aloud. "RS Let Dead Dogs Lie."

Enrique takes it from her and holds it up for a better look. "Too bad we handled it so much. The perpetrator's fingerprint might have been on it. Or on the bird bands."

"That has to be talking about JB, right?" They both nod.

"He's the only recently dead anything you know." Eve says, stating the obvious.

We all stare at the note for a minute,

Eve continues, "I think we should stop investigating on our own and let the police take over. They have more resources and will do a better job."

Enrique and I look at each other, both shaking our heads.

The police won't investigate.

"They thought it was an accident. They're not going to think anything of the gun or other evidence, or lack of, we found in the house." I run my fingers over the tiny paper, smoothing out the folds.

"Well, they might think about it now." Eve says. "That call we had tonight was JB's house. It blew to smithereens. Anything left after the explosion bigger than a button, either burned or melted. The fire chief confirms what we all suspected when we saw it. The explosion went right up the outside walls but left the neighbors untouched. It was definitely arson," Eve whisks ash out of her hair. "Some very high-tech arson."

CHAPTER FIFTEEN

Sheriff Trammel has an interest in our findings, after all. He orders us up to the sheriff's department in Kalispell, the largest city in the valley and the county seat. Eve, Enrique and I get there at seven sharp. I want to open the gallery at nine this morning and can't imagine this taking more than an hour. "What the hell are you doing, withholding this evidence?" Trammel paces back and forth behind his desk, sweating and pissed. He's none too happy about the pigeon's note, as well.

"You know better than this."

"You, sheriff, gave me the key. You told me to look around." I act irritated, even though I am spooked over the explosion, wondering how close we came to being reduced to button sized. "We didn't withhold, we were busy. I tried to tell you at the gallery reception, but your pager buzzed before I had the chance. I didn't think you'd want to hear about the pigeon at two in the morning."

"At least we found something before it all blew up. What did your crew find?" Enrique asks.

"You shut up." Sheriff Trammel jabs his finger into Enrique's chest. "I don't even know what you're doing here. I do know you were in the state pen recently." He and Enrique would have been standing nose-to-nose, except Trammel's height and ample chest kept them separated.

"Let's all calm down," Eve says. "Everyone sit."

Unable to resist Eve's orders, Trammel moves behind his desk and directs each of us to a specific chair. He puts Eve in between Enrique and me, as if separating naughty children. He lifts a large manila envelope out of his side drawer and lays it on his desk, giving me a piercing look before unclasping it.

"Nothing we discuss in here goes outside. You all got that?" Trammel waits until we all nod.

"Now, tell me how long and how well did you know this JB?" he asks me, as he dumps the contents of the envelope onto his desk. I crane forward to see what it is, and he places his arm over it like I'm looking at his test answers to cheat. I relax back into my seat and take a deep breath. The wait is excruciating.

"You know how long and everything I knew about him. I gave you a written statement."

"Oh, yeah," he snickers. "The sugar daddy report." He arranges the piles on his desk in some sort of mysterious order. "Refresh my memory."

I take a couple of deep breaths and close my eyes to shut out the pressure of his stare. "Ok." I hold up three fingers to begin the countdown. "He came out of nowhere, uninvited, and I let him in." I fold one finger into my palm. "He knew every shaker and mover in the village in a few days. Third, everyone wanted to be in his presence, because he always made people laugh." I grabbed the cuff of my sweat shirt sleeve to dab my eyes. "That's about it. Did you find anything that can tell us his well-hidden secrets?"

"First, we have this," Trammel says, as he deals out a pile of cash from its baggie. "It's two hundred sixty dollars we found in the Mustang's console. This fuel bill you found was forty-nine dollars and fifteen cents. Assuming every fill-up costs around fifty bucks and, because of the lower gas mileage in the Mustang, he used at least two or three tanks in each direction, plus something for food and maybe a hotel room, he must have begun with at least six hundred dollars. It seems like a lot of cash to carry."

We sit forward, hanging on every word. "He spent cash for absolutely everything, restaurants, the Mustang and even the house." I glance over and see Enrique and Eve nodding. I quickly recap the rest of JB's story. "I know he went home and changed jackets before coming to see me. He obviously wasn't wearing the jacket with this receipt." I place my finger down on the baggy holding the small square of paper. "Why did he change when he was already forty minutes late?"

"Maybe he took a shower to freshen up," suggested Eve. "We didn't find any dirty clothes." Enrique pointed out. "We actually took those from the house," said Trammel.

"Pretty damn good guess."

Next, Trammel holds up two pieces of yellow lined paper, each in its own plastic slip folder. "These were under the desk where it scooted up next to the open office door. He emptied the wastebasket, so maybe these got kicked behind the door and went unseen until we found them." He hands one to Eve. "They were crumpled into a tight ball, the two sheets wadded together."

"Can we pick them up?" I ask. He nods.

"Whatever they mean isn't obvious," Trammel says. "One page looks like a trip planning list, with the words 'Buy and Throw' scrawled at the top of the page." A line slashes from top to bottom, creating two columns.

Eve learns by hearing, so she quietly reads aloud to us. "The buy column has things like jeans, shirts, shoes, boots, dress, skirt, undies, coat, jacket, sweaters, toiletries, hair dye, iPod, burner phone and car snacks. Each word has a neat line across the middle. The throw column also includes crossed off items like clothes, personal stuff, jewelry and phone."

I take the paper in my hand and read aloud what's scrawled across the bottom of the page, "pickup, bank parking lot." Then I read aloud up the list again, "Undies, dress, hair dye, snacks," I repeat these to myself three times. "Throw jewelry. Who does that?" I finally ask. "And what man buys undies or even calls anything undies?"

"Looks like he didn't quite finish crossing off his list," Eve says. "What did he pick up?"

Enrique pipes in. "Or he might be talking about getting a pick-up truck? Do you think he bought a used truck?"

Trammel stands up, taking the other yellow sheet with him. "He may have had a truck. We're asking around to see if anyone saw or knows anything about recent used trucks being sold. This page is interesting." He walks over and opens an antique cabinet, revealing a machine the size of a computer printer. He slides the paper under a flap, flips a switch and a picture of the yellow paper appears inside a framed white screen on the wall next to the cabinet. I thought the framed white board was Trammel's attempt at modern art.

"What are those random letters around the page?" I ask. Small, neat printing covers the page in some sort of code or shorthand; LA, m8, CO, TX, m3, sfct, m4, tf, c5, b3, c4, w2, h, jz, lc, CA and on and on.

"Hold your horses, I'm getting to that." Trammel comes back to his desk to pick up a hand control, thumbing one button to bring up an overlay grid of small boxes onto the yellow page. The letters fit perfectly into the boxes.

"You can see it's a monthly calendar," I say, pointing out the most obvious thing about the page. "What month is it? And it's six weeks instead of four."

"Boy, you're quick, missy." I can't tell if Trammel is complementing or teasing me.

"If it was current at the time of his death, it would be February, March and April. We assume he used his imagination to fill in the grid but spaced the letters out to correspond with certain days and weeks." Trammel continued, "I don't think he tried to make the information cryptic, because he planned to destroy it. I believe he did it so often he no longer needed an actual calendar. The dates and boxes were in his brain." Trammel points to the lower part of the chart. "If this is current, then he had plans to travel a lot more."

"Why didn't he buy a monthly planner?" I wonder aloud.

After a single knock, a young man carrying a cardboard tray of coffees and a manila folder under one arm opens the door.

"Thank you, Detective. Detective Elliot, this is Eve, Rosetta and… and… him."

Enrique stands and holds out his hand to Detective Elliot. "Doctor Enrique Roca."

"Tom Elliot. Pleased to meet you," he says, smiling as they shake hands. They seem like two friendly dogs greeting each other with cautious tail wagging. Their height, build and age are similar, but Tom has a head of dusky blond curls next to Enrique's tawny brown. Enrique had the dreadlocks cut off, leaving his hair short, but thick and lustrous.

Trammel glowers at the two men. "Elliot, tell us what you discovered."

Elliot tosses his report onto Trammel's desk. "Well, the gun is an unregistered weapon, but it's clean. The serial number indicates he purchased it in South Carolina, where you're not required to register your weapon and you only need a permit if you want to carry it concealed. He didn't get one. There are no fingerprints on the weapon and no scratches on the handle or barrel. Maybe he did some target practice but hasn't carried in his car or a holster."

Elliot points to the free-form calendar still projected on the wall. "Do any of these letters on the calendar mean anything to you?"

We all shake our heads.

"Wait a minute," I say. "Let me think. It's been two months now, but maybe some of those dates line up with the times JB went on his business trips." I think about the days leading up to the incident. I pull my day planner from my purse and open to last month. "If the second row is the beginning of March, it jives with my notes. He returned from a trip on the fifth of March to attend a fund-raising event for the art center the next evening. He spent four thousand dollars on art and services at the auction."

I follow my finger across the page. "The next morning, we heard a varied thrush trilling at the top of the tallest spruce in Tamarack Falls." I glance at Enrique to clarify, "They had been singing around my house near the mountains since late February, but this was the first he'd heard in his life."

I read from the next page. "He left one day later and came back on the tenth for the high school activities appreciation dinner, bringing ten pounds of shrimp we cooked and served at my fund-raising table."

I skim down my list. "He left March thirteenth and returned seven days later for the Tamarack Falls Development Committee fundraiser. We saw a newly arrived pair of sandhill cranes during a bird walk on the morning of the twentieth and he left right after the fundraiser. I met him for breakfast on the twenty-second and drove up to Glacier Park to see if the harlequin ducks were back. He said he'd see me in about two weeks and that brings us up to April fifth, the last day we met at Larsen Lake." I look at the coded calendar.

"It tallies exactly with the letters on this calendar," Detective Elliot says, taking notes on a lined yellow pad, "except it appears he came back a few days earlier and left again without telling you."

"How do you know he came home?" Eve asks.

He points out a couple of days corresponding to when JB came home. "Lookie here. He has a lower-case tf in each of those dates he spent in Tamarack Falls. He also has a tf on April third." Elliot looks at me. "It means he came home before he died, left town again, and came home to meet you, stopping at his house to change clothes and drop off his long raincoat."

Enrique gives a low hmmmmm. "If it's so simple, these other letters could also be place names."

We all gaze at the projection. Elliot takes up his yellow pad again and starts taking notes.

"Ok," says Elliot, "if tf stands for Tamarack Falls, the other small letters, jz, lc, sfct, pb, w, c8, m4, m2, m3, w1, pr3, w2 might stand for town names, too. Or they might not. Then there are the capital letters, FL, LA, TX, MX, ND, MT, CA, and CO."

"Maybe the small letters stand for cities and the large letters are states," says Enrique, "so LA would be Louisiana, instead of Los Angeles. We need to pull up a map of the United States. Can we use your computer, Sheriff?"

Elliot writes the names of places as Enrique points them out. We already wrote the states of Florida, Louisiana, California, North Dakota, Montana, Colorado, Texas, plus Mexico. The cities prove more of a challenge. Enrique continues, "Juarez, Mexico could be jz."

Detective Elliot takes up the game." I think lc could be Lake Charles, Louisiana, San Francisco with ct tacked on, Pueblo, Colorado and Williston, North Dakota."

Eve looks over the list. "Maybe the ct after San Francisco stands for a district or neighborhood," she says. "Maybe it's China Town." Elliot writes it on his list.

"Ok," says Detective Elliot. "If ct means China Town, maybe c means China or Chinese. Eight of something Chinese."

Sheriff Trammel sits at his desk, his face buried in his huge hands. "This doesn't look good."

"What do you mean?" I ask. Everyone looks at me as if I am an idiot. They all know something. "What? Clue me in?"

"Eight of something Chinese." Trammel says, looking at me. "How about eight Chinese girls? How about four Mexican girls? How about one white girl? Etcetera, etcetera, and this is only a few weeks."

Elliot takes up the topic like they were a tag team in debate class. "Those cities, Juarez, China Town, Lake Charles, and the other places, are all centers of known human trafficking operations. Many of the twenty million trafficked victims from around the world that end up in the United States pass through those cities. If he picked up girls or boys, it's like going to the slavery marketplace. And this calendar represents, let's see, twenty-one people for six weeks alone."

Sheriff Trammel reenters the conversation, "If this is truly his business, it would explain all the cash he threw around. Now the question is, where did he take them and where are they now? Who is paying his salary? Did he have partners? We're going to have to start a new investigation into this character's past."

"Williston, North Dakota and the vicinity would be a perfect place to sell young women into prostitution." Elliot points to the map.

"Why did you mention a truck earlier, Les?" Eve asks.

"We thought he might have left the Mustang somewhere nearby and maybe had a truck or an SUV in storage. He only had the Mustang for a couple of months, so he had to have another vehicle. Also, he'd fit in a lot better if he made multiple trips to the area with something less sporty. He likely flew to the far locations and rented a rig to drive the girls. Plus, the Mustang doesn't have many miles on it. If he drove it for business, it would have to be close, maybe less than a hundred miles." Trammel points at me, "We need a copy of your diary."

"Well, I think you're all wrong." I stand up, tossing my planner on his desk. "He wasn't that kind of person. I would have known."

Sheriff Trammel snorts. Elliot and Eve stare at me, bemused. Enrique keeps a neutral expression as he hooks his arm around mine, dragging me from the room before I can say more.

"Oh yeah," I shout, getting in the last word. "I won't need these anymore." I tossed JB's house keys back over my shoulder.

I stare out the jeep window, dazed. A flash of lightning brightens the dark sky. Huge raindrops splash off the windshield, the wipers barely make a path through the flood before we're blinded again. It matches our mood. "If I only pestered him about his life when we first met," I mumble. "I still feel like a dope for never finding out what he did for a living." My hands hurt from slapping the dashboard a few times. "Do you think the business is still going on without him?" I ask Enrique and Eve.

Eve shrugs. "I don't know. And he wouldn't have told you if he did something illegal. There's your clue right there. They didn't find a planner. His phone was a burner. He didn't seem to have a secretary. What kind of person makes, or made, his schedule on a yellow pad? We need to fill in some of the missing pieces."

"We will find out what he did," Enrique says, emphasis on the will. "But it seems like he would need a partner. I feel the dots will connect as we keep searching."

I want to be helpful. "Look, we already know he traveled to other states, bought clothes and traveling supplies, and had lots of cash. He was gregarious, so his job probably involved people."

Eve took up the list. "He might have rented or owned another vehicle to carry more people. Plus, he didn't always tell you his future schedule and never talked about himself." Eve placed a hand on my shoulder from her place in the back seat. "It might explain all the cash. At several thousand dollars a pop—say an average of four thousand per child—would be over eighty thousand dollars for the month."

We brainstorm as the winds buffet the car like a small boat on a writhing sea. Eve continues, "He wasn't very permanent, we could tell by his house. He had few clothes, no personal items depicting family or friends."

We all pause. Then I add, "Talking about friends—some bad ones probably bombed his house to destroy any evidence he may have left behind."

"It could have as easily been an enemy," Eve says. "Why do you think it was a friend?"

"If it had been an enemy, the blast would have been to kill him."

Enrique added, "Yes. By the time the house blew to bits, he had been dead for almost two months. The person only needed to look online for obituaries or read it in the local paper. Maybe it happened now because we started snooping around again."

"If his business or partnership involved other people," I say, "they might want to destroy all evidence of any connection. They can't access his car in the county impound lot and they might not know about the other vehicle or the gas receipt or calendar."

Besides, if he trafficked people who were, what my friends called, victims of societal ills, then I'm also a victim of the same society, except one where we had to find our mates on-line.

What a joke. I am not a victim. Life is all guesswork.

CHAPTER SIXTEEN

It's time to be proactive. My latest paintings are dark; deep woods with hidden traps for unaware feet and darker ponds with whirlpools to pull down the emotions of the viewer. Jackson told me not to hang them. I did anyway, and they sold the same day. I've felt guilty ever since.

I grasp a copy of the gas receipt I'd made before handing it in to the sheriff. I waited over a week. The sheriff had his chance, and they still had nothing new. The address and phone number of the gas station topped the receipt. I know it's a long shot. Most of these stations have no employees in the middle of the night. The odds of anyone seeing anything and remembering it after two months are slim. I take a deep breath and tap in the number. My knuckles turn white from gripping the phone.

"Hello, Wanda's Corner. How can I help you?"

I am pleased to get a pleasant female voice. "Hello."

"Hello?" She invites me to continue.

"Hi. I know this might seem crazy, but my father's missing and I found a gas receipt indicating he bought gas there a couple of months ago. He might even live around there." I forge on quickly, so she can't protest too soon. "Do you have people working there at one o'clock in the morning?"

"Well, yes. We have staff here twenty-four, seven. We're actually a large convenience store. Not as giant as a truck stop, but we have groceries, a Subway, hot dogs, salads, burritos and coffee. We have a lot of traffic in and out of the oil fields. We're the last stop before leaving Montana."

My heart sinks. I hoped the station attendant would remember a man buying gas so early in the morning. "I knew it was a long shot but thought I would try. The chances of someone remembering after all this time would be crazy."

"Actually, it's not crazy at all. Because the rate of crime has skyrocketed around the oil fields, we have a long term, computerized surveillance system. It makes digital recordings of every car, license plate and person driving through, whether or not they buy gas. I'm not busy right now, so can you tell me the date?"

I'm almost speechless. "Yes, that would be great! The fifth of April and the timestamp on the receipt says 1:10 A.M."

"Wait a minute, I'm scrolling down the dates now. There it is. I'll start at one o'clock. Ok. Now tell me what he was driving."

I think a moment. "It may have been a Mustang convertible, metallic silver."

The girl laughs. "Rad. Should I assume it's a Montana license plate?"

"Yes."

"Describe him." I do.

She comes back right away. "Here he is. He's driving the Mustang." She gives me the license number. "But you know what? I've seen him before. Many times, actually. He came through one night with six young Chinese women. That's why I remembered. We don't see too many Chinese people on this side of the state. One girl told me she and a few of the others were moving to Minot to work at a Chinese restaurant. She spoke perfect English. He drove a white Suburban with Wyoming plates. I noticed, because I wondered where those girls came from. Is there anything else?"

"Can I ask what he's wearing? He's disappeared a while ago and we're trying to find him." I lie better than Enrique can imagine.

"He has on a nice waterproof rain slicker like you'd wear on a horseback ride. It poured and wind blew like the dickens, as usual. He appears to be alone. He came in, used the john and drank from the water fountain. He only bought gas and I see he paid cash. This is also very common since the oil boom. Everyone likes to trade in cash." She abruptly stops and I hear angry talking in the background. The name Wendy is repeated angrily many times, and someone asks if she is stupid. A new woman's voice comes on the phone.

"Hello, I'm the manager, who are you?"

"Someone looking for her father," I say in my best young and innocent voice.

"Well, we can't help you. Call the post office or bank or the police department. Here's the post office number. Ask for Sue." The manager slams down the phone before I can thank her. I immediately go to my computer and order a generous bouquet for the talented, helpful Wendy. I don't know what I expected to find, maybe another family, a home base, but here begins a row of breadcrumbs.

The post office is also fruitful. Sue and I chat about the growth of the town these past five years and of the high-school kids who hire on at the oil fields now, instead of attending college. We talk about the quality of the people in the old farming community. How it went down when the oil workers began moving in. They're not all bad folks, Sue assures me, although many of them are idiots or ex-cons. She imagines their crowded living conditions make them like rats in some sort of evil experiment. Their personalities change. And the prostitutes, well, they're too numerous to count, like bacteria in a bad well. She gives me the phone numbers of the police department, the hospital and the local banks.

"We only have one ATM and a small branch bank in this town, so call the major bank in Spencer's Gap and check the credit union, too." I decide to follow the money and start with the financial institutions. Spencer's Gap turns out to have five branches of national banks and the original, locally owned, credit union. What would I do if I didn't want to be in the public eye and easily tracked. Once a major bank has your name, the advertisements for banking options, credit cards and investments fill your mailbox. There could be a problem if you don't have a mailbox.

The small, local credit union might not be so aggressive. Their website claims they founded their business on making a line of credit to farmers and ranchers, managing a few college and car loans and holding accounts for citizens of the community. This one even has automatic payments for bills and a cash loaded debit card system for local kids. I choose the credit union.

"Howdy. Central Credit Union. Ben here. How can I help?" The rusty voice answering the phone sounded as low key as I hoped.

"Hello Ben, I'm managing the estate of a dead friend who worked in the oil fields the past few years." The near truth came out so naturally. "I want to know if he had an account at your credit union. Sue at the post office in Point B suggested I call you." A little name-dropping can't hurt.

"Well now, little lady, I'm right sorry about your friend. I'll need to get some information from you first. What name did he go by and tell me his social security number? You'll need to mail me a certified copy of the death certificate. I'll also need your name and social security number." I rattle off my name and social security number. I tell him I'll mail the death certificate and begin to lie about why I don't have the social security number of my dead friend when he stops me.

"Here, now. Wait a minute. We have an account in your name, so..."

There's a momentary pause.

"What? How? I've never been there." I'm stuttering, struck dumb, and no words come out.

Ben is unaffected by the revelation. "Looks like this account was opened in your name in early March. I happened to be covering the front desk and I remember the feller. Nice guy. Said he had sold his single-wide trailer and opened an account in this name. Had the social security number and a copy of the Montana driver's license. I thought your name was curious, so I remember it. We have lots of fellers opening accounts for their families and loved ones." Ben pauses. He can feel my confusion over the phone.

"A lot of these guys come from other states and even Mexico or Canada. They have their paychecks automatically deposited here and we send a check to their families, once or twice a month."

I don't like him thinking my name curious, but I keep calm and carry on. "How do I go about accessing the account and how much is in it?" I ask.

"Well, now. Since I don't have any personal knowledge of you, except your name over the phone, it would be helpful if you'd bring in two forms of identification, like a valid driver's license and a passport, plus a social security card." Ben waits for me to answer. I am still stunned, unable to speak. "As for the amount, it's seventy-seven thousand dollars."

He waits patiently for me to process this information. "Ok," I say." I'll drive out there. It might take a few days, but I'll be there."

"We'll be here waiting," Ben says in his friendliest Montana voice, and quietly clicks off.

Eve and Enrique are not enthralled with my new idea. I call in the license number of the Wyoming Suburban to Sheriff Trammel before leaving town. I don't mention my plans, even when he asks directly. I'm in no mood for the tirade.

Before any trip, there is breakfast at the Crossroads Café. Eve and Enrique think I should fax the information to the credit union. Jackson wants me to stop investigating altogether.

"Whatever the dude did, you know it was bad if someone had to blow up his house to hide any evidence." Jackson gasps the words out, as though it's a matter of life or death. "What the hell do you think you're going to find? Get the money and come right home. In fact, I should shut the garage and come with you."

I've never seen him so upset. Whatever he suspects, it's much worse than what I'm expecting. "Listen. I'll transfer the money to an account here and probably start right home." I signal our waitress, Sandra, for coffee refills all around.

"Probably—the operative word. We all know you too well," says Eve.

"Remember, curiosity killed the cat," says Jackson. "Let it go. He's dead now. Can't do it anymore."

We all look at him. Enrique comes to the point. "Do you know something we don't?" he asks Jackson. "You talk like you found the answer to the greatest question."

"Listen, I'm only trying to keep Roe safe. What's the matter with you people? Don't you know it's dangerous out there in the oil fields?" Jackson is almost shouting now. The restaurant owner brings our coffee and places his hand on Jackson's shoulder, asking him to calm down.

I'm glad we're sitting outside on the restaurant's deck. People are staring. "I'll be careful," I whisper, patting his hand.

Jackson grabs my hand, holding it tight. "Remember a few years back, a teacher was kidnapped and murdered by a crack-head oil roughneck while she was out jogging? She lived in a town, miles from the oil drilling. This kind of job draws all sorts of crazy people looking to make a quick buck."

"Don't worry. Think about how many people live there who

have never had any trouble," I say. "I'll be extra careful." And I will, too, because he has me more than a little spooked.

He grabs my wrist, practically pulling me across the table and leans close, staring me in the eyes. "You can't be careful against crazy," he loudly whispers, spittle flying across my face.

We all sit in silence for a while. The first breakfast crowd is replaced by the second wave. Sandra refills our coffee mugs for the fourth time, and I order a latte for the road. I already packed my car. Enrique agrees to run the gallery while I'm away, pulling in Pryor to help with cleaning, and Eve taking over when she's not teaching yoga, making jewelry or riding the ambulance. Jackson grudgingly promises to learn the fine art of latte making. It isn't ideal, but it's only for a couple of days.

CHAPTER SEVENTEEN

A few hours later, the winding mountain pass gives way to steep forested foothills, followed by steep grassy bluffs with scattered juniper trees and then to rolling prairie of mixed grass, small towns and wheat fields. John Denver's *Wild Montana Skies* blares out of the car speakers. I recently learned how to plug my iPod into the car's radio system and filled my music mix with sing-a-longs. I belt out my best harmony with John's sweet voice. Wind whooshing through open windows carries our words out across the prairie.

As the highway passes Butte, I glance over at the gigantic mountain around the Berkeley pit, now a lake, an open-pit copper mine abandoned by the Anaconda Mining Company in the 1980s. When they removed the water pumps, the pit filled with both ground water and rain. Now, over a half-mile deep, it is the largest EPA toxic cleanup site in the nation. It's so toxic, waterfowl die after contact. The only thing happening now is a group of people spend their day scaring birds off the water.

I pull into my first favorite latte stop west of the continental divide, Wheat Montana, where they grow, grind and bake with their own wheat. Their cinnamon rolls and breads are to die for, and the soup is fabulous. I have a bowl and chat with a couple of women I've become friendly with over the years. "Hey there, stranger," says Darcy as she rushes by, busing and wiping tables. "Long time, no see."

I smile and wave. A few minutes later, she comes over to sit for a moment. There's a lull in the customers, giving everyone a breather and a chance to restock the cold cases and shelves.

"We read in the paper you'd had a bit of a brouhaha over in your neck of the woods. A house explosion? A mob hit, someone told us, but it's probably natural gas. And you. You had a car accident in the springtime?" Darcy doesn't have lots of time to visit, so always cuts to the chase to mainline gossip as fast as possible.

"Seems to be true." I part my short hair to show her a scar on my scalp.

Darcy shakes her head. "Like I always say, it's hazardous to live in the mountains, where ya can't see what's coming over the next hill until it's on ya."

I laugh. She does always say that. Every time I talk to her. People in Montana like, and live, on either the west or the east side of the continental divide—the mountain valleys or the prairie. They might visit the other side of the mountains to vacation or hunt but would only move there under duress. I come east over the mountain pass often to ski or hike in Yellowstone, go trail riding with friends and bird watch. Darcy has never been, nor had the desire to go west of the divide.

We chitchat a bit more; me filling in certain details I don't mind sharing; her soaking it up. She will have something to talk about for the next week with her regulars who pass through. I start to leave, when I notice the envelope of photos in my purse.

"Wait, Darcy, do you recognize this man?" I hold out a four-by-six close-up photo of JB's profile.

"Say, wait a minute. Let me take this back to the kitchen. Hang on." Darcy plucks up the photo and is off like a shot.

I pick up my purse and make my way to the counter. I order a large triple shot latte and wait. Laughing bursts from the kitchen where all the women, except the barista, now hide.

Darcy comes back holding the photo and smiling, Lizzy in her wake, wearing a long white apron and covered head to toe with a fine dusting of flour. Darcy hands me the photo, a floury thumb-print across the face. "Yea, we remember this guy. Had a mustache at first, but he shaved it off after I said it made him look old." She laughs again. "He was in and out of here for the past few years. No one remembers seein' him since, maybe, late March or early April."

"He's a real jokester, that one," pipes in Lizzy. "He'd have us all laughing off the walls, with one funny story after another. Even the customers were happy when he came in." She grunts. "Sort of charismatic, you might say. Remember the panda joke?"

Darcy smiles and adds, "Always ordered a triple shot, twenty-four-ounce latte, ham and cheese sandwich with the works and two cinnamon rolls to go." Her memory for detail made her the perfect gossip monger.

I broke in. "Anything else you remember about him, like maybe his name or what he drove? Or if he had anyone with him?"

Darcy gave a combination head shake and nod. "No name—he called us the ladies, and we called him the southern boy. Always paid in cash, but I seen him driving a white Suburban once. I was sweeping snow off the sidewalk for the morning, so it was early. Must have been the mid-January thaw. The temp was way up, may-be even forty degrees, and he wore a pink polo shirt. He parked way down at the end, but I remember a few other people in the car. They didn't get out, however. A couple looked small, dark, maybe Mexican or Asian. I don't think they was Indians."

Without a pause she said, "I remember him ordering a few sandwiches for the road and pickin' up a bag of day-old cinnamon rolls and cookies, plus waters, along with his latte." Darcy would have continued, but three hungry-looking groups crowd through the door and start towards us, with great expectation shining in their eyes. Darcy blows me a kiss and starts talking to the next person in line. Lizzy disappears behind the swinging kitchen doors without a word.

"They said what?" Enrique practically yells over the phone.

I call him as soon as I reach the car. "I'm calling to tell you. Do you think he really was trafficking girls?" I try not to be impatient. My stomach does a little flip when I hear his voice. I've been afraid to call in my findings. "I mean, it doesn't sound like they were captives or being coerced. They could have run off. Aren't most trafficked girls transported in U-hauls?"

"I can't say at this point. I'll call it in to the sheriff. He'll be pissed as hell at you out there asking questions."

"Tell the sheriff I'm on a regular gallery trip and it's a fluke I had JB's picture sticking out of my purse. The question is, why hasn't law enforcement been out here asking about him?" Enrique protests and I backpedal. "Wait, maybe you shouldn't ask. What can he say? He didn't tell me not to leave the county and I'm not under arrest." I sigh and disconnect. Who's going to find out anything if it isn't me?

I drive on in silence, while John quietly croons in the background about passing the pipe around. The highway continues past Bozeman and over the pass to Livingston, where I pull off. I weave my way past abandoned buildings, a few warehouses, and a variety of gentrified older homes and finally see the old train station, a beautiful brick restoration on the edge of the cute downtown. I turn at the corner near the historical Murray Hotel and find a parking place on the next block. If I hadn't eaten already, I would pop into the Murray or to the Italian restaurant for a leisurely lunch, but two meals so close together won't make me any happier today.

The beautiful setting along the Yellowstone River and the proximity to Yellowstone National Park, the Beartooth Mountains and the Absaroka Range tempts me to move every time I come here. The street is crowded with tourists and the license plates are from California, Florida and everyplace in between. I stroll down the sidewalk to stretch my legs and enjoy the sunshine and then enter a place of magic.

Lila Littlefield moved from Texas to the Paradise Valley thirty years ago as a new bride. Her farmer-husband met his demise a few months later at the blades of a 'problem' combine he had stopped to repair during the hay harvest. The enormous machine showed no mercy when he gave it a loving tweak that started the stuck blades turning merrily. This is how she tells the story. She says farmers, like earthworms, expect to die at any moment, so aren't safety conscious. Lila and I met during an Audubon State Conference field trip I led ten years ago and have been pals all this time. She is the person who inspired me to open the Stone Mountain Gallery.

She gave me a Tarot card reading to make me a believer, telling me to be grateful for everything to work out for the best. Her home on the edge of town has a few acres of pasture, and I spent a pleasant week here last summer with my horse and dog. We stayed up all night creating chaos, and the flying electrons finally organized themselves around the nucleus of the idea for the Stone Mountain Gallery. "You can do this," she had insisted. "The cards say all is clear and things and people will show up: the space, the art, your partners, the barista, the architect, the builder."

The day I arrived home, an old house in the middle of downtown came up for auction. Like the children's story of the modern city growing up around the little home, so Tamarack Falls had changed to a quaint tourist village around this dilapidated structure. Over the years, the old Victorian housed a family, a daycare, a yarn shop, an art gallery and, lastly, an antique store. It sat moldering the past three years, boarded-up windows and doors, weeds up to the fence top, becoming a not-to-be-tolerated eyesore in the middle of town. I called three friends, artists who recently voiced an interest in owning a gallery, and all miraculously agreed to be part of the gallery, if I purchased the property and built the building. Everything else, including my barista, Enrique, fell into place, as Lila's cards predicted.

Lila's Magic Valley Rocks and Art not only has large, beautiful paintings from some of Montana's prominent artists, like the three original Russell Chatham oil paintings covering the back wall, but she also displays a collection of crystals, fossils and gemstones. Her creations of hunky, chunky crystal necklaces adorn the showcases standing in the center of the generous room, and smaller rings and bracelets drape over deer antlers near the cash register. The old, dark wood floorboards, scuffed by a hundred years of cowboy boots, creak with every step.

"Darling." The word rings out across the store and a colorful, lithesome figure flits over to embrace me in a hug. I'm enfolded inside butterfly wings, with a faint aroma of meadow flowers and sunshine. Her long, blond hair drapes over me as we twirl around the wooden floor, laughing like little girls.

"You seem sad, darling, tell me everything." After a tall pitcher of sangria and one circuit of the hour hand around her agate clock, I'd divulged everything happening in my discombobulated life. I even described my fight with Enrique in the prairie and the ensuing hot flashes when I touched him. I got a high five for the fight and a bag of herbs and essential oils for the hot flashes.

"It takes time to heal ourselves after the death of someone we love, or might have loved," Lila says, patting my hand. "You know he passed through Livingstone in April, don't you?"

"Who? Enrique? No? JB? I did not know."

"I recognized Mr. Southerton right away from his Sugar Daddy profile picture you showed me in February. I pulled up to a gas pump just as he rolled into the McDonald's drive-through in a cute little Mustang convertible. At first, I thought you were with him, then I saw the black knit hat. You know, one of those pulled down over the forehead, but having a loose top, like an oversized beret." Lila wrinkles her nose. "I knew you would never wear that cheap thing."

Suddenly, Lila takes in my short, dull hair and gently strokes my head. "I went down the block to turn around. Traffic was horrific, because Highway 2 had severe hailstorm and high wind warnings, and everyone drove on Highway 90 instead. By the time I got back, he'd left."

"Why didn't you call me? Did you know he died in early April?"

"Of course, I knew. You got the flowers and all those cards, didn't you?" Lila sounds puzzled.

"Yes, and I loved every one of those blossoms and cards," I reassure her. She lives for the acknowledgment and appreciation of her individually painted cards. "I know it was months ago, but do you remember what day you saw him?"

Lila keeps a detailed diary and, as usual, it was only an arm's reach away. The calendar-sized planner has photos of gems and crystals on every page. "Let me see. It was the day I picked up the birthday cake at Albertson's for my niece's birthday party, went to the farm store for cat food and was on my way back from picking up eggs and butter at Beaumont's dairy." She flips back a few pages to the month of April and finds the date. "Here we are, it was on April 4th and like I say, morning, not too, too early. Maybe between eight and eight-thirty. Does this help?"

We sit in silence for a moment. "This jives with the date on his calendar when he returned home without telling me and then left again. I wonder who rode shotgun? A high school girl, Kendra, went missing around the same time as my…" I take a deep breath and want a stiff drink. Like magic, a waiter delivers two chai lattes and croissants from next door. I know she didn't call in an order after I arrived. Is she expecting someone else? She places a hand on mine and gives me a little satisfied smile.

Lila is as intuitive as it gets. "Lila, I need to tell you everything. Maybe your Tarot Cards can help us figure it out."

Of course, that would be too simplistic—a corny shortcut to the end of a story like mine. A cliché. I grasp any straw available. After I shuffle and cut the deck, Lila lays out what she calls a nine-card Celtic Cross pattern. As she turns over one at a time, she tells me lots of things I already know, a few things way in left field, and then gives me a couple of alarming ideas. She clicks a photo of the card spread with her phone and magically pulls the full page photo out of her printer. We jot down a few notes, so I can remember the convoluted path of the reading.

"Don't be afraid," she says, placing a comforting hand on mine. "Just be aware."

I nibble on the remaining croissant, and we chat about wild flowers and birds we've seen lately. Lila fans out a different deck of cards on the table between us. "Pick one," she orders. My card shows two naked people, a man and a woman, stepping toward each other. "Love. Physical love. Your new barista, perhaps?"

I pull a long face and we both laugh. "Can you spend the night?" Lila asks.

A picnic basket with warm banana bread, sliced vegetables, dips, chips, sandwiches and drinks from Lila's kitchen sits buckled into my passenger seat.

"Promise you'll stop on your way home to tell me absolutely everything and return my basket."

"I promise." We hug next to my Prius, looking up at the lingering stars in the pre-dawn.

"Oh, and there's an app for that."

"For what?" I laugh.

"For reporting human trafficking. I read it in my alumni newsletter. A young woman developed it for part of her master's thesis."

I hadn't even mentioned the possibility.

CHAPTER EIGHTEEN

Driving across wildlife-rich earth is not relaxing. An early morning drive brings up one irritation after another. Throughout the first hour, deer, antelope, elk and other critters run across the highway, jarring me into a constant state of foreboding. By five o'clock, the sunrise streams over the prairie, directly into my eyes. I slam on the brakes when what looks like a puppy jumps toward the highway. As I glide by, prairie dog holes and dozens of statue-still sentries perched on dirt mounds come into view. The radio stations announcers preach, rant or play depressing she-done-me-wrong country music.

My latte disappears all too soon and I've left my ancient iPod charging on the bedside table at Lila's. Why hadn't I taken time to sync up my new iPhone with all those lectures and music? I pull into a rest stop to unload the latte and calm my frazzled nerves. There's no cell phone service. Again!

Eve's voice echoes in my head, breathe. Facing the sunrise, I stretch up, fold my body forward against my legs, reach up toward the blue sky again, move, bend and twist my spine every way. I use my breath to lift and open my ribs, rotating and squeezing my shoulder blades together toward my spine, and then relax. All the tension drains from my neck and shoulders. My breathing finally becomes slow and even. Then I switch to exhaling twice as long as inhaling, then three times as long. This quiets the rat race in my brain every time. I finally notice the cows and horses scattered thinly over the surrounding rolling grasslands. A coulee between nearby hills sparkles green and lush from a little spring seeping toward the rest stop, creating a small marsh of cattails and singing blackbirds. Nature has been my only genuine friend—always telling the truth. Maybe it's time to rethink my interpretation of truth.

As I pull back onto the highway, the Zen switches on and my mind wanders. It all began with the damn birthday profile on Sugardaddydates.com posted by my girlfriends. I'm sure my friends never expected it to work so fast. I bang my hands against the steering wheel a few times until they tingle.

The winks, the flirts and all the esoteric computer jargon are, at first, novel and exciting. Then came his flight. Unable to find some paper, I make a note on the back of my Kleenex box to ask Sheriff Trammel where his ticket originated. At least I find it funny instead of embarrassing now, the basics I forgot to find out about him.

After the euphoria of success came the anxiety. What if he ended up being a jerk? What if we were disappointed? Good grief, it's like a damn audition. What if our color choices clashed? I know a dozen people who've found their spouses and partners through online dating sites, but never really thought about it for myself.

Internet dating is very popular in a small community, where you've known most of the men in your age group since kindergarten, or at least middle school. You either meet them online or in the bar. I didn't even have a high school sweetheart.

Several women in town have horror stories of the first half-dozen men they'd met online who wanted nothing but sex, the widowers who needed housekeepers, and others who only talked about their boring lives and probably never had a second date except with their mothers.

I suffered from pre-party jitters as I drove toward the airport to meet JB. As the minutes passed, I tried to conjure up my dating mojo and realized I'd lost that mojo a long time ago.

JB stepped off the plane, and I skipped the horror story and went right for peacock colors. He greeted me cordially with a gentle handshake, as a gentleman should, with no assumptions of friendship. We drove around the valley before heading home to Tamarack Falls; him chatting and asking questions the whole time while admiring scenery around us. We lunched at my favorite café, sharing what kinds of food we liked and decided on a restaurant for dinner. I told him about some of my hobbies; hiking, horses, sheep dogs, bird watching. He said he also liked birds, although he knew nothing about them, and loved to see eagles and hawks soaring along the highways.

For the first time since the accident, I had a clear picture of him in my mind. He had sparkling green eyes. A smile doesn't always reach a person's eyes, but his did. His smile lines were a permanent part of his facial landscape. He had thick, light red hair, sanded with a spray of gray. His physique wasn't super fit, but it hadn't gone to flab. His blue polo shirt stretched nicely around his torso. He looked firm. He also wasn't gigantic, only five-ten. His hips were narrower than his waist, and his khakis hung straight down his legs, the pleats perfectly set.

His pleasant voice had a touch of southern. He talked a lot but could also listen without fidgeting when I strung more than two sentences together. I loved his aroma. Not a strong, acidic aftershave or cheap men's cologne, but something subtle and mysterious, like

Cajun spices and pine trees in spring. In the morning, we met for our second date at White Apron Bakery, up the street from his motel. By the time I rolled in, he sat at the liar's table, the one reserved for locals. The round table for eight now seated nine laughing people, and JB motioned me over, pulling up a chair from the next table. I would have been invisible if I weren't sitting next to him. He could twist any story into something funny. My high school speech coach called it the "yes, and" technique. Soon, waitresses gathered around the table, holding cooling coffee pots. The cooks, their long white aprons stained by morning bacon, took turns standing behind the counter to listen and laugh along. This foreshadowed every date afterward.

We went sightseeing the rest of the day, around my community, then around the valley, then up to Glacier National Park. I drove all morning but got sleepy after lunch and the nonstop day of talking and laughing. He drove us up to the park while I napped. The Going to the Sun Road over Logan Pass was still closed due to snow, so we took a short walk around the small village. We stopped at the spectacular MacDonald Lake to take selfies with my phone camera. Only later did I realize his face turned away in every shot. We had coffee and pastry at the Belton Chalet, the historic railroad lodge at the entrance to the park. No hint of flagging energy in him, but I felt exhausted.

I dropped him off at his motel, headed home to feed my animals and get ready for the Community Fundraiser later in the evening. I finally climbed into the hammock for a well-deserved rest, when JB phoned to tell me he'd found a ride to the event, and I could meet him there. The dinner, the open bar and the auction all passed in a blur.

He was on a first name basis with everyone by the end of the evening. His bids on the donated auction items were high and generous and made the whole evening more entertaining. He gave the items away, several to me and other items he spread throughout the crowd. He became buddies with the movers and shakers in the village, offering financial help for pet projects. Then I heard he'd made an offer on a house at the local golf course, sight unseen.

The next morning, the realtor picked him up, insisting he see the house before signing the papers. A miraculous jump through the space-time continuum allowed the title company to rush through the closing and, a day later, I watched him hand over four hundred, fifty-thousand in cash. I remember feeling thrilled he could be so confident; he didn't have to spend weeks deliberating about this or that property. It went so fast. I imagined he might arrange the wedding first and then ask me to marry him later. But in hindsight, I never saw the inside of the house. I drove by there on my own when he went out of town, but he had the drapes drawn tightly closed.

In the early afternoon, after the house closing, we drove up to Kalispell and as we passed the car dealership at the south end of town, he yelled, "Pull in!"

I did, and he walked right over to a metallic silver Mustang convertible and ran his hand along the side and up the edge of the windshield. It looked like he was giving the car a hug. "Boy, now, isn't this the prettiest thing you've ever seen? I drove one in the seventies for a while. I'd borrowed it to take a girl on a date, but I've never owned one. We should go on a date in this one."

The salesman descended upon us with keys in hand and after a short drive around the block, JB quickly signed the papers, pulled cash out of a money clip in his pocket and paid them the asking price. No quibbling. We left my car there for a few hours and went on a fast, one-hundred-mile drive around Flathead Lake and beyond, him laughing and enjoying the driving and even offering to let me take the wheel. That's when things changed.

At dinner, he told me he was leaving on a business trip in a couple of hours. He'd call me when he got home on the weekend. He dropped me off at my car and disappeared in a cloud of dust.

I sigh yet again. I'd asked Lila's Tarot cards what it means when someone spends cash for every huge purchase, and they answered with the upside down Knave of Swords. "Shady business," Lila interpreted. Lila said she spends cash for almost everything because she doesn't want to be in debt. She didn't like to speculate but suggested it's also a good way to be almost invisible. When I reviewed the notes of her reading, I see she added, "Lies could be used to manipulate innocent people." It makes me view everything in the purpled colored light of paranoia.

I blow past Billings and come out of my Zen musings when I notice the tall rocky Pompey's Pillar National Monument north of the highway. I've been out here a few times, but not enough to remember the landmarks. Rolling hills with pine trees reach beyond the braided Yellowstone River bottomlands and the horizon seems to stretch farther. It's still early enough for the sun to glare off the road ahead of me. The deep blue sky is punctuated by clouds of every shape, wispy cirrus, skinny fish ribs, and far away, a few tall cumulus clouds behind the plateaus in the north. I adjust my cool new sunglasses and take a firm grip on the steering wheel. A sign says Forsyth is up ahead, so another gas and pit stop are in my future. Please, God, let there be lattes in Forsyth.

CHAPTER NINETEEN

My triple shot, sixteen-ounce latte from Cattle Brand Espresso gets me through Miles City, to where the highway heads more north than east. I pull off into three rest areas before I find one with cell phone service. My phone plays Bob Marley's "Stir it Up."

"Enrique," I say. "Thanks for calling me. I thought I should check in and let you know where I am."

"It's Eve," Eve says, asking about my trip. I tell her my location and itinerary.

"You've just passed Miles City?" she shouts. "Why did you take the long way around? You could have shaved off a few hours by going along the Highline." Eve sounds more aggravated than happy to hear my voice.

"I'll come back along Highway Two. I needed more time to think. Driving this way along the Yellowstone River is calming," I defend my decision. "Besides, I spent the night with Lila. Guess what? She saw JB there in Livingston the day before he died."

"Hi Roe, you're on speakerphone," I hear Enrique say. "We have interesting news, too. But you go first. What about your friend, Lila?"

My heart gives a little flip at his calming voice. I wish he were here. "Lila is pretty sure she saw JB at the McDonald's drive-through the morning before the incident. He had someone with him, maybe a hitchhiker, but she couldn't see her or him clearly. What's your news?"

"The sheriff might have a lead on the bomber," Eve says. "A neighbor noticed a dark sedan parked at a pasture gate around the corner the afternoon of the explosion, a guy using the farm ponds for training his golden retriever. The second time she passed the car, the dog was sleeping inside, but the man wasn't around. She wrote the plate number for their neighborhood watch program and to call animal control if the dog got overheated in the car. She completely forgot about it after the excitement of the explosion."

Enrique took over. "Now Roe, don't be more upset by what you hear. Are you parked?"

"Yes," I say. "I'm at a rest stop." I munch on carrots and hummus from one of Lila's containers.

He continues talking in a matter-of-fact way, giving the facts in an easy, conversational manner. I almost choke when he gets to the punch line.

"The mob," I say through my coughing. "Mob of what? A mob of sheep or kangaroos?" I can't put my brain around what he said. "A real crime family?"

Eve takes up the narrative. "We're not really sure of the name, but the fire chief said they have connections on the east coast and consider this area the center of their northwestern drug operation. He's pretty sure it's Mafia related. The sedan belonged to a guy who lives in the forest up toward Glacier and is a known consultant for mob activities."

"That's ridiculous. I would have heard about this before if it's true." This outburst is met with silence on the other end of the phone. "Hey, are you guys still there?"

"We're here," says Enrique.

"So, have you ever heard of this, Eve?" I say, waiting. "Hello?"

"Yes, I have heard about it." Eve says, sounding like she's been caught shoplifting candy. "We learned about it at the law enforcement part of our EMT training about five years ago. They wanted us to know when we come in to help someone, our lives could be in danger from crossfire between criminals, for example mobsters and drug dealers." She pauses for a moment before continuing. I hear her sigh. "At the time, I couldn't bring myself to tell you. You hadn't been back very long, and I know you love this place for its innocence. It didn't seem fair to disillusion you until it was absolutely necessary. I guess this is the time. The Mafia has discovered Montana."

"Well, so what about the guy and the car and the mob? What does this have to do with JB? Give it to me straight." "Ok," says Enrique. "Sheriff Trammel told us the man with the sedan is a known explosives expert. His day job is a road blaster for loggers and developers. Trammel claims this crime family is involved in not only drugs but also prostitution, human trafficking, and gambling. Since the mob is here, maybe it's not a coincidence JB moved here. Maybe he did some of those things, too. Maybe the connection between them and JB needed to be covered up."

"Can the sheriff prove this guy bombed the house?" I ask.

"Well, that would be a little tricky, since nothing remained," Eve says.

Enrique adds, "Listen, maybe you should turn around and come home. The money in the credit union can wait until things cool down a little."

"We told Les what you're up to," Eve says. "I didn't want to be a tattletale, but we're really worried you'll run into something you're unprepared for. Plus, we were spooked after talking with him. I don't know if he tried to scare us, but he certainly did. He's going to call you, so be ready. He wants you to butt out and we agree. It's all getting too creepy. Jackson is frantic."

"Roe, are you still there?" Enrique asks after a few moments of silence.

"I should head on up the road. I need to be at the credit union by eleven." I say, as I repack the food into my basket and pull out a Kombucha to sip along the way.

"You don't sound very surprised," says Eve. "And you're obviously not heading right for home."

"Lila's Tarot cards made me look at things from a new perspective. They said there were lies hurting innocent people. The death card was there, too. It was both past and potentially the future." I pause and look at the clouds over the prairie to think. I start to say goodbye, but remember why I had called. "Hey, wait. Eve?"

"I'm still here, Roe."

"I wanted to ask you about the incident," I say. " How did you all know there had been an accident out in that secluded area? Who called it in?"

"Why, Jackson reported it. I thought you knew."

"How did he know? Did anyone ask him if he saw it? What did he say exactly?"

Eve thinks for a moment before answering. "He said a car hit you and the car sank in Larsen Spring. He said we needed an ambulance, a power socket wrench, a pry bar and a large tow truck. It seemed pretty specific. I'm sure he saw it."

"What was he doing there?" It seemed like minutes before she answered.

"Wait a minute, Roe. Are you saying Jackson may have had something to do with the incident?" Eve sounds incredulous. "Why would you think that?"

"The Tarot cards," I reply. "The moon card came up. It means there are hidden things happening and everything is not be what they seem to be. Before the card reading, I thought he had come when he heard the call on his police scanner. I only knew he arrived first, padding my head and shoulders with his jacket."

"That's certainly a leap, accusing someone who was passing by. It's a public road, after all. He could have been there for many reasons," Eve continues.

"I know, I know. I'm not accusing him of anything. No one would have found me until morning, so I'm sure he saved my life."

Enrique is quiet this whole time. I don't have long to wait for his one-two punch. "Rosetta, I've been thinking. Remember when we first met, out on the prairie, in the breaks?"

"How can I forget?" I answer, snickering in embarrassment, thinking about how stupid I'd acted, how weak, all the crying. Would I ever stop feeling guilty for the beating I gave Enrique? All those emotions well up again. I hate myself. Why did I carelessly agree to meet JB at that remote pond?

Not for the first time, I consider not going back to Tamarack Falls. I sniff.

He feels my quiet pain. "Yes, well, the memory I want you to focus on is your question about how Jackson came to be there. You thought he was jealous, or worried about you. What if he came to see if you were alright?" Enrique waited while I thought about that. "What if he thought you would be stood up? What if he planned to be there because he suspected JB wouldn't show?"

I'm more than a little skeptical. "Did he try to scare JB away?" I look at the clock, waiting for the minute to pass until I ask my next question. "Do you think Jackson sabotaged the car?" The next conclusion follows. "Do you mean he knew JB might run me down?" I reply, trying to use my calm voice, but the high pitch gives me away.

"Not necessarily."

"Or maybe JB was going to harm me in some other way? Maybe by using that gun we found, or strangling me, or trying out one of those unused kitchen knives in my heart? Then it would be easy to tie me to a rock and toss me into the lake. It's always icy cold, so a body would never float up."

Eve says, "Yuck, don't even imagine that kind of stuff. Anyway, I don't think JB was the type of man to get his hands dirty."

I jump in to stand up for the bastard. "What's that's supposed to mean? You've never liked my choice of boyfriends."

"That's not true," she defends herself.

Enrique insinuated himself back into the conversation. "Ok, ladies. Let's get out of junior high for a few more minutes."

"I'm sorry," I tell Eve right away. I never had a boyfriend.

Only friends that were boys.

"Me, too, now and for the past," Eve came right back at me.

"It could be anything. Let's simply say Jackson thought JB wouldn't show up," Enrique offers. "Because he thought JB wasn't coming back, or he expected something to break in JB's car. Or maybe he knew something about JB's health. Any or all of those might be an option. I want to revisit every idea anyone has thought about the incident. The point being, Jackson knew something none of you did and he hasn't shared that information yet."

"I notice you didn't include JB might try to kill me as an option," I add. "So, do you think it really was an accident?"

"I wasn't there, remember? All I know is what I've been told by you and by what I've heard around town." Enrique says.

"Shit," I interject. "They're still talking about it around town?! What have you heard? Does everyone still think I'm an awful person for killing JB?"

"Whoa, slow down," Enrique says. "It's nothing like that. I would put it into the xenophobic realm, like not-trusting-strangers and not-using-dating-sites kind of talk. There is a genuine compassion for you in this community. They support you."

I feel my shell crack. I love it when he says words like xenophobic or other large words I haven't heard used in a sentence in years.

"Listen, I've got to get on the road now. I'll think about what you said about Jackson and the whole affair. I'll call you when I finish at the credit union." My chin quivers as I reach up to disconnect. Before the phone goes dead, I hear Eve say, "She never even had a boyfriend."

Driving in the wide, open spaces of prairie exhausts the senses. After another half-hour, adrenaline from the phone call drains away and the early morning start catches up with me. Glendive falls behind me before I remember I need a caffeine fix. I try singing, driving with the windows open, yogic breath of fire, yodeling and howling like a wolf. Nothing works. The next driveway leads to a swatch of swaying green wheat with a huge pivot irrigator tied to the center of the field, the sprinkler pipe rolling around on plump wheels. I pull over and, with all my windows open, letting the soothing swoosh, swoosh, swoosh of the water shooters lull me to sleep.

In my dream, it's raining, a gentle summer shower. I think about finding cover, but not a tree is in sight. The smell is horrible, like a dairy barn in high summer. Sounds of gusting wind pull at the back of my mind and I run. The rain comes again. Drops pelt my face like frozen, stinging bullets.

I'm sinking. Am I in Larsen Lake after all? I jerk awake to find myself wet. Large water droplets have puckered the map and newspapers on my passenger seat. The irrigation pipe wheel looms ten feet from my open window. I quickly jump back onto the highway and take off.

I change out of my damp shirt and jeans at a vacant parking lot on the edge of civilization. It's late morning by the time I reach the credit union. Luckily, the visor is down and my eyes glance in the mirror. Ugh. A swipe of hairbrush, hand lotion and deodorant barely make a dent.

CHAPTER TWENTY

Central Credit Union is at least twice as large as my credit union. Everyone is busy and there's a long line of customers, mostly men. Ben's door plaque reads CEO, and he's looking out his office window when I walk in. He comes out, extending his hand.

"Hello, welcome to Central Credit Union. How may we be of service?"

"Do you greet everyone this way?" I ask, smiling and taking his hand. I feel him jerk back a little, lifting his head away from me after he gives my hand a brief squeeze.

He has a welcoming smile and a quiet laugh, more like a series of short exhales. "Well, mostly new guests to our branch, but I like people and guess I'm a little nosey when it comes right down to it. So, how can I help you, little lady?"

"Can we go into your office?"

"You bet. Can I grab you a cup of coffee?"

I must look very grateful, because Ben doesn't wait for my answer. He grabs a couple of mugs and the entire pot of coffee and leads the way into his office. After we both have a nice sip and I give a long sigh, Ben says, "You look like you've had a long day already. Did you have an argument with your irrigation system this morning?"

"What? No." I look down at my dry clothes. "Why do you ask about irrigation?"

"You have that distinct aroma of liquid manure fertilizer from an irrigation sprayer." He leans toward me and takes a sniff. "Am I mistaken?"

I tell him about the unexpected shower coming through my car windows. I hadn't noticed the aroma. "Well, never mind. We're used to it around here."

"Boy, you're right, you are nosey," I say, laughing. "I'm Rosetta Stone. I called here two days ago about an account." Ben freezes, his whole body, his arm lifting his coffee cup and even his lips, pooched out like a straw, ready to meet the cup's edge. It's only a split second of suspended motion, the blink of an eye. It's downright spooky. His eyes flicker toward the lobby and he relaxes. I glance around to see what he's looking at. It's an empty leather sofa. The other chairs are full, but I feel he's looking at that sofa. He strolls over to the office window, still smiling, and pulls a cord to collapse the blinds.

"Don't you worry about any little thing now. Let's look at that account."

Ben acts like nothing unusual happened a few seconds ago. He sounds normal, but maybe he's one of those crazies, as Jackson calls them. Why do I attract these people into my life? Enrique turned out to be normal. Or maybe not. I better take a second look at Enrique, which won't be too hard. I figure I can take this guy with no problem if he comes at me. But then again, maybe it's me. Maybe I'm crazy.

"Would you like some identification?" I ask, hoping to move the conversation ahead. I rifle through my purse, grabbing both my wallet and pepper spray, which I pocket, as he glances at my driver's license.

"Did you bring a death certificate for Mr. Southerton? I'll understand if you didn't, because it wasn't the last thing we talked about."

"Yes," I say. I'd gone to the courthouse to get a copy a month ago and kept it in my purse. I thought it would help me realize what really happened. "Would you like to see it?" He nods and I hand it over. "Do you have a photo of him, for further identification, of course."

I scroll through my phone and find one of the Glacier Park photos. JB turning away, almost in profile and blurry. "Will this do?" I hand my phone to Ben, and he nods again. What's with men and words?

Ben keeps nodding, as if jiggling his brain helps him think. He gives an embarrassed, breathy laugh. "That's him alright. I'm sorry if I seem distracted. Let's get on with your accounts. What would you like to do with the one that's in your name?" I hand him a card with my credit union routing and account numbers. "I'd like to transfer it to this account at my credit union. I don't know what I'll do with it yet, but it may as well be nearby." He takes the card, enters my account numbers and turns the monitor towards me.

"There it goes, off into cyberspace, and will be in your account soon." He points to the transaction-completed notice at the bottom of his screen. "Now there's something else we need to talk about. More coffee?" He fills our cups and takes them over to a small microwave that's on an old typing table behind his desk. "Do you mind?"

I shake my head. "Thanks. Now what else could there be to talk about?"

He parks the steaming cup in front of me and walks over to the window again. I glance back to see him peek between his blinds. He exhales and slouches a little, suddenly looking exhausted. Reclaiming his chair, he types a few numbers into his computer. "To access any other accounts with Mr. Southerton's name, you have to be on the account and supply his social security number. Well, I verified he died with your county courthouse clerk and please forgive me, but I investigated you as well. I have to tell you, I doubt you'd find a true social security account for Mr. Southerton, or whatever his name was. Most likely, he was an independent contractor and dealt in cash only. We found the social security number he gave us to open these accounts bogus, belonged to someone who died in the early fifties, maybe his father."

"Whoa, whoa, whoa," I say, standing up. "Do you think his name wasn't JB Southerton? Can you tell me where he worked, Ben?" I lean on his desk, pointing my finger of death at his heart. "You need to tell me everything you know about JB. Did you know his house blew up after he died?"

Gravity threatens to tip Ben over backwards as he attempts to get away from my finger. He holds up his hands, as if I were pointing a gun and he surrendering. I remember Enrique making the same gesture at my threat. I hadn't stopped beating Enrique but decide to give Ben a chance at redemption. I back up and sit down, placing my finger back in its holster.

"Settle down." Ben's chair wheels bump down to the carpet. "I plan on telling you all I know. Safety first is my motto for everything. Afterward, you need to do two things. One, you need to call the sheriff of your home county and tell him what's going on and let him continue his investigation. And two, you need to get back home, as quick as possible." Ben walks over to the blinds and peaks out again.

"What are you looking for?" I ask. "Why do you keep checking the lobby?"

"As I say, safety first. There's a fellow been hanging around. Says JB was his business partner. He's come in at least a dozen times over the past few weeks, wanting to close the accounts and withdraw the money. He hangs out on that sofa, drinking coffee, for hours. I told him not without the social security number, death certificate and a will. He's produced nothing yet and wouldn't even give his name. He strutted in here like he owned the place, new grey Stetson, tall heeled boots to boost his height, huge belt buckle that said Bucking Horse Champ." Ben clamps his lips shut so hard his teeth clack together.

"Yea, right," he mutters under his breath.

"And he always had a damn match stick in his teeth, like he's chewing his cud. Stupid nit. What did he think was going to happen when he demanded account access without identification?" Ben sounds incensed, as though identification is analogous to resurrection.

"Ok, but why does he keep hanging around? Is he waiting for you to change your mind?"

"Maybe he thinks intimidation will work," says Ben. "After you called, I heard one of our new clerks blurt out something about JB's girlfriend coming out here to get the money. We've all been trying to get rid of him and I guess she thought that would do it. She didn't mean any harm. It's been damn stressful for all of us. He practically camped out here yesterday, waiting around to see who you were. The dimwit hasn't shown up today, but best to be on the lookout. He might try to bully you into passing over the money."

"What's the big deal? If he wants some of the seventy-seven thousand that bad, I'll write him a check. Maybe part of it is rightfully his, if they were business partners."

"That's not what he wants." Beads of sweat appear on Ben's forehead. "There are two other accounts. Two business accounts to which you are the sole beneficiary." He pulls a handkerchief from his back pocket to pat his face. His pupils appear dilated, even though the room floods with gentle light from the sunny day. "He stomped out of here yesterday, shouting he knew a way to get back at least some of his money."

"We're trained to spot what you might call red flags, money that might interest police or the feds. Mr. Southerton's accounts don't exhibit any of the digital fingerprints that might indicate illicit activity. However, gut feelings mean something in my world. I planned to report the money, but then he opened the account in your name. It seemed legit. Like I said, he had copies of all your pertinent information, and that's the account we've transferred now. I figured I'd hold off on reporting for a bit to see what happened next." He runs the handkerchief over his forehead again.

"Wait. Did you say two other accounts?" I'm so obsessed with his palpable fear I stopped listening a few sentences ago, holding my breath. "What's going on here? Are you ill?"

"No, but I feel something coming on." He stuffs his hankie back into his pocket. "The two other business accounts stand near ninety-seven thousand and four hundred thousand dollars, plus the biannual dividend we recently paid out. It's well over five hundred thousand total. We encouraged him to invest some of that money in stocks, but he laughed and waved us off. Mr. Southerton added you to these accounts last time he came in. That would be on March 20." He pulls a manila file from a drawer. "He never deposited checks except once last fall, and I pulled that check to save for future inquiries." He hands me a copy tucked in a manila envelope. "Take this back to your local sheriff."

"He died on April 5," I add. "So why did his friend wait so long to collect the money? Were they business partners? Do you think JB embezzled money from the company? What's the business name on the accounts?"

Ben leans back in his chair, glancing at the computer monitor. "The smaller account is JB and Friends Transport and the other is JB's Delivery. JB and Friends account has an automatic payment of six thousand dollars, transferred to a business account at a bank in Denver every month. The larger account has a check sent to an accountant in Houston. It's thirty percent of each deposit, so I imagine it's for income taxes, insurance and possibly other bills. I've included the contact information in this folder, as well. Don't you suspect something is not on the up-and-up here? Some sort of hanky-panky is going on." Ben takes a break to sip his cooling coffee. "Did you know JB for long? You must have been close, but you seem to know little about his professional life. Do you mind my asking how you met?"

I rub my hands vigorously over my face, then through my hair a few times. Who cares what this man thinks about my looks and my life. I'll never see him again. "I know it sounds nuts, but I met him on one of those dating websites for wealthy sugar daddies. My crazy friends created a profile for my birthday. JB and I hit it off when he first came to visit.

Then he bought a car, a house and he seemed to be settling down."

Ben smiles. "I met my wonderful wife on one of those sites six years ago. I think she got the short end of the stick, but we chatted and laughed and, lickety-split, we got hitched. I'm sorry you had such a tragic end to the relationship." He takes off his glasses and pinches the bridge of his nose. "The reason I ask about him is that I'm pretty sure he did something criminal. I do not know what it could be and we can't tell people to take their money elsewhere. None of his deposits were counterfeit or marked bills, and believe me, we have seen those come across our desks." Ben replaces his glasses and looks at me. "His deposits were always cash, never the same amount. He didn't look like a roughneck working in the oil fields. And I know most of the executive types from the many economic meetings we've sponsored."

I guess I didn't need to defend the man any longer. "Since he died, we, meaning my friends and I, suspected his business might be illegal, but we couldn't find any evidence what it might be. Do you have an idea? The sheriff suggested he might have something to do with finding jobs for people or even," I could hardly say it, "selling people. He seemed so happy and generous."

My throat tightens and tears roll. "I'm sorry." I take a swipe at my face. "Why did he target me and my town as a home base? I feel so bad to have put my friends and everyone through this."

ROBIN MAGADDINO

Ben brings over a box of tissues and stands next to me, a hand resting on my shoulder. "I still can't figure it out. JB befriended everyone. No one noticed him being extra friendly to kids or taking advantage of people—in fact, the opposite.

He always gave a little extra at the fundraisers, giving me many gifts and now all this money. Why put me down as the beneficiary?"

Ben gives my shoulder a squeeze. "Well, maybe he loved you."

I look at Ben with surprise. The thought never crossed my mind. I have to get out of here. "So, can we transfer this money in the same way?"

Ben nods. "Why don't we give your credit union a call to tell them what's going on and we'll see what we can do?"

On my way out the door, Ben hands me a heavy, coffee-filled aluminum thermos with the credit union name and logo printed on the side—this month's gift for new members. He says I am always welcome, and he hopes I'll keep in touch. He hands me his business card and adds his personal cell phone number to my phone. I dictate my cell number as he types it into his phone. He makes sure the stalker isn't in the lobby and ushers me quickly out the front door.

"Do the two things I told you to do, you hear me? Go home now and give that envelope to your sheriff." Ben looks relieved as I get into my car and drive out of his parking lot. I guess he wanted nothing happening to me on his watch.

After a couple of wrong turns, I see the highway sign for Point B and Wanda's Corner Gas and Convenience Store. JB's stop that last night. As I gas up, I de-litter my Prius, getting rid of the manure-water soaked maps and newspapers in the front seat. Lila's basket is nearly empty, so I transfer the last hunk of banana bread to my cooler and use the remaining piece of pita bread to scrape out the hummus bowl.

Several women snicker when I strip down to my bra and wash my face, arms, and hair in one of the bathroom sinks. I laugh along, but better to smell like convenience store soap than manure. The paper towels shave off enough surface skin to give me an attractive pink glow. I change into the t-shirt I'd grabbed off a table in the store with the word *Cowgirls* in a curly-cue script over a colorful painting of a western garbed girl on a bucking horse. When I pass the mirror on the way out, I notice, for the first time, there are words below the picture—*Do it with their boots on.*

Next to the door are two different dispensers: one for condoms and the other for tampons. Right next to them is a deck of paper cards stuck on the wall, ready to be tugged off one at a time. It's the hotline for domestic violence saying I can use the gas station's phone if I want to call the emergency number. A small, framed poster fastened on the inside wall of each cubicle shows the National Human Trafficking Hotline with an easily memorized phone number, 1-888-3737-888. The weird blend of promiscuity and cries for help makes me shiver. Sex is a weapon out here. Maybe everywhere.

I refill my new thermos with ice water and approach the check-out counter with a bag of peppered jerky and a bottle of iced coffee.

"Is Wendy here?" I ask the lanky teenager behind the cash register as he rings up my purchases. He looks up at the large vase of flowers on the counter that closely resembles the FTD website bouquet I'd sent two days ago.

"She's gone for a lunch break. Are you one of her fans?" The boy sounds miffed.

"Yes, I am. Why?"

"Since she got these flowers the other day, she's had three job offers and several guys asking to marry her. She's only seventeen, but they figure if she got a thanks like this from a customer, she must be pretty special." He blinks rapidly for a moment. "She is special, I guess." His mouth curves into an adorable, crooked, farm-boy grin.

I smile back at him. "Tell her the flower lady was in and I'm even more grateful for her help."

Stress makes me hungry and nervous eating means the three C's: chips, chocolate and carbonation. I throw the jerky behind the seat for later and rummage around for the three C's in the Yeti cooler, my traveling chest freezer. The Yeti looks like your average beer hauler but has magical qualities. Gallon water jugs stay frozen for two weeks in the right weather and if you don't open it too often. The two jugs tucked into the bottom of my cooler are still hard as rocks.

Parking in the building's shade, I munch my first bar of dark chocolate, alternating with a bite of chili flavored chips and sips of San Pellegrino sparkling water from a large bottle. Along with the paycheck, Ben's envelope contains a copy of the original envelope with the word Payroll stamped across it in red and a company name. I decide to call this Jake's Oil Field Supplies before heading home. First, I call Eve, who doesn't answer. Enrique answers on the first ring.

"Listen, unless it's an emergency, I'll call you right back. The gallery is slammed with buyers and I'm alone. Eve went out on a call. Jackson's coming in for barista duty soon. He turned out to be a natural. Call back in twenty minutes." Enrique disconnected before I can tell him there's no emergency.

Directory services connect me with Jake's Oil Field Supplies. "Jakes ropes and dopes," says the voice answering on the first ring.

"Can I talk to your personnel department?"

"That'd be me, Jake Greco, shop owner and bottle washer.

What can I do you for?"

"I'm calling to enquire about someone who may have worked for you. Are you the right person to speak with?" Background noise of talking and the beeps of a bar code reader fill up the pause. Jake Greco shouts back to match the noise. "I'd be the only person to talk to. We have a lot of turnover in some of our departments." Jake's sounding impatient. "So, who you looking for?"

"His name was JB Southerton," I reply. I hear shouting in the background as Jake put his hand over the phone. There are a couple of whoops, some laughing and muffled shouts over the machines and talking. But before he has the phone completely covered, I hear Jake shout out, "It's her."

Jake said he heard JB was getting hitched soon and lamented about how sorry he was about JB's untimely death. He asks if I can come by the shop and pick up a few boxes JB left there. I'm only an hour from their business, he tells me. Just follow the highway into North Dakota and keep going until I hit Highway 2. I'll see them on the right, down a paved driveway.

Sometimes a word can send the mind reeling off on a tangent, like the blast of wind from a rocket launch or a tornado, amassing stray thoughts along the way. When I heard the word "hitched" and caught the meaning, pictures of the invitations, dress, wedding photos, ceremony, reception, friends celebrating and dancing, honeymoon in Italy and waking in bed embraced in JB's arms roiled through my head, coming to rest like a collage pasted on one page of a memory scrapbook. But it's not memory. It's only my hopes and dreams, visions of things that might have been.

"Hello? Hello?" Jake yells through the phone. "I'll be there," I shout back.

Driving northeast, away from Montana, I notice the change right away; more oil rigs, trucks, dust, litter on the side of the road, people, and single-wide trailers. It reminds me of a refugee camp in a war struck country that never prepared for the onslaught of humans. Friends report grocery stores, superstores and restaurants have yet to catch up. Walmart has only enough staff to forklift pallets of products out to the floor, never even bothering to shelve it. The pallets empty so quickly it doesn't really matter.

Housing is in short supply. Many oil company employees and their families live in any hovel or basement they can find, usually for nightmarish monthly rents. Most don't bring any family unless both husband and wife have jobs. Several people told me law enforcement was in short supply. Recent grants alleviated some of the problem, but oil drilling draws the young, the desperate and the almost unemployable, along with normal folks. The pay is great, the hours lousy and the conditions sometimes unbearable and dangerous. Even Ben reminded me to be cautious and let people know where I was going if I ever came out here. "Better yet, don't go out there," he'd ordered.

The windows are open, letting the spring warmth fill the Prius. I've gone thirty miles before I realize it. I can't believe JB planned to get married, I assume, to me. My attention draws away from my daydreams with the change in the air upon leaving Montana. The breeze doesn't smell or feel quite so sweet. Trailers huddled together in the middle of nowhere, so-called man camps, without suitable septic systems or running water, adding the smell of sewage to the wind. Combined with the truck diesel and fumes from oil drilling, the air feels deadly. Wicked. I pass two tall fire spouts, where natural gas in the oil field burns off into the atmosphere. I roll up my windows and drive faster, eager to finish at Jake's. I'm barely out of Montana and, already, I can't wait to return.

Upon entering Montana from any direction, the aroma comes first, bringing me the same recognition that a salmon feels upon returning to her natal stream. Some months the breeze is a blend of aromatic pine boughs, and an attractive hint of flowing water and sagebrush elegance. Another season it might be a graceful balance of fresh snow, wood smoke and spice tea. On the palate, it's full bodied, well balanced and, the aftertaste, perfection itself.

Leaving Montana is the opposite. Here is dryer air, less colorful, and more brittle. I imagined North Dakotans have a better taste for their atmosphere. Or at least they did. Nothing normal about this air.

I pull over to the side of the highway after crossing the Missouri River and call Eve. The driveway and the big shop are in sight. The wind is steady, a stiff breeze from the southeast. I walk around my car for a minute to collect my thoughts. I heard the winds build up over the day and blow all night long. It's actually chilly across my sweaty body now that I stand in its path. Damn, only one flickering bar of phone service. I feel like I'm on Mars. I send out a group text to tell them I'm on my way to one last stop before starting home.

CHAPTER TWENTY ONE

I reach the driveway of Jake's Oil Land Supply Company and pull over to think. The words "Ropes, Soaps and Dopes" are printed above the logo, with the phone number along the bottom. Ropes, soaps and dopes? A pickup truck pulls out onto the highway, long pipes atop a rack turn away from me as I approach. A large orange flag flapping at the tail end of the pipes almost brushes my windshield. The bed overflows with boxes and cables.

Intuition is begging for my attention again. It can bark at me all it wants, and I can ignore it like it doesn't exist. A small tug in my gut is telling me to turn the car around and go home. I shudder. What if I learn something about JB I'd rather not know? I drove all this way for answers, so continue up the paved driveway to the entrance.

Two dozen trucks are parked along the front and the side of the long metal building. Half of them towing long trailers. I see two smaller warehouses behind the main building with signs over their truck size doors, one reads *Testing* the other *Wire Ropes*. Long lengths of pipe are stacked along one side of the parking lot. I know nothing about this whole technology.

Trucks and trailers are backed up toward the three loading bays at the far end of the main warehouse. A pickup pulling an enclosed gooseneck trailer shoots out of the closest loading bay. As it passes, I read the side, *Jake's Oil Land Supply Company, est. 1990*, on top of the logo and *Portable Warehouse* along the bottom. In the center of the logo is an oil drilling rig resembling a cell phone tower. A cartoon drawing of the same tower is on the back door, except this one has a black spout of oil coming out the top and a red circle and slash across it. Underneath is scrawled *Call Us Before This Happens*. It must be oil drilling humor.

Wondering what I will find, I stop inside the double-door entry, surprised to see a gigantic version of a normal hardware store. Row after row of metal shelving holds everything from household cleaners to hand towels and blankets. Wasp spray, like everything else, is available as one item or a case. Boxes of paper towels and toilet paper fill the rack on the far wall.

I stroll down the first aisle. Cases of car motor oil and other fluids for vehicles are stacked next to window cleaner and seat covers. Rows of bins hold different size bolts, from small to gigantic. Assorted pulleys, hooks, huge wrenches and fasteners of all shapes and sizes fill the shelves. The next aisle has all power tools. There must be a design to the store arrangement, but I can't figure it out.

Cash registers stretch out over a long counter, where two men and two women scan items and credit cards. Coffee dispensers and cups cover a table near the beginning of the winding checkout line.

Standing on tiptoe, I peek through swinging doors at the very back of the store and see a forklift loading crates onto a flatbed truck. I hop back as a girl holding a sheath of papers comes bounding through the door. "Ropes ready for John," she shouts. A young man acknowledges from the front of the store with a "Yo, thanks."

"What ropes?" I inquire. I hadn't seen any coils of rope as I wandered through the store.

"We custom make them to length and strength," the young woman replies. "Some are actual ropes and others are twined metal ribbon or wire, more a cable than a rope. They have ends with loops, hooks, whatever the customer wants. We have equipment to test the strength of ours or any cable rope they bring us."

I stare, wide eyed.

"Hey, sorry for the lecture," she says, smiling. "Looking for something?"

"Looking for someone," I smile back, relieved the natives are friendly. "Jake," I say. "Is he still here?"

"You bet. Follow me." As we walk, she answers my other question about soaps and dopes. "The whole phrase —ropes, soaps and dopes—is from a past era, referring to actual ropes and chains used to hoist equipment, soaps to clean the tools and machinery, plus dopes, which are grease and other lubricants they use by the truck-loads. Now, it indicates we carry every odd-and-end consumable item needed to run the oil drilling rig, from huge cables to the smallest nuts and bolts."

She leads me to the other side of the warehouse, where windows reveal a tidy office complex. In the first room, two men talk on phones, scribbling lists onto order forms. A middle-aged woman occupies the next office, filled with file cabinets and shelves of catalogues on the back wall, juxtaposed with two large computer monitors and keyboard on a modern desk set near the front window. She notices me watching and smiles. Everyone seems busy and happy, but all look frazzled around the edges.

"Looks like you've all had a long day already," I say.

"Oh, we have," she says. "We started at 6 A.M. Some of us will leave soon and another shift comes on until nine. We'll close up the store and only one phone guy will be here taking orders throughout the night. When it slows down, he can sleep in an apartment over there," indicating a door on the side of the first room. "If there's an emergency, he can open the shop for a night-time purchase."

The tall, young woman leads me to a small space with a wall of interior windows, snuggled behind the first two offices. A desk, computer monitor, laptop, a shelf full of catalogues and three chairs are the only furnishings. "Dad?" she says. "Someone to see you." A stocky, dark-haired man swivels toward me from behind the desk. When he jumps off his chair, I look down. I try not to look surprised, or worse, bend over to shake his hand.

"Yes, I'm only five feet five inches tall, Sicilian and one handsome devil. That must be why you're staring at me like that." Jake laughs. The girl smiles like she's heard this a million times. "My daughter, Jenna," he says, standing on his toes, pulling his daughter downward so he can kiss her on both cheeks. I nod at the young woman and can't help running my eyes to the top of her head, probably eight inches above her father's.

"Married a tall, blond Swede," Jake laughs, enjoying my continued surprise. "Go figure. America—where dreams can come true." He gives his daughter a gentle punch on the arm. "So, what can I... wait, are you JB's fiancée?"

I nod, stunned. Was I the only one who didn't know he loved me or was planning to marry me? "I guess I am. You said he left some boxes here. I'll take those and be out of your hair."

Jake glances out a small, barred window at the dust devils dancing across the parking lot. "Give Jen your keys and she can get someone to load them into your car. It's only three small cartons." I toss my key fob to Jen. Jake opens a bifold closet revealing a mini-fridge, a petite espresso machine and a half-full pot of drip coffee. "Now sit, please. Would you prefer a hot or cold refreshment? We have ionized filtered water, Pellegrino sparkling water, several soda varieties, espresso or drip coffee."

"Pellegrino would be wonderful, thanks."

He pulls out a small bottle of the sparkling water, unscrews the lid and pours it into two straight-sided glasses, dropping a slice of lime in each. "Now we talk." He hops back into the chair, propping his stocking feet up on his desk. "It must upset you to lose such a man. He was a great help and friend to me. Tell me everything. I am Sicilian, remember, so I know about romance. Tell me about you and JB, about JB's death. My daughter reads all the newspapers on the computer. She said a house exploded in your part of the state that belonged to a dead man. Was that JB's house?"

For the next twenty minutes, I tell him everything. The carrier pigeon, the gun, the house explosion, and the sheriff's department choosing to ignore the bombing suspect. Jake's face grew dark, the furrow between his eyebrows deepened.

"It's unthinkable," he said. Since he was Sicilian, I didn't mention the Mafia.

It surprised him I hadn't heard the proposal. All JB did when he visited was talk about me. The lack of information I had about JB's personal life, plus the bizarre accident, was like a Sherlock Holmes story to Jake. A story that had to have answers, no matter how obscure. We both dabbed tears from our eyes.

"I have an opinion," he says. "Do you want to hear it? I won't give my view where it's not welcome. Sometimes it's good enough to listen." He throws up his hands and shrugs. "Other times, one runs out of ideas."

I nod and Jake continues. "I think our friend JB led a double life. On one hand, he helped companies, employees, customers and miscellaneous stuff come together. Last year, I wanted to give my people something special from my home country: a certain type of salami that's illegal to import to the States. JB brought a carton of the salami from somewhere and he laughed when I asked him how he had done it. You know how he was so funny, always making a joke."

Jake pulled a second bottle of Pellegrino from the fridge and split it between us. "Another time, we wanted a special wine of a certain year from a winery in California and the entire bottling had been sold-out. My wife and I had it at our wedding. Jen's wedding came and there appeared three cases of this wine. The cost was not prohibitive, so I thought it was fraudulent, perhaps a blend of inferior wines and chemicals. But?" Jake shrugs his shoulders, hands waving as he describes the wine. "I hesitated to purchase the wine. It tasted the same, but I felt it might be stolen property. I watched the internet for months, searching for news of the missing bottles." He laughed at his folly. "Anyway, it was fabulous wine. I mentioned it, JB found it. We used to call him the finder. He was always good to us."

"He told me he was a facilitator who acquired things for people and companies," I said. "Nothing extraordinary, but illegal foreign salami and a sold-out wine seem pretty astonishing to me." I wondered how long he'd been in business. "What about people? Has he ever head-hunted for you?"

"Oh, yes. JB found us several outstanding employees." Jen came in to return my key. "Remember, Jen, the young man who JB brought us last year? What did you think of him?"

Jen gave her dad an exasperated look. "Well, I married him, didn't I?" Both Jen and Jake laugh. "The last one he brought about the time…" she trails off. "Well, it was right before he died." She places her hand on my shoulder. "I'm sorry for your loss, by the way. Anyway, the girl was young, but she was a quick learner. I think she got homesick and took her long platinum hair back to her mama. She didn't show up for work today, no goodbye."

"No, no, no," says Jake, hands fluttering. "This morning, a guy told me he saw her down at the McKenzie Flats Lodge Man Camp late last night. She told me she was the family breadwinner now and would move her mama out here if the money proved good enough. She left us for more pay, but there is no excuse for bad manners." Jake scowls and shakes his head.

"And the other half of JB's double life?" I ask.

"Yes, back to JB. He had a sad side. He has…had…an associate,

Buddy, with whom he argued all the time. I think their business dealings were, perhaps, shady, because JB always took their arguments outside, so I never…". We hear Jake's name called from the store and he excuses himself to rush out.

Jenna grabbed herself a cup of coffee from the pot, reclined back in Jake's chair, and put her feet up on the desk. "Ahhh, that feels good. We start early, rarely sit down and go, go, go until quitting time."

"Can I ask you a silly question?" She nods, smiling. "I've heard the term so many times, but what exactly is a man camp? Surely, the young woman isn't working at one of those disheveled trailer parks I passed along the highway."

She throws her head back and laughs. I never knew Italians laughed so much. "Well, it's not someplace where you'd want to spend any time, but it's way better than those sewer dumps."

She grabs a piece of paper and a pen and draws a long line of little side-by-side rectangles, then another and another. Stabbing the paper with her pen, she points to the drawing, "Most of them are like this: row after row of single-wide trailers, packed in so close you can barely get in and out the doors."

"Power, sewer and water are provided, but not always, and there are usually 4 guys crammed into each steel can. A lot of times, guys bring their own campers or camp trailers and pay to park it. It's expensive. Sometimes the oil company pays and sometimes not."

She draws a big sun shining rays of light down on the rows of rectangles. "They're freezing in winter, with straw bales and cardboard piled around the outside to insulate the pipes. In summer, you can't get enough cool air in there to even sleep. It's tough living."

After another sketching session, she continues. "Other man camps are modular, aluminum sided buildings, fastened end-to-end into motel-like structures called lodges, or some other overblown name. Those lodge setups provide single or double rooms, meals in a dining hall, a recreation room and shower stalls. Most have laundry facilities. I heard some guys even pay to have their clothing washed and bedrooms cleaned. Most of them bring only a few changes of clothing and take the dirty ones home to their wives or moms during their two weeks off."

"The lodge sounds a lot better than four to a single-wide trailer," I say, trying to add something to the conversation.

"Oh, sweet Maria, it's expensive. I've heard they charge a hundred and twenty dollars and up per night. You would only stay there if your company was picking up all or part of the tab." Jenna's paper now held something that looked like a super-sized dormitory. The long center corridor had perpendicular rows of more long hallways growing off like branches along its length. Little boxes lined both sides of each hallway. "The rooms are wide enough for a bed, a little table and a wall mounted television. I think they must be the same size as prison cells."

"What about the camp where the girl is working?" I ask.

Jenna looked blank for a moment.

"You mean Kendra? Oh, I've never been there, but I've heard it's a hybrid of manufactured homes and the modular hotel with all the extras. It's fairly new and supposed to be clean. It's a lodge that has a wing for single women oil workers and for married couples." Deep in thought, Jenna scribbles concentric spirals over her drawing. "I can't believe Kendra would leave us for a hard job like cleaning, slaving in a kitchen or doing laundry at a camp full of horny men, even if it is more money."

Jenna tosses her crumpled paper over the desk and me to a wastebasket in the far corner, above it a miniature basketball hoop and backboard. "Two points." She claps and laughs. "Do you know that girl, Kendra?"

"Not sure. She sounds like someone from my village," I say, shrugging my shoulders, embarrassed to get into a discussion JB might have abducted her and told no one.

"I got to get back to work." We both stand up in silence. She smiles, gives me a quick hug and whisks out the door, yelling across the store to her dad.

I wave at Jenna and Jake while making my way to the front door. Jake throws many kisses and yells Italian endearments at me. My face blazes with red-hot embarrassment as everyone turns, smiles and shouts along with him. A couple of guys actually give me bear hugs and one shoves his phone number at me before I make my escape.

CHAPTER TWENTY TWO

With a dark cloud covering my rainbow-colored day, I turn east onto Highway 2 toward Williston.

Kendra, Kendra, why did you give everyone such a scare? I'm surprised the police couldn't track her down. She would have given her social security number to Jake's company when she started work. Maybe it hadn't had time to work through the system. Plus, today she would have a new employment record for the man camp. This would be her first day. She worked at Jake's for two and a half months after JB's death, then disappeared the day I showed up. Could she have found out I was on my way? No. I didn't know she was here, and my arrival was a complete surprise to everyone.

Why did she never call home? What was her plan? I could see she would want to be the breadwinner in her household. Her mom had been on food stamps and unemployment since she fell on the parking lot ice last January and lost her job. I know it was humiliating for Kendra. She might have felt everyone at school looked down at her. Even so, why vanish so suddenly?

Her dad was a good-hearted ass and pothead. He never grew up, always drinking and smoking away his paycheck. He got into bar fights for the excitement, he'd told judges throughout the years, always ending up in the county jail for a few nights. That's why the court sentenced him to two years for beating a guy to near death in the bar parking lot. The bouncer chucked them both out into the night, but Kendra's dad couldn't let it go. The other guy threatened to take a gun to school and start shooting, maybe killing Kendra and some of her friends. This time, her dad expected the law to reward his diligence for knocking the bum out of commission. The judge didn't see it that way. Kendra and her mom thought he was a hero.

What was JB's role in all this? Did he offer her a job, or did he mean to kidnap her for illicit purposes? Maybe he was no more than a convenient ride. Could all his money be from finding staff for the oil drilling conglomerates, or for cases of precious wine or salami? Jenna and Jake said Kendra was excited to have a job and earn her own money, so why did she sneak away, telling no one where she was going? Was she kidnapped? Naw.

Williston looks like a town taken by surprise. A small midwestern settlement gone wrong. Paper and plastic bags roll down the street, piling up like snowdrifts along fences and intersections. A man pisses against the alley side of a building across the street. I pass three fire hydrants surrounded by piles of doggy doo-doo. They must clean it more than once a day. I passed newer neighborhoods completely housed with single-wide trailers.

A tall billboard, looking out-of-place inside a town, shows a mid-body shot of a man in a suit and tie saying, *"This man wants to rent your daughter."* It says human slavery is a crime in North Dakota and has the trafficking hotline phone number prominently displayed.

I top off my Prius and treat myself to a small five-dollar ice cream bar and a four-dollar cup of inferior coffee. Price gouging is the new normal within the vicinity of the Bakken oil field. Instructions from the convenience store clerk sends me south on Highway 85.

I'd left Livingston at four this morning. I expected to circle north toward the credit union near the Montana border with North

Dakota and then up to Highway 2 and turn west, toward home. It wasn't in my plan to go to Williston, or to the man camp.

Questions spiral through my mind, making me dizzy. "Stop it!," I shout. "It's June 20, it's summer and I am on a road-trip." I shake my body, yawn, and stretch as much as I can while driving. I'm surprised to see it's only half-past two. After a quick visit to the man camp, I can come back through Williston and be back in Montana by late afternoon.

The sun has slightly passed its zenith, and a few more shadows sneak across the prairie. Industrial dusty haze and stench coil across the earth with the wind. Muted colors of taupe and olive green cover the prairie on either side, highlighted by clumps of yellow flowering rabbit brush. White spikes of yucca blossoms dot the area, and a few purple lupine and rosy colored cone flowers add color to the roadside. In the distance, stands of cottonwood and conifers pinpoint springs or homesteads.

The prairie is not as flat as most people think. Dips, flash-flood-cut gullies, rocky outcroppings, buttes and glacial scars crisscross the landscape. Oil drilling rigs cluster over certain pastures with well-maintained roads and gravel platforms. Bulldozers leveled many of the rolling hills and a few creekbeds flow with man-made uniformity. Much of the land used to be planted with wheat and hay, but now farmers plow the fields to keep the weeds down, while leasing their land to the oil companies and earning huge salaries working for the same. Giant dust devils, bound for the Atlantic Ocean, lift topsoil off these fallow fields into the atmosphere. The few fields lush with wheat get crushed into flowing, swirling patterns, where those same dust devils touched down to create beautiful crop circles for alien lovers everywhere.

Side roads have names like Schoolhouse Rock Butte or long-Indian-name Buffalo Jump. Flat-topped buttes alternate with Hansen's, Andersson's, Baumann's or Johansson's Gulch Rd., named for the farmer who owned the land, or more likely, the homestead-er who settled here. In the late nineteenth and early part of the twentieth century, immigrant families from Scandinavia, Germany, Russia, and British Isles and Irish sheep ranchers made up about three quarters of North Dakota's population. Those who couldn't find land moved farther west into Montana Territory.

Around a curve appears a huge billboard advertising McKenzie Flats Lodge. I'd been told this man camp is about a mile down a gravel road where it intersects the power lines and a natural gas pipeline that crossed the prairie. Most camps were conveniently located right on the highway, but this one claimed to be the only camp within one hundred miles, at least when the sign went up.

The gravel road is almost three lanes wide and smooth, so I soon catch up to a couple of trucks going my way and hang back from the dust clouds billowing up thick behind them.

North of the road, the neighboring hay field has a layer of tan dirt as far as I can see. A new barbed wire fence separates it from the road.

Signs along the road notify drivers we are in open range with no fence between vehicles and cows. It means livestock has the right of way and occasional cow pies dot the roadway to prove the point. The road is level, cutting through low tabletop buttes and winding around a few deep gullies. Bridges cross other wide gulches and dry creek beds.

I pull over and pick up my phone. It's dead as a doornail. The charger cord hangs free, not pushed in at all. I plug it in so all the lights flash on, plus the charging symbol. There are five missed calls, two from Eve, two from Enrique, and one from my county sheriff's office. They must have come through when I was out of the car in Williston and then run out of power before I could hear it beep.

I'm in a dead zone again, but according to their billboard, Wi-Fi and phone access are free at the camp. I type a quick text message to Eve and Enrique. *Arriving at the McKenzie Lodge man camp, I will call with good news soon.* I keep the details about Kendra to myself until I find out what's going on. It will certainly relieve everyone to hear Kendra is safe—misguided—but alive and well.

The camp resembles a medium security prison surrounded with barbed wire topped chain-linked fence. The road goes straight into the fence opening with a large stop sign next to the guard shack in the middle. On the other side of the shack, the road exits. In fact, there isn't a gate to be seen. To my right, the road widens into a bypass for vehicles with stickers on the windshield. I pull into the lane marked for visitors and stop next to the shack. The handsome young sentry has that overworked, tired look I'd seen in the faces at Jake's.

"Hi, welcome to Camp McKenzie. What 'cha need?"

His name tag says Tony. He has beautiful skin, hair and good looks, reminding me of an olive oil commercial with men picking olives, a donkey carrying baskets mounded with ripe olives and the greenish oil poured over a caprese salad. Maybe lower Manhattan?

"Hello Tony, I'm writing an article about man camps and would like to take a tour." I do not know why I lied to the man. "Can you direct me to the manager?"

"Sure. Let me make a phone call to find out where you should go."

"Have you been here long? Maybe I can interview you."

"Nope. Won't do you no good. I been here exactly three days. Drove out from New York City and started working an hour after I arrived. Ain't had a decent night's sleep yet."

Tony tucks into the hut to make his phone call. I hear the words "old broad" and decide I will never, ever interview Tony.

"Listen," he says, rather abruptly. "Drive straight and turn left." He gesticulates with a limp-wrist movement, like he's brushing me off on someone else, and good riddance. "The office building you can see from here. Has a wooden arch over the entrance. Across the road from it there's a lunch kitchen. You'll see the signs." With that, he returns to his little, air conditioned glass office and slams the door.

I drive in, but instead of turning left, I decide to look around. The road goes straight in the gate and immediately widens out into parking lots that circle the long building. On the right, a manufactured home with its own fence gives me an idea. I might replace my barn with one of these pre-made structures. Seems a lot easier than building another wooden barn. Plus, with the money JB left me, it would be easy to afford. The gate to the little compound stands open and a green, four-wheel-drive Gator ATV is parked next to the door. I slow to examine its roll bar and knobby tires. Maybe I'll buy one of those for my ranch too.

I follow the road, turning left when I come to the fence line, making a slow circle around the man camp. There are long projections from the center stem, like what Jenna drew for me, plus a larger space behind the entrance that has separate doors labeled dining room and recreation center. Each projecting hallway ends with a door.

At the last turn, a row of four white Quonset huts comes into view. They're disconnected from the lodge, lined up across the road and parking lot, backed up to the perimeter fence. Maybe they're an expansion or perhaps they were here first. Another green Gator is parked in front of one of the Quonsets, the words *Cleaning Crew* stenciled on it.

The laundry and gym are tacked onto this side of the main lodge hallway, along with a few more bedroom wings. The roads and parking lots are graveled and clear of all grass and shrubs. Outside the fence, the native prairie hugs the chain link. The gully behind the lunch place is particularly thick with tumble weed piled eight feet high.

A cheery sign for *The Lunch Room* affixed to the building includes a short list of daily specials, along with amenities like lattes and WiFi. The backdoor is propped open by a huge garbage can, one in a long line of garbage and green recycling bins. The heavenly aroma tempts me to grab a bite before I head home.

Almost back to the entry gate, I see the timber-accented office entrance and park next to the covered stairway. What should I say? Should I tell them a girl ran away from home and I want to verify she works here? Or…?

Four large flowerpots nestle close to the building beside the entry door, out of the breeze. Prairie coneflowers and asters grow in a tall mass of purple and red. Wave petunias cascade over their rims. I imagine hanging plants would be stripped by the wind. It's nice, but shocking, to see vivid colors after driving through the bleak landscape.

The wind whips into a steady four or five on the Beaufort Wind Scale—dust isn't obscuring the sky, but it's definitely lifted in the air. Sagebrush moves like Pomeranians on caffeine, gyrating and vibrating in place, and a few tumbleweeds roll through the parking lot. I don't know how people can live out here. I enter the small lobby through a vestibule, where I'm pelted with a powerful gust of air conditioning blowing from an overhead duct. Maybe it keeps out the dust or maybe I am now decontaminated. A narrow check-in counter stands off to the left and a large, windowed office takes up the space on the right. In the office, two men in conversation face away from me, examining a large map on the wall. One is wearing a suit jacket, the other wears jeans, a plaid shirt and newer looking straw western hat. He's tall and slim like a rancher.

"Can I help you?"

A middle-aged woman examines me from behind the counter. "Have you come about the job advertisement?" I didn't have time to answer, before she leans forward and whispers, "I can't wait to get out of this joint. I have another job lined up at a camp north of Williston."

"Well, so I'd be replacing you at the front desk, Alice?" I say, reading her name tag. Lie on the fly.

I fall right into the game, wondering what's so bad about this job. She flushes rosy-red across her nose and cheeks. "That sounded horrible, didn't it? I need to train a replacement by tomorrow or they won't let me go this week. I'll be closer to my grandkids up there."

I smile, killing time, but hope she thinks I commiserate about her grandkids.

"Did you apply on our website?" I didn't answer, so she asks again. "You did answer the ad, right?" Alice looks worried.

"Actually, I'm writing a story about the oil drilling lifestyle and man camps in particular. I might be interested in the job, though, because writing doesn't offer a steady income."

Alarm crosses Alice's face. "If you're looking for a story, you're in the right place, but I advise you to leave right now." She leans forward, again whispering across the counter. "Get right back into your car and go home or go to another camp. You can investigate from afar."

"Before I go, can you tell me what the age limit is for camp employees? Also, are they paid through wages or as contract workers?"

"Those are mighty specific questions. Can I help you?" Alice flashes me a look that says too *late*.

CHAPTER TWENTY THREE

I turn to face the man behind me. It's the suit from the opposite office. "I'm Sarah Chapman, a freelance writer, doing a story on the oil worker lifestyle." Fly with the lie. Enrique would be proud. "I thought I should start at the top-of-the-line living conditions for oil workers and work my way down. This is advertised to be the best camp out here, right? I know there's one north of Williston I can look at if you're too busy." I meet his stare, pretending I'm not kissing ass and lying through my teeth. I smile a wide, toothy grin, trying to look like a harmless fool.

"I'm Jerry Brenner, the manager here. Do you have an appointment?" He towers over me by at least eight inches, well over six feet tall. His face, pointing down at me, isn't friendly, but not threatening either. It's wrinkled and tired, like everyone else. The expensive-looking sport jacket shows off his broad shoulders and narrow waist, and his long slim legs end in low heeled western boots.

"Ah, no, I don't have an appointment, I'm sorry." He's well within my private space, but I'm not about to back up. I look down and fumble in my purse for the notebook and pen I always carry. "If I caught you at a bad time, I could go to the other camp." I pause, giving him the opportunity to send me on my way. "I talked to people in Williston and a guy recommended I begin at this camp."

"Did he say why?" Jerry asks.

I try not to sound too sappy, but the bottom line at a place like this is the almighty dollar. "He claimed it was the best place he had lived at so far. Best food, clean, convenient, you get the picture and well worth the money. So, I had time to come take a look today before heading home." Now he would know I'm only visiting, leaving soon and maybe the sooner the better. "Like I said, I can visit another lodge for this part of the article."

"No, no," insists Jerry. "I have a few minutes right now, so let's walk and talk. I'll give you a quick tour and you can ask what you want." He heads off at a swift clip through the double doors, taking up the wall opposite the entrance, assuming I would follow.

"You can see our setup is a cross between a hotel and a dormitory. We have this laundry room for both oily and regular clothes." He indicates a solid door labeled Laundry. "Down here is a recreation room with pool tables, card tables, sofas, table lamps for reading and computer consoles." He pushes open the door and I follow. The space is occupied by a few men playing cards or shooting pool. "The television is for communal sports watching or movie night," Jerry tells me, indicating the mega-screen TV on the wall. Lounge chairs with attached headphones extend across the space. We exit through a far door and are back in the main hallway.

"Is it possible to see into one of the bedrooms? I heard they were pretty nice and that each man had his own."

"Here," he opens a doorway down a side corridor and ushers me through. "This wing is empty for repairs right now." This side hallway is almost as long as the main hall. The exit door at the far end is propped open and a couple of repairmen sit on the outside stairs. He unlocks the first door and lets me peek inside. It's as described by Jenna. The prison cell sized space holds a narrow bed and tiny table against one long wall. A three-foot closet notch, plus the door into a shared bathroom, takes up the other long wall. A small television mounts near the ceiling behind the entry door. "There are additional showers and toilets down each hallway," Jerry tells me over his shoulder as he strides down the main hall again.

"Here in the middle, we have the dining hall, serving three meals a day and food available all the time. Some guys come in tired and don't eat dinner and then they wake up hungry in the middle of the night. We try to accommodate every situation." He stops and looks down at me. "You're not taking notes."

"I have an excellent memory and like to look and listen during the first interview. What does this kind of place cost?"

"Depends on our contract with each oil drilling company, how many rooms they reserve, how long their contract. Shared rooms start at about one hundred and then it goes up.

Some guys are passing through between jobs and they pay by the night. There are no hotel rooms available. Anywhere."

"I saw some women outside while I was driving to the office. Do they live here too?" I frown, thinking about the impossible shower situation.

"We have thirty women here right now. They can do most of the same jobs as men on the drilling rigs or as drivers. A third are with their husbands. Couples can earn good wages if they both keep their jobs for a while. The rest of the women are on their own. Then we have a dozen or more women employees, cleaning, cooking or doing the office work. That wing past the dining hall houses women only." He gives me a quick smile and turns to go. "That about covers it and I need to get back to my meeting."

We walk at a fast clip back toward the office, when he suddenly stops. "What was that question you were asking my office clerk about payrolls? You thinking about working here?" He stands in my path, so I have to tilt my head back to look at his face.

"Well, I was considering working for a month to better understand the work and living climate. An acquaintance told me her husband got a lot of money under-the-table and I wondered if that was available in all jobs." It didn't sound convincing, but it was the best I could come up with.

"We are part of a huge, multinational corporation. We deduct taxes and other necessary fees from every paycheck." He glares at me to make the point.

We continue through the door into the lobby, and he takes the few steps more to open the front door for me. I didn't want to leave without finding out about Kendra but felt the direct approach would do me no good. "Thanks for all your help. If I have any more questions, I'll call."

My hand is on the car door handle when I remember about lunch. Leaving my car parked in front of the office, I cross the roadway to the door marked *Lunch Room*. Once inside, the aroma overwhelms me. I order the daily special, meatloaf sandwich, with gravy, to eat here. I pay and pick up my tray. The cashier yells out "Here and with" and turns to the next person. Down the buffet line, the food is served up by a couple of heavy-set guys. I grab a clam-shelled pre-made salad from a hill of crushed ice at the beginning of the line and fill a cup with iced water at the end.

The plate-sized, open-faced sandwich is moist and flavorful. The thick, sourdough bread still has its chewy texture under the mountain of meatloaf, smothered with a perfectly salted, smooth, dark, beefy gravy. I inhale the steam before diving in with my fork. The meal is so huge I don't have room for the salad, which I stick into my shoulder bag for later. I order a latte and sit for a few minutes longer.

My head jerks up at the sound of trays clattering. I hadn't noticed dozing off. I finish up my now cool latte and hope I remember to get another before I leave the lodge. Maybe a little stroll around the compound will wake me up. What can it hurt?

I tuck myself next to the back door of the Lunch Room, where the wind is reduced to a slight breeze. I turn on my phone to find a couple of missed calls and messages. Using the Lunch Room's Wi-Fi, I open my text messaging when a tumble of leaves up the road catches my eye.

There are no trees in sight, so where did these leaves come from? When they finally come to a stop, I see it's a small flock of birds. More to the point, it's LeConte's sparrows. It must be adults with their fledglings. They flutter and run along the ground, digging their bills into the gravel after insects.

Although common here in the prairie, I've only had a fleeting glance at of this species at a bird feeder on a remote farm near Tamarack Falls. I didn't even know La Conte's sparrows traveled in flocks. Bird books show them leading solitary lives except during nesting and migration. I snap a few pictures, using the zoom feature in my new photo application, geo-tag the location and post them quickly to the birding hotline. This will be a coup-count on Jackson, because he hasn't been birding in the prairie for years. He'll see it right away when he gets the hotline text alert on his phone. I smile at my photos and then notice something interesting.

In the photo's background, is one of the green Gators I'd noticed at the prefab building I'd passed earlier. Next to it is Kendra, her long, platinum-white hair shining and blowing around in the sunlight. She appears to be pulling away from the grip of a tall woman in blue coveralls. Kendra is wearing a skimpy sundress, an outfit not exactly her style. The dress doesn't seem like an appropriate cleaning crew uniform. I flip through the photos. In the fourth picture, Kendra seems to look back at the Quonset hut and the tall woman has her other arm raised as if to strike the girl.

I glance away from my phone and back up the road in time to see Kendra jump onto the Gator and speed away. She and the woman are shouting, but whatever they're saying is blown away by the wind.

"What are you doing?" A quiet voice whispers into my ear.

I nearly jump out of my skin. A short, round man in a chef's hat and a long white jacket is watching me. The hat has stains around the rim where it's been touched by greasy fingers. The coat is stained from more meals than the meatloaf.

He notices my nose wrinkle as I examined his whites. "I ran out of bleach and my order hasn't come in yet," he explains apologetically. "So, what are you doing?"

No telling how long he'd stood there. Did he see the ruckus up the road? I was a little creeped out that he was inside my personal space. I turn to face him, disguising my step backward, and hold up my phone between us. "Bird watching. A flock of Le Conte's sparrows landed on the road. Well, actually, it's a host of sparrows. One author calls it a knot of sparrows. There are so many interesting and funny names out there for groups of animals. My favorite is a shiver of sharks." I always babble when nervous, forestalling something bad that might happen.

Chef and I both look up as the six sparrows fly low across the street, through the fence, and into the prairie grasses where they belong. Farther up, a man comes out onto the porch of the hut where Kendra's Gator had been parked. He's yelling and shaking his fist at no one, because they are long gone.

"I had to take a wake-up walk after that fabulous lunch. I have a long drive ahead of me and that excellent comfort food put me right to sleep." Everyone likes compliments about their cooking, and this is no exception.

"Thanks. I don't get many nice comments about my meals. Everyone's too damn tired to care. I'm sure they'd complain if it was terrible, but few take time to say they love it. Still, I enjoy cooking here. I'm the top chef. At home, in Brooklyn, I'm in my brother's shadow. This is better. That was Nonna's recipe for the meat loaf, her American version of meatballs. The gravy is a mix I doctor up with homemade broth. It's pretty good, though."

I agree about the gravy and bid him goodbye. A strong gust of wind chooses that moment to send a dozen tumble weeds over the vast pile on the outside of the fence. Some roll across the top of the building and dumpsters and continue past us through camp. Others drop to join the weeds caught between the fence and the building. As he returns to the kitchen, I hear him mumbling about telling someone to clean those damn tumble weeds off the fence.

CHAPTER TWENTY FOUR

I take off in the opposite direction to see if I can intercept the Gator and Kendra. In moments, the building where I'd first noticed the Gator comes into view. It's enclosed with a high, chain-linked fence that opens with one wide gate. Two Gators are parked side-by-side, so I figure Kendra must be inside. I knock on the front door. There are four steps up to a small porch, so I have to step back down as someone opens the door. It's the tall, lanky woman in blue coveralls.

She roughly looks me up and down. "You're older than the others, but I guess there's a market for everything,"

I stare at her for a moment, trying to interpret what this might mean. She has short, spiky, yellow-tipped, black hair and lots of black liner accentuating her large, telescoping eyes. Her glare stabs right through me. Black lines are drawn out from the corners of her eyes toward her temples, her nose wide, almost blending in with her cheeks. I want to remember this for next Halloween. Her cruel glare reminds me of a Persian cat. Her complexion isn't wind beaten and dry, but pink and plump, like she's stepped out of a spa moments ago. Botox? She looks tough and strong.

"I beg your pardon?" I say. I smile, making her step back and look me over again. I feel like holding onto my story a little longer.

"I'm writing a feature article about man camps and wonder if the cleaning crew lives here. I'd like to get a woman's perspective on working around all this testosterone."

"Oh yea?" she says, "I thought you'd come to join the, eh, crew." Unsmiling, she steps back, allowing me to enter.

The door opens into a great room, part living room, dining room and part kitchen. A bar separates the efficiency kitchen from the small dining table. The large picture window opens out onto the bleak, dust-filled landscape. The perimeter fence runs right behind this building and tumbleweeds roll by in great profusion. This could become a hypnotic screen saver for computer monitors.

Sofas and chairs circle like wagons around the living room. Ten young women in robes, dresses or jeans and t-shirts huddle at the far edge of the furniture arrangement. It looks like an international night at a college. Maybe young girls from around the world apply for these cleaning crew jobs, similar to national park lodges. There are four Asian women, two blond women huddled together, three American Indian women with their long hair hanging in braids, and one Hispanic girl with heavy makeup around her tired eyes.

A buffet of sandwiches, potato salad and fruit fill the kitchen island, and some girls are eating while others sit idle. They all look to be under twenty-five years old, maybe a couple under twenty. They all look spent. It must be long days and hard work, like Jennifer said.

Something's wrong with the picture, though. Two things do not feel right. Cell phones are missing. Young people don't eat, watch television or even have a conversation with a friend, without reading and tapping on their cell phone at the same time. The second thing-no one is smiling. The last was even more obvious. I've never experienced a crowd of women that wasn't full of conversation.

"You're a reporter?" asks the woman. All the girls look at me. "Have you checked into the office yet?"

"Yes, I spoke with Jerry and had a tour of the main hotel."

"And he sent you here?" She snorted a laugh.

"Not exactly," I reply, smiling. "I was hoping to get a few quotes, to liven up the article, from women who work at the lodge and then from those who live and work here in the oil business. Can I ask these young women some questions?"

They all shift their gaze to the cat-eyed woman and then look down. Weird. Not one of them smiles or offers a retort. Usually, young women are all about telling their own stories. "Are you their supervisor? My name is Sarah. Thank you for taking the time to speak with me." I hold out my hand, hoping for an introduction.

"You can call me Boss. They do." She laughs in a slow, deep, throaty way, like Cruella de Ville as she planned to skin all the Dalmatian puppies. Her handshake is like the Terminator. I don't think I'd smile if I worked for her.

"Ok," I say, shaking my hand bones back into order. "Well, Boss, do some of your young women have a few minutes to give me their general impressions about working at this camp? Maybe a couple of specific details; like how they came to work here, if they are happy and how they feel to be away from their families."

"Sure, ask away," she says, crossing her arms, lips pulled in a tight line.

No one volunteers, so I ask the whole room how they found these jobs.

"I answered an ad in the newspaper," came a timid answer from the girl standing near me with a plate of food. "Me too," whispers another.

"I met someone who brought me here," says another. "Me too," adds another girl.

They're not exactly enthusiastic. They don't offer an ounce of gratitude toward their friends. Good paying jobs are hard to come by. Now that I hear their voices, though, I lower my estimation of their ages to be less than twenty.

"Next question," orders the boss.

"Do you like working here?" I ask, thinking it would solicit lots of protests, because no one this age likes to clean their own rooms, much less clean up after a bunch of strangers.

"It's a place to live," says one of the Asian girls, shrugging her shoulders. Others give indistinguishable murmurs.

"How's the salary?" I direct this to the nearby girl. She looks down and away, as did others, after glancing at the boss. Out of the corner of my eye I notice the two blond girls begin to silently cry.

"What do your families think about you working out here in the middle of nowhere?" The two crying girls reach for each other and clasp hands. They look like sisters, maybe even twins, though not identical. "Not too much, I gather."

I'm about to call it quits when Kendra enters the room, now dressed in a hoodie, jeans, and sneakers. She gasps, gives me a startled look and then has a coughing fit, turning away. The two weeping girls get up and exit through the door Kendra is blocking. The girl standing with the plate of food takes one of the vacated lounge chairs. The boss roughly pushes past Kendra and hisses something to the two sobbing girls. I hear one of them cry out and the thump of something hitting the wall.

Kendra stumbles from the boss's swift shove and starts walking toward the buffet. Maybe she doesn't recognize me. She looks straight at the light shade over my shoulder, not directly at me. She is still clearing her throat and starts stretching her arms and rolling her shoulders. It all looks random for a second and then her right hand makes a more deliberate motion. She seems to feign a stretch, bringing her upward turned palm to her chest, then scooping it outward and flipping the hand down.

She does the same motion, alternating her hands and then stretches up and yawns, bringing one hand up to her mouth, wiggling her finger and moving it away from her face a little. She continues on, banging her fist on her heart and then pushing down with an open palm. She does it with both hands and then whips her first finger straight across her forehead, as if wiping off sweat from all the coughing. She grabs a water bottle and chugs it down. "Allergies," she says, nonchalantly. I look down at my notebook where I am jotting my feelings about the girls. It only takes a moment to understand Kendra is asking me to not speak. Hand signing for me to not talk or speak, not to her nor recognize her. She never glances my way.

Two years ago, Kendra came on a bird walk with her sophomore science class, led by Old Jack and me. Kids her age aren't interested in bird watching, so Old Jack taught them Indian sign language while we walked along the nature trail.

The students loved this, figuring they would learn a few keywords, so they could communicate with each other in front of their teacher and not get caught. Little did they know some of their teachers had been taught the same words when they themselves were teenagers on Jack's bird watching field trips. A few kids, including Kendra, came back to visit Old Jack several times to learn new, specific words. Luckily, I had been there, too. No. Speak. It was very clear, despite the stretching and throat clearing. She must be embarrassed for someone from her hometown to have found her. Maybe she doesn't want them to know she had run away from home.

The Boss returns and says, "Well, Sarah, is there anything else we can do for you?"

Kendra looks up sharply as the Boss says my false name. "Listen, I'm going to interview some women who work in the oil fields. If anyone wants to be interviewed for the article, find me outside." I thank the boss, who slams the door behind me.

Both the temperature and wind have picked up by the time I

leave the air-conditioned house. This wind must wear people down. Why else would those young women be so depressed? Pioneer women used to hang themselves or walk out into the prairie and lay down to die after their psyche blew away in the constant wind.

Kendra's rejection stung. We aren't close, by any means, but we do know each other on a first name basis, and she's trusted me with a few of her secrets. I shrug my shoulders. Maybe Kendra will follow me and offer me an explanation. Maybe she thinks I'm a busybody who should butt out of her life. It wouldn't be the first time someone wanted me to butt out of something. Maybe she's lied about her name or age and doesn't want the boss to find out anything different.

Up ahead, a small group of people, including one woman, walk across the parking lot. I catch up to them and can tell they're coming from the cafeteria. The woman and a tall man next to her carry identical lunch boxes and thermoses. They wear matching tan Carhartt coveralls. Maybe I can find out something about Kendra from them. I intercept their path to the parked pickup trucks.

"Hi," says the woman, smiling at me. The men nod and walk on, while the woman slows a bit. She looks around fifty years old. Exhaustion and wind burned, wrinkled skin ages her, and she's probably too tired to care. I can already feel my skin puckering from lack of moisture. Her short hair shows the reddish, frizzy tips of perm burn, and her eyebrows and eyeliner are skillfully tattooed artifacts. I can sympathize with her getting permed, tattooed and waxed into a wash and wear condition, so she can work, shower, eat and sleep, and repeat. "Hello, my name is Sarah and I'm here to research an article on women working in the oil fields. Do you mind if I ask you a few questions?"

"I can talk as we walk to the truck. My husband and I are starting our shift. I'm Carol." She holds out her hand to me.

"Thanks, you're the first friendly face I've encountered. So how do you like working out here with all these men, Carol? Is the work strenuous?"

"Ya know, women are strong and resilient, and I have no trouble doing most of the jobs. Can't say I love it or look at it as a career choice, but it's a job and my husband and I can be together." Carol gives a fond glance toward the tall man walking ahead of us. "We started out working in separate places, but finally figured it out so we could be with the same company, same shift. Makes it easier to bear, let me tell ya."

Carol slows down, widening the gap between the men and us, and then lowers her voice. "We don't have kids yet, but that's coming after we pay off our mortgage. I know, I'm thirty-two already, but we can pop a few kids out before too long. Our house in Kansas is almost paid off, by the way. Our company pays for room and board, and we don't have to fly home every few weeks. Our first paychecks went toward buying a trailer in an Arizona retirement park and we fly there on our weeks off. It's a little more expensive, but it's saved our sanity and kept us working longer than most folks. This is our second year."

I am pleased and surprised by her heartfelt speech. "It must be nice to have your cleaning and laundry done by the housekeepers while you're at work in the field."

She gives me a puzzled look. "The public rooms get a cursory cleaning every day, but I prefer to keep my own space clean."

I continue on. "I visited the women's compound. They were a pretty silent bunch, but they must give good service. Do you know any of them?"

Carol's countenance darkens, and she steps in front, whirling to face me. She looks downright angry, so angry I back up a step. "You're joking, right?" She stomps off but turns and comes back. "Well, it's not funny." She pushes her powerful hand into my chest, propelling me back.

I'm more than a little scared. What brought this on? The men had walked on, but the husband glances back at us. I wonder if he can call her off. What the heck is wrong with her? Wind crazed?

"Are you some sort of kinky, sadistic reporter, working for the National Inquirer or some other trash rag?" She keeps shoving her strong hand against my chest and then grabs my shirt and leans in really close. "If we didn't need the jobs so bad, I'd do something about that, and you can quote me after two months have passed, because we'll probably have moved on to another location by then. You should be ashamed of yourself." Carol swipes at the tears forming in her angry eyes as she turns and hurries to catch up with her husband.

The miniature dust-filled tornado kicks up behind every one of her heavy, rapid steps as she stalks away. This wind makes people nuts. "Weird," I say out loud to no one. "Weirded out by this damn wind." I keep walking until I turn the corner away from the women's compound.

Oil workers were coming and going. It takes many staff rotations to keep the oil fields running twenty-four hours a day, seven days a week. Every so often, I catch a glimpse of the Gator carrying one or more of the housekeepers across the camp. I don't see Kendra going out. Maybe she's finished with her shift. I come across small groups of women, some willing to chat, others in a hurry or too tired. Most are grabbing a meal before going out on the job.

Three of the younger women are truck drivers. They describe their jobs as pretty boring. They drive in a long line of oil tanker trucks, waiting for their truck to get filled with oil, drive to the depot, and wait in line to get rid of their oil. They do this for ten hours a day. They'd be back here after midnight, their clothes, skin and hair reeking of oil. "Even my pee smells of oil," one laughs.

Another woman in her fifties has worked in the oil fields for six years. "I'm a single mom and my youngest of three kids starts college in the fall, so I'll stay another couple of years to pay that off.

They'll all, hopefully, have their master's degrees and jobs, and I never let them forget that they'll all be supporting me in my old age." These jobs represent so much sacrifice and determination. There must be hundreds of interesting stories out here. Maybe I should do some real interviews and write a real article.

CHAPTER TWENTY FIVE

Every public room of the main lodge is accessible from the parking lot and the recreation center has a big sign over the outside door. I slip inside to catch a moment out of the wind. I find myself in a wide coatroom, with long benches against each wall and coat hooks higher up. Doors with pictures of a little man and a dress-clad woman are immediately to the left and right. I have to laugh at the generic skirted figure marking the women's bathroom. I bet they never see that around here.

Crazy hair day! The mirror reflects someone who's pushed her finger into a light socket. I am surprised anyone would talk to me at all. Dirt falls from my hair into the sink, and I dip the top of my head under the running tap, scratching my fingers through the short cut. Grit glues itself into the squint lines across my eyes, cheeks and forehead. I splash cold water over my face, getting a free microdermabrasion, as I coax the fine soil off of my skin. My wet fingers swipe over the sand grains in my ears.

Maybe I should leave, get into my car and drive away like the desk clerk suggested. I can call Kendra's mom and let her take it from here. I splash my face a few more times, and with the wet paper towels, try to smooth down my spiky hair.

"Oh," I groan. "I can't wait for a shower tonight."

I'm parched, like I've been hiking for miles. In the recreation room, a bucket full of iced bottled water sits on the first table. I knock the first bottle back without taking a breath. I slip a second one into my purse and wander over to a table laden with a sad collection of spotted bananas and a few bruised apples, grabbing a banana for later.

Shelves with games, cards, checkers and backgammon boards, puzzles, and books line along one wall. The pool tables are full, four men to a table and others stand nearby, watching and waiting for their turns. Pinball machines, two foosball tables and video games are beyond the pool tables. The television is centered between sofas and easy chairs with headphone jacks. Several guys watch or doze encased in the earmuff-like, noise blocking headphones.

As I stand there considering the room, I see a man who resembles the one who yelled after Kendra and the boss had left. He'd been far away, but his long hair and short beard seemed the same color. I look around the room and notice most of the men have short beards.

Longhair is gesticulating and laughing, obviously telling a story. I sidle over to a vending machine and pull out a bill to buy a soda, as an excuse to stand closer. The four other men at his table laugh along with him. They all have frosty bottles of beer cradled between their hands. He says, "The little bitch was like a damn deer, twisting and kicking and as slippery as a fish. Damn near messed myself in excitement."

"I hear she got off the hook," said another man, joining the table. They all laugh except for Longhair, who now looks pissed.

"I'll get her later. Teach her a thing or two." No one laughs at this, and everyone looks down. Two of the men drift away. Another says, "Catch you later," as he pushes back his chair. They seem like normal guys, accepting abnormal behavior away from home. Apparently, teaching young women a lesson isn't acceptable.

Two new men take over the vacant chairs. One glances at me, so I grab my Squirt and turn back toward the door. I see the manager coming in the outer door and make my way through the interior door into the main hallway. I don't know if he'd like me wandering around by myself, so best to avoid further contact. Right across the hall is the door to the laundry. The front is close by, beyond the office. I could go past the front desk, but then I'd have to explain myself to the secretary. I choose the laundry.

About twenty washers and ten huge dryers line up in two rows and against a wall. The place reeks of oil. Five washers have orange tape across their lids, indicating out-of-order. Another five washers are painted across with black slash; the word "Oil" stenciled over it. Those must be for the oily clothes. It cost five dollars for a wash and four for a dry. Cubicles cluster along one wall. Three guys are using their laptops and a baseball game plays on the big screen television mounted to the wall.

Two men and three women are doing the Laundromat dance of changing clothes from washer to dryer, getting change at a machine on the wall, folding shirts and pants into plastic laundry baskets, boxes or duffle bags. A few offer a nod or a smile, even though weary, bleary eyes and wrinkled brows mark every face. A young Hispanic woman wearing a smock with the McKenzie Lodge name and logo on the front and back is the only one who looks downright miserable as she folds and stacks a gigantic pile of towels. It's actually a little humid in here. Maybe doing laundry will plump up their skin.

Loud talking erupts in the hallway, and I peek out through the window. Jerry, the manager, lingers in the hallway with his plaid-shirted friend. They're deep in discussion and headed back to the office. This is the part where the heroine makes her elegant getaway. He doesn't even know I'm here, and he probably doesn't even care, but why chance it. After they pass, I re-enter the hallway and cross over to the cafeteria.

The dining hall has an exit on the side of the building nearest Kendra's house. I want to give Kendra one more chance to tell me what she's up to and to find out what oil worker Carol is talking about. I'm not leaving here without asking Kendra about JB. What am I even doing out here if it isn't to find out about JB? I have to know if and why he brought her to North Dakota. I want to know why she left her job at Jake's. And I want to know why she signed those last two words to me.

The dining hall holds about twenty round tables, each with eight chairs. It resembles any nice college cafeteria. The long buffet offers a lot of variety. Sodas, iced tea and coffee dispensers line the wall at the end of the buffet. This is an all you can eat, twenty hours a day operation, the manager told me. The closed hours are for cleaning, prepping and cooking. Dinner is in full swing now. Even though I've eaten the filling meatloaf sandwich over in the Lunch Room, the food smells marvelous. I take a stroll along the buffet line. There are mixed greens and a pasta salad, two trays of vegetables, baked potatoes, prime rib, pork chops, gravy, chicken Alfredo and, at the end, spaghetti with meatballs.

The young truck driver girls wave me over to sit at their table. They're getting ready to go on shift and have their loaded lunch boxes and heavy metal thermos bottles filled with coffee. They introduce themselves as Heather, Babs, and Bobbi. "If you think this is good, you should show up tomorrow for chicken pot pie," says Bobbi. "It's to die for."

"You girls are lucky to be working hard enough to burn off all this food." I banter back.

"Not so much." They all laughed. "We've all gained ten pounds. It's sick having all this free food," Heather pipes in.

"Whoa, not me," Babs slowly pushes out the words with a heavy southern drawl. "I did at first but lost it all now. I had to start running before dinner in case it was something I liked. My mama will kill me if I come home a fatty." Heather slapped her arm. "As if."

"Hey, do you girls know anything about the cleaning staff living in the prefab with the fence around it? I tried to interview them, and no one would talk to me. They seemed almost sad."

Bobbi and Babs shake their heads in unison. "We're not here much and in fact, I've only lived here for two weeks," offers Babs. "We all knew each other from truck driving school, so we got our employer to move us to the same camp."

"I've been here for five months now," says Heather.

I persevere. "Did you notice the girl with long platinum hair showing up recently?"

"I did," Heather says, nodding. "Saw her for the first time this morning. You get used to seeing them traveling around on their ATVs with their warden. That's what I call the tall woman in overalls. It seems like she's always there when I see one of the girls. She reminds me of the prison guards in a TV show I used to watch."

"Do you ever see them working? Cleaning rooms or this kitchen or the grounds?"

Bobbi and Babs shake their heads. Heather looks down for a moment. She leans forward, getting closer, so she can whisper. "One of them, a Mexican girl, works here sometimes, but I think they all have other duties. I've overheard some of the guys talking about having sex in their rooms. The rule against bringing prostitutes into one of these lodges is pretty strict. A guy can get kicked out and lose his housing allowance."

She looked around to see if anyone could hear her and leaned closer. "So, I started wondering if they were having sex with some of the single women, well, like us, working in the oil fields. I don't think the lodge manager could do anything about it. But since I've moved into McKenzie Camp, I've known every woman in the oil business that lived here. I would have heard if they'd found a friend with benefits. I mean, we have little to talk about and it would have been prime gossip."

Her two friends look at Heather with a newfound respect.

They'd be talking about this for weeks to come.

I'm getting a bad feeling. I thought about the struggle between Kendra and the boss in the road and then the man yelling after them. At the time, I'd thought maybe she'd broken something while cleaning, or used his computer to e-mail her friends, or even stolen money. A lot of these jobs pay cash that might be hard to hide in those tiny bedrooms.

What may have been the same man, was bragging himself up to his buddies about a woman, and not in a nice way. She had struggled against him. Another man teased him about letting her get off the hook. Now the braggart was going to teach her a lesson. "What are you trying to say, Heather?"

"Well, all the staff eats here in the dining hall. I've seen the manager, the office staff, janitors and even the builders eating here. The guard woman, the one in overalls, eats meals here, too. But I've seen none of those girls at dinner or breakfast. I can't imagine I wouldn't have seen one of them in all this time. I'd say they were kept isolated. Maybe that's why they seem so sad."

"Holy crap," cries Bobbi, jumping up, "Look at the time!" The other two take a quick look, grabbing their lunch boxes and thermoses.

I leap up and follow them to the door. I tug Heather's sleeve before she gets outside. "Heather, you think those young girls are having sex with these guys?" She looks back at me and gives a little nod.

I stand on the porch, watching the three young women run off toward their pickup trucks. They wave as they speed toward the gate, their trucks sending up a plume of dust. I sit down on the stairs, the sun now shining full on this west side of the building. It's hot, but I feel a chill, maybe from the wind, maybe from this tickle in the back of my brain.

All of those girls? Prostitutes? Not Kendra. She wouldn't even think of it. Her mom said Kendra didn't even have a boyfriend. I wasn't her close confidant, so how could I decide what she would and wouldn't do. Did it make sense? Did any of this make sense? Had Sheriff Trammel been right about human trafficking? And earlier today, Eve told me about a crime mob operating in our valley. Was JB involved with them? Did JB bring Kendra to North Dakota for this? No. No. No. It can't be true.

The sun is still high in the sky but beginning its descent. It's only four o'clock and I've been up and traveling for twelve hours. It's one of the longest days of the year, which means it won't be dark until well after ten. The Lunch Room latte kicks in and I feel wide awake.

Kendra's last two signed words made little sense. Maybe they were out of context. Maybe they referred to another time and place, or maybe she'd used the wrong hand signals. The first signed word started with her fist next to her heart, thumb touching her chest. She opened her hand and pushed the flat palm toward the earth. Bad. She could have mistaken it for the sign for sadness, which was a downward facing cupped palm in front of the heart, making a tiny clockwise circle. Neither of us knows many words, so I can't come up with anything else.

The second phrase she signed was white man. There was no doubt about that one. The forefinger drawn across the forehead is indicating the flat line a western hat leaves on the forehead of the wearer. Or some said it was drawing the flat brim of the cowboy hat itself. There was no doubt about this sign, because we used it as a joke. The girls and I bantered about the boys on the bird walks, signing they were bad, crazy white men. The girls used the universal symbol of crazy, forefinger pointing at and circling the side of their heads. I think the boys got a kick out of being called men.

She'd made the first sign twice—bad, bad. Did she mean one man was very bad, maybe Longhair? Or maybe several men were bad? There are many good men behaving like bad boys out here. In the isolated, exhausting world of mineral extraction, whether it be oil, gas or diamonds, men live in unnaturally crowded, all male conditions. Away from family and friends, they can reinvent themselves and become as wild as mad hatters.

I'm determined to speak with Kendra in private. Heading back toward the women's fenced compound, I notice the two men, one in a suit and one in the jeans and plaid shirt, come around the corner of the office porch. I back up and duck behind the cafeteria entrance. The men stop with their backs to the building corner and look around. One points toward the other end of the building and then toward the women's house, like he's explaining the parking lot layout. Plaid shirt turns in my direction. Damn. I see the red head of a matchstick twirling around in front of his clenched teeth. My eyes fall on his belt buckle and cowboy boots. He fit Ben's description of JB's mysterious partner, Buddy.

I immediately crouch down to fiddle with my shoelaces. The two men walk toward me, or rather toward the door nearby. I pivot so my back is facing them. As the men pass, I overhear Matchstick Man mutter something that sounds like "business continues as usual," and the rest is lost when they enter the cafeteria.

As soon as they're through the door, I act. Walking at a normal pace down the side of the building, I make it to the next corner. "I can do this. I can do this." I whisper the affirmation as I cross over the open gravel to the women's house, feeling like a mouse leaving the cover of a wall and entering the wide open predator zone.

I stop and turn away when one of the Gators starts up. The boss woman and one of the girls slowly pull out into the parking lot, driving toward the other end of the compound. I walk the last forty feet like I belong there and enter the house without pausing. Most of the girls I saw on my first visit are still huddled in the living room, staring at their plates or sleeping in their chairs. No phones, books, games, nail polish, or chatting. It seems boring to the extreme and totally abnormal. Not one glances up. They all look younger to me now, curled in self-protective fetal positions, diminished by their lack of vitality.

Kendra is missing, so I enter the bedroom wing. There are two bathrooms and two bedrooms. Each room has six wall-to-wall mattresses covering the floor, under jumbled masses of pillows and blankets. I continue down the narrow hallway and enter the last door. This small room has a single neatly made bed and a metal clothing rack loaded with dresses, blouses, sweaters and pants folded over hangers. Shoes line two shelves. All are high heels, high-topped boots or sling back sandals. Under the window, a long table with lotions, makeup, wigs and mirrors make it look like the dressing room at our local theatre. This place has everything but glue-on noses.

Shaking off my distraction, I head back to the bedrooms, looking for Kendra. She's there, bundled under blankets along one edge of the mattress-strewn room. I don't know how I missed her the first time I'd peeked in. Muffled sobs float from beneath the blanket. She doesn't hear me until I stand right over her bed. "Kendra," I whisper.

She throws off the blanket, looking defiant, with one arm held across her face, as if to ward off a demon. "You can't make me, you fucking witch!" she shouts. When she sees it's me, she hugs my legs, weeping out loud.

"You can't be here," she says, scooting back against the wall, looking terrified and heaving out sobs. "Go home and forget about seeing me. Go! Now!"

"Wait a minute, Kendra. Tell me what's going on. I have lots of questions. I'm not leaving until I get some answers."

Kendra stops crying instantly, like a water tap turned off. "No. Not now, maybe not ever. You have to leave! Disappear, go home!" I must look hurt, because she whines out a pitiful "Please."

"Not until I learn about how JB and you cooked up some cock-and-bull scheme to get you out to North Dakota without telling even your mother. I talked to Jake and Jenna at the shop in Williston. I know you worked there and JB got you the job. Why did you leave it?" I stop, realizing I've asked too much at once.

I back off to ask one question. "Did JB kidnap you or force you to come here?" For the first time, I notice a red welt rising along one side of her face and a darkness crawling across her upper cheek, the beginnings of a black eye. Thumb-shaped bruises dot the front of her throat.

She relents. Taking a quick look at the door, she motions me to kneel next to her. "Yes, JB told me about the job at Jake's. No, he didn't kidnap me," she looks incredulous. "What are you, stupid or something? He's supposed to be your boyfriend, isn't he?"

She said a few other things, but I had already stopped listening. Maybe he wasn't a bad guy after all and, somehow, she didn't know he was dead. I feel a relief so strong I could collapse onto Kendra's bed and fall into a deep sleep. All those nasty things Trammel and the others implied were completely false. It was all an innocent mis-understanding. Kendra wanted a job, JB found her a job.

"So why did you leave Jake's to work here? They said you didn't even give notice. Did you think about how this reflected on JB? I suppose you..."

She now has a grip on my clothes, pulling me to my feet and cutting off my words. "Look, you've got to get out of here. If the boss sees you talking to me, I'm dead. You're dead. We're all dead. I mean dead, dead, as in killed, and no one will ever find our bodies. If you want to be helpful, send the sheriff or someone to get us out. Now get the hell out of here!" She gives me a shove toward the door.

"What are you talking about?"

"We can't talk about anything. I can't tell you. You have to get out! Please get out!" Tears are streaming down her face again, her expression crazed, wild with maniacal fear. The whites of her eyes seemed to fill her face, like the eyes of wild horses I saw driven into a corral with a helicopter. Beads of perspiration appear on her forehead and upper lip.

We both freeze as we hear the revving Gator in the distance. The Boss returns.

CHAPTER TWENTY SIX

I look at the wide screened window at the back wall of the room. No one appears to be around.

"You're coming with me," I say. I quickly arrange her blankets and some borrowed pillows to look as though she's still curled up in bed. Opening the slide window, I lift out the screen and lower it to the ground outside. I close the door to the hallway and pull Kendra over to the window. She struggles, but I shush her and finally slap her across the face to get her attention.

"Look, get outside. Then we can decide what you are or are not doing."

She becomes passive and compliant, almost immobile, so I hoist her up and get her to swing her legs over the windowsill and jump to the ground. I heft myself up and she helps me get through, scraping my belly and thighs on the metal ledge. We replace the screen and work our way along the wall, away from the bedrooms. At the living room, we go down onto our hands and knees to crawl past the picture window. When we reach the back corner of the building, we stand and brush ourselves off.

"Look, Kendra, come with me to my car. We can sit in there and talk out of this wind."

She shakes her head. "No, I have to go back now. If the boss finds me missing, she'll go on another rampage and try to find out where I've gone by beating the others. You don't understand. They told me to be very careful not to antagonize her. I have to go back to protect them."

She tries to go toward the front door. I hold her in what I hoped felt like a grip of steel. She seems to respond, becoming totally passive. I didn't want to slap her. I wonder if they have terrorized her, and maybe the cause of the red welt wasn't only this one slap on her face. It sounds like this boss is one vicious woman. I was getting the picture.

"Wait a minute." I pull our bodies close against the wall. "Look, we're out here now. Come with me for a little while and talk, then you can come back if you want to. I'll help you make up a plausible excuse." This seems to placate her, and she reluctantly nods. "Hold it. Put this on." I pull a black fleece ski hat out of my bag, twist up her long, glowing hair, and shove it under the cap. At least she won't show up like a neon sign.

We calmly walk out the gate and around the corner to my car. I scan the area, relieved no one is watching, and we get in. I start the engine and ramp up the air conditioner. Kendra sits, staring at her hands, as if in a trance. If I didn't know better, I'd have thought she was praying. I notice her lips moving.

"Are you praying?" I ask in a quiet voice.

She nods. "I learned how from one of the other girls. Maria's from Mexico City. She said everyone is Catholic down there and prays constantly. She showed me how and told me not to be afraid. If we prayed right, she said we would all be saved."

"You mean saved, as in the born-again kind of way?"

Kendra gives me that look again. "No, airhead. In the save-our-lives kind of saved."

Enough cutting bait. I may as well go fishing. "So, Kendra, are you being held here against your will?"

"Duh," comes out as a two-syllable word. She rolls her eyes up toward the roof of the car. "What the hell do you think is going on? Haven't you figured it out yet? I thought you were the brilliant one."

"Look, I'm trying to find out what's going on. Investigating," I said slowly, so she could understand. "I have no idea." If I confess my ignorance, maybe she will finally tell me. "Really, I don't have a clue."

"Listen, you jerk. You came here. You saw me. Now you're trying to get me killed. These people are bad. Bad, bad, bad. Mean and nasty. I hate everyone!" Tears gather at the corners of her eyes. "And the people living here turn their heads, ignoring us like we're trash. You have to leave, and I have to go back. The bitch in overalls will kill us, and I mean kill you, all of those girls and me, in a very slow and painful way." I hand her the box of tissues for her runny nose and eyes.

Kendra wipes her face and continues. "She's supposed to take care of us. At least that's what Buddy said when he persuaded me to come with him yesterday. He said there was this woman, called her an advocate, to help me adjust to the new job. He said she would look out for my best interest." Her voice became higher and louder. "Bull shit! She's cruel. She hurts people." Kendra touches her tender cheek, grimacing from the pain or the memory. "Buddy knew what he was doing, bringing me here, and I hate him the most."

"Why did you leave without saying goodbye to Jake? Tell me about this, Buddy."

"Buddy came around nine o'clock, after Jake and Jenna went home, and said he'd fixed it up with Jake. I could leave this job and get one that paid more. Jake hadn't mentioned it to me. I thought we were friends, but maybe no one makes friends with their employees here. People seem to come and go in the oil business."

"How did you meet Buddy?" I was afraid to ask this question. I had been putting it off. I didn't want to know the truth. "I met him the first day I got here. JB and I left really early. It was still dark. We got into Jake's in the late afternoon. Buddy was already there. He and JB were friends, maybe partners, in some kind of business. I first thought they might own Jake's, but then I met Jake and Jenna and figured that wasn't it. I don't know what it was, but it wasn't going very well. We were all in Jake's office when Buddy asks JB to come outside to talk. Before they got outside, we heard Buddy yelling. I thought it was kind of funny—a grown man having a tantrum."

I ask, "How can people yelling be funny?" Kendra couldn't stop talking now.

"You know." She glances at my blank face. "Oh, maybe you don't know him. He was yelling, but never took the stupid matchstick out of his mouth. Couldn't understand a thing he said. I remember Jake shook his head and told me not to worry. He said they fought like bulldogs, but it always seemed to work out."

I feel ill in the pit of my stomach. "Tell me what you are doing here? Is this job better than Jakes?" Kendra shuts down immediately and looks outside. Her hands clasp and unclasp in her lap, and she whimpers, remembering where she is.

"I have to go now," she says quietly, robotically.

"Wait a minute. Tell me more about JB and how you two got together."

"We didn't get together." Kendra looks around and then continues. "He asked me what my plans were after graduation. He told me I could earn a lot of money in a short time. Enough so I could start classes at community college in the fall. I'd have a job with some nice people, friends of his. I thought my mom could come out later if it worked out for me. That's when I quit school and got my GED. I wanted to start work sooner but had to wait for my birthday. JB gave me a small computer to study retail sales and get familiar with the inventory."

"Where is JB, anyway?" She demands but didn't wait for an answer. "JB thought I'd told mom. It surprised him when she wasn't with me when he picked me up at the bank parking lot. He even bought me some new clothes and stuff for the job."

I am completely stunned. Now the list of clothing he needed to buy wasn't such a mystery. "And did you throw anything away, like your old clothes or something?"

Now Kendra intently stares at me. "Yea, how did you know? He had me throw out my old ratty clothes, my gothic skull necklace and earrings, my old, cracked cell phone, and even made me dye the red streak out of my hair. He said I had to look good to work for his friends." She looks away and then back. "Jenna mentioned JB had an accident. Is he ok?"

I ignore the question. "Tell me what you do here. What do all those young women do here?" I can see her lips moving.

She's praying again. I don't know how much her Mexican friend has told her, but I try an indirect approach. "Did your friend ever tell you a famous saying about God?" She looks up at me, her lips still moving, shaking her head. "It says God helps them who help themselves. Maybe you've heard it somewhere before?"

She shakes her head again and appears to be interested. I continue. "Well, it's true. It's common knowledge, in fact. When someone wants to change their circumstances for the better, they need to take steps to get themselves out of the situation they're in. As soon as they are going the right way, God kicks into play and opens doors for them to get what they want or need. Maybe I'm the answer to your prayers. You took the first step in helping yourself when you came to my car. What do you want to happen now?"

I quietly watch Kendra wringing her hands. I don't know the answer for someone who has been brutalized, or raped and who knows what else, even for a day. Maybe she's not able to reason, to decide her own future. I reach over and try to cover her hands, to quiet their gyrations, to calm her. She jumps and pulls away, crowding over next to the door. She looks at me as if seeing me for the first time. I smile and back myself up to my door, giving her space.

I've heard of girls and boys who get kidnapped or tricked into human slavery, become resigned after a brief time. They live isolated from normal people, get addicted to drugs and are told this is what they deserve for the rest of their lives.

There's no contact with families or friends. Acting becomes normal, as if having whatever kind of sex, they perform is the delight of their day. Acting as though the client is the most important person in the world and the best sex partner they've ever encountered. They make him believe they can't wait to see him again. If the acting isn't believable or the John complains, the slave gets tortured, beatings that won't show, isolation, starvation, rape. It's a brutal business few escape, and many don't survive.

I wonder if JB or Buddy got her into this, or both. Maybe the job at Jake's was the tease to get her out here, and then the promise of more money allowed Buddy to lure her here. Maybe they were a tag team, JB luring women into regular jobs and Buddy handing them over to the sex traffickers. Kids like Kendra, with unstructured family life and lots of unsupervised time, are prime targets. I guess I took in more than I thought when my friend lectured about human trafficking.

Sometimes, a kid or young adult who gets caught up as a victim in the slave trade becomes the lure, introducing the target to the friendly, caring adult, who eventfully makes the offer for a job or travel opportunity. In this case, I was the patsy who knew the trafficker. I unwittingly brought the plague to my little village. I indirectly introduced JB to Kendra and other children, by taking him to fund raisers, high school sports events, and school championship celebrations, where he encountered a smorgasbord of potential victims. I had innocently offered the town's children to the Pied Piper.

Judging from her fight with the long-haired man, maybe Kendra hasn't been raped yet. Maybe they haven't had the time. She obviously didn't play her role very well. I imagine she's had a beating across her kidneys, or a painful hair pulling, besides the fierce slap, when the boss got her back to the house.

She's scared and angry. I take some deep breaths, hoping she will begin to breathe with me. I close my eyes and lean back. The door handle clicks before I detect any movement. By the time I look over, Kendra stumbles out the door. In a flash, I'm out and I catch her in a bear hug. She struggles, but I'm taller and probably stronger.

Through clenched teeth I say, "You get back in that car." She's already used to hearing orders, not beseeching. She's hardened to kindness due to fear, so this intervention needs brute strength and force. I meet her energy with my own. I imagine myself mad, overbearing, cruel even. Hissing and pulling, I shoved her back into the car, telling her to stay. I feel horrible. I wouldn't even talk this way to my dog.

I get back into the driver's seat, breathing to calm myself. "What do you want to happen now, Kendra? Don't tell me what you think you should do. Tell me your wildest dream."

She answers me by sobbing, a gulping sob of despair. "I tried to run away last night. I knew right away what was going on. We'd seen a movie on human trafficking last year when the Soroptimist brought all those people in for a week. It freaked us out, but we also laughed about it later that those girls could be so stupid. I mean, it couldn't happen in our little town." She crumbles into more tears. "The boss bitch said they would kill my dad in prison if I didn't stay here. They know people. They have people in prison who run the place and can slit my dad's throat on the way to the kitchen." Her voice is higher and shriller. "They even knew he worked in the kitchen. Some people working here sound like mobsters from the movies, so I figure they aren't lying."

Sniffling, tears slow down as I toss her the box of tissues. "Listen to me very carefully. Kendra, look at me." She keeps glancing at the house and at the office entrance. Trucks drive by, coming and going. Groups of men walk towards the Lunch Room, a few send glances our way. The chef appears by the back door again to catch a smoke. He sees me in the car and waves.

"We have to get out of here. Now." I look over to see Kendra looking outside again and then back at her hands. "Kendra, stay focused. It's a bluff. They don't care about your dad. Everything costs something. You're not even a valuable asset yet." At least I hope not. "I saw you leaving the lodge earlier today wrestling with your boss woman. I overheard a man complaining in the recreation center later. Sounds like you gave him a good fight. You got away. Right?"

She looked at me, not scared now, but mad. Mad is better than scared. "He was the third man they put me with. He was dirty and smelly, and no one was going to rape me, especially not him. The second guy got a hard kick in the balls. It terrified the third one, even though he acted like a tough guy. He tried to force me down, but as soon as I started throwing my feet and knees in his direction, he lost his grip. I scratched his arm, and he started yowling. What a baby. He let go of me to protect his face and I ran out the door."

Now she was looking absolutely radiant. She is Xena, Warrior Princess. I make my move. "What do you want to happen now? Can we leave?"

"What I want is for all these girls to get saved. Maria came from Mexico City and she's my age, eighteen. She came here to work in the kitchen. JB met her in at the Denver airport and drove her up. She said soon after JB dropped her off, his friend Buddy came into her room and raped her. He slapped her a lot, too." Kendra had to stop for a minute and swallow a couple of sobs. "Maria was so shocked she hardly had time to struggle. She's so ashamed. She never wants to go home now because she feels ruined. No one will marry her, and she will live a life of shame. She's sure her parents won't take her back."

Kendra's energy winds up. "I called out her bullshit. She's not a prostitute and we are getting out of here." Kendra was not only mad, she sounded ready to step forward as the hero and help the others. "Right then, I decided I would not be raped. I wasn't giving any blowjobs, either. Right before I kicked his crotch, I spit on the second guy last night and he slapped me so hard I got this black eye. The boss bitch slapped me in the same spot later. She said it was a good way to break me in." Kendra looks over at me. "And then you show up. What gives?"

"JB," I say as an explanation. "Jake says JB brought you there to work in the shop." I decided not to tell her about the law enforcement hunt. Despair kicked her mom into hyperdrive, with a new job at the high school and the scholarship to the community college to get trained as an X-ray technician. A lot had changed in the time she'd been gone. Her mom was determined to earn enough money to keep up the search. Even her dad promised to stay clean and sober and get out of prison as soon as possible.

"It was totally a coincidence they mentioned you. Jake and Jen started talking about other employees JB found for them. Jen thought you'd gone home. She was disappointed when you didn't even say goodbye, but she understood if you wanted to go home to your mom. Jake heard from a customer you were working here."

The Prius keeps flipping to the quiet energy-save mode. I continue punching the air conditioner button to keep it running. Kendra sinks back into the mire. "I thought you were here to work in housekeeping, or whatever, and I came to check it out, offer you a ride home if you were ready to call it quits."

"What, you think I'm a wimp?" Kendra gives me a piercing look. "Why are you out here in North Dakota, anyway?" She glances back at my one small suitcase, cooler, purse, picnic hamper, and the three boxes. I always keep the back seat folded down so I can see and reach almost everything in the compact car. "Didn't JB come with you? I thought you two were tight the way he talked."

"I came out here on business and stopped by Jake's to pick up those boxes JB left there," poking my thumb toward the boxes in the back of the car. There will be plenty of time when we're out of here to tell her about JB's death and all the other things happening at home. "I'm in the art business now. We opened the gallery a short time ago. You'll like it. It even has an espresso bar with a handsome man running it."

Kendra seems to stop listening. "I got into the office in the middle of the night and used the phone to call JB. I wanted him to come fix things. He didn't answer. I don't think he knew this was going to happen. He told me I'd be safe at Jake's. I don't know why I believed his friend. When he said his name was Buddy, I laughed. It's like a dog's name. Isn't that stupid?"

I thought how stupid you didn't call your mom or the police.

"I got caught right away and was pushed and shoved back to that house. I was beaten and locked in a closet without a bathroom or food or water. In the middle of the night, the boss made me clean up my mess in the closet before I could take a shower or change my clothes. It was so gross." She looks toward the direction of the house. "Listen, I'd go with you in a minute if it wasn't for the boss and Buddy hurting those girls. I mean, other than Maria and the three Indian girls, they are all fourteen or fifteen years old." She gives an involuntary shudder and then looks toward me again, her eyes wide with fear.

CHAPTER TWENTY SEVEN

I glance over my shoulder into Buddy's huge belt buckle as he starts rocking the Prius. He bangs on the roof, shouting through the closed window. "You're the bitch who's trying to cheat me out of my cash! The money in JB's account is all mine, and you can't have it." He pokes his face against the glass and points at Kendra. "And that's my property! Finders' keepers, losers, weepers. I already sold it, and you can't steal that, too." His talking about Kendra as a thing really gets my blood boiling. Kendra is quiet and I can see she's undecided. Her sad eyes show resignation. She needs a little encouragement, the feeling of belonging to the winning pack. I am her pack leader at the moment.

"Get the fuck away from my car, scumbag. She's a free woman, and she's coming with me!" I shout at the top of my voice, which I hope doesn't hold the tinge of panic I feel.

He tries the latch. Locked. Banging on the roof again, he kicks the door. As he backs away to heel-kick at the window, I flip the car into reverse and move. He didn't know it was already running. I love you Prius, your quiet, patient waiting—always ready for me to give you a command. His kick met only empty air, flipping him over onto his back. I watch his head give a satisfying bounce against the hard ground.

"Awesome." Kendra springs to life. "Take that, asshole." She sends him two one-fingered salutes.

"Look," I say, while backing out along the road toward the gate. "We'll call the police when we have cell coverage, but we are getting out of here."

"No, we have to go pick up Maria."

"No. We can't help her right now without getting caught. Think! If we don't escape, then no one gets help!" I pull in behind a truck blocking the exit lane. "We have to help ourselves first, then we can save them." I toot my faint car horn, the only wimpy thing about my trusty steel steed.

"He's going inside." Kendra glances back, keeping a lookout.

"Good." I open my door and peer around the truck. What I see is not in our favor. "I think they've called out the troops." There are three men standing next to the open door of the panel truck. The guardhouse jerk, the chef from the Lunch Room, and another man in dark blue coveralls who must be the truck driver. He has one foot up on the running board and one hand holding the door open against the wind. They all look my way when they see me peeking around the truck. They hadn't known I was back there in my little car. Behind me comes two trucks, the first driven by an angry-looking Buddy and the next I can't see, but they are definitely coming our way.

"Watch 'em and hold on!" I shout to Kendra. I put the Prius in reverse, swing the back of the car over into the other lane, so the delivery truck's out of my way, and start forward.

The entry road stands wide open before me. The three men position themselves side-by-side across the road, their hands on their hips, legs spread. They'd put up a long, but feeble looking sawhorse in front of them. I laugh. "Do they think I'm going to run at them on my own two legs?" They have terribly underestimated my petite Prius.

"Damn. This is going to dent my car." It had been with me for eight years. Two hundred thirty thousand stood out on the odometer, as a warning sign that soon, probably this year, the electric battery will suddenly stop working and I will be out at least thirty-five hundred dollars to replace it. My silver steed and I have been through a lot together. There must be a new color to reflect the new me. The me who survived attempted murder, who went camping by herself, fought with her ghosts, and found an unexpected friend. The me who owns an art gallery, a businesswoman, who inherited a shitload of money, and who is rescuing a young woman from sexual slavery.

"They're almost here!" screams Kendra, "What are you waiting for?!"

"Look forward and hang on!" I don't want her to get a whiplash when we collide with the sawhorse and the bodies. I put the pedal to the metal and shoot forward. In my mind, the Prius is going like a bat out of hell as we close in on the men. We fly past the parked truck faster and faster.

The men waver and shift positions, their hands coming forward, as if to ward off an angry child. I swerve at the last minute to hit one end of the sorry excuse for a sawhorse, hoping it won't fly into the windshield. Luckily, it springs out to the side and lands square on the back of the jerk, laying him out flat. As we pass, it bounces off the next man and comes back to shatter my rear side window.

"Whoo hoo," shouts Kendra, pumping the air with her fists. She gives them the finger out the window. She looks back at the sprawling men as the pickups come flying through the gate. "Ouch," said Kendra, telling me the first truck ran over the fallen man's foot. "They stopped to look at him. Now he's getting up, and they moved the sawhorse. Go, go, go!"

We speed around three, then five curves in the road. Behind us, a plume of dust is closing in. Kendra moves into action mode. "Do you have a gun? I can shoot out their tires."

"No gun." I think about what else we can do. "Look around the back. Look in the cooler." Kendra climbs back between the seats. She has to fold her tall body almost in half. She doesn't waver as she opens the Yeti and pulls out the two frozen, one-gallon water jugs. As advertised, they hadn't melted one bit in the past two days. She breaks out the rest of the glass from the broken window. Bracing her legs between the seats and hanging out the opening, she flings one and then the other of the jugs high into the air. The truck speeds into the second jug and its windshield shatters.

The truck swerves and stops for a moment, while Buddy brushes the glass off himself. There goes my three bottles of sparking water, followed by a foot of salami. "Stop!" I shout, grabbing the salami and tossing it back into the cooler as the lid slams down. The three bottles explode on the road behind us, leaving heavy, broken glass across their path. Buddy can't see it because of my dust and, next thing we know, he fishtails to a stop. I look behind him and see the second cloud of dust closing in on Buddy's truck.

"We'll never outrun them. We have to hide." Two curves later, I find my chance where a low bridge crosses a dry creek bed. The Prius scrapes its way down the shallow bank, and we drive up the stony gully. After a hundred feet, the banks narrow, and the bed is choked up with tumble weeds and scrubby trees. These are not creek beds as one might find in the mountains, full of bubbles, fish and coolness. These gullies are carved during flash floods fueled by rain and hail, plummeting down from super cell storms. Ninety-nine percent of the time, they're dry. Moisture lingering below the surface helps plants flourish. Ahead of us, the dry, spiny shrubs grow as thick as an English hedge.

"Go clear a space in the tumbleweeds, so I can drive in. Stack them behind the car for camouflage." She wades into the yoga-ball sized tumbleweeds, pushing them along in front of her body, and I ease the car into the narrow space.

"They're rolling away," she shouts.

I pull a spool of fishing line from my rucksack. Using the little hook clip on the end of the line to loop it around the door handle, I began weaving it through the tumbleweeds. The process is too slow. "Look up top to see if they're coming. Keep low. And use a tumbleweed to wipe out the tire tracks."

Kendra scurries up the steep bank and comes back, smiling. "No dust. It looks like they both stopped."

"They won't take long to change tires and clear the glass off the road. Help me finish this." She pushes up armloads of tumbleweeds, using her whole body to squeeze them together. I run back and forth with the fishing line, like a spider spinning a web, until the spool is empty. It will slow them down, but if they walk up the creek or even come along the top, they will see the car. "Follow close," I tell Kendra.

We squeeze between the side of the car and the high bank, which grows higher as the creek bed narrows. Cliff swallow holes line the top of the bank, and a sudden chatter of birds makes us look up. The swallows mob us, circling overhead, just above the bank. Their loud commotion could draw attention, so we hurry on. In the middle of the channel, an erratic bolder left behind when the last glacier melted, causes the channel to widen. We both scrambled up the boulder and get high enough to see the end of other tributaries in the distance where a few scrubby trees stand sentinel on the prairie surface. I can't see the path for this channel, but I know from the map on my phone, these are a sort of miniature badlands of eroded creek beds. This has to be the main channel, because it's so wide and deep.

We come to a relatively clear spot of bare sand among the trees. "Let's rest a minute. You be the lookout. I'll try my phone." Yippee, four bars of service. I call Enrique first. The call connects. "Hello? Enrique?" I hear silence, a low crackling, then silence again. "Oh

God. If you can hear me, Kendra and I are outside the McKenzie Lodge, south of Williston. They're after us. I hid the car and we're out on the prairie, south of the entry road. Call police." I click off.

"Why don't you call the police, idiot?" whispers Kendra.

I frown. I thought about her silly wasted phone call last night. Waving, I signal her to follow, and hurry forward, faster now as the scrubby trees thin out. This channel runs due west, back toward the camp. It must be the swale behind the Lunchroom building. As we trot along a narrow deer trail through the bushes, I dial 911. It rings forever. No answer. How could I have bars and no service?

"What is the nature of your emergency?" A man's bored voice asks.

"Help! We've escaped from McKenzie man camp. We're about a mile along the entry road from the lodge, on the south side, following the big creek bed," my breath coming in gasps. "Bad men are chasing us, maybe the Mafia. They're holding young girls as sex slaves," I shout at the phone.

Kendra shushes me.

"Right." The word is clipped and abrupt. "Name please?"

"Listen, please send help! They're closing in."

"Name," the voice demands. "Rosetta Stone."

"Listen, what kind of game is this? Lousy fake name, by the way. We've been out there three times on false alarms about sex slaves, human trafficking, and kidnapping. It's hogwash and racial profiling. My family is New Jersey Italian, too, and we are not all Mafia, you bigot. We found nothing out there, so get a life and stop calling us."

"Please, call Sheriff Trammel," I whisper urgently, but the line goes dead. Kendra looks at me questioningly, and I can't tell her the police aren't coming. I take a geo-tagged selfie of Kendra and I and send it off to my Group, comprising of Enrique, Jackson, Eve, Trammel and Ben, telling them where and why, hope they find our bodies, and put those bastards in prison and save all those girls.

"What about fire?" hisses Kendra, excited to be out and on the run. "Maybe we can send smoke signals."

"You are brilliant," I say, giving her a hug. "Not smoke signals, as in little puffs into the prairie wind, but a blaze to bring all the fire departments within fifty miles."

I dig out my fire starter kit. "We need to clear a patch of ground," I tell her. When she hesitates, I add, "Otherwise, we'll be caught up in the fire." Next to the base of the bank, she shuffles her feet to brush away grass, leaves and cactus. "Break up these twigs and small branches while I find something to contain the fire." I reach into my pack and pull out my forty-dollar titanium camping cup. I bought it a few months ago for an upcoming long distance hike next year. It was brand new, with the tag still on the handle. Oh, well. I put a Sterno-soaked cotton ball at the bottom of my cup, sprinkle in a few leaves and short spiny twigs.

"What's that?" says Kendra. A high, shrill whistling pulsates along our canyon.

"It's the bank swallows. The men found the car and are moving this way." I finish preparing my cup of kindling and then notice we're trapped. The fire can go in any direction in the swirling wind of this creek bed. "Let's go." I tell her to grab up the sticks and leaves and we run up the draw. Around a bend, about fifty feet farther along, a smaller creek meets ours. "Check it out," I tell Kendra. "See if you can locate the end and a way out, while I fix a place for the fire up this main branch. We don't want the fire to follow us before we've escaped."

She's back in a flash. "It looks like it goes on and on. I saw what may be the end, in a little group of taller trees way out there." She waves her hands to indicate distance. "I think we can make it to the trees or climb out sooner if we need to."

I put the cup on the ground and point the steel bar in its direction. I scrape the little flint shard along the steel bar. The breeze immediately snuffs the bright yellow spark. So are the next and the next. I lean closer over the cup and started scraping fast, one after another, not paying attention to where they land.

"Yikes," said Kendra, pointing next to me.

I am still scraping madly toward my cup. All the sparks didn't die as they blew away because three small fires smoldering next to me burst into flame and spread rapidly. An inferno blows up beneath my hands, with an audible whoosh, when the Sterno fumes in the cup ignite like a blowtorch. My fire starter flies away as Kendra kicks the cup and pushes me face down into the dirt to put out any flames on my clothes or skin. It's hot but doesn't have enough time to burn me and isn't painful until I feel the cactus needles drilling into my hands, forearms, and cheek.

"Aargh, let me up," I squeal. She rolls me onto my knees and helps me stand.

"Oh, look," she said, pointing at my arm. Three small blades of cactus stick flush with my skin. She knocks them off before I can react. I feel for other spines and find a few, and then look around. The creek bed is filling with smoke. The short wall of flame stretches almost bank to bank thanks to the kicked cup of fire.

"Let's move," I say, heading up the side gully.

We push our way through the thick spiny bushes, flushing a jackrabbit ahead of us. We look back. The fire has created its own momentum now. It's at least twenty feet farther down the draw, heading with the prevailing wind back toward McKenzie camp. Oddly enough, it didn't look like much smoke.

I pull my heavy Swarovski binoculars out of the rucksack and climb a tree, but still can't look over the ten foot high bank. "Listen, Kendra, you go on and wait for me at the head of this draw. I lost my fire starter, so I have to go back and throw some flames above the creek bed. We need more smoke and faster spreading."

'Give me your phone. If you're killed in the fire, I want to be able to call someone."

"Thanks for the vote of confidence," I say, handing her my phone. "You can use the GPS and compass apps to find your way to the nearest highway. Hitchhike out of here if we get separated." She looks at me with contempt. Did I think she didn't know how to use a smart phone? I grab up my binoculars, hanging them around my neck. I wave Kendra on and head back toward the fire.

CHAPTER TWENTY EIGHT

I want to stop and put the binoculars back into my rucksack. The straps catch on every bush, plus they're bulky, knocking against my body with every step. To save time, I stuff them down the front of my shirt.

It takes only a minute to reach the place where we started the fire. A standing line of blackened sticks remain where the fire started. This drought resistant vegetation is so dense it barely burns. The fire is cool and smokeless. Up above, out of the creek bed, there's more grass, a better fuel.

I pull a Leatherman out of the side pocket of my rucksack and unclip my bracelet. I hadn't planned on wearing it but found it under my car seat earlier today. It looks like any macramé design of half hitches from the hippy days of plant hangers and ankle bracelets. This one is special, though. I'd made it with red nylon parachute cord and a plastic clip. Using the needle-nose pliers of my Leatherman, I tease an end out of the center loops of the weave and start pulling. The bracelet unweaves into a length of nylon cord about eight feet long.

I stomp a couple of tumbleweeds into a tight mass and tie it together with the one end of the chord. How to get it up over the high bank is the question. A short, gnarled root sits under a nearby tree, but when I kick it, it remains attached to the tree. It cracks when I kick it a few times but remains dangling by a pesky two inches of wood.

The Leatherman Tool has a small, inadequate looking saw I pull out of its slot. I've never used it. The teeth are coarse, and I don't think it will bite into the hardwood. I'm wrong. It takes only a dozen strokes to free the root. It's heavy, maybe four pounds, and about ten inches long. I tie it on the other end of the cord. I gather up the root and tumbleweed into my arms and push through the blackened bushes to find fresh fire. I shove past a barely burned group of trees and around another bend before I find the live fire. I hug my root and weed bundle closer to my chest and smile, thinking how the fire will eventually meander its way to the Lunchroom and all those tumbleweeds piled up against the fence. The crazy creeps chasing us must be thinking frantically about how to protect the camp. "Got ya, bitch."

My blood freezes. I look back over my shoulder and there stands the matchstick chewer, Buddy. "Who are you? What do you want?!" I'm shouting, hoping my voice will travel to Kendra, urging her to get out of here faster.

"You know damn well who I am. Buddy. JB's partner and the one you stole four hundred K from."

"That's ridiculous. I didn't even know you existed. Look, I'll give you the money, all of it, if only you'll help us."

"Listen, I earned that money. JB and me was partners since we were kids. Doing one business, then another, and finally getting into the concierge business, if you catch my meaning." He pronounces the word in his wide southern drawl, making it into four syllables—cone-see-air-je.

"What do you mean, concierge?" I hope Kendra has enough time to escape. "You mean like in a hotel? Did you plan trips, purchase tickets and make dinner arrangements for anybody? Did you find stuff for people? Oh wait, did you kidnap kids and sell them as slaves?"

I know I've gone too far when he approaches. "Yea, we became modern day slavers. It was only a sideline at first. We made good money in our legitimate business, but the first time we got paid selling some girls, it was as much money as we'd ever made in three months. We still kept up our other deal, JB's finder business. The clients who bought the girls encouraged us to fill more orders for them."

Buddy takes a quick step to the side, so I have to back into the blackened shrubs. "Pretty soon, we found ourselves in the human trafficking business. We were small fry compared to other traffickers. We specialized, you might say. Presorting, I liked to call it, if you know what I mean."

"I can't believe JB was involved in kidnapping and trafficking. You're lying through your teeth. He was a nice man and wouldn't hurt a fly." I back past the burned shrubs, moving closer to the fire.

"We're both nice men." Buddy laughs. "Everyone says so. JB said you wouldn't understand. We kidnapped no one or forced any girl, in any way. In fact, we never do the end marketing, you know, the last move. Someone else does that. It made our business a lot easier. We kept our reputation spotless in case one of those people escaped back to their family. They'd never suspect us." His satanic, leering smile bespoke of pure evil or maybe cleverly disguised stupidity.

"What do you mean, the last move?" I have to keep him talking until an opportunity presents itself. The natural world offers interesting experiences, full of surprises. If you're ready, it can be wonderful, even magical. If you're not ready, if you don't pay attention, stay in the moment and use all your senses, well, bad things can happen. Some of those things are alarming, frightening to say the least, and some can be deadly. I make myself take a few deep breaths and a few more steps backward, following the receding fire. I repeat my question. "Tell me, what is the last step? Is there a first step? Is there a middle step? What is the formula? What does it take to kidnap someone?"

Buddy snickers. "That's just it. Like I say, we don't kidnap anyone. Plus, we don't do little kids. Everyone comes with us willingly. They all want jobs, adventure, escape, maybe even friendship. Whatever they want, we can offer it. See, like I say, a concierge. It's easy to find workers for a highly paid, unskilled labor force with on-the-job training." Buddy takes a moment to chew on his matchstick and the red tip spins in a circle. "We place an occasional ad in the classifieds of a medium-sized newspaper. We target someplace with higher unemployment, maybe a small town. Sometimes the ad might ask for specific people to fill specific good paying jobs in, say... North Dakota, with room and board provided."

"We get over a hundred calls to our ad. We gather applications, interview all the likely candidates and find the ones who can easily disappear. You'd be surprised how many girls are willing, even enthusiastic, to take off into the unknown. They're very trusting. If I had a daughter, I'd slap her silly if she even thought about answering this type of ad and going off with a stranger."

"That's it?" I ask, incredulous. "You put an ad in the paper. Aren't the police suspicious?"

"If they are, they've never said a peep to us." Buddy laughs. "They're pretty naïve, too. Another good pond to troll is in college towns. All those kids are lonely and looking for friends. An adult comes along, maybe throwing parties, buying the drinks at bars. It takes longer. You got to be friendly and win their trust. Then you might offer the bait, take them on an all-expense paid weekend trip to some cool place. I get nibbles right away. A few refuse to go, so I drop them and concentrate on others. I always get a bite or two. We take the fun trip and pretty soon they're willing to go try out the new job. It takes a few weeks, but it's worth it when the paycheck comes in. I can fish the same pond for a few months before parents call to find out about their missing daughters."

"It doesn't seem possible for parents to wait so long," I say. He enjoys bragging about his skill. I have to kill some more time.

"You know how irresponsible kids are these days. Some never check in with mom and go off, doing their own thing without permission. I always start at the beginning of the term, when the parents are relieved to have their kid in college and the kids are homesick. That's what the first weeks are for, finding a kid who's down on her family, for one reason or another. Once they have me, a good-looking, understanding adult, as a friend, they're even less likely to check in with the folks. We drop them at the legitimate job, the restaurant, casino, or warehouse and then leave." Buddy smiles and shrugs. "Whatever happens afterward has nothing to do with us."

He's running out of steam, so I try a different approach. "What about JB? Did he play it the same way? I can't see him hanging out in a college bar. The man I knew didn't seem like the type to drag women into bondage."

"Oh, Mister High and Mighty changed his mind after the first time. It happened by accident. We'd been headhunting for legit-imate employers of different businesses in Las Vegas during the building boom. They needed young people to train as builders and cleanup crew, waitresses, clerks, teachers. We'd been working mainly in the South before that." Buddy notices me backing up to the fire, so he moves closer to the middle of the creek bed to keep me corralled.

"The first time it happened was a complete surprise, you know what I mean?" Most of Buddy's slow sentences ended on an up note, as if he were asking a question. From a little kid, it would have been endearing, but with him, it was plain annoying. "We brought three fresh-off-the-boat girls over from Chinatown in San Francisco to work at a restaurant in Las Vegas. Next thing we know, we get an envelope full of twenty and hundred-dollar bills adding up to nine thousand dollars."

Buddy shrugged and looked up, noticing the smoke for the first time. "Gosh, what a mess you've made here. Anyway, I was afraid to go find out what the cash was for, thinking it was some kind of mistake. JB barged into the restaurant with the cash in hand to get some answers. It turned out to be good old, made-in-America mobsters. They thanked JB for the product." Here, Buddy held up two fingers of each hand to make air quotes around the word product. "He didn't want to do it again, but I convinced him it wasn't so bad. It was a job for those girls and at least they were taken care of and not living on the street."

I'm having some real honest hate for this man. "How did you think they were taken care of?"

"Well, you know, that was over thirty years ago, and I don't think either of us had even heard the phrase 'human trafficking. We thought they were high-end prostitutes. Then we found a few of the women we brought were actually working as maids and a nanny, anyway. We'd never even been to a prostitute and had only a vague idea of a pimp. We were busy with searching out other things, like hard-to-find equipment, machine parts and food products. It was before the Internet, so clients hired us to do the legwork and phone calls. We could find anything." Buddy puffs out his chest. "We were a great team. It's your fault he's dead, you know."

"How's that?"

"He wanted to get completely out of the business. We've been working for a certain client for about fifteen years now. His family manages this camp. I'm sure the owners don't know what's going on, or maybe they do and get some kind of kickback. Who cares?" Buddy is really wound up now. "The Mafia must have taken care of

JB. I mean, they don't let people leave, do they?"

"What about Kendra? I think JB brought her out to work at Jake's store. How did you end up taking her away from there?"

"When I found out JB was dead, I started looking around for our money. He'd been holding it and paying us both salaries. We still had our legit business of finding stuff for people. JB thought it was like a puzzle. That boy loved puzzles. You know, riddles were his hobby. He used to buy riddle books and drive me crazy when we drove across the country." Buddy shortens the distance between us as I keep backing toward the fire.

I can feel the heat on my back now. "Listen," I say. "I'll give you all the money to let us go. It's in the credit union across the Montana border."

"I know where it is, damn it. They got that shit-head manager over there, Ben. He wanted death certificates and all kinds of identification from me. Forget that. I was shocked as hell when I found the money there. We promised each other to never create a paper trail. We got checks or cash for the legit jobs, but only cash for the girls. Income taxes were paid on the legit jobs, too. That money is mine. I figured he had your name on the accounts, because they didn't know me from Adam. I sent for a death certificate, but it didn't come yet. Fuckin' slow government office." He edges closer and looks me in the eye. "I don't think the mob liked the idea of JB quitting the business."

He takes a lunge toward me, and I leap back into an opening next to the steep bank and the fire. I slip the binocular strap from my neck. "Wait, a minute!" I shout. He pauses. It won't be much longer. Mother Nature has always been my best friend and I'll wait. Then I hear what I'd been waiting for.

I take a couple of quick dancing hops to the side, into the fire. Buddy lunges toward me and, too late, hears the buzz of the prairie rattlesnake. He plants his foot right on top of its firm, round body, losing his balance. The first strike goes through his jeans into his cowboy boot. He tries to get away, but I swing my heavy binoculars. As good as David's well aimed slingshot that downed Goliath, it lands square between Buddy's eyes. The snake has time to pull back for a second strike, this one landing on Buddy's knee. He screams and writhes on the ground. I run like the wind while the scaly, arrow-shaped head pumps poison into Buddy's leg.

I realize I'm still hugging the tumbleweed to my chest and it's already on fire; the heat climbing up toward my fingers and the nylon rope is melting. I grab the middle of the cord, spinning the heavy root. I let it fly on the second circle, sending the burning mass up into the open, dry prairie. I don't wait to see if anything catches fire. I scurry up the side channel, following my footprints and then Kendra's. At the end of the gully is the copse of trees. Kendra is nowhere to be seen.

Behind me, the fire is racing up my gully. It must have caught from cinders off of the tumbleweed sling. I shimmy up the shallow bank at the end, squatting behind the trees. The tumbleweed started a new fire up on the prairie and copious grey smoke billows up from where I left Buddy. It doesn't take much to spread a grass fire, a little flame, and a lot of wind. Fires eventually create their own storm, clawing themselves forward like living beasts consuming everything in their path. This will draw attention. I sent a smoke signal and people will come. I shout and wave my arms at a plane flying overhead.

I take a chance to stand up and look for Kendra. Nothing. I call out. No answer. I look back to see if I'm being followed. One pickup sits on the road. Must be the one with the flat tire. Another truck races back to the camp, trying to beat the grass fire, which has spread from the creek bed to the north side of the gully and into pasture fields across the road. My side, the south side, has burned far already, definitely headed toward the man camp. I can't see the camp but hope the girls and innocent people won't get hurt. I look back at the road and then hear fire engine sirens far away. Beyond the smoke, one of the green Gators bumps across the prairie in our direction. I don't think they can see me, but they know where I'd head to escape the fire.

There's a lot of smoke between the Gator and me, which is weird, because they are upwind from the fire. I move around to the other side of the trees. The original fire has started to back burn. It's heading straight for my Prius.

CHAPTER TWENTY NINE

K eeping the trees between the Gator and me, I crouch over and begin a half shuffle, half run through the scrub. "Kendra!" I shout. "Kendra!" The wind blows my words away.

The fire crawls behind us and, once it gets up to the end of the gully, we will be right in its path. We'd never be able to outrun it. "Kendra. Kendra! God, please don't let her be hurt. Kendra!" I've got to move. I stand up and start running flat out, struggling through and over thigh high prickly shrubs, ankle high cactus, squirrel holes, and snakes. Four grouse explode out from under my feet, and I scream.

"Over here!" I hear Kendra shout. She pops her head up from behind a bush about 20 feet farther on. I would have stepped on her if the birds hadn't startled me.

"Oh, thank God. Are you alright?" I run to Kendra, and we hug each other.

"I was waiting for you, but with all the wind, I didn't even hear you coming."

"I shouted. Didn't you hear me?"

"Maybe it's when I was on the phone. I called my mom. Can you believe there's service out here?"

"Did you tell her where we were? Is she sending help?"

"Not exactly." Kendra looks shell-shocked, confused. "She asked if I was ok, and I said yes. She said it was a relief to hear from me. She started to cry. She asked where I was, and I said I was working in North Dakota. Then she said she was at her radiology class, and could she call me back afterward and then she hung up." Kendra screws up her face with a question. "She's going to school?"

"Yes, Kendra. It's like an alternate universe since you left. Your mom got a grant, started taking classes at the community college, and your dad went into Alcoholics Anonymous and is behaving himself, so he can get out of prison early and start looking for you. The whole town, no, the entire valley, is involved in the search." I let it soak in. No need to rub more salt in the wound. I think she's learned her lesson.

"I never thought she'd let me go; you know." I nod. "We should have both come with JB. We could have found good jobs and started a life together out here. We'd have a home set up for when Dad gets out. Maybe he would change if we got him away from his old high school buddies. Mom says they're still all juvenile delinquents. If only I'd told her what I was doing. I should have trusted her."

"Woulda, shoulda, coulda," I say. "Forget it." We trot on, crossing the next creek bed to where the Gator couldn't follow. They'd have to chase us on foot and, by the look of the smoke, they're now in the fire's path. We hear the ATV speed up and see it heading back to the road. "I think they have enough to keep themselves occupied. Why the heck hasn't the fire department arrived? Let me have my phone."

She hands it over. There's only one bar, and the power reads ten percent. I dial emergency services again. If they answered, I don't think they could hear me. "I want to report a fire out at McKenzie Lodge and it's going to burn down the whole place if you don't get here soon." Nothing but static. Damn phone. So much for technology. I shut it down and stick it back in my pocket.

We cross another gully and circle back toward the east and away from the line of the fire.

"It's still coming towards us," Kendra points out.

"Yes," I agree, "but the back burn is much slower, because the wind is pushing it west, toward the camp, for now."

"For now?"

"Depending on the time and temperature of the day, the wind changes direction from morning to evening." I look back. We're now walking at a fast clip, and I feel drained. Kendra stumbles over a bush, falling to her knees. We both have adrenaline lows. My fingers and calves burn from the singe marks. I don't see any blisters, but the skin blazes red and painful where my clothes rub.

Not far ahead of us, a coyote trots across our path headed south, away from the fire. He stops to look straight at us, not catching our scent because we are downwind. Without alarm, he trots on his way. A minute later, another coyote lopes past to catch his friend. As we walk on, I think about getting to the highway and hitching a ride. I boot up the phone and barely have enough power to use my GPS.

"Oh, my God, there's a road up ahead." We take only a few more steps and look down on the blacktop of a narrow county highway. No pickup full of men is sitting there waiting to trap us, thank goodness.

"Quick, get across. We should go farther along. This is an obvious place to intercept us. If we head toward the main highway, we'll be too near the entrance to the camp." Crouching down, we run across the road, crawling through the barbed wire fence on the other side. We run another ten minutes until we tire and then slow to a steady walk. "How are you doing?" If I expected a mere 'fine,' I was mistaken. Kendra started bawling, an all-out, vulnerable show of sorrow. "I'm awful. I'm a terrible daughter and person. I hate myself. I scared everyone. They went through all the trouble of looking for me and I wasn't even in trouble until last night. I can never go back."

"Listen, for now we have to stop with the pity party and concentrate on getting out of here in one piece," I say. "Remember, we have to save those other young women." In horror, I recall what she told me when we were first sitting in the Prius, right before Buddy appeared. "Wait. Did you say most of those girls are only fourteen years old? Did you ask them?"

"Yes, yes. Except for Maria. I didn't make this up. I remembered from the movie we saw most girls are captured when they are young teenagers. One of the Indian girls is from Ronan and was taken only a month ago." Kendra sobbed. "I recognized her from playing against her volleyball team last fall. The twins have been trafficked since they were ten and now, they're fourteen. They've been taken all over the states. At least here they get fed and have a shower. Oh, and they mostly have sex on a bed instead of in an alley." Kendra kicks at bushes as we pass, her fists are held out like she's ready to punch someone. Suddenly, she lets out a blood-curdling scream. "Shit, shit, shit, fuck, fucking bastards, dick heads."

Running out of swear words, she kicks and stomps the ground a half dozen times, sending small rocks flying.

Kendra jerks to a halt. "Something else," she says, looking away. "They held me down for the first man last night. He's some bigwig muckety-muck in the government here. He apparently paid extra for a virgin. When he found out I wasn't, all hell broke loose. He tried to choke me, calling me a slut, but Buddy about killed him, telling him I'm valuable property."

We walk in stunned silence for another minute, letting this news soak in.

Kendra finally glances my way. "What took you so long when you went back to start the fire in the grassland. You should carry a lighter. I was worried."

"We must be on the only unplowed, non-grazed section of land in this part of the state," I say, stalling before answering her question, "because without the rolling hills and trees in the creek beds, we'd be completely out in the open with no place to hide." Ahead we can see rows of tall green cottonwood trees lining a swale. In a few more yards, we come across a yellow sign affixed to a metal fence post. "*State Wildlife Management Area.* Whoohoo. Saved by Mother Nature again, with the help of North Dakota."

I finally answer her question. "I ran into Buddy back at the fire."

"What?" She stops walking. "I knew we shouldn't have separated. What happened? How'd you get away? That asshole made me like him. What a con artist. He's the cause of all this trouble." She catches up to me. "I hope you killed him."

I give her a sidelong glance. There's that useful anger again. "I don't think he's dead, but I'm sure he's hurting a lot. I had some help from a prairie rattler." I look down at my binoculars. "I hope he didn't break these when they landed on his hard head. I won them in a raffle last year and know they're waterproof, but don't know if they're skull-proof."

Kendra looks at me with a little smile on her lips and maybe admiration in her eyes? "Wait. A rattlesnake? I didn't know there were rattlers out here." Her eyes dart from side-to-side and her steps become more tentative.

"Don't worry," I tell her. "They'll try to move out of the way before we get to them or lay still unless we step on them first." Even I stare at the ground for a second. "We have more important things to think about. One, the human snakes hunting us, and two, the fire will change direction at any moment. We need to speed up. Now."

"God, I'm thirsty," says Kendra.

We'd kicked it up to a slow jog. At this speed, the distance between the entrance to the camp and our patch of prairie is stretching quickly. The sun is sinking toward the earth directly behind us. "Let's start cutting to the north to find the highway."

I feel the phone vibrate in my pocket. I thought I'd turned it off to conserve power. I pull it out and the display reads Central Credit Union. "Hello?"

"Rosetta, this is Ben. Where are you? Your county sheriff friend, Les Trammel called trying to get a hold of you. He said he hadn't been able to connect with your phone. Is, ah, everything ok?"

"Ben, oh my God! I haven't been able to answer any of my calls. I left text messages for everyone."

"Stop blabbing and tell him where we are!" yells Kendra.

"Ben, we're east of McKenzie Lodge, a man camp south of Williston. I'm with Kendra, a friend who we thought had been kidnapped. The prairie's on fire around us and a group of mobsters are chasing us. We're probably a mile south of where the highway curves toward the east, at the entrance to the camp. There's a lot of smoke, but we haven't heard any fire engine sirens come near. I thought if I started a fire, we'd get help from the police and the fire department."

I catch my breath and keep shouting at the phone, cupping it in my hands to break the wind. "They're holding girls for human trafficking at the man camp. The Mafia manages the place. I know it sounds far fetched, but it was confirmed by the matchstick chewing partner of JB's, named Buddy, by the way. He's the one who kidnapped Kendra from her job at Jake's. He had me cornered against the fire, but a rattlesnake bit him in the knee, so I was able to get away. We don't have any water and it's getting cool out here now. Can you call someone to help us and call Les back to tell him where we are?" I stop, waiting for an answer. "Ben? Hello?"

I look at the phone screen. It's black... out of juice. "Damn. I hope he heard something useful before the power ran out." I pull out a small solar charger I just remembered having, hook it to my pack and plug in the phone. "This takes forever to charge something, but we might get a little juice out of it despite the smoke."

Kendra groans. "I shouldn't have spent all that time talking to my mom. I'm such a loser."

I want to throttle her but hold back. "It doesn't really matter. Other people know where I am. I sent text messages to my friends before I even reached the camp. Maybe they don't know we're in trouble, but they'll start making calls if I don't check in soon."

"Maybe if I go back, they'll stop chasing us." Kendra stops walking and looks back toward the wall of smoke.

"Stop. This is your fear talking. Tell me, do you think they'd be nice to you if you went back? Think before you answer. Was anyone in charge nice to you?"

Kendra turns in place a few times before answering. "No, and no." Her head hangs down like a whipped puppy.

"Did they let you call your mom or friends?"

"No, you know they didn't. Did you see any fucking phones in that house?!" Kendra is mad, marching off at a good pace, the helpless puppy gone for now.

"Those people are not your friends. They are evil men and women. It's good they didn't like you. You didn't like them."

"I liked JB and even Buddy, for a few hours. JB never came back for me or called. Kind of hurt my feelings. Why isn't he here with you? I thought you were getting married soon. God, he couldn't shut up about you on the drive out here. I couldn't believe you were there in that...that...prison. I was still mad about hearing your name, over and over, and what a wonderful, fabulous, perfect woman you were. God, I almost hated you. I forgot about it while I was working at Jake's. Suddenly, there you were, and it came flooding back. I almost choked."

"I could see you didn't want me there. My feelings were hurt when you sent me away without telling me what was going on. It seems pretty trivial now." I want to tell her every thing, but not yet. "I almost left but was determined to hear how JB happened to bring you out to North Dakota." She's pouting and doesn't hear a thing I'm saying. "By the way, that was quick thinking about the Indian sign language."

Kendra smiles and gives me a gentle punch in the arm. "I didn't know if you'd get it, to tell the truth. Maybe you are the coolest woman ever." She looks like a mischievous angel when she grins over at me. I realize she's taller than I am. She seemed shrunken when I forced her into my car.

I laugh. "Maybe you're pretty cool yourself. That might be the smartest thing I've ever seen anyone do. We never would have been able to connect if you hadn't thought of it."

Kendra's step is a little jaunty now. "You're damn right, you know. They are horrible people. How can one person be so cruel to another person? It's good they didn't like me, right? I hate them." She clinched her fists and kicked the next rock out of her way. "They wanted to use me to make money and all those other girls, too. I wonder if anyone has died out there. Do you think they'd have killed me if I didn't give in? The others did what they were told, but I couldn't. Those men who use the girls should be arrested." She takes a shaky breath.

Kendra finally understands what happened. An acceptance of a horrific, but real, experience and of her serendipitous escape. "Those people are criminals. They tried to physically and mentally beat you into submission." I say. "All of them, Buddy, the cat eyed woman and the men who use the girls as toys. They may as well be riding their snowmobiles or shooting beer cans off of a fence post with their long, pointed guns for the amount of pleasure they get. It's a power thing. That kind of man should be castrated and publicly flogged."

Kendra snickers. I laugh, too. "Haven't you ever heard of cowboy justice?" Kendra looks at me, waiting for more.

"Maybe we'd have to call it cowgirl justice, instead; not exactly retaliation, but more a kind of social aversive conditioning."

"Shut up," she says, clapping her hands at the prospect. "Could that really happen?"

"Only if women ruled the world," I reply, chuckling. "But it's fun to think about it."

Kendra's expressive eyebrows furrow together. "Why didn't you ask JB why he brought me out here?"

I guess now is as good a time as any.

CHAPTER THIRTY

"I didn't know your disappearance had anything to do with JB until I got to Jake's this afternoon. JB didn't offer the information, because..." I slow down to talk. I don't feel like crying anymore. "Because, as he arrived back in Tamarack Falls, the evening after dropping you off, he had a fatal car accident. I was injured, too, and spent weeks in the hospital."

"What? Oh, my God! I can't believe it. When Jennifer said he'd had an accident, I didn't even ask how he was." Kendra, returning to her emotional teenage self, grabs me into a brief hug. "Are you ok?"

"Yes, yes. Fully recovered," I lie. My hips and back are killing me.

"Look." Kendra points back toward the camp. The smoke is clearing, going straight up into the sky and a bright red ball hangs where the sun should be. "Hey, did you notice the wind dropped?"

"What a relief," I sigh. We stop in a swale between two low hills to feel the stillness, listening to the quiet.

"I've wondered if JB really was friends with Buddy. I mean, at Jake's, Buddy was nice. He came so late to pick me up. Said he'd cleared it with Jake already." She looks toward the sky. "I could tell he'd been drinking. By the time we got to the camp, he was yelling about how he was getting back at JB." Kendra held my arm. "I didn't get it. JB must have cheated him somehow."

"Yes, he did," I confess.

"I wonder if anyone understood any of our messages or if anyone is coming to help us." Kendra whimpered. She's feeling vulnerable again, wanting to be held, helped and saved. Do I feel the same? I've always been so independent. Vulnerability hasn't been my strong point, and neither has care giving. I don't ask for help and I'm usually not asked to help. Maybe I do observe from the outside rather than connecting with people, like the hospital therapist suggested, but I'm not a cold fish.

I put my arm around Kendra's shoulders and give her a squeeze. "We're a team now. We can do what needs to be done. We're saving ourselves, but if someone comes to our aid, that's icing on the cake." I switch on my phone again. One bar of power and two bars of phone signal appear. "Five text messages?" The latest, from Enrique, said *turn north now.* "Huh?" I scroll on.

"What?" asks Kendra.

"Jackson said, *flew over and saw you. Turn due north.* My God, the plane. That was a while ago."

"Not so long," Kendra points out. "Maybe twenty minutes."

"Is that all?" I look at the phone and pull up the compass application. We turn due north, taking a long sighting on the left edge of a butte in the far distance. There wasn't much to look at from this vantage point. "We have to keep that butte in sight."

"Any other messages?" Practical Kendra got me back on task.

"Yes. Ben says he got my message and called Sheriff T." I was suddenly very grateful for my network, the cloud of souls circling around me like guardian angels. My eyes well up and a couple of tears escape down my cheeks before I can turn away.

"What's the matter?" Kendra comes closer and grasps my arm. "Bad news?"

"No, good news. Never discount or trivialize a friend, no matter how new, or how much they irritate, pester, or ignore you. Friends are always there, lurking around in the shadows, until they are called forth to fulfill their purpose."

"Yea, whatever. You're tired. Come in this direction a little more." She gently pulls me back onto the due north pathway. "The wind is picking up again. Look at the smoke."

I look up at the haze between the butte and us. "The wind changed direction for the evening. We better take closer sightings. No telling how thick the smoke will get." A sudden flair of black smoke completely closes off our view of the butte.

"Don't worry, I took a couple of sightings on those scrubby trees," Kendra says. "We'll be close enough." Kendra realizes she's still holding my arm and lets go. "Besides, the sun is burning the left side of my face. It's pretty easy to tell direction out here at this time of day."

I look at my phone. It's black now. "It's turned itself off again." I shove it into my backpack. "Sorry I didn't carry water in here." I pull out a small empty bottle. "But I have this ultraviolet pen to kill the bacteria when we find a creek."

"Fucking fat chance of that," Kendra says, snorting.

Twenty steps later, the land stops and a gaping gully opens before us. At the bottom of the thirty-foot cliff lies a pool of water. Seven heads fly up, stabbing us with black, bulging eyes, and suddenly the gully is alive with motion. The white behinds of pronghorn zigzag across the dusky creek bottom and up the other side in a few bounds. I smile at Kendra. "Oh, ye of little faith."

We take a sighting across the gully in the direction we want to head when we climb up the other side. After a short walk along the cliff, we find a wide stretch where the bank sloughed off and an animal trail traversed down the slope. We reach the bottom, sliding on our behinds at the end, and make our way back to the water. The small pond is opaque with silt, but the hole is deep and probably part of an underground stream. Smoke makes the gully much darker than up on the prairie. I see why the animals felt it was safe to drink here.

My cup is gone, but I find a couple of zip lock bags in my pack, handing them to Kendra. I remove the UV pen and a roll of cheese-cloth from a plastic bottle. Sliding a three-inch square piece of the cheesecloth over the bottleneck, I screw on the lid. I pull open the spout, squeeze air out of the bottle and hold it under the water. "It takes a little while to suck up the water, but we need to filter it into the bottle. The ultraviolet light won't kill the bacteria if the water is too murky."

Kendra goes to the other end of the hole and splashes water onto her face and arms. "I'm so gritty and look at the scratches on my arms." She holds them up and I can see a million little scabbed over trails. I imagine my arms look the same. "I'm going over there to pee." She heads toward a clump of shrubs down the creek bed.

I squeeze air out of the bottle again, sucking up water until the bottle is full. Removing the lid, I stir the ultraviolet pen into the water and push the button. It lights up for forty-five seconds and switches off. This water fills one of the small zip lock bags Kendra left on the sand. I change the filter and repeat the process. "Come and get it," I holler. No answer. I fill the second baggy with water, replace everything into my pack, and walk toward the spot where I'd last noticed Kendra. I see her, still squatting, frozen in place. She turns her frightened, tear-streaked face toward me and that slight movement starts a loud buzzing next to her hip.

"Damn. We don't need this. Don't move and don't talk." Where was a stick when you needed one? I walked around in a wide circle, kicking at bushes, trying, unsuccessfully, to break off a limb so I could use it to slide the snake away. I scoop up a handful of gravel.

"Don't nod your head or move anything until I say." I kneel close to Kendra, with the snake in between us, throwing one pebble at a time toward the snake. It's a skinny little thing, but every rattle-snake is as poisonous as the next. I finally hit it and the rattle starts up again. It looks in the pebble's direction, instead of Kendra. Her behind is as still as a stone.

I continue to fling pebbles, occasionally hitting the snake. It rattles less and less as it becomes habituated. I throw a pinch of pebbles and the snake rattles again, but with no target, he's getting discouraged. He's finally had enough when a handful of dirt lands on his face. The snake packs up his rattle and fangs and slithers away.

"Ok, you can move now."

Kendra is still squatting, eyes closed, face red, fist clenched and arms around her knees. She pees, sighs and relaxes. Tears roll down her cheeks. "It started rattling as soon as I squatted. Thanks for coming after me. Again."

She guzzles down her bag of water in a few gulps. By the time we scramble up the path taken by the pronghorn, the prairie is thick with smoke. I point toward the west where the camp lay and the sun is barely showing through the pitchblack, billowing smoke. "I think the Lunch Room is on fire. I didn't know a prefab building would actually burn."

"Listen. Sirens." Kendra gestures to the north. "Finally."

"Let's go faster. The smoke is making it really dark, and I don't want to walk out here with snakes when I can't see." Kendra grabs my sleeve and picks up the pace.

The wind is not in our favor. Visibility is way down and we both bend over coughing. I pull my shirt up over my nose and give Kendra my handkerchief to tie around hers. We can only see about a hundred feet ahead. The sun is our only navigation point now. Keeping it on our left cheeks, we trudge on. "Look over there, at about ten o'clock."

Kendra looks at me as if I am bordering on delirium, and then looks up at the sky, puzzled. Most kids don't even know what a clock face looks like, much less how to read one.

"Look." I stretch my arms straight out in front of my chest and joined my palms together. "We're standing in the middle of a big clock face on the ground and both my hands are pointing at the twelve." I open my left arm out to a little past forty-five degrees from my chest, as if I'm pointing at ten on the clock face.

She suddenly understands and looks in that direction. "Police lights," she says, whooping. She jumps up and down and gives me a quick hug. "We did it."

"We did it." I say, trying to sound as if I'd had no qualms. The highway is close, maybe a ten minute walk. From our vantage point on a small rise, we can see a couple of cars parked along the road. Both of them have flashing lights and one looks like an ambulance. I head in the direction, and suddenly notice Kendra isn't next to me. Looking back, I see her standing still, fisted hands clasped to her stomach.

Maybe she's having a reaction to the water? "Are you ok?" I hurry over and rub my hand on her bent back. "Do you feel sick?"

Her breath comes in shuddering gasps. I recognize this as a twin to the panic attack I had on the day I met Enrique. "I can't go back. Everyone hates me. My mom will never trust me again."

"That's not going to happen." There are cruel, unthinking people who try to blame the victims. "Truthfully? There are people who barely know you, who've never met you, and whom you don't know, who are going to give you grief. Remember, you blamed the girls in the movie who had been captured and put into prostitution rings?"

I hope she isn't blocking out my words. "At first, some ignorant souls will not understand. They won't understand a teenager coming to Jake's to earn money for her family. They don't want to admit or understand what's happening to those girls back at the camp and what almost happened to you. We don't care what they think, and maybe we can educate them. The most important people do understand, and they will support you. Your parents and friends are crazy about you. That's what you will focus on."

Her arms are around my middle, her head buried in my shoulder. "Listen, there's something I want to share with you." I give her a brief list of events surrounding the accident, glossing over the details. "After I came out of the hospital and rehabbed enough to go to town again, I was disgusted at how many people seemed to blame me for JB's death. I thought some of them hated me for bringing him to town. I imagined some thought me a troublemaker and a bad person all around. It was only my trauma talking. My imagination needed a reset." I look out over the smoky prairie. She's unwound herself and stares into my eyes.

"A friend told me I was the only one beating myself up and everyone in town was on my team. I was so steeped in self-pity I couldn't see everyone supporting me. I'm telling you, your parents, friends and the community love you. You will see sympathy and compassion in people's faces. You might mistake it for something else, like hate or pity. Time heals. The best thing is to go back, share your story over and over again. Find a purpose for this tragedy. Help save other girls from the horror."

She looks at me as if I am her aged grandmother who's headed for the loony bin. I persevere. "You're strong and you're brave." She gives me a one-armed hug. I know she thinks this is a bunch of hooey I'm feeding her to get her to go home, something she desperately wants to do. Too bad we don't have a pair of ruby slippers right now.

"I'm sorry about JB. He really loved you," she says before releasing me from the hug.

I feel nothing—not a tight throat, not a teardrop, no ache in the pit of my stomach. The guilt is gone. "So, I hear," I say, taking her hand and walking toward the flashing lights. "So, I hear."

Enrique and Jackson shout and wave and run out to meet us.

CHAPTER THIRTY ONE

Fire engines from the Bureau of Land Management, Bureau of Reclamation, others from a nearby town, plus a couple of private water tanker trucks from local farms, raise a wall of dust as they head home. A few trucks and a dozen firefighters stay behind to mop up the hot spots on the prairie and in what was once the lunchroom. They started coming within 20 minutes of our smoke signal, but we couldn't hear from our place on the windy prairie.

After the ambulance crew checked us over and bandaged the few serious burns and scratches, we loaded into the sheriff's Suburban and drove back towards the camp. The lunch room building had burned to the ground. Amid the debris, pots, cabinets and tables lay in wet ash and smoke. The deputy escorted Kendra and me to see the young girls gathered in their original house. The Boss drove out of the camp as soon as she heard about our escape. She's a survivor all the way.

A few of the girls called their parents and others had no one to call. Their future was a blank wall of homelessness and getting picked up by a new pimp. Maria was not among the girls, but came running when she heard Kendra was back. They hugged each other, laughing and crying.

We park on the road's shoulder next to the gully where I'd hidden my Prius. Four yellow-coated firemen trudge from around the bend, their legs streaked with black from the charred shrubs in the creek bed. They've rescued the ice chest, JB's boxes, Lila's picnic basket and my suitcase from the scorched car. The firemen agree it was lucky that I'd filled the gas tank in Williston, or it might have exploded.

They load everything into the back of the County Sheriff department SUV and stand with us to watch the straining tow truck drag my reluctant, blackened Prius out of the gully and onto the road. Both back tires melted flat from the heat of the burnt tumbleweeds and leave deep grooves in the sand. We decide not to wait for the trailer that has been summoned to haul it away.

The sheriff hands me a plastic evidence bag into which I empty the glove boxes, console and junk from under the seats. We drive off when I remember something. "Wait," I shout. Running back to the Prius, I pull open the driver's door and reach up to the ceiling. Clipped to the visor, so I could glance at it while I drove, is the profile photo I took of JB the first day when we went to Glacier National Park. Enrique, who's followed, puts his arm around my shoulders, guiding me back to the SUV, where Jackson and Kendra wait with the sheriff.

Jackson wanted us to check into a motel and rest after our ordeal. I protested and wanted to go home. We stop at a nearby truck stop to wash our face and hands and change out of our filthy, torn shirts. Enrique protests when I toss out my Cowgirl t-shirt. Jackson grabs sandwiches and drinks, and heads to the airport. He makes a deal with the sheriff to send my boxes, cooler, and suitcase to us by bus.

"Buckle in," Jackson says, as the engine of a four-passenger Cessna roars to life. Now that we're out of the smoke, we can see the sun is still above the horizon.

"How did you get here so fast? And why did you come?" I finally remember my call to Enrique, when he mentioned Jackson as acting barista.

"You can thank the birds," Jackson says, completely deadpan.

"Huh?"

"In your haste to post that LaConte's sparrow picture to the birding hotline, you probably didn't even notice Kendra in the background. As soon as I saw her, I called a friend who owns a charter jet service that flies oil workers between Williston and Kalispell. He was leaving Kalispell and offered to let us fly back with him. We closed the gallery, sped to the airport, and flew to Williston in about an hour and a half. The local sheriff provided transportation from there."

I explained about noticing Kendra on the road after I'd posted the photo.

Jackson nodded. "When I saw her, I knew something bigger was going on, and we'd already read your text about checking out the man camp. I was truly disappointed in your carelessness."

The Cessna 172 Jackson rented to fly us home holds four passengers, but not much else, so I clutch Lila's basket and the salami to my chest. The plane looks startlingly old, but he swears it's the best plane ever built. We lift off and make a wide circle, giving us a view of what looks like the lights of city high-rises. On closer inspection, they turn out to be oil drilling rigs, tightly packed across the prairie. We swing south to see McKenzie Lodge is alive with the flashing lights of law enforcement vehicles, and more flashing lights thread along the highway, headed that way. The prairie fire burned only the mile stretch along the entry road until it met a fallow plowed field on the west and newly sprouted green wheat on the south.

I fall asleep to Kendra's lively monologue, waking briefly when we land in Great Falls to top off the fuel tank and empty our bladders. Again, my growling stomach reminds me of the sandwich and energy drink. Not long afterward, we bounce over the complete blackness of the Bob Marshall Wilderness, my shield against the ugliness behind us. A full moon lights the mountain tops, glowing bright where snow still hangs on the north slopes.

I search the dark, moon-struck forests below and know my true love is there. My hunting among men, for the fictional, elusive unicorn of affection, will cease and desist. If it's out there, it can damn well find me.

I don't sleep rolled up in a fetal position for a week. I don't go the hospital for a checkup. Epsom salt baths, swimming in the frigid lake, hikes up steep mountains and horse rides through the forest, purging my old aches and pains, replacing them with better ones. I drop the cane and do more to help myself heal. I pull my vegetable juicer off the bottom pantry shelf, pick kale, chard, parsley, cilantro, peppers, celery and cucumbers from my garden daily, and begin drinking my way through a ten-day juice detox. I join a three-day backpack with the Montana Wilderness Association.

In ten days, boxes arrive from the Sheriff in North Dakota. Jackson washes the smoky ash off of the cooler and suitcase and stores them in my garage. He stacks JB's boxes on the covered porch, but the smell of smoke permeating every cardboard pore reminds me of their presence. My detachment seems complete. I'm not eager to reopen that chapter of my life. I'm not fearful about the relationship, the incident, or anything to do with JB.

I sit in my gazebo, hugging furry Meg and my latte, thinking about all the wonderful opportunities that have opened their doors. The credit union money is a wonderful gift, and I have an overwhelming desire to use some of it to help those girls from the McKenzie camp. They need a place to live while they recover. An organized support system is necessary to help these young women integrate into society.

The girls are living in a women's correctional and rehabilitation facility in North Dakota, not only because it is the only place available for a large group of women at short notice, but because their drug addictions make them easy prey for more traffickers. The place seems to have the therapeutic and medical help they need, but the courts will decide if these teenagers can be considered adults and charged with prostitution. No one understands that attitude. Do they think the girls were living the good life? Kendra is joyfully reunited with her mother, and her dad is home on parole.

The weekly local newspaper sits in front of me, folded back to the feature article. Upon my return, I found a letter from the county attorney informing me that my name was on the deed and now owned JB's lot at the Larsen Lake Golf Course and the Mustang. The incredible amount of house insurance coverage will make it possible to rebuild if I want. The local newspaper reporter, Marry Kat, interviewed me in front of the empty lot, where I told the world about the local human trafficking and how we have to close it down. "I'm going to make it a priority to shine a light on whoever is perpetrating this horrendous crime against humanity in our backyard," said the quote. I felt ripped opened and drained by the reporter.

Further down in the article, another quote is attributed to me about hoping the perpetrators burn in hell. The truth is, it was the reporter's opinion. I said, "I hope they get their balls cut off with a dull knife and are forever flogged in the town square by all the women they've harmed or meant to harm. I hope they have to mop the floors and clean the toilets of whatever prison they rot in. And I hope they have to spend three hours a day meditating on what a wonderful world it will be when every woman and child is safe from human predators and there is no more slavery in the world." Too many words said the reporter.

"Hello?" I'd brought the phone out to the table with my latte, even though I didn't expect a call this early. The distorted phone ID voice chirped, "New York Times," and I suspect that they're selling subscriptions. Normally, I don't answer calls selling something, asking for donations, or when my phone shouts out the warning of "caller unknown."

"Hi, this is Bill Bright from the New York Times," the calm voice replies. "Can I speak with Rosetta Stone?"

Before North Dakota, I would have given a long, sarcastic answer to this. With a Spanish accent, I would say, *This is the Pope. Rosetta is cooking our breakfast and cannot come to the phone but listen to my latest sermon.* Instead, "Hi, this is she."

"I read the story about you in your local paper. Do you mind if I ask a few questions?"

"About what?" I squeak. I try not to be paranoid, but the harder I try, the more paranoid I become. "Is there a way you can identify yourself? How do I know you're a reporter?"

"Well, let me explain a little about my research. That will give you time to log onto the New York Times website and find my bio. And then I want you to call the number on the website and ask for me. Ok?"

"Newspaper reporters do research? Wait, sorry, I didn't mean that. You mean you're investigating something special."

"Don't worry about it. Yes, I'm an investigative journalist. My area of interest is human trafficking." He pauses a moment. "I understand you had a human trafficking experience up-close and personal. Is that right?"

"I have the number, let me call you back."

It only takes a few choices through the dichotomous key of questions, to reach the newsroom secretary and get transferred to Bill's phone.

"Listen, Mr. Bright, I'm sure if you've investigated human trafficking, you know way more than I ever will. I had an accidental encounter. I was looking for a missing neighbor. Anything I tell you will be confusing, especially if you're trying to stop it." I take a couple of deep breaths to calm down my emotional upwelling. I don't want to cry over the phone. "Except for the burn-in-hell quote, the rest of the article is pretty accurate. The young woman who escaped with me has her own story in the newspaper. My friend, Marry Kat, did a thoughtful interview with Kendra and her family. I hope you can give her some name credit in your article. Did you see it?"

"Not yet, but I'll look it up." Bill sounds sincere and persistent. "You have a unique perspective, you know. You personally knew the perpetrator and I believe you might know more than you could tell that reporter. They come in with questions to help them write the type of article their editor wants. Yours was almost a feel-good story, not exactly an investigative report. See the difference?"

I consider the difference for a minute. "I think I see it. How can I help you?"

We end up talking for over an hour. I tell him the Mafia is in Montana, and he tells me about their interest in human trafficking—about the finders, the lures and many things I'd never heard of. "They call the finders *scouts*, as in talent scouts. Most of it comes back to lonely kids getting sucked away by a lying, so-called friend, or answering a job advertisement and getting groomed to disappear into their system and normalize that life. The teens end up as captives, slaves." I am furious when Bill tells me the girls from McKenzie Lodge were charged as adult prostitutes. He adds that a national trafficking advocacy group is working to get the charges removed. This is a big problem in some states, he says, and many do not have laws that pass the advocacy group annual evaluation. There are still places which charge both the victims and traffickers as criminals. The flip side is the girls will now get help at the women's rehabilitation facility in North Dakota.

I tell him Kendra's friend, Maria, was folding towels in the laundry when the raid went down, didn't get caught up in the arrests. She stayed in North Dakota and transferred to the Lodge north of Williston at the recommendation of Alice from the front desk. Maria and Kendra talk on the phone several days a week and Maria plans to visit Tamarack Falls next month.

Bill tells me the sad fact, sometimes children or women are kidnapped, but many kids are used by their parents, foster parents or an uncle. It's a profitable small business. Grooming by a new acquaintance, using the familiar candy-to-kids routine, breaks down a person's life to get them to accept selling their bodies is normal. It often turns into beatings, withholding food and water, intimidation and drug addiction. Even though hundreds of thousands of Americans are abducted into the trafficking trade every year, there are roughly two to four million trafficked people in the United States, including new immigrants stuck in indentured labor situations.

I start scrolling through my mind about the last time I had my nails done in the Vietnamese nail salon. "When the price seems too good to be true, it's probably slavery."

He tells me, globally, it's estimated private businesses benefit to the tune of one hundred fifty billion dollars. Kids are put to work in jobs as diverse as rug weavers, sex slaves and camel jockeys. These days they are even used as egg and organ donors. And, of course, there is the ever-present mercenary marriage. Their stories are all beyond cruel, beyond horrible. He goes on to tells me it's happening in my backyard.

"Listen, I've told you stuff even the police don't know yet," I say. "Can you give me a day before you publish? I need to tell my local Sheriff."

"Don't worry. It will come out as a small part of a longer article this evening, so most people won't see it until the morning. I hope that's enough time," Bill says. I pin his cell phone number and direct link to his desk on the corkboard over my phone.

"By the way, did you know there used to be a wealthy evangelist with your name?"

"It was the bane of my childhood," says Bill. "Please call me if you remember anything else."

CHAPTER THIRTY TWO

I froth and brew my second latte of the day. The aroma of good coffee is so comforting and precious. The whole process of foaming my homemade almond milk, grinding the beans to release the first molecules of scent and then listening as the pressurized water forces its way through the grounds is something I look forward to every day. My new machine both grinds and brews the beans, but my beautiful, wooden, handcrank burr grinder sits in a place of honor in the kitchen hutch.

I rock myself back to reality on the porch swing, hugging my insulated travel mug of steaming latte. Morning mist surrounds the cottonwoods and sun sparkles through jewel-like dewdrops hanging along the edges of purple and yellow iris. Old-fashioned lilacs bloom around the yard and small Korean lilacs give off a sweet fragrance from their fragile unopened buds. Lavender plants waft their musky sweetness up the path but won't bloom for another few weeks. Meg is chasing after early morning robins, who systematically tug earthworms out of their tiny holes.

It takes time to calm down from the conversation with Bill. I was doubly upset after I read in our local paper a summer resident, a gazillionaire philanthropist, whom I previously admired, might be involved in big-time trafficking. If your rich enough, money can make all your troubles disappear. It makes me weep for the human race.

Dripping with dew and a chase through the creek, Meg shakes and spins in excitement, spreading her shower of joyful wet border collie aroma. The shawl I'd left draped over the back of the bench swing last night has a patch of black, orange and white hair from the calico cat that moved in while I was in the hospital. The cat is now very pregnant.

The overwhelming smoky smell from the burned Prius is so strong on the boxes stacked at the end of my porch, I can't open the front door without the stench flooding the house. I briefly think about calling Sheriff Trammel before opening them, but instead use a kitchen knife to slice the packing tape. For inventory purposes, I mark identifying numbers on each box to keep the evidence sorted. What if there is a magical combination of particles and products that fit together to have more meaning than the parts? What if it can give me answers? With a yellow pad on my lap to write down the inventory, I part the flaps on the first box and, right away, note how orderly it is. There is a piece of paper on top that both seals the box from infiltrating dirt and offers a brief list of contents. How convenient. I snap a picture with my phone.

The list is perhaps a clue, or maybe a confession. I'm calm and detached, trying to explore without judgment. At the top of the page list is a heading for cell phones. Underneath are the names Karen, Cheny, Lupe, Carlos, Kara, Margarita, Mary Jo, Bao, Ann, Lin, Tian, Maria, Jan and Jackie, Kendra. Seeing Kendra's name is bad enough, but I almost lose it at Tian, which means something like heaven or celestial. Beloved daughters missed or sold by their families. Sad, so sad. Did he keep these as trophies? Who knows? Lifting up the paper reveals a clear zip lock bag full of old, mostly flip, cell phones, many of them cracked or scratched, all with initials marked on the face. The next bag is full of an odd collection of cheap necklaces, rings, and bracelets, each item or group in a labeled plastic baggie. On top is a big, gothic cross, once belonging to Kendra. There are half a dozen skull-shaped rings.

A narrow, three-ring binder reveals a few details about each person corresponding with the phones, plus over one hundred more names, both female and male. Each page is like an interview form asking for name, age, parent's names, skills, education, interests, the town of origin and destination. Green card application details. The front page is Kendra's interview and the one behind it is Maria, her friend from Mexico City. I flip to the back page. It's dated almost fifteen years ago.

If nothing changed for these people, as it did for Kendra, maybe they could still be found in their original destinations. They traveled mostly to cities and the end locations include legitimate jobs in restaurants, oil businesses like Jake's, a trucking company, mechanic shops, beauty salons, nail salons, hotels and athletic club. I replace everything in its original position and close the box. Whatever else is in it belongs in police hands.

Box number two is also tidy. The list begins with books, travel guides, maps, travel music and ends with travel food, water bottle and coffee mug. Clothing in plastic compression bags included a fleece jacket, new polo shirts, t-shirt, undershorts, socks and cash. This must be something he took on every trip, a sort of survival kit. I lift off the paper and examine the books.

The first one I pull out is *The New Earth*, by Eckhart Tolle. This has me totally stumped. How could a person involved in human trafficking read the most recommended transformational book in the world and remain in that sort of work? I flip through the pages, looking for notes or bookmarks. JB's study aid of choice was a yellow highlighter. He'd used it sparingly at first, but by chapter four, he seems to be more engaged. Some pages are totally circled with yellow.

He'd bookmarked chapter seven, about discovering your true self. I can tell by the yellow highlighter he'd read the whole book, but his bookmark is here, like he'd gone back to read it again. Was he transforming? If he was, then why take Kendra, plus attempt to murder me, and then commit suicide? Did he have a relapse? It's like the guy had a dual personality. Buddy said JB liked the benign side of the business; finding people jobs, supplying hard-to-find items, finding employees. Maybe these books pushed JB over the edge and gave him the strength to get out of trafficking. I chuckle at an Oprah book club novel. There are three, dog-eared folders of Tony Robbin's CDs. The next layer contains a thin Will Shortz puzzler book, Ziploc bags filled with granola bars and nuts, road maps, sealed water bottles and underneath that, cash.

Box three has a strip of clear packing tape across the top. The other two had their flaps tucked into each other and looked well used and worn on the corners. This box is new. I rip off the tape, but no list awaits me. Zigzag slices of brown paper packing material fill the box to the surface. I wonder if something will jump out at me if I lift the top layer. I stir my pen through the shredded paper, gently probing deeper until I thump onto something solid. I reach in and bring out a football-size something, tightly duct-taped in bubble wrap. I carefully snip the tape with a pair of scissors.

I peel off the layers. Out comes a metal box about ten by twelve inches. It isn't very thick, nor does it feel or sound full when shaken. It isn't locked. One side of the lid has one long hinge and one side has two latches, like one of those ammunition boxes sold by the Army-Navy surplus stores. Undoing the latches, I point the box out toward the yard and gingerly lift the lid. Nothing jumps out. Only three items rattle around in the box.

The black and white framed photo shows a young woman and a little boy. She's kneeling next to him in front of a palmetto, one of those low palm-like bushes that grow in the southeast. They're both laughing and he's reaching his tiny arm over her shoulders like they were pals. I slide the cardboard out of the slot on the rear and the photo falls out onto my lap. There's no date on the back of the photo, but a neat script proclaims "Happy 5th Birthday, my JB. Love you so much, little man. Mama." I replace the picture into the frame and set it aside.

The notebook looks identical to those I used in college to write exams; almost square, black, hard, the covers joined with red binding tape. The first page is blank. "For Rosetta Stone" pops off the next page. It is so neat it looks commercially printed. It isn't and I recognize the printing from the sheet of paper the sheriff found in JB's house. The next page starts with *If you are reading this, I'm either missing or dead.* As I jump up, shocked, the metal case slides off my lap, crashing to the concrete and a small black box bounces out of it into the flowerbed. Meg rushes in to investigate, pushing it around with her nose, tasting it.

"Leave it!" I yell, grabbing her collar and fishing the box from beneath her muzzle. She cowers down, startled and guilty. "I'm sorry, girl," I croon while rubbing her ears. "I thought you were going to take it away before I could look at it." Her tail thumps a few times, forgiving my momentary transgression in dog owner etiquette. I push open the front door so she can hide inside.

The box is the size and shape of a jewelry box, but you never know these days. I thumb it open and, sure enough, it contains a pair of rings. The first, a wide, undulating ribbon of gold, holds a large, beautifully cut diamond. The other is a narrow band of white gold, with two small sapphires. The two rings magically nestle together to make an attractive combination of intertwined yellow and white, with the gemstones touching. The diamond must be nearly a carat. I'm not a diamond fan, but this is a beautiful piece of art.

I can't help but slip it on to see if it fits. It's perfect. He must have guessed at the size, which is pretty amazing, considering we hardly held hands. I only surmise this ring is mine. All knowledge of our upcoming marriage is second-hand. He was a weird duck. Maybe he had some sort of behavioral affliction that wouldn't allow him to express his emotions. We'll never know.

The Reggae rhythm of *Stir It Up* bursts out from my cell phone, pulling my attention away from the wedding ring.

"Hello?"

"Roe, where have you been? Your phone's been busy for over an hour!"

"I was talking to someone. What's up Enrique?"

"Wonder if you remember we're having an art opening tomorrow and the village Art Walk is this evening." I can hear voices in the background. "I opened the doors and people are already browsing. Are you coming in this morning?"

"Oh, gosh." I glance at the clock and see it's past ten. "I'm sorry. It's later than I thought." I look at my clothes, the open boxes on the porch and the unfed dog and cat. "I'll be there in forty-five minutes."

With Meg brushed and the cat feasting on breakfast, I dress in Indian print harem pants and a light silk blouse. I quickly push the boxes inside the house, line them up along the wall, and lock the front door. The house will stink like smoke when I return, but now they seem like evidence, and I need to protect them. For good measure, I grab the cat hair endowed shawl and cover the boxes. Now, they look like a hassock. I add a couple of throw pillows for good measure. My phone rings with the theme from the television show, *M.A.S.H.* "I'm on my way," I tell Eve.

As I search for my glasses, I notice the metal box with the notebook and ring is still on the kitchen counter. I toss the ring case into the towel drawer and slide the notebook into my purse. I'll take time to read it later. I lock the back door, something I never do, on the way to the garage. "This is overkill," I tell Meg, as we hop into my old pickup and drive away.

As much as I expect stress in the gallery, it proves to be a joy. The best part is none of the summer tourists know my story. No one asks me how I am and how I managed to burn hundreds of acres of prairie and rescue a teenage girl from human traffickers. There is no mention of snakes, bad guys, internet dating, sex, or crime of any kind.

Eve gathers me up into a hug and tells me how terrific I look. "Getting out into the mountains always does you good," she says, holding me out at arms-length.

"Hey." Enrique looks me up and down, all smiles.

Meg runs to sit at Eve's feet, whining up at her. "What did you do to Meg? She's telling on you."

"Traitor." Meg wags and licks my hand when I squat down to ruffle her fur.

Although Eve keeps adding to the inventory from our store-room, I can see it's going to run short in a couple of weeks. If the business keeps up at this pace, I might have to commit to becoming a real working artist. Tomorrow's opening is our first special show by a non-owner. We have twenty miniatures and larger paintings on consignment from a Montana wildlife artist who lives on the border of Glacier National Park. The way most galleries make money is by selling art from a variety of artists and taking a percentage of the selling price. It works out well for everyone involved. The artists don't have to own a gallery and we don't have to produce all the art. The artist will invite his friends and clients, as well, so we expect quite the turnout.

Eve and I spend most of the afternoon moving artwork around to accommodate the special show, then serve cookies for the Art Walk and finally lock the doors at seven. Enrique invites us up to his apartment for dinner and we enjoy the setting sun pouring in through the west windows while gobbling up his moist homemade enchiladas and Spanish rice.

"I haven't had a chance to tell you I opened JB's boxes this morning."

They stop eating, forks in mid-stroke, between plate and mouth.

"Oh, and a reporter from the New York Times called me for an interview. He's investigating human trafficking. The article should be out already." I thought about my promise. "Oh, damn, I forgot to call Sheriff Trammel. I wanted to tell him about the reporter and the boxes."

Enrique hands me his phone. "Here, I have his cell phone on speed dial. Number three."

I push the number and hear the tiny ring through the speakerphone. "Yea?" I hear Trammel's voice, aggravated, as usual, when he has to talk to Enrique, who he still doesn't trust. "Hi, it's me, Roe. Hope I didn't catch you at a bad time."

A snort explodes through the phone. "Yes, you did catch me at a bad time. I just got off the phone with the FBI. They're pissed as hell about the New York Times article and by the fucking fact I didn't know anything about you talking to them." He pauses a moment. "Oh, sorry, but what the hell were you thinking?"

"I meant to call you right away but got busy at the gallery and forgot all about it." I'm done with guilt. "I'm calling you now."

"Do you realize the position this puts me in? And the danger it puts you in?" I can hear him cover the phone to shout at someone else. "Now the crime family knows we know about them and will be planning their defense. Worse, now everyone in the valley knows they're here and will be expecting me to do something about it and I don't have anything on them."

Eve, Enrique and I look at each other. "I forgot. I haven't even seen the article. He said I was going to be a tiny portion of a larger article. Is it that bad?"

He sounds a bit less threatening and sighs. "Oh, that's probably what he planned, but then he called Kendra and her parents. Now your fiasco rescue dominates almost the whole article. It was the special feature, with sidebars covering the general information. Damn, Roe, it's online. The whole thing has gone viral."

We listen, stunned it had so much impact. "Tell him about the boxes," Eve prompts.

"Listen, Les, I opened JB's boxes. They're full of evidence. You should go pick them up right away. They're inside my front door." I tell him where the key is hidden.

"I'll get someone out there as soon as possible. Did you tell the reporter about the boxes?"

"I don't think so." I thought about it. "No, I'm pretty sure I didn't tell him. I opened them after he called this morning."

"Good. That's one good thing. Sometimes that's all ya get." Trammel slammed down the phone.

CHAPTER THIRTY THREE

"Do you think he's really as mad as he sounds?" I look at my two companions. "I mean, it can't be that bad. Does he even know what viral means?"

Enrique taps away on his iPad. "Hmmm. Well, I see that three people have shared the article on my Facebook timeline and I don't even have very many friends on here. My Abuela wants to know if this crazy woman is the one I met in the desert. She thinks any land outside the village is the desert."

"That doesn't mean anything. They know you live here and they thought you'd be interested," says Eve to Enrique, trying to downplay it for my benefit.

"Clicking the article takes me not to the newspaper website, but to a site that copies and sends out top articles of the day. I see the Huffington Post reposted it, and when I go to share, it says it's been shared over one million times since it was published a few hours ago. I have no idea what constitutes viral, but that's a lot of people reading this article." Enrique continues to click from page to page. "Hey, look at these comments. Looks like you're the next superhero, Roe."

He hands over the iPad and I read comments ranging from hero worship to crazy woman to wishes I would be more careful.

"Look at these," I say, pointing down lower on the page. They drag their chairs around the table so we can read together. "They look like threats."

Eve reads out loud, "Keep your nose out of other people's business." "Watch out, you might be next." "Stop talking about something you don't understand." This one's short-"Stupid Bitch."

Enrique takes back his iPad, "Well, at least there aren't too many bad comments. It looks like most are in favor of what you did. We don't really care what anyone says, we love you anyway." Eve and Enrique glance at each other behind my back. Enrique continues, "Actually, this stupid bitch statement could have been posted by any law enforcement officer between here and North Dakota. Sheriff Trammel and his counterpart in McKenzie County were pretty pissed off you got yourself so involved. They said things you'd never want to hear."

I repeat for them the dressing down I got from the dispatcher. "They're the ones that deserve those criticisms. The sheriff's department blew me off when I called for help. And besides, they might not have rescued those girls for months, or ever, if it hadn't been for my interference." Waving my hand in dismissal I say, "It's past history. We got out alive and that's all that matters."

"Please, don't go off on your own again," says Eve, as she carries dishes to the kitchen sink.

I stand up to head home. Eve beats me to the door, waves and runs down the stairs. "See you tomorrow. I'm on call until two in the afternoon and making jewelry between callouts, but will pop in to help out. The catering is all set up with Kelly this time. They'll bring everything." The back door clicks shut.

"I'll see you early tomorrow." I carry the rest of our plates over to the sink and Enrique says he'll wash up. "I bought a shelving unit for the gallery and Pryor made a beautiful bench out of rough cut larch for the larger pieces. We need to attach the legs. It seems like a million little details need to happen at the last moment." Enrique walks me to the car. The sun is still up, and I consider jumping off the pier for a swim before heading home but it's not to be.

Yosemite Sam's fierce face lights up my phone screen, accompanied by a shrill old-fashioned phone ring. "Hey, Sheriff T," I give the jaunty greeting hoping he has recovered from our earlier call. "Did you get an invite to our opening tomorrow? It's from five in the afternoon, until eight. There will be lots of food."

"Yea, I'll be there if I can. Where are you? Are you headed home yet?"

"Leaving the gallery right now. Did you get the boxes from my house?"

He sighs. "Not exactly." Another long sigh. "Nothing is easy if it concerns you. As my deputy was coming down the highway, he almost got t-boned by a black SUV barreling out of your driveway. We tried to pull the license plate number from his car's dashcam, but no luck."

"Is my house ok?" I hold up the phone so Enrique can hear. "Everything seems to be neat. We'll need you there to verify if anything's missing. We couldn't find any cardboard boxes, so maybe they got them." He sighs again and mutters something. "My deputy is still there and two highway patrolmen joined him, as backup. When can you be there?"

Enrique calls over my shoulder, "We'll be there in ten minutes."

"You don't have to come. There are three officers waiting for me."

He put his hand on my shoulders to steer me out the back door. "I'll follow you out there. You have a lot of work to do here tomorrow. I don't want you getting lost along the way."

We pull our cars in next to the three law enforcement vehicles. Neighbors are on the front porch with the officers, concerned about what's happening. Maybe they were the ones who posted the *stupid bitch* comment, for bringing danger to our rural neighborhood. We all live across pastures or through the woods from each other, a loose association of farms and homes. Still, we tend to take care of each other's homes and animals like an unorganized, but effective neighborhood watch program. These neighbors live behind me and noticed the flashing lights through the woods.

"We stopped by to see if you were ok," says Mrs. Don Harris. They aren't much older than me, but I started calling them Mr. and Mrs. when they moved in two years ago and never changed. I don't even know her first name. Mrs. Harris slips her arm through her husband's, to lead him away. "Wanted to make sure you were safe, dear, after your little adventure," she says in her no-nonsense way. "We'll leave you to it, whatever it is," she adds, waving as she marches Mr. Harris down to their car. They'd parked way off the driveway, probably on one of the sprinkler heads.

The sheriff's deputy turns out to be Detective Elliot, whom we met at our first interview with Sheriff Trammel. He and Enrique shake hands and he introduces us to the two highway patrolmen.

"I put your key back in its hiding place. It doesn't look like anyone got into your house, but we couldn't find the three boxes."

I lead the way through the door. Relief rushes over me, as I scoop up the scarf and pillows. "Here they are." The three boxes sat as I had left them this morning.

"Good disguise," says Elliot. "We'll take these off your hands now." The two highway patrolmen help him carry the boxes to the trunk of his car. They drive off as Elliot returns to the house. "We're going to send someone here to stand watch tonight."

"Thanks, that would be comforting, but would they come back after almost being caught?" I'm grateful, but it's awkward to accept the help. "Am I'm taking advantage of the sheriff's department? You have more important things to take care of." A few months ago, I would have protested loudly and send them packing. I want them here, but I still don't want to appear helpless. "I store a loaded shotgun by my bed, so maybe I'll be ok."

"That's your right, Roe, but don't get trigger happy and blow the deputy away. I'll warn him to stay outside the house. He's bringing his German shepherd, so please don't shoot her either."

"Look out for grizzly bear, mountain lion and coyotes around here. He should keep her on a leash, so she won't run off and get eaten," I say.

"I'll let him know that, as well." We all turn to watch a car come down the driveway. "Here he is now." The deputy and his German shepherd jump out of the car and rush up the path. "This is Deputy Clive Johnson and Camie." We all shake hands and fuss over Camie. I convince Enrique to return to the gallery in case it gets targeted. We wouldn't want anything to happen there tonight either. Elliot promises he will send patrols through town all night.

I make Clive a thermos of strong coffee and clean the kitchen. It's then I notice the empty metal box and remember the book in my purse. I should have given it to the sheriff. If I can get through a few pages tonight, I'll feel better about giving it up tomorrow. Instead, I reread the first page, stick it under my pillow and fall into an exhausted sleep.

The house and the gallery are still standing the next morning. Pryor shows up early to help me hang the shelf and assemble the heavy table. Jackson brings scones hot from his oven and Enrique pulls espresso shots and hands out creamy, smooth lattes to all of us. Is this heaven or what?

"Will you adopt me?" Pryor asks, closing his eyes as he takes another bite of the buttery huckleberry scone. We'd moved four chairs out onto the sidewalk to soak up the morning sun peeking through the mountains, trees and buildings across the street.

"Who, me?" Jackson asks. We all laugh, and Jackson puts his arm around Pryor's shoulders. Pryor shrugs him off with a groan.

"No! Roe. She leads a charmed life." He leans over to look at me around Jackson's barrel chest. "Things you love seem to show up in your life. Can't beat this morning continental breakfast, the sunshine, the art, and who doesn't like hanging around town with friends early in the morning before all the crowds show up?"

Nodding agreement, I smile at him and lean back against the wall, closing my eyes. Is that what last week was? Something I wanted in my life? Am I an adrenalin and danger junkie? "Not always," I say. "Sometimes things happen by accident."

"You might see it that way," says Enrique. "But by taking the first step, and then the next, and the next, the unexpected happens. It could be construed as an accident, but if you follow the crumbs, you'll find your way back to the starting point."

"You're talking about the quantum entanglement theory, Dude," Jackson adds. "Because you knew Kendra, your particles finally got together with hers. You knew her, JB knew her, the credit union dude knew JB, and people you met at the oil drilling supply shop knew Kendra and JB. It's like a web or a net. It was inevitable. You never thought about finding her and you never would have if you had been looking for her," says Jackson. "Funny how ideas keep coming around. Remember when we started hearing about this in the '60's?"

"Dude, you were only a baby in the '60's," Enrique points out, mimicking Jackson's overuse of the dude word.

"My mom was into all the new science stuff. She was ahead of her time. She thought famous scientists were rock stars," Jackson huffs. "She actually flew to California to meet Einstein at a physics convention before I was born. Imagine graduating from Stanford with a degree in physics, then you get married and end up teaching general science in Tamarack Falls, Montana. I always felt bad for her. Whenever one of us kids wanted to try something new that Dad didn't approve of, which was most things, he'd say, 'You may as well fly off to see Einstein.'"

I sigh. "Sometimes it's a relief when someone negative leaves our lives." They all lean over to look at me, eyebrows raised. "I didn't mean it like that, Jackson. It's not good that your dad is dead. I loved your dad. And he just didn't know how to cope with people thinking outside the box." I try to redeem myself. "But, as long as we remember and feel the guilt, shame or a sense of inferiority from something someone said to us as kids, they may as well still be here, sticking it to us every day."

"Damn," says Pryor. "Now I'm feeling bad about what I said to a kid at school last April when I was subbing for middle school woodshop. Told the little shit no one would ever love him if he didn't shape up. It seems kids are behaving worse and worse in lower grades every year." He looks down at a cigarette butt someone had thrown on the ground yesterday. "I'll be more careful next year." He uses his napkin to sweep up the butt.

After a few more minutes, Enrique says, "Well, it's been fun exploring the inner psyche over our morning coffee, but maybe we'd like to come back to Roe's charmed life, which is really a lot of hard work."

As we stand, the first cars creep down the street heading for the café and shopkeepers appeared with brooms to sweep sidewalks. The village is doing its morning stretch and everyone waves and smiles. I love this place. Even with the flaws, it's nicer than anyplace else I've lived.

Pryor and Jackson fold the chairs, I gather the mugs onto the tray and Enrique holds the door for us.

Jackson rearranges paintings, sorting the new show into some magical order for hanging. He certainly has a knack that I don't. When he's finished, the wall looks like one piece of art. He adds my three huge paintings, a triptych, that I haven't had the courage to show. A little card taped to the wall next to it shows an exorbitant price and the title: Through the Thin Veil.

Pryor and Enrique carry boxes and shelves into the gallery from the storeroom while I heft the toolbox from my car. We set to work, reading instructions and assembling, completely absorbed in our tasks when the door opens.

"Well, isn't this cozy," smirks Sheriff Trammel. "Roe, when you decide to do something, seems like the whole town gets involved."

"Aren't you exaggerating a bit?" I say, trying to smile at his sarcasm. "By the way, thanks for your help last night. We made it without a hitch."

"Yeah, well, we sure could have used those boxes right away. If those guys had got 'em first, we'd have never found some of these girls. Now it looks like there are over a hundred we have leads on."

Enrique steps up next to me. I think he's more offended than I am at how Trammel tells the story like it was my fault in the first place. "Isn't that great? If Roe hadn't taken the initiative to go pick up those boxes, no one might have heard from those girls again."

Unphased, Trammel continues. "One box was empty except for packing material. What can you tell me about that, Miss Stone?"

Oops, I should have put something in that box, maybe the metal container and the ring. I'm not quite ready to give up the notebook. "I must have thrown it into one of the other boxes and not noticed." I'm still a lousy liar and my face turns red as the men look on.

"Those other two boxes have inventory sheets. The third box didn't have a list." Sheriff Trammel crosses his arms over his ample chest, waiting.

Oh, what the hell. "It was a ring and a notebook. I'm sure I packed them into one of the boxes." Trammel glares at me. "No? Then maybe they're at my house. I'll bring them to the reception tonight and you can pick them up here. How about that?"

"Don't forget," Trammel says, hitching up his utility belt and striding out the door.

All thoughts of gallery show come to a screeching halt and my co-workers stand in a line, as though awaiting my blessing. I owe them an explanation. Maybe Pryor won't be so excited about that adoption now. "Ok, ok. I guess I forgot to mention the boxes, Pryor." I go over to the espresso machine to pull another shot for my second latte of the morning. "Anyone else?" They all shake their heads. "Can we work as we talk? This has to be finished in the next hour."

They slowly pick up their tools and stand poised in a tableau of carpenters, awaiting my next word. I sigh and pick up the electric screwdriver. I run the power tool over the next half-dozen screws lined up on the side of the bookshelf. I'm screwed, I'm not screwed, I'm screwed, I am not screwed. I can't decide if I should celebrate, or if I should hide out from whoever was in that big black SUV yesterday. My merry men can do nothing but follow my example and work.

CHAPTER THIRTY FOUR

"First, we have to be on the same page. You cannot mention any of this, to anyone." I look each one in the eye. "Agreed?" They all nod.

Information about inventory sheets, cell phones, applications and books pour out in a helter-skelter order. "The third box was fresh, a new box, completely sealed with packing tape. Inside was a metal box, maybe an old ammo box, something you could pick up at Army Surplus. Not like a shoebox. More a cake carrier." I notice Enrique's lips compress into a thin line and his eyebrow caterpillars squeeze together. "You know, sort of flat and wide. Almost square."

I pick up a shelf and Pryor helps push it into pre-cut grooves. I screw the six screws through the end and into the shelf through the pre-drilled holes. Enrique taps wooden plugs into the pre-sunk holes to cover the screw heads. "Everything is pre-done on these kits. Why isn't life preset?" I ask. "It would take out so much of the guesswork."

"Boring," says Jackson.

We set the shelf upright against the wall. It was slightly A-framed, with the bottom shelf about two feet longer than the top. I don't love it, but maybe it will be ok for this show. Enrique runs the vacuum over the particleboard crumbs on the carpet and I dust the shelves.

"And?" Pryor looks expectant as he places small drums and pottery on the top shelf. I'm sure this adds the right amount of suspense to his otherwise predictable day.

"In the metal box was a wedding ring set. Very artsy and shiny."

"Whose ring was it?" Pryor asks.

I had to think about that. On the flight back from North Dakota, Kendra told the others about JB's plan to marry me. It didn't seem relevant to pass that information on to anyone else. I guess people will find out now.

"It was for me, Pryor. JB wanted to marry me." I shrug my shoulders. "He hadn't had time to tell me about it."

Pryor looks stunned, as though the thought of my being married never entered into his mental universe. "Wow. Would you have said yes?" He looks around at the others. "You would have been married to a criminal. That's scary." In his mind, he must already be adopted. He sounds very protective. "Listen, if we knew then what we know now, she wouldn't have accepted his proposal." Jackson tried to steer the conversation out of this loop. Pryor would have none of it.

"You need protection from yourself and your girlfriends. Weren't they the ones who signed you up on that stupid dating website? Those things should be banned." He's on a roll now. "Maybe you should run it by us, next time you accidentally get involved with a strange man."

I lock eyes with Enrique. With a snort, I pack up the last of the tools and take them into the storage room. Involved—a word with many meanings. Enrique was the strangest man I've been mixed up with, but not in Pryor's sense of the word. More like entangled, as Jackson would say. It makes me shiver.

"There was also a notebook in the box, which I happen to have right here." I reach behind the counter and pull it from my purse.

"You, Ms. Straight-laced, lied to the Sheriff?" Pryor says, suddenly blushing, having blurted out loud one of the nicknames they all had for me. The three men look at me, eyebrows lifted, Mona Lisa smiles on each face. I guess I've made up for my poor taste in dating partners.

"You boys finish arranging the show while I read you a story." They scurry to grab paintings and weavings to show their keenness. I begin at the simplest place, the beginning.

For Rosetta Stone. If you are reading this, I'm either missing or dead.

I look up to see if they're working and wait until they get into motion.

My darling lady, by now you may have found out I am involved in an unsavory profession. It was never my intention to make my living by hurting folks, but that's how it turned out. I finally risked a change over the past few years. Kendra is working for my friends at Jake's Ropes and Dopes in Williston. I made her promise to call her mama, but you know how kids are. If you have these boxes, then you already understand. Many of the others are working in Williston, or elsewhere in North Dakota. I negotiated high salaries and decent living space for all of them.

The next page has Jake's address and phone number, plus a description of the location, including a little hand-drawn map, as well as Kendra's job description. "Every application had a detailed destination at the bottom," I explain to the men. "A few employees were sent to other states, like Wyoming, Pennsylvania, and Texas."

Enrique looks at me. "Dead men can't know how easily their earthly plans go awry."

JB's neat writing continues.

> *I started as a small-town Texas boy, knowing I was some-how destined to help folks. I had no idea how it would happen. Our town was so poor even the possums left. I found a Dallas newspaper in the motel trash one night and saw a job listing that fit my high school English teach-er perfectly, so I told her about it. When she got the school administration job in Dallas, she sent me two hundred dollars from her first paycheck in a thank you note. That was more money than my mama and I saw in a month of Sundays.*

> *After that, I started going to the county library, reading the classifieds every day. My friend, Buddy, helped me copy down the jobs, and I started a list of local people who had skills for those jobs on the back of old library catalog cards the librarian gave us. I read the rest of the newspaper and found there was an infinite world out there waiting for me. After I found jobs for two more people, folks started calling me to ask if I knew anyone who could do such-and-such or if I knew of a certain job nearby, they could do. A lot of the jobs were temporary, but there was no job service to sign up at, so I guess we were the first.*

"Sounds like he had a good thing going back then." Pryor continues to place drums and small weavings on shelves. Jackson follows behind to rearrange.

> *I'm telling you this to let you know you would have loved me back then. Maybe you love me now, but I'm not sure. I've shut down the vulnerable part of my mind. It would burn up my heart to empathize with the people I've sold into slavery. There's no other word for it. I read in the newspaper they are calling it modern slavery. There's*

nothing modern about it. It's the same old sex and labor dealings that have been around for thousands of years. Entire countries and industries were built with slave labor. If you're reading this and I'm not right there in front of you, you already know all about me. It makes me sad because I stopped doing it over a year ago and I wanted to explain in person. I even told the Godfather I was quitting. I've helped him out so many times with other needs, he is letting me go. At least that's what he told me.

This was news. Buddy didn't know or he would have told me.

"Sounds like the poor guy was trying to go straight," Pryor sounds sorry for him.

"Damn him." Jackson slams his fist on the shelf, causing all the drums to roll to the side and the paintings hanging on the wall nearby to slant off-kilter. "He should have never started. The dude knew it was wrong from the get-go. He should have kept his sorry ass out of here."

"He must have known about this area from his connection to the crime family," Enrique adds. "He wanted to stop, but he didn't."

"What?" I ask. "How do you know?"

"Remember that calendar Detective Elliot showed us? It had other girls on dates throughout the month and even beyond the time he helped Kendra."

Jackson mumbles under his breath, "If you can call that help."

"He might have thought he was stopping, but he was delusional," Enrique adds.

"He claims to have placed those girls in legitimate jobs, like Kendra," I say, pleading a case for JB's innocence.

"Yea and how'd that work out?" said Jackson.

I put up my hands to stop him from continuing. "We won't know anything about the people on his list until the sheriff checks them out."

"It's sort of sad and pathetic. He couldn't walk away from it," Pryor says, still trying to sound, for my sake, like the guy wasn't a complete waste.

"I'd always thought no one could quit the Mafia." I look down at the notebook. "Maybe he was strongly encouraged to do a few more before he quit." I made air quotes around the word quit. "Maybe they would have killed him if he stopped doing his job."

"Maybe that's what they did," Enrique says and looks away.

I point to the words in the notebook, leaning close, trying to keep my voice steady.

> At the Central Credit Union, you will find three accounts in your name. One is only in your name, and you are the beneficiary on the others. I used to share those with my business partner, Buddy. I took him off almost a year ago and started paying him a salary. He can go through money like hot molasses running through a sieve. Hopefully, you'll never meet him. He loves the hurting part of the job. I don't know how he ended up like this, since we were so much alike as youngsters. I'm sure the credit union will sort it out. The house at the golf course is in your name, as is the Mustang. I hope you enjoy them both if I am gone. If I'm in prison, maybe you can wait for me. I won't hold it against you if you don't.

I look at my friends. The Mustang insurance payoff was high, considering its short life. I'd donated the money to the volunteer fire department for helping me out at Larsen Spring Lake. Most of the forty K went to help pay off the new ambulance and the rest toward training new recruits. I turn the page.

> I'm fairly sure the local Mafia knows all about you, where you live, your gallery. I can't see them bothering you since you knew nothing about my business. Here are the names of the

worst of them and the most likely to cause local trouble. A few names are not on the list; my misplaced loyalties. After time passes, maybe I'll get over it and add those names, too.

The boys came to peer over my shoulder, reading down the list of mostly Italian names. We'd never heard of them, except one, for whom Pryor had installed kitchen cabinets.

You would never know from looking at them their whole life is funded by crime. I had some good times with these guys and their families. They seem so normal. Maybe they are. They moved here because it was a better place to raise their kids and grandkids. They are like everyone else, looking for the same good things in life. Their older kids, of course, hate it. I think most of them will move back to the city after a short time in the quiet country.

"The sheriff needs this list." Enrique brings out his phone. "Not yet," I say, holding up my hand. "Let's see it to the end."

I scroll quickly, page after page, to the last section. "The last half of the book is labeled *Insurance Policy*. What can that mean?" I thumb through the pages, reading to myself and the blood drains from my face.

Jackson acts as my chauffeur, driving me home to change for the reception and feed the animals. On the way back, we stop at his place to pick up his version of dressy clothes, consisting of clean jeans and short-sleeved shirt, a summer weight tweed jacket from the thrift store and an antique silk tie I gave him last Christmas. We decide to walk to the gallery; even at this early hour, downtown parking is a headache. The evening is hot, but the trees and the river make it feel ten degrees cooler.

We rest against a stack of firewood behind a neighborhood garage, catching the cool breeze coming up the slope. We descend the long stone and cement staircase leading into the village. The lush foliage of ivy, tall purple phlox and columbines line the stairs, and willow trees shade the path. Slippery patches of moss grow along the edges of every step. "Oof." Jackson suddenly lurches forward, almost collapsing on my back. He grabs the central pipe railing, catching us both at the last minute.

"What happened?" I ask, turning to steady him in my arms. "Are you all right?"

"I don't know. Look at my back and tell me." I maneuver around and find a huge dirty spot in the middle of his jacket. He leans down to rub his twisted ankle.

"Look." I point to the ground. A short, thick branch lay on the stairs next to us. "Could that have fallen off the tree and hit you on the back? It looks heavy."

Jackson doubles over, gasping, trying to catch his breath. He takes me by the arm and begins to descend the stairs. No more strolling. "Yea, that's it. Let's get to the gallery before anything else happens." His limp slows our descent, but once on the flats, we rush down the middle of the street.

We make the two-block traverse without getting involved in any conversations. It's hard to smile and walk on when everyone you meet wants to gab. I invite them all to the art opening to make up for it and hope we have enough food. Members of the Chamber of Commerce, all women, are unloading and stacking orange cones along the side of my building. "A Chamber woman's work is never done," I say. Indicating the cones, I ask, "What's this about?"

"Fourth of July Parade in a few days. Can we store these here until then? Sorry we didn't ask earlier, but I discovered it on the to-do list this afternoon." Benny has been the Chamber Chairperson since January. She'd started a clothing design company in the office space over the liquor store three years ago, and finally has time to volunteer for a few of our hundred-and-one town projects. She couldn't know everything the first year. She'd moved here alone from New York City, by her accent, even though she always claims it was Maine. She's friendly, but no one knows her very well. I tease her about being in a witness protection program, which is my go-to answer to all mysterious people.

"Sure, they're not in the way. Are you making it to the reception tonight? We'd love to see you here." Benny nods and heads back to her studio. Jackson disappears into the gallery and returns with Enrique at his side. They look worried—frowns slash across their faces, foreheads wrinkled. "Is Kelly late with her catering crew?" Kelly agreed to have the Firehouse Café cater this art opening. After the fiasco of our first one, I hope it will be without a hitch. "What's up?" They lead me clear to the back and into the storeroom.

Enrique turns to me. "I hear you had an accident on the downtown stairs."

"Not me, but I saved Jackson's sorry ass from a tumble." I punch Jackson on the arm. "How's the back and ankle? You're not limping too much."

He holds up the jacket. The dirt brushed cleanly off, but there is a thin gouge right in the middle of the back. "It's not complete toast, but I'll need to visit the thrift store to replace it soon."

"Listen, I'll pay for it. Get what you want." I hang my purse in the closet and take a few steps into the gallery.

Enrique grabs my arm. "Wait a second." I turn back to look at them and see trouble written all over their faces. "Jackson didn't want me to say anything until after the reception, but I knew you'd be upset to learn it later. I think we should all be forthcoming from here on. We're dealing with hard-core criminals and must stay vigilant for our everyone's safety."

"What happened? Is Eve ok? She should be here by now."

"She called to say she'd be here in thirty minutes. They had to rescue people from a boating accident, but she's off shift now. No, this is about the stairs." Enrique looks to Jackson to take up the story.

"It sounds crazy," says Jackson, "but that wood didn't fall off the tree, it was thrown."

"What?" I didn't mean it to come out so flat and nasal, like the looser buzzer on a quiz show.

"Listen, you don't have to believe me." He gives Enrique the I-told-you-so look. "It would have hit my head or shoulders if it fell from the tree. This thing hit so hard in the middle of my back; it knocked the wind out of me. Besides, I recognized that branch from the stack of firewood we were leaning against at the top of the stairs."

"So, maybe it was kids. Was it attempted murder by firewood?" Damn, not my best answer. "Sorry. So, what does it mean?"

Jackson says, "It means the mob is threatening us. Giving us a taste of what's to come or maybe what's going to happen until they accidentally kill us off." His fingers bent into quotation marks around the word accidentally. "We need to be careful."

"They think we know things. They think JB told you about them and their operation and that you are going to tell the sheriff or the FBI. They assume you've shared that information with your friends and partners."

"Well, he didn't tell me anything. We figured it out by ourselves. I shared some of it with that New York Times reporter." My hands fly up to cover my mouth. "Oh, God." I realize the little mistakes I've already made. "I shouldn't have read you those journal entries. We'll let them, whoever they are, know that I know nothing."

"A little late now since that reporter's story went viral," Jackson says. He paces around the storeroom to calm down.

"We don't know how or why JB died, but we do know he was trying to get out from under the mob." Enrique touches my shoulder. "It could have been a coincidence he died within months of telling them."

"Or not," mumbles Jackson. "You know they won't stop until we're all dead. We're nothing but loose ends to them to be cut off and discarded. We'll need to be on high alert for the rest of our lives."

"We don't need to be cautious; we need to be smarter," I say. "We need to give them a reason to protect us."

The aroma of warm cookies drifts in from the gallery. Let the party begin.

CHAPTER THIRTY FIVE

Eve presses a red dot onto the label of one of her small weavings to show it is sold. At least two dozen other labels around the walls and shelves indicated sold art pieces. Our featured artist is a hit. I figure a hundred people have come through our doors so far, and we're only halfway through the three-hour reception. Many of the early guests have already left for their reservations at local restaurants. The familiar pattern of dinner, followed by a live musical theater production, began in May, and will continue through August.

Eve and I circulate, promoting the artwork. Enrique runs the cash register and Jackson mans the espresso machine and wine bar. The caterers keep the food platters fresh and help with the wine. It is like a well-choreographed dream, as Pryor pointed out this morning. Only three people mention the Kendra connection. It's already stale news.

Eve beckons me over to introduce a potential buyer. They're standing in front of the three large paintings I'd finished last month. As I lay in the hospital, the vision of the painting came to me. It had to be large. I'd always painted smaller works but felt the idea seemed too unmanageable for one painting. I couldn't wrap my brain around how to move the piece, so I divided it into thirds, a triptych. To me, it's one painting, as I had seen in my vision.

I hold out my hand. "Hi, how can I help you?"

Eve introduces us. Leo Bonato takes my hand in both of his. "You are the artist of these paintings? You must have been truly inspired."

I tell him about my vision and my long hospital stay. It never hurts to show some vulnerability to potential clients. "I guess it was a forced vacation, the kind where boredom sets in after two days and your mind finally starts to wander."

"Oh, that sounds wonderful," says Leo. "I don't think that's happened to me since I was a boy." He turns back to the paintings. "What were you trying to say here and here? There are so many interesting places to go in this landscape." He gazes into my eyes, questioning. My heart turns a somersault. No one has ever admired and analyzed my paintings before. "It is a landscape, isn't it?"

Art lovers are never wrong because everyone has an interpretation relative to their experiences up to this point in their lives. "Yes, it is sort of a landscape. What do you see?"

"Come." He links his arm around mine and guides me across the room. The paintings are so large they benefit from a longer view. "From here, it looks like mountains with forests in the background. Not the thick pine forests of Montana, but maybe cottonwoods along the rivers. It could even be open oak forests of the eastern seaboard."

I haven't heard that phrase for a long time. My mother used it when she talked of visiting my dad's family who spread themselves between Connecticut and Delaware, in that little armpit at the top of the country, before it reaches out toward Maine. The eastern seaboard—I suppose the expression is still in circulation. In Montana, we don't spend much time thinking about anything east of eastern Montana.

"Are you from the east then?" I look at Mr. Bonato. His clothes are expensive and nicely tailored to fit his chunky frame. Nicely styled salt and pepper hair covers his handsome head. He's fit, but not a runner. He might lift weights at a gym or hike in the summer, or maybe ski. I guess his age to be between fortyish and sixty.

"Oh, yes. Most of my family is still there. You know how it gets into your heart that you must move to Montana, but it gets into everyone else's head this is only a primitive frontier?"

"I know exactly what you're talking about." We have a chuckle over all the things people mistakenly think about Montana; snowed-in all winter, wolves on your back porch, nothing to do, no place to shop, running out of food, out of fuel, out of heat.

"Nevertheless, I built a home in the north valley, not too far out of town. It's a beautiful property, with a creek and pond in the pasture and tennis courts near the barn. Things to entertain the family and friends when they come to visit. I expect the grandchildren to learn skiing so they will come in the winter also."

My business brain begins to kick in and I bring him back to the artwork. "What do you see in the rest of the painting?"

"Here, here and here," he says, indicating places on each painting. "These seem to be ethereal beings, perhaps angels. Perhaps they are having a picnic, maybe a party or a business meeting. Who can know?" He laughs. "What do you say they are doing?"

I've never dissected one of my paintings this way. Maybe I'm turning a corner in my art. I've never considered them as having meaning. It has always been fun and challenging to reproduce a waterfall or a wolf, but I never found the story. This is different. It came from somewhere deeper. Talking about these paintings, as if we were in the Louvre, examining the Mona Lisa for hidden meanings, makes me laugh. "Oh, your interpretation is as good as anything I've come up with. Inspirations don't come with an owner's manual. It's a blueprint, an idea that needs to be expressed.

I like the idea they might be at a business meeting. I'll have to think about the business interests of angels." Falling back into my current default mode for a moment, I fleetingly think maybe this is their last supper, a business meeting to end all meetings.

Leo buys the three paintings, plus a few drums, necklaces and a weaving. He asks that I deliver them personally to advise him on where to hang or arrange the pieces. We chose a time the next morning. Jackson agrees to let me borrow his hippy van and help me deliver. Leo says it isn't necessary, as he has staff to help with the lifting. He adds a promise of the best espresso I've ever tasted and we part company. With a little bow, he is gone.

I follow him to the door and watch as he approaches a silver Cadillac parked up the street. A man hops out of the driver's seat and scurries around to open the back door. Beyond them, I notice Benny walking with friends toward the gallery, wearing one of her flowing, colorful creations. I have to get one of those tunics to further promote my new, artistic personality.

Leo steps out to meet her, gesturing to her clothing. She waves her friends on toward the gallery. Good, I thought, more business for more people. I pull out the little notebook I carry, to jot down instructions to Leo's house and mark the tags of artwork he purchased. These must have been truly inspired, as my new friend Leo suggested, because this is more money than I've made from my previous life of occasionally selling artwork. Leo talked about his family, but never mentioned a wife, nor did he wear a deflector ring on the third finger of his left hand. Maybe the cliché was true, when one door closes, another door opens.

A few minutes later, Leo's gleaming Caddy passes the gallery. I expect Benny to come flying in and tell me exciting news about orders and sales. She never appears, so I return to the front of the gallery. Through the window, I see Benny slowly wandering down the sidewalk. Did she forget about the reception? I open the door to yell after her, but she tucks her chin and runs across the street, pushing through the door to her studio. That's weird. Back at the wine table, I find her friends are unconcerned. One of them offers, "You know how she is. When an idea strikes, she loses all focus on the outside world until she gets it on paper."

Sheriff Trammel enters with the next wave of guests, looking dapper in his old corduroy jacket and chinos. A bolo tie strung through a huge elk antler burr stands out against his dark blue shirt. A path seems to part before him, as he walks right up to Eve. She gives him a friendly hug. I don't think he gets enough hugs. She walks him over to the wine table and chooses a glass of red. He looks around, sees me and doesn't look so happy anymore. Eve takes his arm to steer him on a tour of the new artwork. People greet him as they move about the gallery, but no one else hugs him.

"Do you think it's lonely?" I say to Jackson. "Sheriff is such a powerful position. I wonder if he has many friends."

"Oh, I don't know. The dude is gruff, but most of his longtime acquaintances see right through it."

I nod. Jackson is right. I have a hard time taking him seriously, but he is good at his job. As if reading my mind, Jackson adds, "I heard he was a shy kid in high school, despite the sports trophies." Jackson probably didn't realize I had been there. "But he was near the top of his class at the law enforcement academy. My dad used to talk about it every time we saw Trammel on television. Dad always shook his head in amazement that anyone he knew as a kid could possibly grow up to be successful. Once a kid, always the same introverted kid, with the same kid problems, according to dad."

"Never a prophet in your own hometown," I say, paraphrasing the Bible.

"This is going very well," says Enrique, appearing behind me. "We should celebrate the sale of your paintings. How about dinner out for all of us? Your treat."

Jackson crosses his arms. "Maybe that sale will pay for the wine everyone is drinking up tonight. I don't know why you served it instead of lattes. Do you think we should go to boxed wine next time?"

Enrique and I shrug.

"The visiting featured artist requested it so, we wanted to be accommodating'" I say in mock apology, clinking wine glasses with Enrique. "Let's look for sales and explore wineries. We'll figure it out after a few more receptions."

I motion toward the wine line. Jackson heads toward the wine table to help one of the caterers open more bottles but makes a hard left towards the door when Angel enters, her slinky red jungle-patterned blouse and black silky slacks clinging in all the right places.

"I saw him hauling all that junk out of his house one day and the next, noticed her car in the driveway," I whisper to Enrique. He nods knowingly as if he's been part of our extended family forever. Who is this guy that makes me smile and keeps me on track? I thought he'd be here a few weeks and disappear back into the cottonwoods along the Missouri River. "How's your book? Getting much writing done?"

He smiles. "Actually, I was going to tell you after the reception tonight. I found a publisher."

"What? How? When did you have time?" I give him a quick hug. "That's wonderful." I want to kiss him but think better of it. Not here, not now. I step back a little. First Mr. Bonato, now Enrique; what's the matter with me?

"It's been almost two months since I came here. In the beginning, I organized my old notes and wrote at night. I found that I already had too much material. After consulting an editor friend, I worked on narrowing the focus. It's all done. I might go float the river in September to take some fall photos. Will you chance coming along on a second camping trip with me?"

I laugh, but my stomach both tightens and flutters. "I don't know about that. That idea brings up memories, both hilarious and pathetic." He chuckles and rests his hand on my shoulder. "It could be fun, though," I say. "You set a date and I'll see if I can swing it."

Trammel appears in front of us like a stealth bomber swooping in for the drop. "Hey, big guy, glad you could make it." Enrique seems to be at peace with the sheriff's animosity towards him. They shake hands and Trammel's mouth curves into a closed-lip, introvert smile.

"Thanks for inviting me. It's been…" he looks back at Eve, who's talking to complete strangers like they were long-lost friends. "Good. It's been really good."

"You look nice tonight. I love the bolo tie. They're the in-thing right now." I reached up to examine it closer. Now I could see that the elk antler burr was carved with a delicate outline of a bull elk, with a thin line of blue stone set in the groove.

"Thanks. I made it. My mom showed me how when I was a kid, but I never really got into it. You know how those antlers pile up, season after hunting season." Eve had told me about his stash. "My garage attic is full. Mom always told me the elk gets rid of them every year and so should I, so I figured I better learn to make something." He slips it over his head and hands it to me. "Last summer, I ran out to spend a week of my vacation time with mom, to get a few refresher lessons and eat huckleberry pie. The winter nights are long, so I made a good dent in my antler pile."

"Your mom is still alive? Why didn't I know this? Where is she?"

"She's still living in her little log cabin down past the State Forest Camp, a mile up Camp Creek Road. A couple of the forest rangers and their wives look in on her a couple of times a week and we talk every morning. She had her eightieth birthday last December."

"That's so exciting. I'd love to meet her."

"Yes, well, I'm going back to town now, so I'll be needing that notebook." Trammel stands to his full, overbearing tallness, now instantly all business. The accidental personal reveal is over.

"Right here." He follows me to the storeroom, where I pull the notebook out of my bag. He flips through it.

"Are some pages missing here at the back?" He fingers the smooth edges.

I look at the book. "I don't know. That's how I found it." He stares at me. I don't think he will ever believe anything I say again. For my magician distraction, I hold out the black velvet jewelry box and flip open the lid. "Here are the rings that were with the notebook." He holds them in his open palm, examining them for a full minute. "And here is the photo, and this is the metal box that contained it all." I point to the box on the floor.

"Ok, then." He tosses the ring case, photo and notebook inside the box. "I'll get these back to you after we finish our investigation."

I swear to myself to go home and read those pilfered pages before he gets more suspicious.

CHAPTER THIRTY SIX

I pull into the grocery store parking lot before turning up the county road to Leo's house and check on the artwork in the back of the van. I can't find my toolbox. The picture hangers, hammer and corner pads, my pliers, and other assorted art paraphernalia aren't here. My apprehension from this morning has morphed into determination. I've toughened up during the forty-minute drive. I quickly replace my toolbox contents by buying them from a local framing shop in the mall across the highway.

After driving four miles up the gravel road, I notice the higher addresses and double back towards Leo's driveway. An imposing steel gate blocks the entrance. I noticed this as I passed the first time, but scrutinized the intricate metalwork for so long, that I completely missed the gold-plated address numbers on the stone gate pillars. I stop on the roadway to look at the gate again. I don't know the artist, but I must seek him out for my gallery. The metal herd of Montana animals looks real, and some are life-sized. Blends of dark and pale patinas add shading and highlights to create the illusion of three dimensions. They interact with each other in friendly ways as they gallop along.

I press the intercom button to announce myself. "Is that you, Miss Stone?"

"Yes." I'm surprised to hear Leo's voice. A surge of excitement fills me to see my paintings on the wall of this house.

After reading the rest of JB's journal last night, I also feel sick.

The gate slowly opens inward. The break comes between a leaping deer and a running mountain lion. With the gate closed, they're touching, and look as though they run in tandem. Now it seems that the lion is chasing the deer, outstretched claws raking her flank as she's leaping for her life. I shiver. I wonder if the illusion is intentional.

The driveway snakes through an idyllic aspen forest. The house, barn and fences are stained a lovely shade of dark brown that stand out beautifully against a tall edge of deep green Douglas fir forest running along the far end of a large pasture. A long covered porch extends across this end of the house and there stands Leo, with two tall doors opened behind him. He comes down the few stairs, pointing for me to park at the end of the porch.

"Welcome to my home," he says, opening the van door for me. "So lovely to see you again so soon. Come, come, we will have refreshments." He ushers me onto the porch before I have time to respond. I eye the van, needing to get the artwork out of the sun's heat. "Don't worry, I'll have someone transfer everything into the living room right away. Come. Leave your care in my hands." One hand on my elbow and one hand on my back, he leads me through the portal into his world before I can say another word.

The sumptuous entry is cut off by another set of doors that stand open. I don't have time to examine the beautiful solid wood doors as he hurries me down the wide hallway lined with portraits and antique furniture, resembling a sumptuous castle. We pass other closed doors and finally find a way out at the end.

Leo leads me through a wide arched opening into a beautiful kitchen. A bank of tall windows opens toward the northwest, framing a view of the pasture, dark green forest and the ski mountain in the background. In the distance, inside the trees, is a series of smaller homes. "Are those your neighbors?" I thought that if I had the money, as he does, I'd buy up the view from my house.

"No, no." He smiles as he flips on his espresso machine and waits while it heats up. "Those are guest houses for when family and friends come to visit. It is much easier for them to have space for themselves and their children. I save the house from wear and tear and meet here only for drinks or for business. Over there is the, what do you call it?" He gestures toward the building I'd taken for a barn. "Ah yes, recreation center, filled with games and lots of room for festivities."

"This is lovely. Do you live here alone?

"No, no. Family and business associates come out for meetings or to relax." He smiles. I remember at the gallery that he said he never relaxed. "Right now, is only my staff."

Leo fills a small metal pitcher with milk and clips a thermometer near the handle. His brow furrows with focus. The espresso machine develops very high pressure, so the milk steams quickly. He stops midway to swirl the milk. He finishes steaming in a few seconds. He then pulls two shots of espresso into two cups, the kind you find in Europe, where they haven't developed the need for the jumbo mugs that Americans prefer. He smoothly pours the frothy velvety milk into the cups, stopping below the lip. He tops each with a few spoonfuls of milk foam.

"Tell me how you like that."

I inhale the bittersweet aroma and draw in a tiny sip. "Ah, heavenly." I close my eyes and take another sip and another. Leo claps. "Bravo, this is my best critique. I have the coffee roasted locally and blend it myself right here in this kitchen. I shall call this blend Stone Mountain, after your gallery." We both finish our cappuccinos and then Leo repeats the procedure to prepare seconds. He takes a moment to decorate the top with liquid chocolate circles and run a toothpick through to make a design. We take these cups to the edge of the patio, where the morning sun baked the flagstones. The radiated heat warms my feet and legs. A tall man comes to move the freestanding umbrella into position to keep the sun off our heads.

"Thank you, Carlo. This is Miss Stone who painted those wonderful pictures. Please bring the ladder to the living room so we may hang them after we finish our cappuccinos.

"He's so tall, we may not need a ladder," I kid.

Leo becomes serious. "Yes, he is tall. His first year of professional basketball left him with a serious injury to his kneecap, ending his dream of a sports career. It was a shame, but he came to work for me afterward. That was six years ago. He is very loyal."

I thought that was a funny turn of phrase. "You mean some of your staff are not loyal? What do they do, give away family recipes?" Was it too snide? I didn't know if he'd get the sarcasm. "I'm sorry, it's none of my business."

"It's ok." Leo smiled and nodded. "Most of my employees are with me for a long time, but a few choose different paths. That is their choice. The benefits of staying with me are great." He shrugged, bringing one hand up in an "oh, well" gesture.

I wonder if there's a downside to quitting.

He tells me how wonderful it is to have me as a guest in his home as we finish our second coffee. We talk about the property, the clean air, views of the ski hill and his ski lessons last winter. I'm surprised. "It's a new world," he says.

"Come." He leads the way through open double doors farther down the patio. The living room is as marvelous as the kitchen. A long dining table, made with gouged and saw-marked boards filled in with resin, is stained three different colors and varnished to a high gloss. Ten matching chairs surround the table. "This is delightful," I say, running my hand over the cool wood.

A seven-foot wide fireplace is framed by three feet of stonework on each side and above is a cracked and twisted timber of dry tamarack tree as the mantelpiece. I love everything about this house. The whole place is magical.

The paintings lean up against the hearth. "Choose the order in which to hang them and Carlo will take care of it." I run a line with my laser level, measure and mark spots for the nails and Carlo hangs the paintings. "Now that is delightful," he says, borrowing my word. "What do you think?"

I back across the room, looking at the paintings from different angles. "I have to admit, it looks like the wall was made for them." A bittersweet tightness in the pit of my stomach reminds me I'm parting with something I love. These paintings came from my inner being. My creations. My children. It's hard to leave them. "They are part of me, but I release them to your keeping." I make an exaggerated bow.

He gives me a puzzled look. Carlo nods and seems to understand. He had also lost part of his life, letting it go due to injury, and given himself to Leo. I wonder if he has any regrets.

"Well, I can't take it with me, as a friend recently told me. I can't hoard my inspirations. I have to let them go so that more can come my way." No, there will be no regrets.

Leo shrugs and nods. He hands me one of the drums and he and Carlo carry the other two. We walk around the room, setting them here and there, finding the right spot. "I would hang two on the wall and set this painted one on the bookcase next to it."

We agree on the proper arrangement and Leo sends Carlo to bring the weaving. It's a large tapestry, five feet by four feet.

Leo leads us down a short hallway to what must be his bedroom. This room is so different from the rest of the house that it could be a movie set. The furnishings appear to be old but well kept. He notices my surprise and laughs. "From humble beginnings." He shrugs and laughs again. "This is the bed where my mother brought me into the world. The rest is the furniture of my parents' small home in Naples."

He lovingly runs his fingers across the top of a plain dresser. Two curving arms support the mirror, and their carvings match the bed head and a tall ornate bureau standing against the nearby wall.

"It's very elegant, old-world simplicity. They must have been very proud people and you must have loved them very much." What I thought was that this man wants to prove that it was a long, hard climb from his poor childhood to his present opulence. Or, that the birth into a regular working family is a free pass to being what he is today. Being poor, once, makes everything excusable and his ability to wield power all the more justified.

We hear this drivel from almost every presidential candidate, except if it happened to be a Kennedy or a Bush. It means that he was born into the middle or lower class like you, Everyman, so you can trust him. You'll never make it as far as he has, but you can ride along on his coattails if you play your cards right. I never had much respect for that sort of nonsense, and it must show on my face. Leo is bent over, examining the tapestry spread out upon the bed. I'm sure Carlo is a mind reader. He steps between Leo and me with the protective posture of a bodyguard.

Leo points to the wall opposite the bed. "We should hang it over this fireplace. The muted colors go very well in here, yes? Tell me the meaning again."

"It's called Winter Count Ten. Many Native Americans painted the story of the tribe's year on a buffalo hide, sort of like a journal or diary. It included important events, like hunts, hunger, deaths, births, raids and celebrations. This weaving is number ten in a series showing the important events as if Montana was the tribe. The artist used to do it herself, but the past couple of years, our women's drumming circle has made the list and helped with the weaving."

I am literally saved by the bell from explaining further. My new message alert is the sound of a boxing ring gong. Yosemite Sam glares from my phone.

OUT OF THE DARKNESS

I read the text. *"Bonato is Mafia Don."* I nod to myself. *"Me and the troops are parked outside the gate. Will storm the place if you're not out in twenty minutes."*

"Who is that? Is it important? I hope you don't have to rush off." He seems genuinely disappointed.

"A message from my friend Sheriff Trammel. It's nothing that I didn't already know." I text a short *"all's well"* reply and slip the phone back into my pocket. "I think that's a great place for the tapestry." I explain to Carlo how to hang it and he goes to fetch the ladder, looking back at me as a warning to not do anything foolish.

"I have something for you." I pull out an envelope from my fanny pack and hand it to him.

"Is it a bill for the delivery?" He smiles. "I plan on being very generous with the extra gratuity." He lifts two, folded, one hundred dollar bills from his pocket and thrusts them into my hand.

"No," I say, trying, unsuccessfully, to give them back. "The delivery is on the house. This is something else."

Carlo brings the ladder, hammer, tape measure and nails. He pulls a stud finder out of his back pocket to locate the wood behind the stucco wall for his nails. Leo nods his approval and Carlo blushes with pleasure. "Let us go to the other room." We end up back in the kitchen. The padded chairs around the mosaic topped table mirror the outside colors of deep green trees and cerulean blue sky.

Leo accepts my refusal of another coffee and settles down with the contents of the envelope. He spreads the pages across the table and begins to read. His face first blanches and then turns bright red over the next few seconds. He flips through the four pages quickly, scanning to see that they are similar in content. The date of the first entry is fifteen years ago. It and all the others were clearly rewritten into this one notebook.

The page titled Insurance Policy has an explanation of what follows. Over the past twenty years, three noteworthy criminal events from each year are explained with detailed information of the crime, the proof, the places where evidence is hidden and the importance to this particular crime family. Sometimes the evidence is a paper trail or objects, other times it is people, both living and the murdered. I've redacted the actual clues to the discoverable evidence with a black marker.

"JB started the diary as an insurance policy for himself and his friends when he began working for your organization twenty years ago. It was his winter count," I tell Leo. "JB's sudden, unexplained death in early April set a clock in motion and, from some unknown source, the first five years' worth arrived at the appropriate police departments in the districts where crimes were committed and a copy sent to the FBI."

It's only a matter of time before these agencies begin to find and seize property.

"I'm no fortune teller, Leo, but I predict a long line of court cases in your immediate future. They've had this information since April, so I imagine solving these crimes are works in progress." A purple tinge crosses his forehead and cheeks. I hope he doesn't have a heart attack. That would be sad because he has so much to answer for and death would be such an easy way out.

"I gave you the most recent page, from this year, because there are only two entries; the McKenzie man camp, which is taken care of, and the other, drugs carried to the Bakken oil field will need to come to a halt, because I've already turned this over to the Drug Enforcement. I still have years six through nineteen."

"What is the meaning of this? I had nothing to do with JB's death. He was like a son to me. I do remember him mentioning something about this list, his so-called insurance policy, long ago. He said it as a joke. I thought he was kidding."

"Yes, but he was one of the sons that voiced his disloyalty. He wanted a divorce, a nullified adoption, he wanted to quit the business of human trafficking."

"That is meaningless. You think a normal human being can keep up such a vile activity for long? No. They burn out, as you Americans like to say. We direct them to another profession, one that has less personal contact with people. JB had many talents. His partner did all of the human trade, anyway, and that kind is kept as a mere business associate. I loved JB and treated him well. He would have kept on finding other things for me. It was no problem or threat. I can't believe he didn't trust me."

"Not trust you? No one trusts you, Leo. You're the Mafia, for God's sake." I lean back in my chair. This is a surprise. If Leo didn't have JB killed, who did? "What about his house? Did you blow it up?"

"One of my Captains strongly suggested this action, because we didn't want to take time to search the house. His local man watched and reported you going into the house one afternoon. He decided it was time." Leo waved his hands while he spoke, jabbing the air for emphasis.

"I came to show you that list and to let you know that I've sent my pages out to ten different attorneys around the world in sealed envelopes to be opened in case of my death or if I give the word."

Leo sits up tall looking me in the eyes. "I'm not afraid of this shit. You could disappear at any moment, when you least expect it." His cheeks are bright now, his eyes filled with rage. "I can ruin you, your life, your business, your friends. Plus, they can be taken care of without leaving a ripple."

I lean closer. "If any of my friends, old or in the future, die or are harassed under suspicious circumstances, I will give it all to the FBI. If anyone's business is compromised by a threat, real or imagined, I'll give you up. Harassment means trying to harm in any way, including throwing firewood."

"I heard that you had an encounter with one of my people." Leo chuckled. "It was only a small action made by one trying to please me."

"Small to you, but we could have been badly hurt." I seethed as he smiled at our misfortune. "Hey, this includes Benny. What did you say to her in the street the day you came to my gallery?"

He first looks puzzled. "Ah, my lively Maria," he said, tenting his fingers, as he rested his elbows on the table. "She was the *sposa*, the spouse, of one of my employees. She found out his business and turned state's evidence of his operation in exchange for immunity and protection. I usually find this kind of person, but she eluded me, so it was a happy accident that I came to your gallery on that special night."

Wow. I've finally guessed right about witness protection. "She is included in my friends, regardless of her connection to you," I say, getting right up into his face and pointing my magic, loaded, I-mean-business finger. "What's past is past. You are to send her twenty thousand dollars for one dress order and tell her all is forgiven and forgotten. If she's having difficulties, I might ask you to order another dress, not for ten thousand, but a proper amount. Your granddaughters will love them."

"If any child, man or woman from my area disappears, I'll turn it over to the police. I can't imagine right now how vast my area is, so play-it-by-ear. If more gambling, whoring, or an abundance of drugs infiltrates Montana, I'll be watching." Leo relaxes. His color returns to its normal Mediterranean complexion. "This is a minor setback. Lawyers can juggle like circus clowns, keeping cases open for years, until time passes, officers retire, or litigators lose too much money. A mosquito bite, nothing more."

We both notice Carlo looming at the kitchen door with his hammer.

My voice loses its calm façade. "Say what you want, Bonato, but know that I might call in favors once in a while. A school or organization might need a financial boost, a scholarship fund might need building, or a crime might need solving." I stamp my foot and shout out, "If you're going to live here in Montana, you're damn well going to support it."

"So, you are going to enter the world of extortion." Leo smiles and leans close. "Excellent. In that, I can give you training. I am going to enjoy our association."

Without flinching, I turn and walk out the door, shouldering past Carlo at the entrance.

EPILOGUE

July 4th parade watchers, bands, floats, tumbling troops and politicians fill the street. Myself, Enrique, Pryor, Eve and Sheriff Trammel, who's become her regular companion, perch on the narrow balcony above the gallery entrance. Marry Kat is here with our other neighbor, Gerry, a young recluse that we both agree needs to get out more.

Jackson and Angel sit across the street at the beer garden, laughing and sipping from frosted steins in the noontime heat. Sharing their table is credit union Ben and his lovely, much younger wife, Adele.

The gallery apartment is filled with other friends, who pop out to watch the parade for a while, before returning to the buffet and wine covering the purple kitchen counter. The food wagons down the street give off the mixed aromas of Indian fry bread, Hawaiian soba noodles or French crepes, depending upon the direction of the breeze.

Early this morning, Jackson cornered me in the gallery with news about the Mustang. After Leo insisted that he had nothing to do with JB's death, I'd claimed the vehicle from the police impound lot and had it towed to Jackson's garage.

He'd worked on the vehicle several times, customizing it to JB's wishes.

Jackson also knew the engine inside and out. After two hours of a point-by-point inspection, he found a magnetic box stuck on the outside of the direct fuel injection system. Tests were inconclusive, but the best he could come up with was that it somehow sent a signal to the Ecoboost system, accelerating the Mustang without using the gas pedal. One thing was for certain though, it was remotely controlled. The device had to be set off by someone close by.

"I called the sheriff right away, and guess what," Jackson smiled. "Sheriff Trammel found records of a round trip flight from Williston to Kalispell on April fourth. During the time that JB was driving home from delivering Kendra to Jake's, someone flew here. That someone was Buddy."

Jackson continued the story while we prepared platters of snacks for the parade party. "He hadn't even used a false name. Trammel got the North Dakota Marshall to lean on Buddy." We already knew he survived the snakebite and was now locked up in Watford City, awaiting a decision about jurisdiction over his crimes. Jackson shook his head. "It's sort of pitiful. Buddy broke instantly, confessing through tears, that yes, he had planted the device on the Mustang when JB delivered Kendra to Jake's and murdered his best friend."

JB's boxes sat in the Sheriff's evidence locker for days. Yesterday afternoon at three o'clock, I received an excited call from Trammel. "Why didn't you tell me about the cash?"

"I wanted you to experience the same terrifying thrill." I didn't ask him why he took so long to do a thorough search of the box of traveling supplies to find the money underneath the clean shirts and underwear.

The cash turned out to not be a few hundred bucks for gas money, but a compression bag full of hundred dollar bills— seven hundred thousand dollars' worth. A handwritten note that could be read through the bag told the total amount and source. This was JB's split of the trafficking money from Buddy for the past five years. It further explained that the FBI would confiscate this cash, but that there were other savings accounts in the Central Credit Union in Spencer's Gap, Montana, that were earned from the legitimate business. Records for tax payments are in the account book included at the bottom of this box, plus the name and phone number of his accountant. Buddy's trafficking cash was at his apartment in Denver and JB included his address.

Jackson already explained about the pigeon. He'd inherited the coop full of birds from the owner of the old house where my gallery now sat, and wanted to warn me off the investigation. He thought a carrier pigeon would be so bizarre that I would pay attention and stop looking for answers. We both laughed.

"Listen, Roe, I knew JB had something to do with Kendra's disappearance. I didn't know how to tell you without sounding like a twit. You're so sheltered and strait-laced, I didn't think you'd believe me." Jackson said. "My niece was kidnapped fifteen years ago and we all learned everything there is to know about human trafficking." The niece had been rescued a year after her disappearance but she committed suicide after she'd been home one week.

"The reason I came to Larsen Lake that night was that I'd called the Montana Highway Patrol to report Kendra's abduction and give the car description." Figuring that JB would be stopped, arrested and never come home for the big date, Jackson hadn't wanted me to sit out there and wallow in my disappointment all night.

I wave off everyone's questions about the visit with the Godfather. I tell them, instead, about the interesting gate and fabulous house, the excellent coffee and the perfect hanging of the artwork. I don't tell them what happened with the list. Enrique, Jackson and Pryor know about the existence of the list, and I hope they won't share it. It's a lot to ask. Even they didn't know the details past the first year of crimes that JB recorded in his journal, where I'd stopped reading aloud. They would recognize those crimes when they reached the evening news. I'll never tell what else I did.

I announced that thanks to an anonymous donation, a halfway house and facility for women victims of trafficking would be built on a beautiful, private farm in the valley. My architect is already on it. Most of the women will have some sort of post-traumatic stress disorder and drug addiction that's best handled outside their family homes. Angel already agreed to take psychology and counseling training and set up a survivor advocate program for the girls. And the new house on the golf course lot will be sold through a fundraising auction for the new rehab program.

The hot sun is right overhead when the local dude ranch fire truck drifts by spraying the throng and managing to get a straight shot at our balcony. Screams of dismay and delight fill the air from the crowd below us, as we run inside to escape. Here in the present, I have a lot to be grateful for. I squeeze Enrique's hand. "Pryor's right, this is like a dream come true."

The parade's tail end is swallowed as masses mob onto the street, strolling and greeting friends. What an enjoyable place to live. Secluded from the world, we welcome outsiders every summer and send them home with pleasant memories and works of art. I towel off the water that hasn't already evaporated in the heat of summer and go downstairs to unlock the front doors.

The End

ACKNOWLEDGMENTS

Becoming brave enough to publish a book is huge. My family was there from the beginning when we brainstormed a crime that is in plain sight and could exist unnoticed in a small town.

Authors of the Flathead and Montana Women Authors contributed much to my success, as they encourage me to persevere and keep honing my craft. My last writer critique groupies, Dee and Shannon, pushed me over obstacles and encouraged me to finish. Thanks to my many readers, especially my dear friend Lolly Franklin, who read an early draft and honestly told me where it didn't work. To my many early readers, thank you for your support, advice and encouragement.

To my many friends who make me laugh, thank you for words and ideas. I told you when I wrote something down through tears of laughter that I was using it in a book, so don't be surprised. To those who shared their expertise, thank you and I won't tell anyone to blame you for my author interpretation

Thank you to my publisher, Gloria Coppola, for coaching me back from the cliff, my proofreader, Patty Pascua for her input to fill in the gaps, and my cover and layout designer, Carol Anne Hartman, for creating a cover far beyond my dreams. If it wasn't for PPP Publishing, this book would still be in a box.

Special thanks to my daughter Martina for reading snippet after snippet and helping me come up with the title.

NATIONAL HUMAN TRAFFICKING

National Human Trafficking Hotline. 1-888-373-7888

Text 233733

Our protagonist Rosetta is well educated, strong and focused on her life. She doesn't believe trafficking is happening in her back yard. It only happens to those people over there.

Our antagonist JB is a "nice guy." They are the perfect storm.

- 300,000 children are sold for sex in the US every year. Labor trafficking is larger, but less likely to be reported in the US.
- The average age of girls forced into the sex trade is between 12 and 14. Fewer than 2% are rescued.
- With more than 40 disappearances reported annually, Montana ranks the 5th highest state for number of missing and murdered indigenous persons.

PAY ATTENTION to who provides your services; know the signs!!!!

If you are buying sex off the internet and connecting to someone through a phone, that person is most likely underaged and trafficked.

If you are at a Super Bowl or large amusement park and getting a quickie, that little girl has been transported there by a PIMP, a human slaver, where he can earn up to a thousand dollars a day from each child.

Slavery exists in other ways.

- Does your nail technician only speak her native Asian language?
- Is your Au Pair from an online service?
- Local manufacturing companies, restaurants, hotels, cleaning and landscaping services often use slave laborers.
- Kids selling door to door or in a mall as part of a traveling sales scam are slaves.
- Foreign agricultural workers picking our food are often indentured labor for large farms.

https://www.soroptimist.org/our-work/

https://www.pbs.org/wgbh/frontline/film/
sex-trafficking-in-America/

www.polarisproject.org https://
50forfreedom.org/modern-slavery/

Half the Sky: Turning Oppression Into Opportunity for Women Worldwide, by Nicholas D Kristof and Sheryl WuDunn. Download free PDF or read online for free.

National Human Trafficking Hotline. 1-888-373-7888
Text 233733

ABOUT THE AUTHOR

Robin Magaddino is a follower of dreams. After college, she studied wildlife and plants in the Okavango Delta of Botswana under the guise of a Peace Corp Volunteer working with the United Nations. Later, the mountains of western Montana called and she became a wildlife refuge manager of lakes and a mountain left in the aftermath of glaciation. Surrounded by bison, elk, deer, pronghorn and horses to ride, she found her heaven. She lives on a small Montana ranch with her husband, horses, and border collie. Now a Yoga teacher and writer, she continues to hike, kayak and enjoy all the wild world has to offer.

Made in the USA
Las Vegas, NV
26 April 2022

48047758R00187